THE
SAVIOR

BOOK YOUR PLACE ON OUR WEBSITE AND MAKE THE READING CONNECTION!

We've created a customized website just for our very special readers, where you can get the inside scoop on everything that's going on with Zebra, Pinnacle and Kensington books.

When you come online, you'll have the exciting opportunity to:

- View covers of upcoming books
- Read sample chapters
- Learn about our future publishing schedule (listed by publication month *and author*)
- Find out when your favorite authors will be visiting a city near you
- Search for and order backlist books from our online catalog
- Check out author bios and background information
- Send e-mail to your favorite authors
- Meet the Kensington staff online
- Join us in weekly chats with authors, readers and other guests
- Get writing guidelines
- AND MUCH MORE!

**Visit our website at
http://www.kensingtonbooks.com**

THE
SAVIOR

FAYE SNOWDEN

Dafina
Books

KENSINGTON PUBLISHING CORP.

http://www.kensingtonbooks.com

DAFINA BOOKS are published by

Kensington Publishing Corp.
850 Third Avenue
New York, NY 10022

All Kensington titles, imprints and distributed lines are available at special quantity discounts for bulk purchases for sales promotion, premiums, fund-raising, educational or institutional use.

Special book excerpts or customized printings can also be created to fit specific needs. For details, write or phone the office of the Kensington Special Sales Manager: Kensington Publishing Corp., 850 Third Avenue, New York, NY 10022. Attn. Special Sales Department. Phone: 1-800-221-2647.

ISBN 0-7582-0750-6

First Trade Paperback Printing: October 2004
First Mass Market Printing: September 2005
10 9 8 7 6 5 4 3 2 1

Printed in the United States of America

To Bertie, Eric, and my favorite uncle.
God bless.

PROLOGUE

Violet Hamilton sits on the edge of a twin bed in Room 303 of The Elite Hotel. Her father—who had once worked at the hotel—told her that in the old days, even before he was around, ladies with black ostrich feathers in their hair and men in top hats would stay at The Elite to get away from the city. They would catch a play at the famous Dunhill Theatre or eat in one of the county's fine restaurants. That was in the mid-1930s, when The Elite's Greek columns gilded with gold allowed the place to live up to its name.

But, oh, Daddy, if you could see it now.

At night, The Elite swallows up an endless stream of drug addicts, drunks, and whores. The rooms that once held two king-size beds and sitting areas with matching divans have long since been divided into two, sometimes three smaller rooms. Though Violet had been at the hotel for several weeks now, the small rooms were usually rented by the half hour. The once famous Elite Hotel had become an infamous whorehouse.

Violet grips the side of the bed with such strain that her arms feel like they are held together by rusted wire instead of vein and sinew. Her tiny bow-shaped lips wrinkle like wet paper as she closes her eyes. A drop of sweat rolls between her eyes and alongside her wide nose. She wipes it away and opens her eyes, only to be assaulted by the brown color of the knotty bedspread, the faded hardwood floor indented with scratches and stained with piss and vomit.

She stands up and paces back and forth between the narrow bed on the west wall and the splintered door on the east. She alternately hugs her waist and beats her forehead with the heels of her large-boned hands. The pain distracts her from the withdrawal symptoms. With cold sweat wrapping around the back of her neck, she sticks her large hands under her armpits to kill the shakes that have already started.

She catches a glimpse of herself in the cracked full-length mirror nailed to the grease-slicked walls. Violet is a tall, broad-shouldered woman with wide cheekbones and deep-set eyes. They now glitter helplessly as she waits for her fix. Today, on the day that she will die, she wears a denim shirt she got from the homeless shelter a couple of weeks before, a pair of wide-legged men's pants, and some run-down house slippers that do nothing to hide the gray ash covering her black feet.

In the past, to keep the withdrawal symptoms at bay, Violet Hamilton would go to a place where she felt safe. It is no different now. She closes her eyes on the picture of herself in the mirror, and listens in the darkness until she hears a stream trickling over stones. When she smells the water, she opens her eyes and finds herself sitting against the trunk of a tall redwood. Uneven bark imprints a pattern of swirls and lines on her back, and she knows that her shirt is being stained a rusty red. A breeze cools the sweat on her forehead, and she holds her breath as a spotted deer approaches cautiously with its brown eyes focused on the apricot lying in the curve of her hand. Of all the rehab centers she had lived in, that one by the river with the wild deer had almost been the one to cure her. Almost.

A spasm racks her body. Instead of water trickling over stones in the river, she finds herself doubled over in the corner of Room 303, vomit leaking out of her mouth. Her eyes move from her curved palm to the snapshot of her daughter held to the wall with a single straight pin. That picture has seen countless hotels like The Elite. It has lain crumpled in her hands in alleyways. She has clutched it to her chest in flophouses. No matter how high she has been, she has never forgotten it—not once. *My daughter,* she says now in a voice that makes her throat hurt, *my daughter Kendra, the doctor.*

And now her daughter, clear-eyed and smooth-faced, stares back at her with a smile. For a moment, Violet almost gets it. For the first time since sticking a needle in her arm, she almost remembers what she's lost. But then she feels sweat slip down her back, hot and threatening. She turns away from the picture.

A knock at the door interrupts her thoughts. She snatches it open and sees the man she has been waiting for standing in the doorway like a god. It seems as if she has waited for an eternity. Violet Hamilton bursts into tears.

He doesn't give her what she has waited for right away. Instead, he insists they share a drink first, a toast. As Violet looks at him, her only thought is how clean he is. He is clean from the corners of his eyes right down to his perfectly filed nails. And his cologne reminds her of baby powder.

He tells her in a voice that sounds like singing that she still has a choice to make. "Throw the drug away, Violet. I will help you. I will see to it. It is for your sake, for your daughter's sake." But she only smiles, the bourbon they share tasting like smooth flame in the back of her throat. And she waits. Finally, he presses a clean syringe and two dime bags into her open hand and leaves.

After he's gone, Violet's vision blurs against the spoon and the flame as she cooks the heroin. Her nose runs in anticipation. She sits on the narrow bed and twists a belt around her arm. She touches the needle to the vein now tattoo green

and bulging. She closes her eyes—and, yes, she could do this
with her eyes closed—and feels the sting of the needle. She
empties it, and waits to rest in the arms of God.

But instead of the infusing peace she expects, hot dyna-
mite explodes in her chest and flames stream from her mouth.
She tries to twist away from it, but her body disobeys. She
falls face down on the bed with her eyes wide open. She
knows she is about to die, and she is afraid. So she dreams
that the foam oozing from her mouth is the deer licking her
cheek in payment for the apricot she had let him eat from her
dark hand.

CHAPTER 1

The letter didn't mean a damned thing. Another crazy, that's all. Richard T. Marvel, homicide team lead for the Dunhill County Sheriff's Department, picked up the letter and looked at it for the third time. There was no return address or anything that might tell him who it was from. The date had been blacked out with permanent marker, and the letter was unsigned. The paper itself was yellow, the ink faded and scratchy. Rich read it again.

> *Those who know who I am call me The Savior. I have been charged by God to deliver the children, and I've delivered many so far . . .*

Rich stopped reading. Crazy talk, his father would have called it. He opened the bottom drawer of his desk and threw the letter on top of the others. This one would make number four. Just another thing that he couldn't do a damn thing about, despite his new assignment as homicide team lead.

Dunhill really didn't *need* a homicide division within its sheriff's department. It was not that people didn't die in Dunhill. Oh no, that happened with a frustrating frequency. But it was the way that people chose to dispose of themselves that did not require intensive investigation, nor was it terribly interesting.

Back in the early seventies when businessmen folded up their clock factories and their watch factories and their aircraft parts factories and took them all back east or to—God forbid—Mexico, many longtime residents made rich by the factories jumped out of windows or shot themselves with their antique double-action Smith & Wesson revolvers. Ever since that first rash of suicides, Dunhill County, California, seemed to fall in love with death.

And today was no different. Teenagers from the middle-class neighborhood known as The View drove their vehicles headlong into trees on drunken larks. Poor people of The Pit still chased each other around with stolen twenty-twos or injected drugs that froze their hearts in mid-beat. Rich people in The Point got confused sometimes, and flew their toylike planes nose-down into the rolling hills surrounding the county.

The fact of the matter was that people in Dunhill died early and often, but with sufficient and satisfactory explanation. Everyone accepted this as a fact of life. Everyone accepted it until James Freehold decided he wanted to be sheriff of Dunhill County.

Rich thought about the recent sheriff's election as he watched a TV so old that he had to wrap the antenna in foil to get a decent reception. It was officially Easter Sunday, and Rich and his two partners were on the downhill slide of a graveyard shift in the newly formed Dunhill County homicide department. A dyed-blond reporter told of the latest Amtrak train wreck while her teeth glowed green and a bright splotch of red crawled over one blue eye. Rich watched the crumpled cars, the fire licking out of the shattered windows, and thought about God winking. Those people had probably boarded the train thinking about their next destination and what they would do when they got there. They never thought the journey would end in sirens and broken glass.

God winked at the old sheriff, Bill Connors. Connors had never thought that he would lose the election to Freehold. He relied on Dunhill's romance with death, the community's total acceptance of the way things were. But Freehold took advantage of Bill Connors's complacency. He'd talked about how many homicides were left unsolved. Freehold insisted that his opponent—whom he nicknamed Boweless Bill—was too afraid to reach out to the people in The Pit. He claimed Boweless Bill was content—no, actually happy—to see those disenfranchised citizens killing each other. One less welfare mother, one less crack addict, one less heroin hound.

Of course, Rich knew that Bill Conners thought none of this, but the incumbent sheriff could not defend himself. It was fact that of the 104 deaths ruled suspicious in The Pit that year, only six had been cleared in the strictest sense of the word. Most of the cases were like the files on Rich's desk. The police knew who the perps were, but those perps were either temporarily or permanently unavailable.

Rich stood up and stretched to his full six foot, four inch height. He drew his black hand over his stiff hair, which was so precisely engraved into a fade that his hairline looked sharp enough to cut. His mouth had that three o'clock-in-the-morning dry feel. He looked at the clock hanging loosely on the brick wall and saw it was almost four. He yawned and felt the sides of his mouth crack.

Two weeks ago the new sheriff, James Freehold, named Rich acting team lead of the sheriff's department homicide division. Before James Freehold stepped on the scene, Rich sat in a chair with a wide, cushioned seat and wheels oiled so smooth that no one heard it move until he was halfway across the room. That chair had "Lieutenant-Commander"—the post he had worked his entire career for—written all over it.

Rich now leaned as far back as his current cheap metal chair would allow. He put his feet on his wooden desk, which warped upward at an angle. No matter how hard he tried, he couldn't pull open the two attached file drawers. He had to keep his files on the top of his desk. The only drawer working was the bottom one, the one that contained those crazy letters.

Under the watch of the old sheriff, the department had been remodeled. The new design did not take into account a new homicide division, and perhaps did speak to Bill Connors's lack of vision. Every inch of office space—down to the last stick of furniture and the last pencil—was accounted for. When the new sheriff, James Freehold, announced his plans to the press to create a homicide division, he needed to find some place to put it. And he did.

He tucked the department away in a defunct cafeteria, barely ripping out the kitchen equipment before raiding the basements of county buildings, and most likely Goodwill, for furniture.

Rich looked up to catch the glance of one of his partners. "How you holding up, old man?" Gregory asked.

Gregory Atfield's eyes glinted from the glow of his desk lamp. He was a white man as thin and long as a Popsicle stick. His sexless manner had earned him the nickname of The Priest—a name no one had dared call him to his face.

Gregory had been with the sheriff's department for about four years. He had transferred from a precinct in San Francisco, and though Rich had known Gregory since the academy, he didn't know why his friend had left his old job. Talk and rumors swirled around the department regarding Gregory Atfield, with his farmers' hands and soft voice, but Rich knew that the talk dissipated like smoke when Gregory ambled into the room. Not only born with a silver spoon in his mouth and bottle-fed from Waterford crystal, Gregory had a family with political connections that caused colleagues to think before they challenged him.

Rich did not know what had possessed Gregory to become a detective, but become one he had. And in Rich's opinion, Gregory was one of the best. He was the type of man who wielded silence like a weapon. During interrogation, perps found themselves wanting to talk just to kill the silences. Gregory usually worked the day shift with a patrol officer assigned to him, but earlier, around eleven-thirty that night, he had strolled in wearing a wrinkled sports coat and complaining that he couldn't sleep.

Now Gregory lifted an eyebrow waiting for Rich to answer his question, but Rich just shrugged and said nothing. Rich looked across the room at Beau Blair, the third and last member of the homicide division. Beau was a big cigar-smoking, cowboy-boot-wearing, skinny-tie-with-the-turquoise-stone-sporting southern prick. At least that was the way Rich always thought of him. But the farthest south Beau had been was Bakersfield. When he was young, he'd obviously overdosed on reruns of *The Dukes of Hazzard* and *Gunsmoke*.

Beau didn't look as if he were paying attention to the TV or Rich or Gregory. Instead, his feet were propped on his desk and crossed at the ankle while he flipped through the pages of an outdated—and probably confiscated—porn magazine.

Sheriff Freehold gave Beau Blair the homicide assignment because the young rookie patrol officer had become a local hero by talking a gunman out of his nine-millimeter MAC 10 machine pistol and saving a nursing home full of old people—a valuable commodity in Dunhill County. Being the media's darling boy was what got Beau the assignment. But Rich was a different story. He didn't like to think of the reason he was offered his job, so instead he thought about the reasons he took it.

When Sheriff Freehold had faced Rich—the self-assured clean-cut black man raised in The Pit and engaged to a judge's daughter—he had appealed to Rich's ambitions, his ego, and his career aspirations. Rich remembered what the sheriff had said: *Just think how good this will look on your résumé. Pretty soon, this could be a permanent assignment, and you could be promoted to commander. It's your ticket. Write it, Rich.*

Rich thought of the conversation and felt the sudden need to take a shower. Dunhill County needed a homicide division like Beau Blair needed a membership to PBS. Rich convinced his partner, Gregory Atfield, to take the assignment with him. And most nights were like this: Rich watching early-morning CNN news and Beau flipping through filthy magazines.

Rich's dreams—all of his dreams of getting that promotion and getting the respect he deserved—were about to come true. All he had to do was sit in a cafeteria turned squad room, watch the late-night news, and feed the press stories about how effective the new homicide division was.

Rich returned his attention to the hazy images of the destroyed Amtrak train. The newscaster, female and appropriately disheveled, reported the tragedy with a voice edged in disbelief. Rich caught the phrase *four killed instantly* and thought about all of those dreams, how they had simply exploded in one bright second.

CHAPTER 2

The phone's ring on that early Easter morning so stunned Rich out of his cocoon of boredom that he just stared at it for a second or two, thinking, *I didn't know it could do that.* Two weeks had passed silently by since the inception of the homicide team, and there had not been one single phone call. The patrol division had cleared the one real murder that had happened during that time.

Rich snatched up the phone after the third full ring.

"Yo," he said as he flipped his notebook to a blank page. Out of the corner of his eye, he saw Gregory Atfield grimace at the informal greeting. But Rich did not think too much about it. Hell, it was probably a wrong number.

But it wasn't.

"Is this the Dunhill County homicide division?" The squeaking voice on the other end of the phone advertised incompetence. Rich guessed that it was probably a rookie from the patrol division.

"No," Rich said. "It's Pizza Hut."

"Oh, Um, I'm . . ."

"No, no, man," Rich interrupted. "This is Rich Marvel. What do you have?"

"This is Officer Franklin. We have a dead body over at The

Elite," he said. "We need someone from homicide to come over . . ."

Rich had been jotting down the time and the officer's name, but when he heard those words, *The Elite,* he stopped. He abruptly threw the pencil down and watched it roll on the lined notebook paper. He leaned back in his chair and scratched his temple with his index finger.

"The Elite, huh?" Rich asked more slowly. He looked up. Gregory's faded gray eyes searched Rich's face questioningly, but Rich held up his hand before Gregory could ask.

"Yes sir." Officer Franklin cleared his throat. "It's a female, about forty, slumped over the bed . . ."

"With a needle in her arm?" Rich finished for him.

"Yes sir," Officer Franklin answered, a little surprised. "How did you know?"

Rich let his chair fall level to the floor. There would be no ride out this morning after all. They would sit here scratching their asses until Officer Paget for the day shift arrived.

"Because every corpse found at The Elite has a needle in its arm, or white powder around its nose . . ."

"Yes sir, but this is different. I think someone from homicide needs to come and check it out."

"Tell me one reason why I need to waste my time on a drug overdose?"

The younger officer fell silent. Out of his peripheral vision, Rich saw Gregory stand up and glide over to his desk.

"Let's check it out, old man," Gregory said in his slightly musical voice. "It may be good for a few moments' distraction."

"Hell, I'll go," Beau boomed.

Rich winced. The man's voice was as loud as a freight train. Officer Franklin remained silent, but Rich knew he was still on the phone because he could hear the man breathing. He took one more look at the TV. The picture had become so distorted that the fiery scene of the Amtrak wreck had become suffused in white TV snow. Hell, it would be good to get out of the office.

"Okay, Officer Franklin," he sighed. "Give it to me one more time."

Rich took down the time, place, and the officer's badge number. He told Beau to grab a notebook and the homicide kit.

"Let's roll," Beau said enthusiastically.

Rich looked up at the pitted ceiling in disgust. "Just get the homicide kit," he said.

Beau retrieved a duffle bag from one of the cabinets. Rich had created the kit right after Freehold assigned him to homicide, scrounging the Polaroid camera, gloves, and paper bags from other departments. Freehold hadn't gotten around to giving the department an operational budget.

Rich shrugged into his sports jacket and adjusted his holster, which contained his nondepartmental-issue Beretta 92 FS pistol. He had bought the weapon out of his own pocket after he lost a gunfight with a local drug dealer. His standard department-issued six-shot Smith & Wesson revolver was at his apartment in his gun safe. Useless as hell and probably getting rusty. He was adjusting the collar of his jacket when Gregory spoke.

"I haven't seen that jacket before," Gregory said. "Is that one Dinah gave you?"

Rich felt a sting of irritation at the question. Dinah Webster was his girlfriend. No, strike that, she was his fiancée and the daughter of a judge. Not just any judge, either, but a state superior court justice, the big daddy of them all. Though Dinah was accomplished and beautiful right down to her pink-painted acrylic nails, she had a nasty habit of buying him expensive things like the silk-blend jacket she had brought back from a business trip to New York. They fought about it, but she couldn't understand why it made him so angry. And Rich didn't know why, either, really—or, rather, he didn't want to acknowledge the reason.

"What makes you think that she gave it to me?" Rich asked.

"Because you can't afford that on your salary, old man." Gregory smiled.

"Hey, Gregory," Rich said. "What's with all the 'old man' shit? You're older than I am."

But Gregory was already turning away. Rich suddenly stopped at the door as if remembering something important.

"Wait," he said. "If we go, who's gonna mind the store?"

"I love it when you say 'gonna'," Gregory said and laughed.

Rich noticed the look of confusion in Beau's blue eyes and knew what the big man was thinking. Rumors abounded that Gregory swung the other way. Hell, Rich had wondered himself a few times. But even though Gregory and Rich had been friends for over ten years and roommates for two, Rich had never asked him. True, he never saw Gregory bring a date home or go out with a woman. But neither had he seen him with a man. *Figure that out, Detective,* he thought. Beau probably thought that Rich swung the other way, too. Rich could care less, but Beau's demeanor annoyed the hell out of him.

"I set up the voice mail," Beau said in a faked southern drawl. "If someone calls, we'll get beeped." He showed them both his pager as if holding up a flash card. "I can call them back. I'll be damned if I'm gonna get stuck with phone duty just because I'm the new guy. Why should you two girls have all the fun?"

Beau turned his back on both of them and headed for the door. Rich took a breath to respond, but Gregory stopped him by placing a deceptively fragile-looking hand on his arm. Rich looked down at Gregory's rough grip, the only un-gentle thing about him, and let his breath out without saying anything.

The unmarked white Monte Carlo sedan screamed "cop" from its front bumper right down to its rear end. Rich gripped the steering wheel as a familiar feeling crept over him. It was the feeling that he got when he knew that at any moment he would be staring down death once again. Even though he had worked the last ten years in narcotics, he'd had the dubious honor of working homicides many times.

And before the viewing of each crime scene, a thousand butterflies tapped a ballet against the wall of his belly. The slump of the body, the lack of life, made him think of his own mortality. He'd see the detectives and the paramedics and the firemen—including himself—milling about the body like it was nothing but a sack of blood and guts—not a person who once lived and laughed and breathed. And he knew that was how it would be for him when he was the one lying in a pool of blood.

But he got used to it after a while. The bodies all melded into one, especially since he found that in most cases the victim was almost as despicable as the perp. And he learned that, regardless, the souls that had once inhabited those bodies simply discarded them as if they were damaged luggage. Hopefully, they sat at the throne of their God—Jesus, Buddha or Allah, or whoever. That is, if they deserved it. As he thought about what awaited him at The Elite, Rich negotiated each curve through The Pit, stopping dutifully at each yellow light.

"Shouldn't we put a move on it?" Beau said from the backseat.

Rich looked in the rearview mirror. Beau's balding head gleamed in the early dawn.

"Why?" Rich asked. "The body is dead. It's not going anywhere."

They drove south, passing an abandoned clock factory. Once the area known as The Pit had contained a clean collection of light industrial plants and row houses built for returning World War II veterans. But now shattered windows and creased metal doors scarred the factories; junkies used the shell of row houses to hibernate between fixes.

The old clock factory they now passed was tagged with blue and red swirls of spray paint from the first floor to the fifth. But the oddest thing about the factory was a clock perched on the pointed roof. The large black Roman numerals stood against a circular field of blinding white. And because the damn thing still worked, people in The Pit called it the miracle clock.

Gregory's voice broke into Rich's thoughts. He was telling Beau what to expect when they arrived at the scene and explaining the importance of taking notes and measurements. Rich abandoned the conversation again for his own thoughts when Gregory started droning on about methods for searching the crime scene.

He looked at the vacant lot flowing past his window. A chain-link fence protected yellow weeds cracking in the early morning breeze. A basketball hoop, netless and rusted over, stood silent sentry over three feet of crumbling concrete. When Rich was a boy, the three feet surrounding the hoop had stretched over the entire area now defeated by weeds. Rich remembered playing basketball and shooting the shit with boys he would later end up arresting. There was Raymond Smalls, a.k.a. Ray Ray, and Clifford Rhone. Ray Ray was a known drug dealer, and Clifford was serving life in San Quentin for murder.

As Rich passed the dilapidated court, the weeds winked golden for a moment in the rising sun. He saw in his mind's eye shadowy figures wearing shorts and running as they passed a basketball between them. Shaking the image away, he nosed the car around a corner. The Elite was on Fifth and Main, a couple of minutes' drive from The Pit's rundown BART train station. The usual pack of junkies and prostitutes lingered at the double doors of the narrow building. But when they saw the Monte Carlo, they scattered like roaches under sudden light.

"So much for securing the scene," Rich said as he walked into the hotel.

Beau and Gregory followed without comment. The high registration desk was surrounded by bulletproof plastic. The foyer itself was narrow and deep and empty. Not a soul in sight. The black-and-white tile floor that once sparkled in the hotel's heyday was now faded and missing tile.

"Should we take the elevator?" Beau pointed to a creaky elevator with a scrolled iron gate.

"Hell, no," Rich said as he headed for the stairs.

When he opened the door to the stairwell, fresh urine and old vomit washed like a wave over his face. He ignored the gagging noises coming from Beau and simply took the stairs two at a time until he reached the third floor.

Rich opened the door to a carpet worn with holes. Two officers stood at the opposite end of the hallway. Rich recognized the old man with them immediately but didn't acknowledge him.

"They teach you how to secure a crime scene at the academy?" Rich asked Officer Franklin before the man could speak. He knew it was Officer Franklin because he recognized the badge number. "There should be a patrol officer at the stairwell door, man."

"Now, Rich," Gregory cut in. "Take it easy."

Rich ignored him, and kept his attention on Officer Franklin. "If you are going to call me down here and treat it like some homicide you can't deal with, at least secure the scene like you care."

"We did secure the scene," Officer Franklin explained. "In there."

He pointed to the closed door of Room 303.

"I'm the only one who's been in there besides Mr. Jiffy. He discovered the body." Officer Franklin's voice trailed off so low in the end that Rich could barely hear him. Even Gregory had to crowd in close to hear what Officer Franklin was saying.

"You secured the room where the body was," Gregory explained. Still in training mode, he turned to Beau. "But if this were a shooting or stabbing there could be a secondary crime scene in the stairwells or the elevators which could have been used as escape routes."

"So, Officer Franklin," Rich started again. "What happened?" He hated coming back to the old neighborhood, but knew he shouldn't take it out on the young cop.

"We were called to the scene by—"

"Mr. Jiffy?" Rich couldn't keep the annoyance out of his voice.

"Yes, uh, Mr. Jiffy," Officer Franklin answered. His large Adam's apple bobbed up and down. Rich got the feeling that the man suddenly realized how ridiculous that sounded. "Anyway, Mr. Jiffy wanted to evict the victim."

"And the victim's name?" Rich asked.

"A Violet Hamilton, sir," he offered eagerly.

Rich could have sworn he saw Gregory stiffen for a second. Gregory's hooded eyes fluttered lightly.

"You knew her?" Rich asked his partner.

"No." Gregory's entire body relaxed with the word. "That name just rings a bell."

"Hamilton's a pretty common name," Rich said.

Beau was listening intently. He stared at Gregory as if he wanted to dissect him. "But not Violet," he said.

"Look, can we move on?" Rich asked.

"Mr. Ji—" Officer Franklin went on, "I mean, the landlord knocked on the door of the victim's room several times about an hour ago. When he received no answer, he used a master key to unlock the door, and then he found the body."

"You canvass the other rooms yet? Anybody hear anything unusual?" Rich asked.

Officer Franklin nodded. "We talked to what residents we could find. No one's claiming to have heard anything, sir."

Rich swiveled around, placed his hands on his hips. He wasn't surprised at Franklin's answer. If anyone did hear anything, they wouldn't tell the police about it. After all, in The Pit the police were the enemy.

Beau whipped out his notebook. He questioned each officer in a voice so curtly professional that both Officer Franklin and his partner would have known that Beau was new to homicide. Officer Franklin did most of the talking. The other officer, a young black man named Henderson whom Rich had known, stood apart from his partner. Rich knew that they had probably argued about even calling homicide out on this. The patrol division probably could have handled this one. It was most likely a simple drug overdose. Rich caught Officer

Henderson's eye. Henderson nodded, his face expression-less.

Rich motioned to the old man behind Officer Franklin. "Jiff," he said, "come over here for a minute, man."

Jiffy shuffled over to where Rich stood. Rich placed an arm around his shoulder in a friendly gesture. Even though he was rewarded with a sour stink cloud, Rich didn't pull away. He steered Jiffy back toward the stairs out of earshot of the others. Dirt streaked Jiffy's pale face, and his hair hung down in greasy lanks over his fat forehead. He wore a shirt so filthy that Rich could only guess at its true color.

Rich looked down and saw the hem of Jiffy's gray pants floating a full two inches above his flip-flops. The shoes were too small for him and molded to both of his encrusted feet. Yellow toenails curled up at Rich in a greeting.

"You remember me, Jiff, don't you, man?" Rich asked him, keeping the warm smile on his face despite the bile turning in his stomach. Anyone looking at them would have thought that they were lifelong buddies.

"Of course I do." Jiffy giggled with a little smile. His one tooth, bright yellow, slipped over his bottom lip. "You was one of them Marvel boys. I knewed you when you was little."

Rich didn't bother to remind him that he was still one of them Marvel boys. The only reason Jiffy used past tense was because Rich had gotten out of the neighborhood. All of them had—he and his three brothers and eventually his mom and dad.

"I knewed you would end up in here one day," Jiffy said. "I just didn't think it would be like this."

Rich jerked his head back toward Officer Franklin, whose mouth was moving furiously as he talked to both Gregory and Beau.

"Jiff," he said. "Why didn't you tell the nice man your real name?"

Jiffy stopped his shuffle. He looked up at Rich with wide, innocent eyes.

"I did tell 'em my real name. Jiffy."

"Jiffy's your real name?" Rich asked.

"Yes siree, it is." Jiffy confirmed. His head bobbed up and down for emphasis.

"Is that your first name or last name?"

"Why my first name, of course," Jiffy said, puffing his shirt up in mock indignation.

"So if Jiffy's your first name, what's your last name?"

Jiffy pursed his lips and considered for a moment. He finally answered in a funeral-eulogy voice. "Pop."

"Pop?" Rich questioned, his eyes still on the old man, his arm still around his shoulder, and his nose still filled with the stench of him. He didn't laugh. It was early Sunday, and he was going to miss church and then brunch with Dinah and her father. Again. He was tired, and there was a dead body in Room 303 that they would eventually have to look at. The former Violet Hamilton probably had a syringe the size of a rocket ship sticking out of her arm. Someone would have to take it out and bag it, risking AIDS or hepatitis in the process.

"That would mean your name is Jiffy Pop," he said. "Like the popcorn."

"No, not like the popcorn," Jiffy huffed. "Jiffy as in a pop 'em in and pop 'em out of the hotel. You heard my slogan, ain't you? Rooms by the half hour."

Rich chuckled then, but not out of humor. "No, Jiff, I need your real name, as in the name your mamma gave you. I need it for the police report."

"Hmmm . . ." Jiffy stalled. He tried to shuffle an escape to the stairway door. But Rich clamped his shoulder tighter and guided Jiffy back to the others.

"As in the name my mamma gave me? Y'all gone do anything with that?" Jiffy said, gazing up at Rich.

Rich shrugged in reply. "We have to check it out to see if you have a record. Procedure, you know."

Jiffy scratched his chin. "I have a record, but I ain't

wanted for nothing. I guess it won't do no harm to give you my real name."

They had reached Gregory, Beau, and the two officers, who now regarded them questioningly. Gregory rocked back on his heels and let his notebook dangle from his long fingers. Beau leaned one arm on the greasy wall and tapped his silver-tipped cowboy boot against the threadbare carpet.

"My real name is Shirley," Jiffy said, not realizing all eyes were on him.

Gregory said nothing. Rich said nothing. Officer Franklin looked down in embarrassment. But Beau and Officer Henderson laughed loudly.

"Now, ain't nothing wrong with being named Shirley," Jiffy said.

"What's your last name, Jiff," Rich said.

"Sherman. Shirley Sherman," Jiffy said and smiled his one-toothed yellow smile.

"When you found the body, Mr. Sherman . . ."

"Aw, come on now," Jiffy protested. "Call me Jiffy. You been calling me that since you was little. Done called me that just a minute ago."

"Okay, Jiffy," Rich agreed, no emotion in his voice. "Tell me what happened."

"That Violet woman is one of my longtime customers," he said. "She's been rentin' here for a couple of weeks now. Of course, she been rentin' here on and off for about the last fifteen or sumpthin' years. But this time, she been staying at least two weeks."

"And that's a long time?" Beau questioned.

"Usually Jiffy rents by the hour," Rich explained to Beau. Beau had never worked the beat in The Pit. It was common knowledge that he was assigned to the stationhouse in Dunhill Point, the richest neighborhood in the entire county, right after the academy.

"Half hour," Jiffy corrected Rich. "I usually rent by the half hour."

"Go on, Jiffy," Rich said.

"Well, Violet hadn't been paying no rent. So this morning, I done had 'bout enough of that. Plus, these rooms was filled all up, and I needed her space." He shuffled over to Beau, who took two steps backward after catching a whiff of him.

"So I was all prepared to tell her to pay up or heat up the street. I knocked some, and when I didn't get no answer, I got the master key. I found her all on the bed like that."

"About what time was that," Beau asked from a safe-smelling distance away, raising his voice so Jiffy would hear him.

"Four or so."

"Four in the morning?" Beau asked.

Rich sighed and didn't wait for Jiffy to answer.

"Did you go inside, Jiffy?" he asked.

"Nope," Jiffy said. "When I saw her stretched out like I did, I just closed the door and called the police station."

Rich then turned his questions to Officer Franklin, but the young officer was so nervous that he did nothing but stammer and sweat. Rich kicked himself mentally for intimidating him earlier. He was in a foul mood and he was letting it get in the way of work. If the officer missed telling him something because he was too nervous, it could screw up the entire investigation.

"It's okay, Officer Franklin. You're doing fine," Gregory said, looking into the young man's face. Officer Franklin paused and took a breath.

"Female victim," he said. "Early fifties or late forties. Black. Black hair. Her eyes . . . I couldn't catch the color, but her hair is black and uncombed. There are no obvious rips in her clothes to indicate another possible cause of death. She is cold, sir—"

"And getting colder," Beau broke in, but everyone ignored him.

"I didn't see any blood, and she is lying on her stomach,

crosswise on the bed," Officer Franklin finished and sighed in relief.

"Did you examine the body?" Rich asked him.

"Definitely not, sir," Officer Franklin said. "Only to ascertain if she were already dead. When I realized that it might be something other than an overdose, I secured the scene, left the body, and called the homicide division."

"What makes you think that it was not a simple overdose?"

Officer Franklin didn't say anything for a minute or two. Instead, he stared at his shiny patent leather shoes, then looked at Rich. Rich could tell by the resolute expression on Franklin's face that he didn't have much.

"There are two glasses and an expensive bottle of whiskey on the table. I thought somebody else might have been involved."

Rich nodded, matched Franklin's earlier silence with one of his own. He wanted to tell Franklin that they were wasting their time, but instead he said nothing.

"Good work," Rich said. And for the first time, Officer Franklin smiled. "We will need your help taking a report on Jiffy. Think you can do that?"

"Yes sir."

"Okay," Rich smiled, feeling a little better. He clapped Officer Franklin on the shoulder.

"Rich," Gregory urged gently.

"Yeah, yeah, I know," Rich responded tiredly. "It's time for the show."

CHAPTER 3

Rich opened the wafer-thin door of Room 303 of The Elite Hotel. Gregory and Beau stood behind him without speaking. Although this was a natural state for Gregory, it wasn't for Beau. Violet Hamilton would probably be Beau's first body.

Rich thought about the first time he had been called to a homicide, well over ten years ago. Rich had tried his best to swagger, pretend it was nothing when he saw his first victim. The body had been left outside during a heat wave and was in an advanced state of decomposition. After he left the scene, Rich spent the next half hour with his head in a toilet.

"You all right, man?" Rich asked Beau now.

"Fine," Beau said.

Rich stood just inside the doorway. The room was so small that he couldn't help but notice the body sprawled across a twin bed with a fist curled toward the door. But Rich ignored it and told Beau to get the Polaroid out of the homicide kit. He heard Beau drop the film a couple of times and sputter curses under his breath.

Rich felt those butterflies start their ritual dance inside his stomach. He didn't advance into the room. Instead, he stood in the doorway, taking it all in. A straw bag sat next to the twin bed. It gaped open to reveal most of its contents—a can opener and an unopened can of Campbell's soup sat on top of some clothes balled into a bunch. A lone fringed rug added no warmth to the hardwood floor. A full-length mirror covered in a layer of film and cracked in several places was attached to the wall.

"Rich," Beau boomed behind him.

"Damn, man," Rich said. "Do you have to yell?"

"You gonna let us in?" Beau countered. "I've been calling your name forever."

"I didn't think you wanted to come in," Rich said as he stepped inside the room.

He continued to look around as the flash from the camera illuminated Violet Hamilton's body. Rich didn't know how Officer Franklin knew that it was a woman. She was huge and dressed in men's clothes. Half her face was buried in the bed, pink foam leaking from her open mouth.

The body was just as Officer Franklin had described it, though. Violet Hamilton lay across the bed, facedown. Her torso covered the breadth of the twin bed. One long arm was tucked across her chest. The other one, with the belt tied around it, reached out toward the door. Her hair, relaxed straight in some places but nappy in others, sprung from her head like the points of a harlequin's cap.

Thin curtains billowed in the wind from an open window. Rich heard the sounds of laboring cars and blasting radios float upward from the streets below. He saw the whiskey and the glasses that had brought them here on a small table to the left of the window.

Rich noticed everything at once, letting his observations drop into neat little boxes inside his head. He rarely had to take notes, but he did because that was how he was trained. He could remember everything about every homicide he had investigated. Someone would say the name of a victim, and walls would raise and slide backward to reveal a neat row of boxes he had set up in his head for that particular unfortunate. And he could tell them all sorts of things about the homicide—the position of the body, the person's name, if they lived alone or with somebody, if they were dumped or killed where they lay. He created a new row of boxes this Easter Sunday morning, a new row just for Violet Hamilton, a dead junkie.

He noticed vomit in one corner of the room. The vomit meant she had probably been going through some withdrawal symptoms before this last fix. Rich pulled on latex gloves—thinking, thinking, thinking for the thousandth time, *What in the hell am I doing here? How did I get here?*

Gregory and Beau walked in carefully around him, and then Gregory did what he always did at homicide crime scenes. He made a beeline for the body.

"Oh, man, come on," Rich said. "She's not going anywhere. She can wait."

Gregory didn't reply. While Rich preferred to take in the scene around the victim, Gregory always went for the body. He would check the body for signs of rigor or lividity or bugs—all the other shit Rich hated. After examining the body, he would stand and pronounce the time the victim died and whether or not they had struggled. Then he and Rich would place a ten-dollar bet, and usually Rich would lose. Ninety percent of the time, Gregory was better than the medical examiner. This always spooked Rich, but also comforted him in its sameness, its consistency. So before he started a thorough search of the room, he waited for this one small comfort in a world of death and uncertainty.

Gregory stooped, put his face close to Violet Hamilton's. When he rose, he didn't speak.

"You okay?" Rich asked.

"Fine," he replied shortly.

"Well?" Rich waited.

"Well what?" Gregory questioned. "I can't get a feel for this one. We'll have to wait for the medical examiner to determine time of death. Besides, I'm too tired for all that foolishness this morning."

Rich accepted it. He was disappointed, but he accepted it.

Gregory walked over to where Beau stood and instructed him on the sketches. His voice was not as assured as it normally was, not as soothing. Rich cataloged this fact, and dropped it in the appropriate box. He didn't know why he put it there, but he did. They worked the rest of the scene in silence.

"Whoo weeee," Beau squealed from the worn dresser. "Lookee here."

Beau held a Polaroid that Rich at first thought he had taken earlier.

"This window was most likely open last night," Gregory said without acknowledging Beau. "I wonder if the neighbors heard anything peculiar."

Rich laughed but didn't turn to his friend and partner. "Didn't you hear Officer Franklin? Besides, the 'neighbors' have most likely moved on," he answered. "What you got there, Beau?"

Rich strolled over to Beau, silently wishing the medical examiner was there so they could get on with their morning.

"Looks like Cinderella and her ugly stepmother."

Beau held the picture out to him. Rich took it carefully, only touching the edges. A tall, big-boned Violet Hamilton smiled out at him with every single one of her teeth. Her sporadically relaxed hair was combed in a fat circle around her head. She rested her cheek on top of the head of a young woman. Violet's arm was so tight around the woman's shoulder that her fingers dug into the flesh.

The woman in the picture was dark. Her hair corkscrewed from her head and scraped her shoulders. She wore a close-lipped smile, and her arms were folded across her chest. Rich looked at the younger woman too long, and resisted an urge to run his thumb across the face. He knew who it was, knew it the minute Beau handed him the snapshot.

"She's a looker, ain't she?" Beau asked, a sleazy smile on his face.

"I'm not looking at her," Rich lied. He pointed to Violet. "Where's the cross?" he said to no one in particular. By this time, Gregory had joined them. He now peered over Rich's shoulder.

"What?" Beau asked in confusion.

Gregory, as if reading Rich's mind, went over to the body, and gently moved Violet's head to reveal the folds of her neck. Her eyes were wide open and staring.

"Nothing here," Gregory said. "Only a couple of bluish scrapes."

"Oh, you talking about the cross that she's wearing in the picture?" Beau said, finally catching up. "She probably pawned it. I mean she was a junkie, for chrissake."

"Maybe she was. However, I think someone may have appropriated it from the looks of these marks on her face and neck. Looks like she was in some kind of fight," Gregory said.

"Whatever," Beau said, shrugging his shoulders. Rich took the picture and placed it in a Ziploc.

"Hey, Richy Rich." Rich turned when he heard the smoky female voice behind him. It was the medical examiner. Her name was Rita Sandbourne, and Rich knew she had a thing for him. He played it for all it was worth, getting special favors when he needed them or participating in a little harmless flirtation when things in the office got too serious.

Rita was a white woman, around forty and thin as a reed. Her dark, messy hair hung around her face, and slipped out of the knot at the nape of her neck. She ringed her drooping Bambi eyes in black eyeliner and heavy mascara. Her nose was so small that Rich had to look one, maybe two times before he noticed it.

"Hey, hey, Rita," Rich smiled at her. "What did you do, pull the short straw?"

"Something like that," she answered, her voice husky. Though Rich was not attracted to Rita physically, he knew that she had a voice that could drive a man crazy. And he knew she drove Beau, fifteen years her junior, crazy.

Rich smiled. "You know, Rita," he said. "You can even light up a crime scene."

She didn't smile back. "Cut the bullshit, Rich. I'm tired. I'm just one hour out of pulling an all-nighter," she said.

"All night?" Rich said. "What did you do with the kids?"

"My mother," Rita said simply. "And you better believe I'm going to be paying for it. You want to tell me what we have?"

Beau pushed Rich out of the way.

"What we got is a dead body," he said, looking at Rita so forcefully she winced. "Looks like an overdose."

Rita walked over to the body, her navy blue windbreaker crunching loudly in the small room. She looked at the body from every angle as she pulled on a pair of latex gloves. She gingerly pulled the needle out of Violet Hamilton's arm and corked it before placing it in a plastic bag.

"Oh yeah?" she asked. "What gave it away?"

"Hello, Rita," Gregory said from the other side of the bed.

"Hiya doing, choirboy?" she answered him without looking up. "What does this look like to you?"

Rita was the only person who could call Gregory a choirboy and get away with it. Gregory didn't answer right away. Rich strolled over to him. He didn't stop until he was close enough to smell the last remnants of Gregory's cologne fading away with the night. For some reason Rich couldn't explain yet, he wanted to be close to Gregory when he answered this question. He needed to know what Gregory's reaction would be.

"Well," Gregory let out the word on a rise of a deep breath. He lifted his long fingers to indicate the glasses on the table. "The crystal is odd," he said. "And her jewelry is missing."

"Jewelry?" Rita barked a laugh.

"Yes. A cross. But no telling when that was taken from her, though by those marks, I'd hazard it was recent."

"So what are you saying?" Rita snapped, a little impatient.

Gregory smiled with his mouth closed. "I'm simply saying that sometimes a duck is just a duck. But we shouldn't jump to conclusions, at any rate. I'd be interested in the autopsy results."

Rich let out a sigh of relief, and with it, all doubts that his partner was holding something back. If Gregory did know something about this, he'd be so anxious to close the case that he would have said that Violet died of an overdose. The end. Case closed. But still . . .

"Hey, man," Rich said, jerking his chin toward the bottle and the whiskey on the table. "We still better get that stuff tagged and down to forensics. I'd be interested to see if it's as expensive as it looks."

Gregory didn't say anything at first, then he nodded.

"I'm pretty sure it was an overdose," Rich said to no one in particular.

"There you go, choirboy." Rita winked at Gregory. "You've just been outvoted. Three to one."

"Three?" Gregory questioned.

"Three," she confirmed. "I'm pretty sure it's an overdose, too, or more correctly, some pretty bad dope. Had to be, if the needle is still in her arm." She pointed to the side of Violet's mouth. "That foam there is a pretty good clue."

Beau stood right behind Rita, her thin backside near his crotch. She would move one way, and he would follow as if magnets joined them. Rita stood up abruptly.

"Are you all done here?" she asked, annoyed. "Can we get her out?"

"We are pretty much finished," Rich said, grinning a little. "Body is all yours."

"Are you sure you don't want to get a crime-scene investigation team out here?" Rita asked.

Rich thought for a long time. If they needed a CSI unit, they would have to put in a call to Oakland. The Dunhill Sheriff's Department used the Oakland team only when they ran into a case that wasn't cut-and-dried. But on simple cases like this, they used their own people to process the scene. Beau had taken a million pictures, done all of the necessary sketches. And besides, this one was going to be a cakewalk. And he wanted out of The Elite Hotel as soon as possible.

"Nah," he said. "I think we got what we need. Now it's on to the next step."

"What's that?" Beau asked, looking over at Rich. Rich saw his face drop about four feet. He knew that Beau wanted to stay with Rita.

"Next of kin," he explained before walking out the door. He didn't look to see if Gregory and Beau followed, but the three of them walked out into the full morning light. Rich looked at the lopsided moon, its silvery light fighting to be noticed.

He closed his eyes a minute and let the crisp morning wind bend over his face. He wondered again how he had ended up here. He imagined himself still in high school, standing on the pitcher's mound as he struck out one of his victims: his fingers curl around the baseball, his arm extends as he releases it from his hand like it has a will of its own. He imagined himself seventeen again with a future of pro ball in front of him. That reward—not law enforcement—was supposed to be his ticket out of The Pit.

He had conquered the first step with a college baseball scholarship back East. He was good enough. Damn it, he was. Then came the bullet that sliced his knee almost in half and his dreams of baseball into bright red and blue pieces. Law enforcement was his new way out of The Pit. And it had worked, and it was working still, to an extent.

When he opened his eyes again, he realized how much that ticket out had cost him. The first thing he saw was the meat wagon across the street, the second was the perps. They were everywhere. Even toddlers in knitted sweaters tugging at their mothers' hands were perps in Rich's eyes. Perps slipped into corners, and averted their eyes from the oh-so-obvious three plainclothes policemen standing outside the doorway of The Elite Hotel. Instead of escaping, Rich had simply become the enemy in his old neighborhood.

CHAPTER 4

Rich opened the window to escape the smell of the other men in the confines of the Monte Carlo. They had been on duty all night, and the cheesy smell of the old cafeteria-turned-squad-room clung to them like incense.

"Where to, man?" Beau asked.

"I don't know about you two, but I'm headed home for a shower and change," Rich said.

Gregory, who had his head hanging out of the window, whipped it back into the car. "I thought we were notifying the next of kin."

"The next of kin can keep," Rich said. "You stink, Atfield. You too, Blair. I'm tired, and my eyes ache. Besides, I need to—"

"Check in with Dinah," Gregory finished for him.

Rich gave him a sidelong glance. He knew how Gregory felt about Dinah. Gregory knew her. After all, they were part of the same social set—the set that Rich had been trying to join since his dreams of baseball died. He now clutched the wheel to keep from snapping at Gregory. Instead he managed to answer him in an even voice.

"She's expecting me, man. I just need to tell her that I won't be there."

"We've got business to perform," Gregory answered. "We need to notify the family and continue the investigation before this entire thing goes stale.

"Look, Gregory." Rich did snap this time. "There is no *thing* here." He banged the side of his hand against the wheel. "What we have is a dead junkie who got ahold of some bad dope. Nothing more, nothing less. I'm tired of this bullshit about treating every death as a suspicious death. I can't believe I let Freehold talk me into this. Good for my career, my ass."

"If you cared about your career like you keep insisting you do, you'd realize that not caring about these people is exactly what got the last sheriff removed from office."

"Don't preach to me about these people," Rich said. "I grew up with these people, remember?" Rich looked in the rearview mirror just in time to catch Beau's big mouth stretched into a grin.

"What's this, a lover's spat?" Beau asked.

"Fuck you," Rich said snapping his chin down for emphasis.

"So, where to?" Beau said, unperturbed.

"Since Rich is team lead, I'd suggest we follow his orders: we take a break," Gregory answered, looking at Rich. "A small one."

Rich dropped Beau off at the house Beau shared with his mother in Dunhill View. Beau's mother lived in one of the narrow World War II tract houses to the north of The Pit. The tiny homes were built right after the war for GIs who returned home by way of Oakland and decided to stay in Dunhill County.

"Forty-five minutes," Rich said to him as Beau began to lumber from the sedan.

"Got it, man." Beau said.

But before Beau could close the door, a tail-wagging Labrador mix, golden in the sparkling sunlight, jumped on Beau and pushed him onto the backseat of the car.

"Shit," Rich yelled, instinctively reaching for his Beretta.

Rich hated dogs. When he was about nine years old, he had to pass an old junkyard to get to school. Every morning, no matter what time he passed, a black pit bull mix with fur shimmering over rippling muscles would clatter against the chain-link fence, intent, Rich was convinced, on killing him. His razor-sharp teeth would bite at the fence, and warm spittle would fly from the snarling mouth. Every single morning, Rich was treated to the music of the clanking fence as the dog tried to break free in order to kill him.

Then one spring morning, Rich forgot about the dog. He didn't remember why, but on that morning he was happy. Maybe it was the last day of school or the first day he didn't have to wear a coat because spring's promise was just around the corner. But he remembered whistling and walking with his hands in his pocket and his backpack bouncing pleasantly against his back. Maybe the dog sensed Rich's inattention, because for a long time it remained silent as Rich walked by.

Then, at the right moment, the dog jumped high enough until his face was right up against Rich's. Rich remembered marble brown eyes and sharp teeth the color of bleached bone. Spittle burned Rich's brown face. A kid, what was his name? Rich didn't remember that, either, but this kid pushed Rich's face against the fence and held it there, laughing. The dog went crazy. He jumped up so many times in a row that it looked to Rich as if the animal simply hovered in thin air, licking and biting and spraying spittle everywhere.

On that day, dogs were forever ruined with him. He hated dogs. All kinds of dogs—mean dogs, little dogs, big dogs, fat dogs, friendly dogs—it didn't matter to him. He hated them all.

"Beau, Goddammit," he now shouted as the memory dissipated. "Get that animal out of the car."

But in the confusion, Beau didn't hear him. "Cougar," he said, laughing. "Ain't you a sight for sore eyes? How did you get out? I missed you, man."

"Beau," Rich said, feeling his heart beating in his chest. "I'm warning . . ."

Gregory stepped abruptly from the car. He walked to the passenger side of the door and cajoled the big, friendly dog out. Rich heard Beau mumble, "Yes, yes, sweetheart, I know. Daddy's home, uh huh."

"I'm going to throw up," Rich yelled. "Right here, right now, I'm going to blow."

Beau sat up, his red hair rising from either side of his balding pate like gauzy wings. "What's the matter?" he asked. "It's only Cougar. He's a teddy bear."

"He's allergic," Gregory said dryly. He held the dog tightly by the scruff of the neck because Cougar had no collar. The dog sat on his haunches panting, his tongue lolling out of his mouth as he watched them. He picked one paw up and down, over and over, making scratching sounds against the sidewalk.

"Beau . . ." Rich warned.

"Okay, okay. I'm out." Beau heaved upward and got out of the car.

Gregory folded his long body back into the passenger's seat. Rich watched Beau lumber up the walk. Cougar loped beside the big man as they made their way up to the front door.

"That's one rather dumb, untrained yellow mutt," Gregory commented.

Rich didn't reply. Instead he drove in silence to the apartment they shared on the ninth floor of a sprawling complex just on the other side of what was still considered one of the good parts of Dunhill. Almost every stick of furniture and every piece of African art in their apartment came from Dinah. She disguised each as a gift so Rich would take it. The leather furniture was for his birthday. The zebra rug and coffee table? Why, their first anniversary dating. And the art was for this Valentine's Day or Easter or Christmas. Eventually, Rich stopped fighting.

But then Gregory suddenly bought into the whole retro-seventies thing. Rich thought it was just to spite Dinah. Because after the zebra rug, he started filling the apartment with stuff he found at garage sales. He bought a kitchen table with lime green Formica and puke-yellow vinyl chairs from an old couple in Sacramento, paying too much for them, in Rich's opinion. It was amazing how fads could make people crack open their wallets to pay for junk. Then there was the Coke vending machine, which, after Gregory restored it, dispensed Coke in short glass bottles for the exact change.

Dinah asked Rich constantly why didn't he move out. He told her it was because they needed to save money. But the truth was, he liked living with Gregory, and he liked the way that Gregory annoyed the hell out of her. Maybe secretly, but he still liked it.

Rich threw the keys on the coffee table and walked to his room. He could hear Gregory call the station and ask about Violet. Rich stripped and took a shower—a long shower. As he shaved, he appraised himself in the bathroom mirror. How would he describe the man staring back at him? Before he could stop them, a string of words came to mind. Male. Black—no, African-American. Early to mid-thirties. Hair black. Eyes, light brown. Height, tall, about six four. Small scar on his left cheek, missing part of his left ear.

He stopped suddenly. He was describing himself as a perp. He looked closer. His face was square, and his hair cut into a fade. His features were perfectly proportioned, his nose long and straight, but his nostrils were wide and flared a little, especially when he was angry. His eyebrows were thick, and he did have long eyelashes that his mother said looked like a girl's. Then there was the ear. He reached up and brushed the rim of the black flap with his index finger. Another souvenir from The Pit. All in all, he was not *bad*-looking. He could certainly find someone with a better personality than . . .

But he cut himself off before he finished the thought. He loved Dinah even though she could be a little pushy at times.

Now was not the time to start having second thoughts, not when he had almost made it. He cut the thoughts of doubt away from his mind and dressed quickly. Sitting on the edge of the bed, he emptied his mind before picking up the phone on the nightstand and dialing Dinah's number. She answered in a voice that was low and sexy. She obviously knew it was him.

"Hi, babe, it's me," Rich said anyway, and waited.

"Oh, no. Oh no, Rich," she said into the silence. "You are not going to cancel on me again, are you?"

"I don't know," Rich stalled, not wanting to say it right away. "What time is it now?"

"What time is it now? What do you mean, what time is it now? You called me, Rich, remember?" He heard her fumble around and knew she was turning the digital clock on her nightstand to see the time. "It's eight. You can't finish up what you need to do in the next couple of hours and meet my father and me at First Baptist?"

"No," he said. "I got a call. I'm sorry, baby."

Neither of them spoke for a while. Then Dinah said, "This is the second time, Rich." Quietly.

"I know," he confirmed.

"When you are the official commander instead of the acting one, you can assign someone to do this, right?"

Rich said nothing. He didn't tell her how far that was from the truth. He would work just as hard when he did get promoted. He couldn't do anything less. But that was the carrot he held in front of her. He needed the promotion so he could spend more time with her. He needed it so they could afford to buy the house in The Point. But more importantly, he needed it to prove to Judge Webster that his daughter was not marrying Pit trash.

"Did you ask him yet?" she asked now.

"No."

"You haven't asked James Freehold when he is going to make your promotion official? Come on, Rich. Do you want to get married or not?" Her voice blared into the phone. Rich could almost see her sitting up in bed, the strap of the pink satin nightgown she always wore falling over her honey-colored shoulders.

"Dinah," Rich challenged her in spite of his earlier thoughts. "We don't need that house in The Point to get married, and you know it."

"I know that's what you think because of where you came from and all, Rich," Dinah said. "But, look, I'm almost thirty-five, and I lack both the inclination and youthful patience to buy some raggedy-ass starter home in which I'll have to fight the roaches for floor space. Besides, I need a decent place where I can entertain. I have responsibilities, Rich. And pride, just like you do. If you would just take the money from Daddy . . ."

"Me look? No, you look, Dinah," Rich said. "I'm not taking money from *Daddy* or anybody. If you want to call this engagement off . . ."

"No, please," she said. "I'm sorry; I'm just disappointed, that's all." Dinah's voice had changed as if she knew just how far that she could push him.

Rich sighed. "That's okay. It's my fault, too. It's been a rough night," he conceded. "Look, this is a pretty simple case. I may be able to finish up in a hurry and meet you and your father at church. And if not church, brunch."

"Okay," she said. "Call me on my cell phone if you can't make it. At least let me know what is going on."

"I will," Rich said and hung up. He didn't say good-bye, because for some reason, he felt he had just been handled.

He sat on the edge of his low, king-sized bed and thought of Kendra Hamilton, the woman in the picture posed with the now dead junkie. Of course he knew Kendra, but that wasn't exactly right, was it? He knew of her, and had met her officially once. The meeting was an unpleasant one he didn't care to dwell on. They had had a run-in about two years ago when he still worked narcotics.

It happened, of course, in The Pit, where a simple arrest

had turned into a near riot and caused him to have the first and only official reprimand placed in his file.

Max's Fine Liquor was a dirty yellow structure that sat at an angle on an acre of black asphalt. Directly across the street, bars protected the windows of a single-story run-down motel. And on the south side of Max's liquor, an alley served as an office for a low-level drug dealer named Peanut. Peanut had a spotter posted in front of Max's whose job was to lead the potential customer to the alley for the drug buy. If the spotter, usually a boy about ten or so, thought the customer was actually a cop, he would shout a warning to Peanut, who would then escape into the network of alleys and houses next to Max's.

Besides being a drug dealer, Peanut was also Rich's informant. The bust was not planned, but Rich was angry with the man (who was actually shaped like his name) for leading him down the garden path for weeks now. Rich had been trying to get Peanut to roll over on Raymond Smalls, who was one of the biggest dealers in The Pit. The bust of Raymond Smalls in Rich's personnel file would have practically guaranteed the promotion Rich had worked so hard for.

But Peanut led Rich on for months. Oh he gave him lots of leads, but they evaporated like ice cream on a hot day when Rich investigated. He believed that Peanut would be more in a mood to cooperate if he were facing a full-body cavity search.

Rich noticed the people milling about on that March afternoon as soon as he and Officer Henderson stepped from the police cruiser. It had been raining unmercifully for weeks. This was the first day that the washed blue sky revealed itself, and warm sun splashed everywhere. People at the motel had placed plastic patio chairs on the pavement to enjoy the weather. Rich noticed a big biker dude with both arms covered in jailhouse tattoos sitting in a plastic lawn chair that cracked under his weight. The biker's bare feet rested on the seat of his Harley, and he held a silver visor to his bearded face to catch some rays.

There were several whores in the doorways of the motel, all in various states of undress, holding plastic tumblers probably filled with Kool-Aid or booze. Some brazenly strolled the parking lot with their fingers curled around cans of Schlitz. A group of thugs, stocking caps covering their heads, leaned against the liquor store balancing bottles of malt liquor on their knees. Rich also noticed kids with back-packs walking home from school or wherever, bouncing basketballs on the cracked sidewalks.

But all of them—every damn person on the street—trained their eyes on Rich and the other officer the minute they stepped from the cruiser. The kids even stopped to gawk. Though cops were not rare in this neighborhood, it was rare to see just one cruiser.

"I don't like this, man," Officer Henderson said. "Maybe we should wait until there's less activity."

"Don't be such a wuss." Rich laughed as he tucked his shirt in back of his jeans. He adjusted his dark glasses and quickly wiped his nose with his forefingers as if getting ready for a run or a workout. "We'll just do this fast and get the hell out of here."

The plan was simple. They would take the spotter into custody and then go for Peanut. But as soon as the spotter saw them approach, he began to cry. Loudly. His shoulders heaved with each sob. He covered his face with his hands as clear snot ran through his little-boy fingers. Rich wiped the sweat from his forehead and grimaced. Maybe this was not going to be as simple as he thought. He bent down on one knee until he was eye-level with the little perp.

"Look here," he said. "We are just going to take a ride. Now why don't you be nice, stop crying and get into the ve-hicle. I won't even handcuff you."

The boy began to cry louder. The sound grated against Rich's ears.

"Oh, for Christ's sake," Rich said, standing up in disgust. And that's when he heard the first boo. He whipped his head around, trying to figure out who said it. But the faces around him were as silent as moons.

Peanut walked from the alley with a confused look on his face. Looking at the crowd, he walked a little farther with his head cocked in question. Maybe something in Rich's face gave it away, or maybe the sky warned him. One minute the day was clear, sun-drenched. In the next instant, a heavy field of clouds rolled by, and the sky grayed over. Still air suddenly gathered itself into a wind that blew leaves and gum wrappers into spirals of funnel clouds. It blew so hard that the thin trunks of the palm trees lining the streets bent almost to breaking.

Before Rich could speak, Peanut broke into a full sprint across asphalt. Rich took off after him, his breath catching in his throat. Out of the corner of his eye, he saw a whore in a flash of blue satin run from the doorway of one of the motel rooms and into the liquor store parking lot. He didn't see it then, but later he figured it had to be her who beckoned to the boy and hid him among the crowds on the street.

Cursing, Rich reached Peanut and lunged out into a dive. He tackled Peanut, who hit the asphalt face first. Rich caught the asphalt on the left side of his own face, and his knee— the bad one—came cracking down as well.

"Ow, ow, ow!" Peanut screamed, as Rich closed handcuffs around his wrists. "I'm hurt, man. I'm hurt!"

"Shut up, and get up," Rich yelled, and yanked Peanut up as hard as he could.

Rich's knees were bleeding, and his hands were scraped raw. He hoped the wetness he felt on the left side of his cheek was rain but knew that it wasn't.

He walked Peanut toward the cruiser. Officer Henderson had the whore in handcuffs. She looked defiant and righteous, which made Rich even angrier.

"Where is he?" he yelled.

"Who?" she asked in a voice that was not at all concerned.

"That young-ass perp standing here just a minute ago."

"He has a name, you know," she spat at him.

"Look, girl, right now I don't care if his name is the Jolly Green Giant. Where the hell is he?" He jerked Peanut back and forth for emphasis.

"Hey, hey, man. Easy, easy," Peanut said, trying to twist away from him.

"Shut the fuck up, Peanut," Rich said. He jerked him back violently once more. "I can't believe you ran on me, man."

"Nothing personal," he whined back.

Rich threw Peanut to Officer Henderson. "Search this fucker," he said.

He then took a step toward the whore. She stepped backward. The cruiser stopped her, and she leaned her head back to look up into his scraped and bloodied face.

"You are under arrest," he said, his index finger pointing down into her face. The crowd booed again.

"For what?" she breathed.

"Aiding and abetting, obstruction of justice. For starters!" he said. The crowd booed even louder. He heard someone say, "Hey, man, leave her alone." Officer Henderson tugged on his arm after he had secured Peanut in the cruiser.

"Yo, Rich," Officer Henderson said. "We'd better jet."

"Did you search her yet?" he asked Officer Henderson, ignoring his advice.

"What?" Both Henderson and the whore said at the same time. She was wearing nothing but a royal blue satin robe that stopped mid-thigh.

"I said . . ." Rich began.

"I know what you said, man," Officer Henderson replied. "She's not carrying anything."

"I'm not wearing anything under this," she said in a hurried whisper.

Rich could see it was true. The rain had started to come down in fat, warm drops, causing the robe to cling.

"No one, and I mean no one is getting in that cruiser unless they are searched first. And that includes"—Rich said, looking at her—"half-naked whores." The crowd started yelling. But Rich didn't care. He had let his anger take control over him. A brick whizzed past his head.

"Man, I'm telling you . . ." Officer Henderson started.

"Do it and get it over with." Rich drew his weapon, held it in the air so everyone could see it.

Officer Henderson searched the whore gingerly, apologizing the entire time. Rich watched, saying nothing, looking at the crowd around him. The sky emptied as lightning streaked across the sky. Warm rain stung the raw place on Rich's face. Someone threw another brick, and this time Rich fired his weapon into the air. The crowd stepped back, but only a bit. When Officer Henderson finished searching the whore, Rich noticed that her chest heaved in anger.

Officer Henderson started to walk toward the trunk of the cruiser.

"What are you doing, man?" Rich asked him.

"Getting a blanket for—"

"Leave it," he snapped. "Let's go."

This time, the biker with the tattoos walked over threateningly. Rich observed that the thugs in the stocking caps were sauntering over to them, too. He asked himself several times afterward what would have happened if the whore hadn't spoken.

"Come on, you guys," she said tiredly. "Leave it alone. It's not worth it, okay?"

They hesitated, and Rich took that moment to get her into the cruiser. The crowd closed around them as the cruiser pulled away. Rich heard loud thumps as they kicked the sides and banged on the trunk.

"You want to go back and arrest them, too?" the whore asked sarcastically from the backseat. Rich said nothing. He just dabbed at the blood on his face with a handkerchief as Officer Henderson nosed the cruiser out of The Pit.

The whore turned out to be not a whore at all, but Dr.

Kendra Hamilton, who was visiting her strung-out mother in that grungy motel across the street from Max's Fine Liquor.

Rich still wanted to push the charges, but the then sheriff, Bill Connors, was so angered by his recklessness, he not only dropped the charges but gave Rich a dressing-down he had never forgotten.

Rich heard three quick knocks on the bedroom door. He looked over and saw Gregory poke his thin face into the room.

"Hey, old man," Gregory said. "Are you ready?"

"Yeah," Rich said. "Come on in here for a minute. I have to get my shoes on."

Gregory opened the door wider and slipped in. Rich tied his shoes, and contemplated Gregory from across the room. Gregory Atfield of the New England Atfields was a thin man, about two inches shorter than Rich. And in Rich's room, with the dark satin comforter and the black lacquered furniture, Gregory looked even whiter than usual. Standing in the middle of the room with his hands shoved in his pockets, Gregory also looked uncomfortable as hell.

"You know I can wait outside," Gregory said.

"No, no, man. I'm almost done." Rich sat his foot on the floor and reached for the other shoe.

"Did you find out where this Kendra Hamilton is?" Rich asked him.

"Yes." Gregory scratched behind his ear. "She works as a resident at Doctor's. But she also volunteers at the free clinic on weekends and nights."

"So it's back to The Pit, huh?" Rich said, as he planted both feet flat on the floor.

"Yes, so it is," Gregory answered. He smiled a little, and considered Rich with searching gray eyes. "Is there something you want to say to me, old man?"

"Do you remember her?" Rich asked, ignoring the question.

"You mean Kendra?"

"No," Rich said. "I mean Dr. Hamilton."

Gregory answered slowly with a wry smile on his face. "I don't think we ever met. However, I do know the circumstances under which you two met. Very odd."

Rich stood up. He let the silence in the room play for a minute. "Did you know the mother?" Rich asked.

Gregory didn't answer right away, but his face hardened.

"Why would I know her?" Gregory asked.

Rich's voice sounded loud in his own ears in comparison with Gregory's quiet one.

"Why wouldn't you, man?" Rich said casually. "You're a cop. She's a junkie. That wouldn't be so strange would it?"

Gregory conceded by nodding his head. "It would not be strange, you are right. But we've never met."

"Are you sure?" Rich persisted. "You were just acting a little weird back there at The Elite."

Gregory folded his arms, and then stroked his chin with his flat fingers. "How long have we known each other, Rich?" he asked.

Rich shrugged his shoulders. "Ever since the academy."

"That's right," he said. "And you'd think by now that you would have learned to trust me." Gregory's New England accent thickened as he said the last words, and Rich knew that he was angry.

Rich laughed. "Come on, man. You know I trust you with my life."

Gregory didn't laugh. He took a step toward Rich and said in a quiet voice, "Then trust me when I tell you that I never met Violet Hamilton before today." He turned away from Rich and started toward the bedroom door. But when he reached it, he turned back to Rich. "Ever," he finished.

Rich caught up with him, and they walked together to the front door of the apartment. As they were about to walk out, Gregory stopped him.

"Tell me this, Rich," he began. "Am I a suspect?"

Rich didn't smile before answering him, though he knew

he should have. He just looked at Gregory. He studied his quiet gray eyes, his blond, almost white hair wisping over his forehead.

"How can you be a suspect when there wasn't even a murder?"

A shadow passed over Gregory's face, but he didn't say anything. Rich regarded him for a few seconds, trying to read him. He concentrated on measuring his breath in and out to keep from speaking of his suspicion once again. He had known Gregory Atfield his entire professional life. He didn't know much about him personally, even though they were roommates. But Rich did know when Gregory was lying.

April

April Hart's chanting ended with a scream when a rat with delusions of being a tomcat sauntered across her bare feet. She screamed out of surprise more than anything. The rat had gotten bolder as the hours turned into days and the days into nights in the garden shed that had been her prison for the last twenty-four days. But the chanting had allowed her to forget about the rat until she felt his reedy claws on her feet. She brushed away the scratches he left and ran to the wooden door of the shed. She beat her fists against it, and her wounded wrists throbbed with each blow.

"Help," she yelled. "Somebody help me! Help."

Silence—just plain mean grim-faced silence—answered back. The bracelets of sores tightened around her wrists, and she felt fresh blood leak onto her forearm. Deflated, she walked back to the bed and sat down.

"My name is April Hart. I'm from Red River, Texas, and I'll be sixteen years old on April twenty-ninth."

Sometimes, when she remembered how she had ended up here, she would laugh until her sides ached and her baby flipped inside of her. It was simple and plain as the dirt on her face. But it was complicated at the same time. She ran away from Red River when she was thirteen years old because she didn't want to become a ward of the state. She ended up in Los Angeles—first a whore, then a heroin addict, finally pregnant. And scared shitless.

She turned to a man that a lot of girls knew, a man they said had connections down at the free clinic. They told her that he would help her—help her and not ask any questions. Shit, she didn't even know his name. He put her up in a room and told her to sit tight. Everything was going to be all right. She thought it was for an abortion, and he let her think that for a while.

But then, one day when she felt she had waited long enough—maybe too long—he told her that it was not for abortion—but for adoption. He had a woman who would take care of the baby somewhere in Napa. When the child was well enough, a family—a good family—would adopt it.

She cursed at him, called him every dirty name she had learned on the streets, and tried to leave. The stinging slap across her face didn't scare her all that much. But the ropes and the blindfold and later this old garden shed emptied of its tools and reminding her of a burrowed-out pecan shell put the fear of Jesus into her.

April started chanting again and continued until the words felt like a small ball of fire in her mouth. Her grandmother, her Nana, told her once that when she felt particularly nervous, she could chant her name or pinch herself hard enough to leave a mark. At least for that moment, she would know that she was alive and held a space in the universe.

And now, since April was not feeling just nervous but terrified, she added a couple of more things to the chant—like her birthday and where she was from. Her hometown was a little place called Red River, exactly fifteen and one half miles outside of Lubbock.

She squeezed her eyes shut and tried to remember exactly what Red River looked like. It really contained no river at all, just a tail of stagnant water that the town eventually dug under with a backhoe to keep the mosquitoes from breeding.

But right now, the month of April, the ground would be wet and the air sweet with the scent of tea roses from Nana's garden. About eleven million pecan trees, their bark knotted with swirls and ridges like old faces, would be stretching along a narrow road for two and one half miles—the entire length of Red River.

April imagined herself walking barefoot along that road in a pink cotton dress, her blond hair freshly washed and shining in the sunlight. She imagined her feet stinging from the hot sand of the road. She saw herself bend, scoop up a handful of pecans, and crack them with her teeth.

But the magic of Pecan Row only lasted for a minute, and the simplest thing, like the branch now scraping against the murky window of the garden shed, put her right back where she didn't want to be. And that was in Dunhill County somewhere in Northern California—the unwilling charge of a crazy man.

CHAPTER 5

"April, did you say?" Dr. Kendra Hamilton asked the frantic woman on the other end of the phone.

The woman's name was Mildred Hart. She was calling all the way from Texas—or at least that's what she said when Kendra answered the phone. "I'm calling all the way from Texas, and I'm looking for my granddaughter." Kendra received these kinds of phone calls all the time. Parents and grandparents assumed that their runaway children would eventually wind up in the only free clinic in Dunhill.

Kendra pressed the phone to her ear, wanting the distraction. She had a full day ahead of her for an Easter Sunday. A pregnant teenage mother waited for a prenatal check, and an old black woman with skin like shoe leather lumbered in with a cough that didn't sound good at all. To top it off, Kendra had just finished closing a stab wound on a thirteen-year-old boy called Boomer because he bebopped through The Pit with a boom box on his shoulder. But instead of Lil' Kim and Puff Daddy, he listened to jazz, the old jazz of Duke Ellington and Ella Fitzgerald. The wound came from his mother, who mistakenly stabbed him during a fight with her boyfriend. The boyfriend split afterward and was probably halfway to nowhere by now.

Boomer had been waiting for her when she arrived at the clinic that morning. He begged her not to call the police, insisting that his mother didn't even know she had cut him. Kendra knew if she reported the incident the boy would end up in a foster home.

"Are you listening to me, Doctor?" Mildred Hart asked.

"Yes, I am," Kendra responded, trying with all her might to give the woman her full attention, "April Hart."

Kendra could hear the desperation in the woman's voice. "My granddaughter. She's been missing for a couple months now. I mean that's when I last heard from her—a couple of months ago. She actually left home a couple of years ago. Anyway, she was living somewhere in Dunhill. She sent me a postcard."

"And you think she might have been seen in the clinic? Did she tell you that before she disappeared?"

A pause then, a long one, before the woman spoke again. "She ain't told me nothing, but when I called the hospitals out your way they told me to call the clinic. They thought that you might have seen her."

Kendra understood Mildred Hart's silence and knew why the hospital told her to check at the clinic. A young girl living on the streets of The Pit could only mean one thing. She was most likely a whore. And whores paraded in and out of the free clinic looking for condoms or AIDS tests all the time.

"I don't remember an April Hart, Mrs. Hart. Maybe if you called the po—"

"I've been talking to the police, Dr. Hamilton. But they ain't doing much about it. If you could just check. . . ."

"Okay, I'll check my records, and call you back."

"Oh, bless your heart," the woman said. "I'll send you a picture . . ."

Kendra didn't hear the rest of the woman's words because Richard T. Marvel swaggered through the double doors of the clinic like an oversized avenging angel. Though two other men were with him, she saw Rich first. She knew who he was—recognized him from that mess at the liquor store a couple of years ago. Richard T. Marvel—emphasis on the *T*—was from the old neighborhood. The word on the street was that he no longer worked narcotics but instead headed the newly formed homicide division for the sheriff's department. Richard T. Marvel was James Freehold's promise to the voters fulfilled and incarnate. It helped that he was also handsome enough and black enough to grace the eleven o'-clock news when James Freehold needed to win points with his constituency.

He grew up in the same part of town she did, but Rich was not a nomad like Kendra. He and his brothers had lived in the same paint-peeling Victorian from birth to adulthood, while she had traveled from motel to motel and from flophouse to flophouse with her drug-addicted mother.

When the Marvel boys reached eighteen, they did what normal kids did. They flew properly from the nest one at a time to attend private colleges on scholarships or to work data-entry jobs or deliver pizza in San Francisco to earn enough money for college. The narrow streets separating the Marvel boys from Kendra and her mother might as well have been the first battle line drawn between them.

Kendra turned her attention to the two other cops who accompanied Rich. One was a balding man with a face as smooth and red as a baby's except for the mustache that hung unevenly over his pink mouth. He was dressed like a cowboy in black snakeskin boots and a belt that was all silver buckle. The other one, a slender gray-eyed cop with wispy blond hair, looked vaguely familiar. She had seen him before. And, no, he hadn't been with Rich Marvel at Max's Fine Liquor, but she couldn't quite remember where she had met him. His gray sports coat swung from his bony shoulders and did nothing to complement his faded blue Dockers. It was like his electricity had been suddenly shut off that morning and he had been forced to dress in the dark—or blindfolded, maybe. The man had a distant look on his face as if he wished to be any place instead of The Pit's free clinic.

And, frankly, Kendra wished he were somewhere else, too, because deep down she knew what they were all about to tell her. It was the phone call, the knock at the door in the middle of the night; it was the moment that she knew had been coming for years.

"Damn," she muttered under her breath as she hung up the phone from Mildred Hart.

Still, she didn't acknowledge the cops but instead turned to her assistant. Maria volunteered with Kendra to work at the clinic on the weekends. She was a short RN with bouncing black hair that scraped her shoulders. Now, as Kendra looked into Maria's flashing brown eyes, the truth of what was about to happen passed between them. Kendra ignored the salty taste of tears trickling down her throat. She took a mental inventory of the waiting room and decided now was not the time to turn on the waterworks.

Kendra turned her attention to the woman with the hacking cough. The woman, swathed in several blankets and smelling of menthol and candle wax, huddled in the corner. Kendra had almost forgotten about her, but she remembered how she had first appeared at the clinic over a week ago, sitting in the corner like an old black crow. Like a bad omen. A blinding white rag encircled her dark head, and every minute of her miserable life conspired to carve a map of wrinkles on her shiny black face.

Boomer had seen the cops, too, and was almost as nervous as Kendra was. He took a step backward while holding his bandaged arm by the elbow. Kendra strode over to him. She didn't want fear compelling him to say something that he would regret. Boomer turned his liquid brown eyes to her in worry as the cops sauntered over to them. Kendra clamped a firm hand that meant *quiet* on Boomer's shoulder. She knew that they were not here for him. Rich stopped in front of the boy, who stood shaking like a leaf from his skinny shoulders to his Nike hi-tops. Rich stooped down until he was eye-level with Boomer.

"What happened to your arm, little man?" Rich asked

him. His voice almost sounded concerned in Kendra's ears. Almost.

"He broke it," Kendra said before Boomer could answer.

Rich looked at Kendra. The man was still as good-looking as the devil, but he had that same air of cynicism and arrogance that disgusted her two years ago and disgusted her now. And it didn't help that his light brown eyes as they searched her face held compassion.

Rich touched the bandages gently. "That doesn't look like a cast," he said.

"He broke it," Kendra said again and swung away, heart thumping in her chest. *Please God,* she thought as she walked away, *let it be something else, please.*

The clinic didn't have an office for the doctors who volunteered their time there. It and a pawnshop were the only spaces open in the bedraggled strip mall. The space the clinic occupied had been many things—an old clothing store, a Mexican restaurant, a pool hall. It changed its identity more times than a person with multiple personality disorder. Finally, Luke Bertrand, a philanthropist and former doctor, bought the space and added two exam rooms that were as tiny as prison cells.

Kendra went into the first exam room, fully expecting them to follow. Rich and the blond cop, the one she thought she recognized, walked inside the room with her, but the cowboy waited outside the door. Once inside, she turned to face them with her arms folded across her chest.

"What can I do for you, Detectives?" she asked in a voice so iced in formality that it startled even herself.

"This is my partner, Gregory Atfield," Rich said, then stopped.

She waited for him to continue, but he just stood there, silent. And so did his partner. Their hesitation surprised her. She figured that in their line of work they did this sort of thing all the time. She wasn't about to make it easy for them. Instead she waited. Gregory looked at a point over her shoulders. But Rich? He didn't take his eyes from her face.

"For God's sake," she finally snapped. "Just say it."

Rich sighed. "Violet Hamilton is your mother?"

Kendra swallowed. She shook a coil of hair from her forehead and felt everything fall apart in her at once. She closed her eyes and willed herself into control.

"You know she is." She was surprised at how strained her voice sounded, like a stretched piece of silk.

"That's right, we do," Gregory said, and he finally looked at her.

She returned his gaze with steady eyes. She felt not one tear in her eyes. Not yet, anyway. He continued in a voice that reminded her of a priest in a confessional.

"Your mother was found dead this morning at The Elite Ho—"

"How?" Kendra cut him off. He fell silent, and his fingers fluttered together like sparrows. She could almost see the nervous energy emanating from his body.

"What do you mean, how?" Rich said before Gregory had a chance to answer.

She used her palms to heave herself up onto the exam table. She gripped the sides with both hands. Tissue paper rattled noisily in the small room. She bowed her head and fought back tears with every ounce of her being. Pride was the only thing that kept her from breaking down. She waited until she felt her voice strengthen into a tight rope in her throat.

"How did she die?" She stared down at the floor, afraid that if she looked at them the tears would come.

"Doc," Rich started, "you knew that your mother was—"

Kendra's head snapped up before Rich could finish. "A what?" she challenged. "A junkie?"

"I was going to say addict, Dr. Hamilton," Rich finished gently.

"You still haven't answered my question," she persisted. "I want to know how."

"Your mother died of a heroin overdose," Rich replied.

"What?" Kendra breathed in surprise. But they didn't answer her. "That's impossible," she whispered into the still room. Then her voice rose in the face of their silence. "You hear me? That's impossible."

She looked from Gregory's gray eyes to Rich's brown ones. Rich remained still as a stone under her gaze, his hand knotted into a fist on his hip. His open suit coat revealed his badge, which glinted in the harsh light of the exam room. Gregory walked over to Kendra and touched her shoulders.

"Your mother was found at The Elite Hotel dead from a drug overdose. The needle was still in her arm. Obviously, she came into possession of some bad drugs," he said, his voice pattering around her like a gentle rain.

Kendra jerked away from him.

"If you found my mother dead from a drug overdose, then somebody killed her," she said. Though her voice was calm, the words struggled out of her mouth and caused sharp points of pain in her throat.

Gregory lifted his own hands to Kendra in a gesture that said he had given up.

"Dr. Hamilton," Rich said, "what makes you so sure that your mother *didn't* die of an overdose?"

Kendra jumped from the exam table and walked over to Rich. She folded her arms and regarded him intently. Violet had once told her that she had not been afraid to die. She always said that a little piece of her would be carried forward in Kendra, and Adam, who was Kendra's brother.

But as soon as those words had left Violet's lips, Adam died from a cop's bullet on one blinding afternoon on the streets of The Pit. After that, Violet became so fearful of death that she refused to walk past a cemetery or step foot into a hospital or cross Main Street against the light for that matter. She didn't share needles or buy her heroin from someone she didn't know or trust. If she had to come to the clinic where Kendra volunteered or to the hospital where she worked, Violet would stand with one foot in the street while cars whizzed by and drivers honked their horns. Violet would talk endlessly of the death pall hanging over Dunhill, how she needed to leave the town before it mistook her for a goldfish and swallowed her whole.

Kendra wanted to tell Rich all of this, but the words failed her. One look at his judgmental brown eyes told her that he couldn't, wouldn't be convinced. She tried anyway.

"Let me tell you something about Violet Hamilton," she said. "She was an addict for over twenty years. She may have been a junkie, but I tell you that she was a damn good one. She would have never allowed herself to overdose. She just wouldn't have."

The interest she had seen in his face earlier left all at once. He sighed and took a step back. "Look," he said. "I'm sorry."

Kendra knew that it was unreasonable, but she hated the tone of his voice. All polite and official and noncommittal. She glared at Rich Marvel. The sound of the old woman's cough floated in from the waiting room.

Gregory Atfield pressed his lips into a thin line. She could see that he was slightly embarrassed, and she thought that he was embarrassed for her. She knew everyone in the waiting room could hear them. But she couldn't help it. If her mother had to die, why did Richard Marvel have to be the one to tell her about it?

"I just bet you are sorry," she said in a quiet voice bathed in anger. "I just bet, by damn, you are."

Rich didn't reply, so she went on. "You are standing here, Richard *T.* Marvel, not caring one whit about your dead junkie. You are just standing here thinking how my mother ruined your Sunday, wondering how you can finish up with this case and get back to all your uptown Point friends. You don't care who killed her or why she died. You don't care because she was a junkie. Her death is not important to you and your precious homicide department, is it? James Freehold will probably dance a jig tonight when you tell them that he is rid of one more addict."

Rich stared at her. Anger warred with compassion in his eyes. Finally, he spoke.

"No one killed her, Doc. She killed herself."

She turned away then and angrily swiped at the tears in her eyes.

"Get out," she said. "Do you hear me? Both of you, get out."

They both left without a word, their steps like whispers. Kendra stood for a minute in the tiny examination room with its pitifully small tissue-covered exam table and attempted to deny her primary emotion.

Relief.

The word clanged in her head like a rusty church bell. To escape it, and she had to escape it, she swung around and grabbed up the tissue paper and white sheet into a ball. The festive rustling sound sent her to her knees. She rested there for a minute thinking of what she would miss about her mother. But the brief, angry tears she had shed a minute ago disappeared like smoke. She couldn't think of one thing she would miss about her. Not one goddamn thing.

And that was horrible to her.

Violet Hamilton, she thought, *my mother, Violet Hamilton.* As she repeated the name—dry-eyed and dry-throated—she couldn't help but think about growing up with a junkie. As early as five years old, there were the endless dramas of searching for Violet. And finding her—in shooting galleries, in alleys, and in cheap motels. Then there was the endless succession of foster homes after the state took Kendra away from Violet for what should have been forever. She had been ten years old then. She was made a permanent ward of the state, but through it all she always kept in contact with her mother. Violet's world enveloped Kendra like a placenta and marked everything that she did.

When her knees started to ache, Kendra stood up and took a deep breath. Wearily, she separated the cloth sheet from the tissue paper and stuffed the paper into a small trash can. She placed her fingertips on both cheeks and searched for Violet in her own face in the mirror over the sink.

But Kendra's features could not have been more different.

Where Violet's eyes were narrow, Kendra's were wide and round. Where Violet's nose had been small, the strong line of Kendra's nose angled at the tip. And where Violet's lips were tiny and bowlike, and where her teeth were like broken buttons in her mouth, Kendra's mouth was full, her teeth even and straight.

Kendra leaned closer into the mirror, her fingers on her cheeks like long brown tears. Then she found what she was looking for. In some way, her mother had been right about living in her children. Scraps of Violet Hamilton lay in Kendra's high cheekbones, and in the haunted look in her brown eyes.

She took her hands from her face, lifted the faucet lever, and let the water run in a clear, cold stream. The water she splashed on her face chilled her back to reality. Violet Hamilton was gone, and that was that. The only things to do were to find out who killed her and make them pay.

CHAPTER 6

The old, black crow woman swathed in white glared at Kendra when she returned to the waiting room. She focused her lidless crow eyes on Kendra without blinking. Kendra thought the woman found and condemned every ounce of relief in her. If Maria hadn't rushed to Kendra's side, she would have leapt on the old woman and shaken her until her nose bled.

"I'm so sorry, Kendra," Maria sputtered. "If there is anything I can do . . ." Maria reached down and took Kendra's hand in hers. Kendra felt as if she had just stuck her hand into an oven mitt that had been used to take something hot out of the oven. Maria was one year from fifty years old and had just entered menopause. She was so excited about this fact that she would squeal in delight at the onset of each hot flash. She would press Kendra's palm to her face so she could share the heat.

Nowadays, no matter what the weather, Maria wore sleeveless shirts that exposed the black freckles on her shoulders. And when Maria was at a loss for words—like she was now—she thought she could make up for it by touching people—by placing a hot hand on a bare shoulder or squeezing a waist with a grip so hot Kendra often wondered if it were possible for someone to be branded by a touch.

"No," Kendra said extracting her hand from Maria's. "I'm fine. Where is Boomer?"

"I sent him home while you were talking to the detectives," Maria explained. She swiped sweat from her forehead before continuing. "I told him to come back tomorrow so we can check his bandages."

Kendra nodded heavily and looked around the room. Two rows of plastic chairs faced one another across a linoleum floor. The floor itself was covered with black scuff marks and a layer of dirt and grime. The first weekend that Kendra and Maria were there, they tried scrubbing the floor with Comet until the palms of their hands were raw and a line of blood rimmed the skin beneath their fingernails. But in the end, none of it worked. The floor looked the same as it did when they started. Dirty, walked on, and a little hopeless.

"What happened to the pregnant girl?" Kendra asked.

"She left as soon as you walked to the back with the cops. That old woman is the last one here, but I'm going to drop her off at a shelter when I leave."

"I don't understand," Kendra said. It was barely ten o'clock in the morning. The clinic was supposed to be open until seven that night.

Maria's tone was brisk as she grabbed a canvas bag and began stuffing her *Redbook* magazine and her lunch into it.

"I put the closed sign on the door," she said. "If they really need help today, let them call nine-one-one. You've got business to take care of."

Kendra looked at the door and saw that the blinds had been pulled down. She felt too weak to protest. She gave Maria a smile as she shrugged out of her lab coat. She was thinking about a cool bath when the blinds at the double doors rattled. Maria and Kendra turned toward it. The old crow woman heaved herself—blankets and all—forward to get a good look.

"Be still," Maria said. "Maybe they will go away."

They waited for a while, and then they heard the rattling again. The knock told them that whoever was behind the door had no intention of going away. Kendra walked over to it and hesitated for just a second. Then with one swift movement, she turned the key still protruding from the lock and opened the door to Raymond Smalls.

Even though Kendra had her back to Maria, she could feel her assistant's entire body tense. Raymond Smalls dealt in drugs—heroin, coke, crack, speed—you name it. And if he didn't sell it he would point you to someone who did. He told Kendra that he was just a businessman. He simply gave people what they wanted. If they didn't get it from him, they would certainly get it from somewhere else—like East 14th in Oakland or South of Market in San Francisco.

To the dismay of law enforcement, he was also the hero of many boys in The Pit. He sported handsome designer clothes and owned several cars. Some were sleek, like the Porsche he drove so fast that he was forced to turn corners balanced on two wheels. Others, like his silver Mercedes, lumbered through the neighborhood like an old woman on a walker.

But more importantly, Raymond Smalls was the boy Kendra grew up with. Neither one of them had ever known where their parents were. Kendra and Raymond were the same age and attended the same schools. They used to skip pebbles off the surface of the water in the Bay as children. While sunlight fought its way through white clouds as thick as cities, they would sit well into the night and tell each other their dreams. She was going to be a scientist and find a cure for her mother's addiction, and he was going to be . . .

But he would suddenly stop, and tell her he couldn't imagine his life after the age of fifteen. For him, the road to the future was bleak and starless. Two of his brothers were dead—in their graves before they were fourteen. And the one remaining had given his life to San Quentin after a fight over eleven dollars left a man dead from a single blow to the head with a fully chalked pool cue.

As she was being sent to her first foster home, Raymond Smalls went to his first juvenile facility for spotting for a local drug dealer. But that was the only time Ray Ray was caught. Now he was careful as a silver fish swimming in the company of sharks. The cops couldn't touch him.

When Kendra used to visit Violet in The Pit, Ray Ray would find his way to her and talk of old times or of going legitimate, getting married- -and having a real family. He talked of leaving The Pit forever, at which point he would look at her in a sidelong, searching glance. But Kendra would not let herself fully grasp his true meaning. His words would lie upon her consciousness like a leaf on the surface of still water, and in the end she would drive them down, pretend she did not fully understand.

Now, as he stood before her with his handsome face twisted into a mask of compassion, Kendra looked at him and saw him—really saw him—for the first time. His face was square, and his skin smooth as black marble. She could see points of light glitter in his black hair, which was cut low and perfect. Velvet eyebrows arched fully over his almond-shaped eyes. And Kendra noticed for the first time how unfathomable his eyes were, how like the color of an empty night.

He pursed his full lips and came toward her with his hands outstretched. Kendra could not take her eyes from the gold bracelet that slipped over the bones of his right wrist. He reached down and grabbed her still hands in both of his. Ray Ray's hands, which were bare of jewelry, felt soft and muscular. She looked up at him. The diamond earring in his left ear glittered as wildly as the lights in his hair. *How much did it cost in pain and suffering,* she thought.

"Kendra," he said, his voice rich as cream. "I am so sorry. I just heard."

Kendra did not respond. Instead she stared at him as if she were looking into the face of a stranger she didn't like or trust very well. Her hands remained limp in his.

"You've got some nerve showing up here—especially now," Maria hissed from behind Kendra.

Kendra saw Ray Ray's eyes whip out a warning to Maria. Kendra looked over her shoulder and saw Maria take a tiny step backward. Childhood friend or not, Raymond Smalls was still a drug dealer. He was a dangerous criminal that many people wanted locked up or thrown away like curdled milk.

"Maria," Kendra said in a tired voice.

Maria flashed Kendra a look. "He's got some nerve showing up here before your mother is even cold in the ground." Maria punched a fist into the sleeve of a blue crocheted sweater, then looked over at Ray Ray. "You might have been the one who killed her, Raymond Smalls. You might as well have put a gun to her head." Maria brought her thumb and index finger to her head to mimic a gun. Ray Ray stared pointedly at her and then coolly raised an eyebrow.

Maria didn't miss the intent in that raised eyebrow. Using a wide hip to bump Kendra out of the way, she darted to him. She stood in front of Ray Ray and pointed her index finger into his face.

"Don't you threaten me, Raymond Smalls," she said. "Don't you think you can scare me, either."

"Maria," Kendra took her by her shoulders and gently pushed her away. "It's all right. Please."

"Please? Please what?" Maria challenged. "Besides, how does he know she's dead? You barely know yourself."

"It's all over The Pit," Ray Ray explained.

His eyes trained on Kendra as Maria buzzed around him with all the impact of an annoying fly. *Just like the cops,* Kendra thought. *He knows how to evade them all.*

"Maria, it's no use," Kendra said gently.

"Fine," Maria said, snatching up her canvas bag. "Throw your life away on this piece of Pit trash. Your mother's dead, and he probably sold the dope that killed her. I'm leaving."

Without having to be told, the woman with the white rag on her head stood up and followed Maria out the door. The blankets weighed her down so much that she had to walk bent over, her body shaped like a question mark. Her beady eyes fixed on Kendra as she passed them in a haze of menthol. After the door closed behind her, Ray Ray looked at Kendra.

"I don't sell bad dope," he said. "You know that, Kendra. It's bad for business."

"Stop it, Ray Ray," she said.

She wanted to strangle him, but she felt weak as she realized for the first time in her life how alone—*really alone*—she was. Adam was gone, and now Violet. And Kendra finally figured out what she would miss about her mother. It would be the Dove soap smell of her skin on her good days, and the feel of her jutting hair. Kendra would even miss the *I'll-get-better* promises that flowed from Violet's lips like water.

Deep in her heart, she knew Ray Ray was worried more about how this would affect their friendship than he was saddened about Violet. She opened her eyes wide and saw the defeated waiting room of the clinic—the faded, plastic chairs, the grimy floor, and the ripped curtains. The hopelessness overwhelmed her, and quite by accident, her face crumpled. She tried her best to not allow the sob to escape her throat, but couldn't. It bubbled over and spilled out of her mouth. She immediately felt Ray Ray's arms around her and heard his sigh of relief.

CHAPTER 7

Kendra Hamilton had always thought April a strange month. It was that time of year when it seemed Mother Nature did not know quite what to do with herself. One moment it would be so hot that sweat beads would form in the small of Kendra's back and under her armpits. But the next moment the sky would turn mean and gray before spilling buckets of stinging rain into the surprised mouths of yellow daffodils that bloomed without mercy all over Dunhill County.

On the morning Kendra boarded the BART train at a station in The Pit to go see an old friend in San Francisco, a hormonal April decided to throw a surprise frost all over Northern California. Ice crystals pricked at Kendra's face and made her wish she had worn her pea coat instead of the gray Berkeley sweatshirt with its torn collar and patched elbows. Once outside Embarcadero station, she followed the daffodils' example and ducked her head as far into the collar of her sweatshirt as possible. She slipped the oversized sleeves of the sweatshirt over her hands, ignoring the few curious glances she received for doing so. As she dodged the endless stream of people dressed in suits and skirts and designer pumps, she thought about what had brought her to this particular point in her life.

Three years earlier she had been a relief doctor in a refugee camp in Africa, mostly battling flies, treating machete wounds, and administering medicines for diarrhea and dysentery. She was physically miserable, but she loved it.

And just a year and a half earlier she had been working a neighborhood in Washington, D.C., that was so embattled in drug wars she couldn't walk two feet without stepping over a syringe or an empty dime bag. It made Dunhill seem tame in comparison. She carried a seven-inch knife in her purse and sometimes slept in the bathtub to avoid stray bullets that might find their way into her apartment. She slept with every single light burning, and her electric bill was one hundred and fifty dollars a month for a one-bedroom apartment. She was scared to death and having the time of her life. She didn't have to think about Dunhill or Violet, only had to put one foot in front of the other and survive.

But Lucas Bertrand—the man who had put her through medical school and helped her land those assignments— called her and told her that Violet had been in decline. That's how he put it: *decline*. He asked her to come back home to be near her mother, and help out in his free clinic located in The Pit. Since she had spent a lot of effort escaping The Pit after medical school, Kendra had refused him for months. She capitulated only when the request came from Violet Hamilton herself.

Now Kendra was going to the man who had been helping her since she was ten years old. She was going to him because he was rich and influential and could get things done. And right at the moment, Kendra Hamilton needed something done. She needed it in a big way.

Yesterday morning, Richard Marvel had awakened her from a Sominex-induced sleep to tell her that the medical examiner had completed the autopsy report on Violet Hamilton. Without a good morning and without waiting for her to answer, he went on to tell her what he had been sure of all along. Violet Hamilton died of a drug overdose.

The tension between them—that had always been between them since that episode in front of Max's Fine Liquor—buzzed so that it was as if she were holding a tuning fork to her head instead of her cordless phone.

"Okay . . ." she trailed the word out slowly. She didn't quite know what to expect. She wanted him to slow down so she could think, but he didn't give her a chance.

"It's what we thought," he repeated. "Bad dope. A drug overdose, nothing more."

He paused then, and Kendra let the silence hang between them as his last words raced through her head.

"Doc . . ." Rich started.

But Kendra cut him off. "Can you just stop for a second and let me think?" She tried to make her voice reasonable but knew how hoarse she sounded. Her throat felt like it was lined with cotton batting. Finally, she spoke again.

"How do you know?" she asked. "Are you telling me that you've seen the final autopsy report?"

Rich sighed. "I've spoken to the medical examiner myself," he explained. "She saw signs of pulmonary edema," he stopped for a second. "That's massive flooding of the lungs due to—"

"I know what it is, Detective," Kendra snapped. "What else?"

"There was also cerebral edema consistent with drug overdoses," he said impatiently.

Kendra didn't respond. She could sense that he wanted to be done with this phone call, but she didn't give a damn. Kendra let the silence play for a while. "Who did the autopsy?" she responded finally.

"Dr. Rita Sandbourne," he said. "Do you know her?"

"I know of her, but she's missing something."

"Tell me, Dr. Hamilton," Rich challenged. "What's she missing?"

Kendra opened her mouth to speak but quickly closed it again. She knew if this were a face-to-face conversation, she would look like a hooked fish. But they weren't face to face, and Rich couldn't know how that question made her heart beat faster, made her want to pack her one bag and leave Dunhill County forever. Rich's next words cut into her thoughts.

"Your mother died of a drug overdose," he said. "The case is cleared. You need to move on and make arrangements to remove the body from the morgue." He said this last gently, and she could tell he was really trying. She knew that he wanted to say more, because she heard his sharp intake of breath. But she placed the phone back in the cradle before the words left his mouth.

"Hey, lady," a voice said, "you got a quarter?"

Kendra blinked. Skyscrapers and cable cars and well-dressed men and women surrounded her. She didn't know where the voice came from until she actually looked down. At her feet was a homeless man with matted hair sitting with his back against a building. She had stopped at the corner of First and Market in downtown San Francisco.

"What are you, deaf or something?" The man squinted up. A white line like chalk surrounded his brown lips. "I'm thirsty as hell. I say, have you got a quarter?"

No, Kendra did not have a quarter. She didn't even have a purse. Her license was wrapped in a twenty-dollar bill in the left back pocket of her Levi's, and her BART ticket was in the other. She reached into her back pocket and unwrapped the twenty from around her license. Without thinking twice, she gave it to him. She barely registered his whoops of joy and cackles of thanks.

The office building the homeless man used as a backrest boasted forty full floors. Once inside Kendra noticed several people milling around the three elevator bays. Suddenly, she found herself engaged in the spot-the-cop game she and her mother had played on the streets of The Pit. She knew that buildings like these had plainclothes guards to keep out San Francisco's homeless population.

One woman with messy blond hair that looked like it had been cut with a hacksaw nervously tapped her high-heeled pump against the marble floor. She clutched a newspaper and a cup of Starbucks coffee to her skinny chest. She wasn't the cop. She looked like she was late for work or for a meeting with a client.

A short man with a shiny bald spot in the middle of his head squinted at the legion of offices listed on the wall. He was lost or looking for someone. There were a few other people doing what people always did at elevators. They waited silently and prayed like hell that they wouldn't catch someone's eyes and be trapped for a few seconds in idle conversation.

But then there was another man who seemed to blend into the building. He was tall and white and young—not more than twenty-six years old. His shoulders were square, his face and eyes clear. His hair was cut as neatly as his perfectly tailored suit. *Bingo,* Kendra thought. *Cop.*

It wasn't until he returned her gaze with a steady blue gaze of his own that Kendra was aware that he had registered her presence. He stuffed both his hands into his pants pockets and strolled over to her. A beige phone wire trailed from his ear and disappeared into the collar of his white shirt.

"Where to, ma'am?" His voice was abrupt, but polite.

That stopped Kendra for a moment. She hadn't expected him capable of speech.

"I beg your pardon?" She blinked.

"You haven't selected a bay," he said and pasted a smile on his face. "What floor are you visiting this morning?"

Kendra looked around and saw that even in San Francisco she was the only Black person near the elevator bays.

"What makes you think I'm visiting?" she asked.

His nod and thin smile told Kendra he had expected the challenge. "I haven't seen you in here before, and your attire would suggest you are not working—"

"Thirty-eighth floor," Kendra interrupted him.

"Then you would need the third elevator bay. Here, let me get it for you." Kendra watched the button light up under his index finger. He smiled at her again and then resumed his casual guarding of the first floor of 525 Market Street.

Inside the elevator Kendra's own face stared back at her from the silver-backed elevator doors. Teak banded by gold trim paneled the elevator in formality and wealth. It reminded her of a coffin raising itself heavenward. No matter how she tried, she couldn't escape the analogy, nor could she escape the fact that she had done nothing to remove her mother's body from the morgue. At least not yet. She could stall the morgue's office for a couple of more days.

Lucas Cornelius Bertrand's wedge-shaped office covered almost an entire corner of the thirty-eighth floor. His secretary, Evelyn, sat behind a cherry wood desk, her glasses perched on her nose. Evelyn was in her early sixties and had worked for Luke for years. Kendra had known Evelyn since she was ten years old.

"May I help—" Evelyn stopped when she recognized her. "Why, Kendra!" She came from behind the desk and pressed her papery face against Kendra's. Kendra's nose filled with the powdery smell of Evelyn's perfume.

"Is he in?" Kendra asked before stepping back. She hoped her face would tell Evelyn that she didn't feel like chit-chat.

"Yes, he is, dear," Evelyn took her by the hand and led her to a leather armchair. "Why don't you sit down? I will check to see if he can receive you. It's so nice to see you again. You don't come down often enough."

She patted Kendra's knee and then walked to the black lacquered doors leading to Luke Bertrand's office. Kendra sat on the very edge of the leather chair and thought about the man she had come to see.

For some reason, well over twenty years ago Luke had taken an interest in her mother. He tried helping Violet overcome her heroin addiction, and when that didn't work, he took an interest in Kendra. She was ten years old at the time. He mentored her through high school, college, and later medical school. He told her of an organization that sent doctors to trouble spots around the world. As a result, after medical school she found herself in Africa, and later Washington, D.C. At first she worked for that organization because she thought she owed Bertrand. Later she did it because she loved doing it.

Kendra stood up and rubbed her hands together. She looked

around the office wondering what was taking so long. Besides Evelyn's cherry wood desk with its gold lamp, there was a burgundy leather chair and loveseat. Monet reproductions shared the patterned wallpaper with certificates and plaques from charitable organizations. She stood and read them to pass the time. *To Lucas Cornelius Bertrand,* one plaque from the Salvation Army read, *without his help many would still be hungry.* There were other framed certificates from the Chamber of Commerce and Children's Hospital.

Though Luke used to be a practicing pediatrician, he was now strictly a philanthropist who spent his time raising money for charitable causes. He had inherited most of his money from an eccentric White man who had once lived on a sprawling estate in one of Dunhill's richest communities. Because he didn't have family, the old man surrounded himself with Siamese cats and fish and parakeets and left his fortune to the son of the woman who worked for him. That son was Luke Bertrand.

When the old man died, Luke spread his money around with a Midas touch. When he grew tired of giving his inherited money away, he threw lavish parties and cajoled his rich friends to add to his charitable coffers.

The relationship between Kendra and Luke had been strained this past year. Even though he had called Kendra back to Dunhill to help Violet, he had questioned her about the hold Violet had over her. He wanted Kendra to commit Violet to a state facility. He wanted Kendra to distance herself from her own mother. He himself, he had told her, would have nothing more to do with Violet.

"Kendra, my dear!"

Kendra turned and saw Luke Bertrand approach her with outstretched hands. Luke was not very tall—only about five seven—but he had a way about him that made him seem much taller. He walked with his shoulders squared and his head tilted upward. He took even, loping steps that allowed him to cover more ground than a man of his height should have been able to.

There was not a single wrinkle in Luke Bertrand's polished brown face, though he had to be nearing sixty. The only thing that marred his perfect face was a ribbed scar that sliced the eyebrow over his left eye clean in half. His nose started from the crease between his eyes and stopped just short of his etched lips. Luke's eyes were dark brown and now kind as he gazed at her.

She felt a smile flicker across her face. He dropped a heavy hand on her shoulder.

"You have to forgive me," he said. "I had a phone call I simply had to finish."

Luke guided Kendra into his office. Windows consumed the entire back wall. The low hum of a humidifier filled Kendra's ears. Gray carpet covered the floor, and a thick glass desk sat center stage in the middle of the room. On it were three stacks of paper and a gold pen and pencil set, glittering as if they had never been touched. Two Siamese cats, their eyes crystal blue and unblinking, stood guard in opposite corners of the room. Kendra would have believed them statues if one hadn't swished its tail forward over its front paws.

Luke sat down on a low bench decorated with Chinese artwork. He patted the place beside him. "Is there something wrong, Kendra?" he asked when she sat down.

"Mamma's gone," she replied.

Luke sighed, a long, deep, compassionate sigh. "I am so sorry, Kendra, though I'm not surprised," he said. "Is there anything I can do?"

She laughed bitterly. "Funny you should ask." She stood up and walked over to the window. From this height, she could see the ferry come in from Sacramento and the Transbay bus terminal. She could see the torn outlines of the new stadium still in the throes of construction. For a second or two she hesitated. She wished she hadn't come. She wished she had taken her mother's body out of the morgue and left Dunhill as fast as humanly possible.

But she couldn't have done that. She knew she still owed Violet something.

"Luke," she said. "They won't investigate."

She heard Luke's soft steps on the carpet. He didn't speak until they stood shoulder to shoulder. "I'm assuming it was the drugs. Is that true?" he said.

She nodded without looking at him. "That's what they are saying."

He sighed. "Doesn't that seem logical to you, my dear?"

She trained her brown eyes on him, stared at him until he dropped his gaze. "You know that can't be true, Luke," she said. "There has to be something more."

"What did the autopsy say?" he asked in a low voice.

"Pulmonary and cerebral edema—" Kendra began.

"Well, there you have it," he said easily. "Kendra, sometimes that's all there is. The logical assumption is in most cases the correct one."

"This isn't logical, Luke," she said. "My mother wouldn't take drugs from just anybody. She didn't have any reason to be so stupid."

"Kendra," Luke said in an almost pleading voice. "Maybe she got desperate and went to a different source for her drugs. She could have received a bad batch."

"There would have been no reason for her to go anywhere else. My mother was obsessed with being safe—or what she *thought* was safe anyway."

"What can I do for you?" he questioned. "Can I help with the arrangements?"

"I can handle the arrangements, Luke." She turned to him and did her best to pin him with her eyes. "You supported James Freehold in the election, didn't you?"

"I did indeed," he said. "As I recall, I contributed a lot of money to his campaign. I also endorsed his candidacy."

"I was thinking, then, Luke . . ." She stopped and swallowed. "Maybe you can talk to him, have him look into what happened."

Luke held up both hands, displaying the Rolex wrapped snugly around one wrist.

"I hate interfering in police business," he said. "That is

not why I supported James Freehold. This would put me in a very awkward position, Kendra."

Kendra remained silent, waiting.

"You know you are like a daughter to me," Luke said.

The phone rang. They both ignored it. Kendra could see Luke struggling. He didn't want to help her for reasons she only partially understood. But on some level she knew that he knew the consequences if he didn't. It might mean a permanent rift in their already tenuous friendship. One of the Siamese cats meowed loudly, and Luke reached down and picked him up. He stroked the cat, which closed its eyes and ducked its head as if to avoid a blow.

"Now, now, Jupiter," he clucked. "Papa's busy." Kendra felt his gaze fall over her face once again.

"I'll talk to James Freehold for you," he said quietly. "However, I cannot promise that it will come to anything."

Kendra nodded and turned toward the window. She wasn't surprised at his next words.

"You know what this could mean, don't you?" he said. His voice was almost like a warning.

"Yes, I do."

"Are you ready for it?" he asked.

She swallowed before sending him a glance. "I'm ready for anything. The question is, Luke, are you?"

His laugh was musical. "My dear Kendra," he said. "Obviously you have no idea what a protective shield money can be. I've squirmed out of more scandals than your young mind can imagine. But I may not be able to offer you that same protection."

He stopped petting Jupiter, and stroked Kendra's cheek. "Don't you worry anymore," he said. "I will talk to James Freehold."

His voice reminded her of sheet music. He turned back to the cat and kissed the top of its head. Kendra waited for the relief to wash over her and was surprised when it didn't come.

CHAPTER 8

Kendra thought about Luke Bertrand all the way back to The Pit's free clinic, and wondered if she had done the right thing. When she arrived she noticed an old woman with iron gray hair sitting on the curb. The woman wore a powder blue pantsuit, the double-knit kind from the seventies. As Kendra approached, the woman stood up so fast that she teetered sideways. Kendra didn't know why, maybe it was the lines etched on either side of the woman's mouth, but she went over to her as if she knew what she wanted. She didn't. She had no idea.

"Dr. Hamilton?" the woman said as Kendra reached her.

"Yes?"

"I'm Mildred Hart, April Hart's grandmother. How do you do?"

Mildred Hart held out a flat hand for Kendra to shake. Kendra instantly recognized the name. It was the woman who had called on Sunday looking for her granddaughter. Guilt washed over Kendra. She hadn't done anything with the information so far. She had been so wrapped up in her mother's death that she had forgotten all about it.

"I thought you lived in Texas," Kendra said, puzzled, stalling for time.

"I did," she said. "I mean I do. Lord, I'm so confused and worried I don't know what to do. Can we go somewhere and sit down?" she asked, her fingers working in and out of the bright blue scarf around her neck.

"Sure we can," Kendra said.

They went to a Denny's near the clinic. Mildred Hart laid her purse on the chair next to her and unwound the scarf from her neck. She smoothed the knit jacket over her stomach and fussed with the gaps between the buttons.

"I haven't had this suit on in almost twenty-five years," she said nervously. "I guess it's just a little out of style. I just wanted to look nice when I saw you bec—" Mildred stopped and looked away. She folded her square hands neatly on the table, started again.

"In answer to your earlier question, I do live in Texas," Mildred continued. "But I took an airplane out here to find April. I had to borrow most of the money, and I still couldn't afford enough for a real ticket. I had to buy one of them non-refundable things, and I've got to get back on Thursday."

Kendra covered Mildred Hart's hands with her own. They were as smooth and soft as powder.

"I'm sorry," Kendra said, not knowing what this woman wanted of her. "Have you been to the police?"

The woman took her hand from under Kendra's and pressed it to her mouth. She squeezed two fat tears from her eyes.

"Mrs. Hart," Kendra said. She felt sorry for this woman, but knew that there was nothing she could do for her. And, hell, she had problems of her own.

"Call me Nana," she said. "Everybody does." She waved her free hand around her face, indicating the tears now freely rolling down her cheeks. "I'm sorry about this. I've been doing it a lot lately, ever since April ran off."

"The police?" Kendra prodded gently.

Nana Hart sniffled. "That's the first place I went. I didn't even get past the man up front. I think he was the desk sergeant, or at least that's what he called himself. He had me fill out some paperwork. 'We'll be calling you'—that's what he told me. Son of a bitch wouldn't even look me in the eye. . . ."

She stopped, looked horrified at Kendra. "I'm sorry, darling," she said. "I hope I didn't offend you."

"You didn't, Mrs. Hart," Kendra said, unable to call the woman Nana. "I still don't understand why you are here."

Mildred Hart picked up the cup of coffee the waitress had set down in front of her earlier. She drank half of it without pausing.

"I lied to you the other night when I said that the hospital told me to call," she said flatly.

Kendra started to speak, but Mrs. Hart held up her hand. "I mean, it wasn't a complete lie. They did tell me to check out the free clinics in Dunhill. And in Oakland. But that's not the main reason why I called you."

"What was the main reason?"

"April talked about you a lot," she replied. "I mean you are kind of famous around these parts, I guess. I don't know if she's ever actually been to your clinic, but she did know who you were."

"I still don't get it."

"April knew that your mother was a junkie," she said. "And how you grew up poor and all, how you left and could have gone anywhere, but you decided to come back to help the people here. Did you check your records? Did she ever come to the clinic?"

Kendra stammered, "Well, I didn't—"

Nana Hart waved the excuse away.

"Don't worry about it. That's one of the reasons I came. I knew from the way April talked about you that if you saw my face, *her* face maybe, you'd be more likely to help. April said that you were decent that way. It's hard relating to a voice on the phone."

Mildred stopped talking, then picked up her purse and reached inside. She held a picture out to Kendra, facedown. Kendra let it hang in the air, knowing what kind of statement she would make by taking it. Nana Hart understood, too, and steadily held the picture out to Kendra, waiting.

"My granddaughter got into some bad things, Dr. Hamilton. I know that," she said. "Whoring and drugs and Lord knows what else. But she is a good person and deserves a second chance. Like you had. Somebody needs to find her."

Kendra backed away from the table and shook her head. "This is a matter for the police, Nana Hart," she said, knowing how ridiculous it sounded. The police received hundreds of missing-person cases a day and would definitely not be working overtime to find some two-bit whore in The Pit just because the grandmother flew all the way from Texas and showed them her face.

"No, it's not," Nana Hart contradicted. "And you know it's not. I've got to get back. I need you to look for my granddaughter. I need your promise that you will find her."

"You don't understand," Kendra said, leaning across the table, trying her best to trap the older woman's steel blue eyes with her own. "I wouldn't know where to begin, and I've just had a death in my family. I can't take this on right now."

Nana Hart's hand and the picture fell to the table with a thud. She sighed heavily, and nodded. "I understand a little of what you are going through. I heard about your mother. But I do believe that you could find my grandbaby. You know this neighborhood and the people in it way better than the police."

Kendra swallowed, said nothing. Of course Nana Hart was right. And another thing, while the people of The Pit would cut out their own tongues before they talked to the police, they would talk to Kendra. But she shook her head sadly, unable to help.

"I can't help you," she said, thinking of Violet, of finding her killer. "My life is too complicated right now."

Nana Hart didn't answer her. She put the picture back in her purse and clicked it closed. She wound the bright blue scarf back around her neck and stood up.

It was then that Kendra made a mistake. She looked April Hart's grandmother full in the face and saw for the first time the blue eye shadow haphazardly drawn over each lid and the uneven rouge on her cheeks. The makeup highlighted her desperation. This woman, who had probably never left Texas, was laying it on the line for her granddaughter, who might grow up to be just like Violet. An incurable junkie.

Nana Hart started to walk past her, but Kendra grabbed her arm. Without a word, Nana Hart unlocked her patent leather purse, took the picture out, and handed it to Kendra.

"Just find her," she said. "Find my baby."

April

For the first time since he had taken her, he hadn't tied her to the old metal bed with clothesline. She thanked God for that because the heavy rope had left sores that reached all the way around her wrists, and they had become infected.

After prayer that morning, the man looked at the sores bleeding pink blood and puss, then at her belly that had taken on a mind of its own in the last few months, and announced that today he would leave her unbound. That was what he called it—unbound. April couldn't quite remember what that word meant. She blamed it on the hunger, the fear. But a voice in the back of her mind blamed it on the fact that she dropped out of school in sixth grade.

Before he had untied her that morning, he forced her to her knees and clasped one dark, heavy hand around her bleeding wrists. He lifted his other hand to the bare ceiling and began to pray.

She would have felt less scared if he'd prayed about just one thing like the preacher back in Red River. That preacher, in his black pants and black silk shirt, would pray and rant for a darned long time. But at least he stuck to just one subject each Sunday. Don't covet; don't bear false witness; respect thy mother and father—that would be worth at least three Sundays.

But this crazy man would start out with a little child shall lead them and wind his way to Revelation and the mark of the beast. The morning prayers sometimes lasted two hours. He would come before the sun rose and force her to her knees—already worn raw from the other mornings—and pray until the sun washed red across the tiny window.

Now, hours later, she hung her head, barely noticing the blond curls thick with dirt fall over her face like a curtain. She was thinking about the next morning, when he would come again to pray. And with that thought came another. What would happen on that final morning, when the reason for him keeping her here became clear? What would happen when she had the baby—if he allowed her to do that? But she figured he'd at least give her that much. He had told her that he cared more about what she carried inside her than he did anything else in the whole wide world.

"Help me," she said again, the words scraping her throat like sandpaper.

"Now, ain't no cause for all that yelling." The voice speaking from inside her head was Nana's, her grandmother from Red River. She was probably at home wondering what foolishness April had gotten into this time.

But underneath her Nana's voice, she heard his. His voice was as smooth as freshly churned butter. His words rattled around in her head, empty and dangerous. *I just want to help you April. I want to help you and your baby.*

April closed her eyes. Her lips were peeled and her tongue fat with the effort of chanting her name. When she fell asleep, she dreamed of Red River, and in her dream she found a time when the river was full and deep, the water as cool as blue ice.

CHAPTER 9

Richard T. Marvel knew that the sun sparkled in the midday sky only because Dinah called to tell him. He and his partners were in the makeshift homicide squad room working a dayshift for a change. He'd finally been able to convince Sheriff Freehold that they didn't need to staff homicide 24/7.

When the phone rang, he had been reading another one of those damned letters. Like the others, this letter was unsigned, and no return address appeared on the envelope. But unlike the others, it was short, about half a page, and written in a tight cursive that he had to squint to read.

God came to me one day riding on a smoke cloud and he smelled of vinegar, of sulfur. He told me that I was his vessel. He sent me forth to protect the children, to protect them from parents who would feed them to the Devil one finger, one toe and one tooth at a time.

He was halfway finished when the phone rang, and he answered absently, thinking that the letter could be important. Dinah's honeyed voice wiped the thought from his mind.

"Rich," she said. "I'm so disappointed you didn't call me Sunday. Daddy was disappointed as well."

Rich folded the letter, pulled open his desk drawer, and threw it on top of the others. Despite her words, Dinah didn't simper. In fact, Rich couldn't ever remember her simpering. Not once. And now she spoke in clipped businesslike tones. Rich could see her sitting at her desk, her glasses perched on her nose. Rich sighed and rubbed his lined forehead with his fingers, waiting for the thunderclouds to burst.

"It's a beautiful day outside," she continued, unperturbed by his silence. "Why don't I pick you up for lunch?"

Rich picked up the baseball on his desk and threw it up in the air. The ball was a tenth-birthday present from his father. He had told Rich that the autograph on it was real—the genuine signature of Reggie Jackson. But even at ten, he knew that his father had probably forged the name, using his left hand so Rich wouldn't recognize the handwriting. Now Rich watched the ball spiral over and over in the air before it fell with a satisfying slap into the palm of his hand.

"I can't," he lied. "It's busy here, Dinah."

"You have no intention of apologizing, do you, Rich?" Dinah replied in a deceptively casual voice.

"Do you want me to say I'm sorry?" Rich threw the ball up again, this time concentrating on the signature from the Sharpie permanent marker. Was it really a fake?

"You think that's going to please me? Sorry?" Dinah's voice, hard and unforgiving, interrupted Rich's musing. "What am I to you, Rich?" Dinah continued. "The woman you are going to marry, or some lay you can fuck when it suits you?"

Rich leaned forward on his desk and pressed the phone to his mouth. "Come on now, Dinah," he whispered. "Do we have to do this now?"

He looked up. Beau had headphones clamped over his ears and was as oblivious as stone. Rich could hear a tinny-voiced Shania Twain drift over to him. But Gregory, a cold-case file opened like a good book in his hands, searched Rich's face. He frowned slightly.

"Then when are we going to do it, Rich? I never see you. You said you would call Sunday, and today is Wednesday. Now, why is it I find myself calling you?"

"Dinah," he said, "I got caught up, baby."

"Caught up?" she replied. "You couldn't carve ten minutes out of your busy day to call me?"

Rich swallowed and pressed his lips into a hard line. "Don't do this, Dinah," he warned.

"Or what?" she challenged. "Or you won't marry me? Every time we try and have a serious conversation, or I bring to your attention your shortcomings, you threaten, Rich. So, like I said before, what am I to you?"

Rich looked up at the ceiling and noticed a fluorescent light blinking in and out.

Dinah's face flashed before him. He could see her rich honey-colored skin and flashing green eyes. He saw her hair arranged in shiny black clouds around her perfectly madeup face. She probably wore a suit today—an expensive one she'd bought from a boutique in San Francisco—and a thick but tasteful gold chain around her soft neck.

"The woman I'm going to marry," he finally conceded.

"Because of the money? Is marrying me your entrance into Dunhill's high society, Rich?"

"You know damn well that's bullshit, Dinah!" He had been trying his best to hold on to his temper, but now it suddenly exploded. Beau turned off his CD player and looked over at him, a question on his flat face. Gregory went back to the file, pretending not to notice.

"Well, you had better get it together, Rich," Dinah replied shortly. "And you still haven't said you're sorry."

The phone clicked sharply in his ear before he could respond. He held it there for a full ten seconds after she hung up. He debated whether or not to call her back, but he knew that wasn't the smartest thing in the world to do. Dinah could say something inexcusable and get away with it. But he knew that if he tried that shit, he'd have hell to pay. Dinah was sensitive about his reasons for wanting to marry her. He placed the receiver back in its cradle, and the phone rang again almost immediately. He snatched it up without thinking.

"And why do you want to marry me?" he said before he could stop himself.

"Ex . . . excuse me?" The voice was watery and tentative. Definitely not Dinah Webster.

"I'm sorry," Rich said, recognizing the voice of James Freehold's assistant. "It's been a rough morning."

"Then maybe you need to get outside, Rich," Tammy countered. "The weather is beautiful today."

"Yeah, I know," Rich answered in a tired voice. "What can I do for you?"

"He wants to see you," Tammy explained. "You and Gregory."

"Who wants to see us?" Rich said.

He felt his good humor returning, but just a little bit. He liked Tammy. She was an older woman, a civilian, and always wore cotton summer dresses splattered with spring flowers that reminded him of the dresses his mother wore.

"Who do you think?" Tammy questioned, a little laugh in her voice.

"I don't know," Rich shrugged. "God?"

"Close." All the lightness drained from her voice. Even she couldn't stomach the new sheriff. "James Freehold. He wants to see both of you immediately. So don't dawdle."

"We will be there," Rich said. He hung up the phone and looked up. Gregory was already standing. He held out a roll of Mentos to Rich.

"Would you like one?" Gregory questioned around the Mento already in his mouth.

"No," Rich said. "We are going to talk to the man, not tongue-kiss him."

"Not in the mouth, anyway." Beau snorted.

Rich tapped the back of Beau's head as he walked by him. A swath of red hair fell over his bald spot. "Hey," Beau protested as he pushed Rich's hand away.

"Don't fuck anything up while we're gone," Rich shot at him.

Rich and Gregory walked through the glass tunnel connecting the older part of the sheriff's department to the new addition. Both Dinah and Tammy were right about the weather. Sunlight spilled on the glass walls and so heated the tunnel it was a good ten degrees hotter than in the homicide squad room. Sweat formed on Rich's upper lip, but he knew that it was not only because of the heat. Part of it was worry. The sheriff had barely deigned to talk to him after that initial parade in front of the TV cameras. Rich knew that Freehold didn't and couldn't trust him. Rich had been too good of a friend to the old sheriff, and, plus, he had grown up in the crime-ridden Pit.

Rich opened the double doors at the end of the tunnel and walked into a wide room. Desks covered the glossy white linoleum floor. Some were stacked high with papers while others were whistle clean, depending on who used them. Uniformed officers and plainclothes detectives clacked away on computer keyboards. A few of them stood leaning against computer monitors as they talked on the phone.

A podium stood like a gate in front of the public entrance. A uniformed officer stood behind it looking down at a brown woman with a baby on her hip and an earring in her nose. Rich couldn't hear all of what she was saying, but snippets of her voice floated above the din and he caught a few words—"Asshole . . . restraining order . . . saw . . . black ass." Rich saw the back of the officer's head nod on occasion as he ran his fingers along a clipboard. He could tell by the slump of the man's shoulders that he was bored as hell.

But not as bored as I was just a minute ago, Rich thought, remembering the room he had just come from. He had been throwing that fake autographed baseball in the air and arguing with his fiancée; Gregory had been working on cases so cold Rich was surprised that he didn't get frostbite; and

Beau had been listening to that Shania Twain CD for at least the hundredth time. As he looked around the main floor of the sheriff's department, Rich realized that he had traded real police work for a chance to move his career upward and for a chance to prove to Dinah's father he was worthy of marrying his daughter.

A few people stopped long enough to call a greeting to Rich, but not many. He knew that his colleagues thought of him as Sheriff Freehold's golden boy. But that couldn't be farther from the truth. An old black uniformed cop glared at Rich as he passed. The old cop sat at a desk in front of a computer monitor with a hand frozen over the mouse. White punctuated his woolly hair like drops of snow.

"Grady," Rich nodded at him.

Grady forced his lips into a smile and jerked his chin down in a mockery of a greeting. Rich had known Grady in his rookie days, and the old man had schooled him on the ways of the sheriff's department. Rich had long ago passed Grady in both rank and skill, but Grady hadn't seemed to mind. Every single promotion Rich received was followed by a card or email from Grady.

But when Rich took the assignment as acting homicide division lead with the promise of a promotion, he received only stony silence from Grady. There were no cards this time, electronic or otherwise. Rich knew that the man thought he had betrayed Sheriff Bill Conners.

Rich smiled at Tammy as he and Gregory approached. She caught his eye but didn't smile back, which made Rich even more nervous. *Just what in the hell is going on,* he wondered.

"Go right on in, boys," Tammy said. "He's been waiting for you."

They walked into James Freehold's office. The sheriff stood up, his hand extended and an innocuous smile on his face.

"Rich. Gregory," he said, pumping the hand of each man in turn. James Freehold was a short, balding man in his early fifties. He coaxed his remaining hair into a friendly flap over his bald spot. The comb-over made him seem a little ridiculous and naive. He would have been a handsome man except that his nose was as flat and wide as a pancake griddle. Rich could tell by the pictures on the wall that the man had been physically fit in his youth. Now his politician's belly strained against his dark shirt.

When Rich first started seeing Freehold's campaign ads plastered on billboards and his face all over television, he thought the man was a joke. But when he met him in person and got one look into Freehold's marble blue eyes, he quickly dismissed that thought. James Freehold reminded Rich of a junkyard dog.

Freehold looked past them before speaking again. "These are the men who are going to get homicide under control in our fair county, Luke," he said.

Rich whipped around in surprise. Gregory turned, too, though more slowly. Luke Bertrand sat in a deep leather chair by the door. Rich felt the tension of the morning slip away.

"Luke, man," he said, his voice filled with the goodwill he felt. "I didn't see you sitting there." For a brief moment, he wished he had taken that Mento.

The kids in The Pit were like other kids in slums around America. Their heroes consisted mostly of sports stars, coupled with brief adoration attacks for Malcolm X or MLK depending on how militant the family was. When Rich was growing up, it was Reggie Jackson and Martin Luther King. For today's kids, it was Shaq and Alex Rodriguez. But both generations in The Pit had one hero in common, and that hero was Luke Bertrand.

Though Luke didn't come from The Pit, he invested in the community like no one else had in Dunhill County's short history. He held summer picnics, owned several shelters and boys' and girls' clubs. He even owned the clinic where Kendra Hamilton worked. He cajoled or inspired or shamed the youth of The Pit into wanting a better life. And when his words failed him, he pulled out his wallet and spread money around like butter on toast.

Unlike most other philanthropists, Luke dressed the part of a movie star. He wore swinging camel-hair coats over three-piece designer suits in the winter. As the weather warmed, he switched to light leather coats and cream slacks. He wore gold rings around his clean, black fingers, and Rich didn't think he had ever seen him in need of a haircut.

"Rich, my man," Luke said. He shook Rich's hand with both of his own.

"I didn't see you sitting there," Rich repeated without realizing it. "Hot damn, man."

"Well, you see me now," Luke said in a deep voice. Power radiated from the man like sunlight. Then, "It's good to see you, son." Luke stopped smiling. His voice turned serious and caring. "Especially like this, with your life finally together."

Rich nodded, knowing what Luke referred to. Years earlier, bitterness and hate had almost destroyed a young Rich. At seventeen, he'd thought of only one thing—being a baseball player. It was his ticket out of The Pit. But before he could take advantage of that baseball scholarship from a no-name college back East, some asshole mistook him for a rival gang member and shot him.

The bullet ricocheted off the wall behind his head and tore a groove into his left cheek. That wasn't the worst of it, though. Another bullet caught him in the leg, right behind the knee. He was running, and the asshole tried to shoot him in the back. He had to have his knee reconstructed, and there was no way he could play baseball. After he lost that scholarship, he thought his world had ended. Hate took a hold in his gut and sprouted like a weed.

Then came the medical bills raining down from the administration offices of Doctor's Hospital. He knew that his family couldn't afford to pay them. He wanted to die, and he wanted those around him to die. He especially wanted the boy who shot him to die—the boy who had the nerve to plead not-fucking-guilty after ballistics matched the bullets fired to the gun the bastard was carrying when they arrested him.

Desperate, Rich's mother called the neighborhood hero— Luke Bertrand. Luke not only paid the medical bills, but he coaxed Rich out of his depression. He helped him leave the hate far enough behind to get his life back together. It was Luke who suggested the academy.

Gregory cleared his throat, and Rich left the memory behind. He blinked a little, and looked out the window behind Freehold's desk, watching the white oleanders press against the glass.

"Oh, yes," Luke said as if suddenly remembering the others in the room. He turned his eyes to Gregory. "Gregory Atfield, am I right?" He smiled with his mouth closed.

"Mr. Bertrand," Gregory replied.

"Please," Luke said. "No need for formalities. Everyone calls me Luke." He shook Gregory's hand briefly.

"What's this all about, Sheriff?" Rich asked with his hands on his hips. The warm feeling from seeing Luke again was beginning to leave him. An alarm sounded faintly in his head.

"Why don't we all sit down first," Freehold said. "Gregory, bring one of those chairs by my desk so we can all sit together."

As they all sat down, Rich wondered what his partner was thinking, but his gray eyes gave nothing away. Freehold's executive leather chair creaked under his weight. He bellied up to his desk and spoke.

"This won't take long, gentlemen," he said smoothly. "Luke"—he gestured toward Luke, who now plucked neatly at his slacks—"Luke has a request for the sheriff's department."

"What's that?" Rich replied, as he thought of spending another day in some recreation center making another cops-are-your-friends speech to a crowd of skeptical future gang-bangers.

Luke looked at Rich only. He sighed deeply, a slight smile on his handsome face.

"You, I understand, and Detective Atfield . . ." Luke began.

"Please, call me Gregory," Gregory said in a stony voice.

Luke's face tightened briefly, then melted into politeness. He continued, "Gregory, then. You participated in a death investigation of one Violet Hamilton."

Gregory sat up. Rich's hands tightened on the arm of the chair. Sheriff Freehold tapped a gold pen noisily on the glass covering his desk. No one spoke for a moment.

Then Gregory broke the silence. "We indeed did," he said.

"She is the mother of a good friend of mine, a Dr. Kendra Hamilton. Do you know her, Rich?" Luke cocked his head toward Rich.

"I know her briefly. We've met once. Or twice."

Sheriff Freehold raised an eyebrow. "But I thought you grew up in the same neighborhood? In The Pit, correct?"

Rich shuffled in his seat uncomfortably. "We did," he explained. "But Kendra's mother, I mean Violet Hamilton, was a known jun—" He stopped, remembering Kendra's challenge. "I mean she was a known addict, Sheriff. My mother was strict. She would have kicked my ass if I even thought about hanging around with someone like Kendra Hamilton."

Rich felt their eyes on him. He looked at Freehold's red face and turned away. Rich knew he had said something politically incorrect, but suddenly he didn't give a shit. Instead he continued, "I barely remember her in The Pit. As a matter of fact, I didn't recognize her the first time we met."

"Like so many lost ones in The Pit, Kendra has found her way," Luke said. He paused and looked pointedly at Rich. When no one spoke, he continued. "I've known her since she was a young girl, gentlemen. In spite of her mother, she managed to complete college and medical school while working for pennies to cover gaps in scholarship funds. I could barely get her to take money from me." He steepled his fingers together before looking at each one of them in the eye. "She is a good woman and an even better doctor."

"Your point, Mr. Bertrand?" Gregory asked.

"My point is that Dr. Hamilton is of value to the community—"

"Are we talking about a woman or a saint?" Rich broke in.

"We are talking about a woman who deserves to be listened to, gentlemen," Luke responded, the smile never leaving his face.

Suddenly Rich understood. He stood up and walked behind his chair. Gregory rubbed his face with his long bony fingers. Rich fixed his gaze on the gold pen Freehold was nervously clicking against his desk. The sheriff's name was engraved on the side in cursive. Rich looked into Freehold's marble blue eyes.

"What are we doing here, Sheriff?" Rich asked him.

Freehold let the pen drop on his desk, then he pushed his chair back. "I just thought you'd like to hear what Luke has to say," he said.

"Uh huh," Rich said and glanced at Luke. "So she went to you, did she?"

Rich could almost see Luke carefully arrange the next words in his head before he spoke.

"She came to me with some concerns, Rich," he said. "She feels like Violet's death was not adequately investigated. She feels that this department did not properly investigate because of Violet's economic status and her medical disability."

Gregory laughed gently before rising and walking toward the door. Scorn filled his next words. "Her medical disability, Mr. Bertrand, was that she was a junkie."

Freehold shot them both a warning look. "Rich. Gregory," he said. "Sit down, and hear him out."

"Come on, Sheriff," Rich protested, still standing. He turned to Bertrand. "Luke, you know how I feel about you, man, but you can't interfere in police business like this. It's not right."

"Rich! Gregory!" Freehold pounded out. "Sit!" Freehold

waited until they both sat again. He took a deep breath before speaking. "I agree with both of you about interfering with police business, but Luke has some valid points."

Rich leaned forward in his chair and stared into Freehold's round red face.

"We investigated that death," Rich said as he stabbed his index finger toward the floor. "And I tell you, it was an overdose, pure and simple. Why should we waste our time on this, Sheriff?"

Doubt wavered over Freehold's face, but Luke answered before the sheriff could respond. "You should waste your time because it will affirm your campaign promise to the community. When I supported you, James, it was because you seemed seriously concerned about crime in The Pit. Kendra Hamilton is well known there, and respected. If you satisfy her, you satisfy the community as well as your supporters. The press will see you making good your word."

It happened right before Rich's eyes. Sheriff Freehold was transformed from a law enforcement officer into a politician in a nanosecond. Leaves scraped at the glass window behind Freehold's desk as they all sat in silence.

"Luke is right," Freehold finally said.

"We have real murders to investigate, Sheriff," Rich said, even though he knew that was slightly untrue. The perps in the open cases he had on his desk were either dead or in jail. But, hell, they were still open.

A look passed between Luke and Freehold, a look that told both Rich and Gregory things had been decided before they walked into the office.

"I am aware of that." Freehold now nodded at Rich. "And to make sure you are free to give this investigation your full attention and to help the public understand how seriously we take such deaths, I'm transferring your existing homicide case load back to the patrol and investigative division."

Rich stiffened. He looked over at Gregory and saw all the color drain from his friend's face.

"That's bullshit," Rich said softly.

"You may think it is," Freehold conceded. "But if the Hamilton death went down the way you say it did, it shouldn't take you that long to confirm your original findings. So . . ."

"Humor us," Luke finished for him. "Humor her."

Gregory turned his gaze to Freehold. "So who's running this department, you or Bertrand?" Gregory asked in the soft voice that had earned him his nickname.

Rich didn't miss the flint in Freehold's eyes. He touched his partner on the sleeve before the man got himself into more trouble.

"Come on, Gregory," Rich said, "let's go."

"I expect a report on my desk every day regarding this investigation, Rich," Freehold said.

"Yeah, sure."

As they walked out of Freehold's office, Rich could almost see Gregory's anger.

"Bastard," Gregory breathed.

Grady caught Rich's eye as they passed his desk. Though he didn't speak, Rich could have sworn the old man wore a look of smug satisfaction on his face.

Rich didn't care that it was the middle of the day. He was going home. His plans didn't consist of clearing a murder, but going home, stripping to his underwear, and watching a basketball game on TV while downing a couple of beers. The sweltering heat caused him to break into a full sweat as he crossed the parking lot to his 1986 Firebird, his own private car. He had bought that car eight years ago and restored it. He knew it was some holdover fantasy from his youth but really didn't give a shit. Besides, the thing sat in the parking lot of the sheriff's department most of the time. He usually drove the department-issued Monte Carlo and only drove the Firebird when he was feeling particularly nasty about his job, like now.

He sat behind the wheel for a while, thinking. Why would Sheriff Freehold give his newly formed homicide department this impossible case? The answer was easy. This would be an easy way for the sheriff to disband their department and still save face. If Rich didn't find a murderer, a trophy for him to hold up in front of the press, the department would be history. And so would Rich's career. Bye-bye promotion and bye-bye Dinah. A horn blared from behind the Firebird, breaking into his thoughts. He saw a car waiting for his parking space in the rearview mirror.

"All right, all right," he said absently. "I'm moving."

When he opened the door of his apartment, he saw Dinah standing by the window. She wasn't wearing the designer suit he had imagined. Instead, she wore a cream silk short-sleeved shirt and a pair of tan slacks. The flat gold necklace did, however, encircle her neck. He said nothing, just waited with one foot in and one foot out of his own apartment.

"Well?" She arched an eyebrow at him. "Aren't you going to come in? This is your apartment, Rich."

Rich sighed as he closed the door behind him. "How did you know I would be here?"

"I called for you earlier," she stated. "Detective Blair said you and Gregory had left in some sort of a huff." She looked around. "Where is Gregory, by the way?"

"I have no idea," Rich said, shrugging.

"He goes off a lot like this," Dinah said casually. "Don't you ever wonder where he goes?"

"It's none of my business." Rich felt a war coming on, and he didn't want to fight. "Look, Dinah, I'm tired and—"

"I know," she said. "You don't want to fight. Neither do I. I simply want to get things settled between us, Rich."

She sat on the black sofa and patted the zebra-skin throw. "Come sit beside me," she said.

She sounded as if she were talking to one of her clients. He did sit down, but barely listened to her patter about understanding and respecting each other. Instead, he thought about how they had met. She and her father had been at a charity event that Gregory had dragged Rich to at the last minute. She was like no other woman he had ever met. She was cultured, polite, and wore her wealth like expensive perfume—understated but noticeable.

She told him later that she approached him at the party not only because of his good looks, but because he looked lost in that crowd. And she thought it was sweet the way he tried to cover it up by looking bored and uninterested. She liked it that he wasn't part of the in-crowd. But that didn't stop her from trying to mold him, to make him more acceptable to her family and friends. And Rich knew that one of his failings was he wanted that, too. But was that so bad? Was it so bad that he wanted to put distance between himself and his life in The Pit?

". . . so I think if we are going to have a successful relationship, we need to respect each other's time. Rich, are you listening to me?" Her prattle broke into his thoughts. He turned to her.

"Of course I am," he said having no idea of what she was talking about. "I'm sorry I didn't call you on Sunday," he admitted as he turned to her.

Her green eyes glowed like jewels. When she smiled, he knew that everything, with Dinah at least, was going to be all right.

CHAPTER 10

The Courtroom Bar & Grill was on Ninth Street, about two blocks from the Dunhill County Sheriff's Department and about one from Doctor's Hospital. Mostly cops and hospital personnel gathered there, not for the food, but to be with other cops and hospital personnel.

Bruce, the owner of the grill, used to be a sheriff's deputy back in the days when the sheriff's department consisted of a sheriff who volunteered on the weekends and two deputies. Bruce was a large man, about six eight, with faded tattoos covering his bulging arms. Eighty if he was a day, he swore he bench-pressed three hundred pounds every morning and could still shoot the hole off a gnat's ass. Bruce whistled a tune as he flipped omelets and adjusted the crocheted beanie cap perched on top of his shiny bald head.

Rich checked his watch for the eighth time. He had told Kendra Hamilton to meet him at the Courtroom at seven sharp. It was already ten after. He told himself that it was her lateness that caused the irritation he felt. But in reality, it was his nerves. His career, every day of the last goddamn thirteen years of it, hinged on the outcome of this case. And, besides, he didn't feel like having the fight that he knew was coming with Kendra Hamilton. For some reason, she acted as if she had the right to judge him and, having done so, found him wanting. He should have not reacted, but he found himself always on the defensive with her. Always justifying his ambition, or, as she would see it, his abandonment of the old neighborhood.

Loud laughter from four uniforms a couple of tables removed drifted over to Rich, taking his mind thankfully off Kendra Hamilton. The two girls Bruce had working for him brushed past Rich's table leaving clouds of cheap perfume and body-lotion scents in their wakes. A kid at another table by the window pushed a full glass of milk to the floor. The pink-cheeked little brat had a hard glint in his eyes and didn't start crying until the glass shattered against the tiled floor and milk splattered on the mother's bare legs. Rich rubbed his eyes against the sight of the breaking glass and the scolding of the horrified mother. Maybe this wasn't the right place to meet. Just as Rich considered leaving, Bruce set the Denver omelet Rich had ordered earlier in front of him, casting a glance at the commotion by the window.

"Sorry this took so long," he said. "I'm shorthanded today."

"No problem, man," Rich said.

"Anything else I can get for you?"

Rich started to answer but stopped abruptly when Kendra Hamilton walked in wearing shapeless hospital greens and holding a brown envelope. Rich heard Bruce's voice assuring the mother and the howling child that he would get the mess cleaned up as if Bruce were talking in a tunnel. All other sound faded away as he watched Kendra search the room for him. Rich couldn't help but compare her to Dinah. Pulled back by a rubber band along with fat curls corkscrewing around her face, Kendra's hair was a mess. Her face was bare of makeup even though dark circles rimmed her brown eyes. But when Kendra smiled at Bruce, her face radiated the beauty she hadn't taken the time to accentuate.

Rich thought about that night at Max's Fine Liquor, how the rain had pressed the short robe to her body, and he knew she didn't have an ounce of fat on her. Despite her rumpled hair, she had a pull he couldn't deny—which complicated matters even more. When her eyes found him, he waved her over.

"You're late," he said without preamble.

She regarded him suspiciously as she pulled the chair from the table and sat down.

"And good morning to you," she said, not smiling.

Rich's eyes wandered over her face. Letting the silence flow around them, he took in the high cheekbones, lingered on the full mouth so unlike Violet Hamilton's. Bruce came over with a cup of tea.

"Strong, hot tea, Doc," he said. "Just like you like it."

"Thanks, Bruce," she said, flashing him another smile.

Rich resumed his stare after Bruce left. He watched Kendra as she stirred sugar into the tea. Finally, she shifted under his gaze and looked at him.

"Can I help you, Detective?"

"How you holding up?" he asked, ignoring the light of irritation in her eyes.

"Is that why you summoned me here, Detective Marvel? To find out how I'm holding up?"

Rich picked up the Heinz ketchup and shook half the bottle onto his Denver omelet. He then shook Louisiana hot sauce on top of that, knowing all the while that Kendra was waiting for an answer. They reached for the creamer at the same time. He looked up at her, and their eyes collided.

"May I?" he asked, lifting an eyebrow and ignoring the shock that went up his hand as their fingers touched.

She snatched her hand away and stared down into her tea.

"What's in the envelope, Doc?" he asked.

"Nothing," she said.

"Is it for me?"

"It's nothing," she said, staring at him hard. "Why am I here, Detective Marvel?"

Rich took a bite of his eggs, wiped his mouth hard with a cloth napkin before speaking. "You heard that the case was reopened?" he asked, scooping up another forkful of eggs.

She brought the tea to her mouth, then set the cup down.

"Yes, I heard something about that."

Rich snorted. "I bet you heard more than something. Luke couldn't wait to tell you about it, I bet. What's up with you two, anyway? You sleeping together or something?"

She stared at him as if he had slapped her.

"He's old enough to be my father."

"That doesn't mean a damn thing," Rich said dryly around a mouthful of eggs and ketchup. He took a gulp of his coffee, the liquid still hot enough to scald even though he had dosed it with creamer. "Why does he take such an interest in you?"

"What's it to you?" she snapped back.

He put his cup down and regarded her fully for a few seconds.

"Personally," he said with a shrug, "it doesn't mean a damn thing to me. You could screw half of Dunhill County's retired population and I wouldn't give a shit. But professionally, I need to know. It may have a bearing on this case."

"Bullshit," she responded.

He stopped chewing, stared at her. "What?"

"You hard of hearing?" she asked. "I said bullshit. You don't need to know about me and Luke Bertrand. You are upset because you're on this case, and you are trying to harass me, to make me uncomfortable enough to drop it. Well I got news for you, it *ain't* happening."

Rich folded his napkin and put it next to his plate, all the time silently acknowledging that she was partly right. He didn't like Kendra Hamilton—her self-righteous attitude and her almost legendary hatred of cops ever since her brother was killed by a sheriff's deputy almost a decade ago. And that incident at Max's Fine Liquor, and now this—this forced investigation—did little to endear her to him. He wanted to see her squirm.

He pushed his plate away, leaned both elbows on the table, and looked into her eyes.

"You telling me you are not cooperating with this investigation? That you are going to answer only the questions that you are comfortable with?" he asked.

She sighed, crossed her arms over her chest. "I've known Luke Bertrand almost my entire life," she said. "He tried to help my mother stop using. When that didn't work, he all but took me in. He paid for college, helped me with medical school. He's like a father to me, not a lover. Are we clear?"

Rich nodded but said nothing, partly because he wasn't clear. Not at all. There were a hundred kids in The Pit with parents as addicts. Why did Luke Bertrand take such an interest in Kendra Hamilton?

"Is that all you wanted to know?" she asked. "Is that why you asked me here?"

Rich shook his head, held her gaze, replaying the Sunday-morning scene at the clinic as he did so. She held his gaze steadily now, but that morning, that morning, she had dropped her eyes, couldn't quite meet his.

"I need to know why you are so sure Violet Hamilton didn't die of a drug overdose," he said.

"I told you," she said. "My mother was careful."

Rich thought that if he looked hard enough, he would be able to see her heart beating, the wheels turning in her mind as she tried to make the lie sound believable.

"You're hiding something, Doc," he said softly. "I want to know what it is."

Rich waited as the seconds ticked away. Kendra swallowed, smoothed a curl from her forehead.

"I don't know what you mean," she said finally.

Disappointment welled in Rich for a reason he didn't want to name. He laughed softly. "You are lying your ass off, girl," he said.

Kendra slapped a hand on the table. Several people turned their way at the sound.

"Don't you *'girl'* me, Richard T. Marvel," she said. "Don't *even* pretend that you know me well enough to 'girl' me."

Rich held his hands up in surrender. "I don't have to know you to know that you are lying," he said. "It's my job, what I do."

Kendra shot up to leave. He grabbed her wrist. "Sit down,"

he hissed. She tried jerking away, but he closed his hand around her wrist tighter. "You want to find out who killed your mother? Sit down."

She snatched her hand away angrily but eased back into her chair, never taking her gaze from him.

"When was the last time you saw your mother alive?" he asked her, all business.

"Several weeks ago," she said tiredly.

"How was she?"

"What do you mean, how was she?"

"I mean how was she?" he pressed. "Was she strung out? Sober? In between fixes? Hanging out with anybody new? What was her state of mind? I mean how was—"

"She was fine," Kendra cut him off.

He gave up. He was not going to get anything out of this conversation. He had hoped to get Kendra Hamilton here at the Courtroom and find out what she hadn't told him and Gregory on Easter Sunday.

"Instead of harassing me, Detective Marvel," she said breaking into his thoughts, "why aren't you out on the streets asking questions?"

"Oh, you think we haven't been on the streets?" Rich asked. "Well, we've been there, sweetheart. I've had uniforms canvass every inch of The Elite, finding out who was there that night and if anyone saw anything unusual. No one knows anything."

Kendra stared at him in amazement.

"And you believe them? You send uniforms with shiny badges and batons into The Pit and you think people are really going to tell you anything useful?"

"Why wouldn't they?" he said. "Besides, I have informants—"

"*An* informant," Kendra said, staring at him as if he had two heads. She held up a forefinger. "One. Peanut. And everyone in The Pit knows that he is your informant, Detective. He's been spoon-feeding you for years exactly what he and everybody else in The Pit wants you and the cops to know."

She sat back in her chair and stared at him. "My God," she whispered. "How can you *not* know that?"

Rich felt his face grow hot. He knew in a way that she was right. People in The Pit hated cops almost as much as he hated perps.

"Just what in the hell do you expect me to do?" he said.

"I expect you to do your job," she said. "I expect you to get off your ass and go back to the neighborhood you grew up in and find out why it's the way that it is. Not send a couple of uniformed rookies to do it for you."

Rich laughed in spite of the anger crowding his throat. "You really believe that bleeding-heart shit you're spewing? How can you sit there and lie to my face about what you know and don't know and judge me at the same time?"

She leaned in close to him. Their eyes caught and held. "What about Jiffy?" she asked him now.

"What about him?" he asked warily.

"You sure he told you everything about what happened the night my mother died?"

Rich pushed his plate away. He leaned both elbows on the table and stared hard at her.

"Why wouldn't I be sure, Doc?"

"Did he tell you that there was someone else there with my mother that night?"

"And how would you know that?" Rich asked.

"Because I've been doing what you refuse to do, Detective. I've been asking a few questions myself. . . ."

Her voice trailed off. Rich believed it was because of the look on his face. He had tried to keep his face still, but he felt his jaw clench. "Let me get this straight," he said into the silence surrounding them. "You force us to investigate this case, then you decide to go off by yourself asking questions?"

"Somebody has to," Kendra said icily. "You obviously are not going to do anything."

Rich took several breaths to calm down. He spoke only when he trusted his voice again. "There is something that you need to know," he said. "I don't care how I got assigned to this case, but it's mine, do you hear me? My case." She said nothing. He continued. "If I hear that you are sniffing around playing cop, I'll yank you off the streets so fast that your head will spin. Stay out of it. The only thing I need from you is the truth. I need to know what you are hiding."

Kendra shook her head. She stood up to leave, clutching the brown envelope she had carried into the restaurant. "I've made a mistake," she muttered, more to herself than to him. She looked at him. "You asked what was in this envelope. I thought it was something else that you could help me with, something that you might have been glad to help with. But I see you are too far gone even for that."

Rich stood up and leaned close to her. The antiseptic hospital smell clung to her like perfume. He tried to still the spinning anger in his gut without success.

He nodded. "If you are hiding something, anything, Dr. Hamilton, then you *did* make a mistake. I plan to investigate the hell out of this thing. I'll be at the hospital questioning everyone about your mother, whether or not she had any enemies, about the relationship you had with her. I'll question your friends, your neighbors, even your goddamned mailman. How is that for getting off my ass and doing my job?"

He felt a small prick of satisfaction when she flinched. He knew that he had shaken her, but when she spoke, her voice was icy again, controlled. "You mean you plan to harass me, Detective Marvel? Is that it? You are trying to intimidate me?"

He held up his palms. "You asked for it," he said.

"No," she responded in that same chilly tone. "No, I didn't. I asked you to look into who killed my mother. But go ahead, question my friends, my neighbors. . . ." She stopped and took a step closer until they were almost touching. "Question the goddamned mailman. I've been harassed by cops before. But in the end, you had better show Sheriff Freehold a murderer, hadn't you?"

He said nothing, but admitted to himself that her perception surprised him.

"You can't stand it, can you? Your career riding on the death of a junkie?" she finally said slowly, softly.

They watched each other a little while longer. Suddenly, she turned away and walked out of the Courtroom, the bell jangling behind her.

"Well," Beau started sarcastically. "You certainly handled that—"

"Shut up," Rich countered without missing a beat.

He removed his wallet from his suit pocket and creased it open. He threw a ten-dollar bill on the table. It bothered him that his conversation with Kendra had been so intense that he hadn't heard Beau or Gregory come in. Who else had seen them? It was almost as if the place disappeared for him when she walked in the room.

"Aren't you going to finish your breakfast," Gregory asked quietly.

"I lost my appetite," Rich replied as he stuffed his wallet back in his pocket. "We start with the glasses and the bourbon. We ask questions around The Elite and try to find out who was with Violet that night. We find out where she got her dope."

"The marks on her neck?" Gregory interrupted. "Probably a good idea to find out if they were pre- or postmortem."

"Right," Rich mumbled. "Pre- or postmortem."

For some reason, he felt rejuvenated. Maybe it was Kendra's mention of his career. Maybe it was because he wanted to prove her wrong about her mother's death. She needed to understand that Violet—and only Violet—was responsible for her own death.

Rich cut a glance at Gregory. "What the hell you doing here, anyway?"

Gregory held up Rich's pager. "You left in such a hurry this morning that you forgot your pager. This bloody thing's been going off for an hour now."

Rich snatched it from him and hit the RETRIEVE PAGE button. He immediately recognized the number on the LED screen. It belonged to Dr. Rita Sandbourne, the medical examiner.

CHAPTER 11

The morgue was in the same compound as Doctor's Hospital but set well apart from the main building. Gray cinderblocks made up the single-story building, and though the refrigeration unit worked for the dead bodies, the air-conditioning for the live employees couldn't be counted on. Rita and her assistant used a trash can to prop open the front steel entrance door.

Rich sat in the driver's seat of the Monte Carlo parked just outside the morgue, alternately glancing at the propped-open front door and then at the hospital in the distance. He couldn't help but think of Kendra Hamilton. He knew that she worked there during the week while giving her week-ends and some evenings to the free clinic. That couldn't have left much room for a social life, though he didn't examine why he should really care about that.

"We going in, man?" Beau shifted in the passenger seat of the Monte Carlo. He had insisted on coming to the morgue with Rich. But the minute Gregory heard the word *morgue*, he made some lame excuse and hurried away. He had once confessed to Rich that the morgue actually gave him the spooks. Rich remembered now that was how Gregory put it—the *spooks*. Just being in one was enough to make Gregory physically ill. This from a man who could look at signs of decomposition and make a pronouncement about the time of death even better than some medical examiners. But Gregory couldn't stomach a body lying exposed on a cold steel table.

But Rich was just the opposite. Though he had grown used to dead bodies during his years in narcotics, he still got that deep butterfly feeling when looking at death in the field. He could look at a scene and play the crime over in his mind like a video, like he was there when it happened. It reminded him of his own mortality, making his dreams of being respected and living in a fine house with even a finer wife and enough kids for a baseball team seem not to matter. Not to matter at all.

He better tolerated bodies when they were sanitized, analyzed, and tagged. When he gazed upon a body in the morgue, clean and shiny, he felt nothing. He was as cold and detached as if he were looking at the polished body of a new car he had no interest in buying.

Rita's morgue attendant didn't look up when Rich and Beau pushed through the heavy steel door. He was an older man with thinning hair dyed a greasy black and horn-rimmed glasses covering his owlish eyes. His pale yellow shirt made his skin look sallow, used-up. He nibbled and chewed on the side of his index finger like it was a piece of very tasty baby corn. If it had been his first time in Rita's office, Rich would have thought that the man was actively eating food. But Rich didn't have to look at the bare desk to know that there wasn't a morsel of food in sight. Clint simply liked to nibble on himself. Rich recalled countless conversations with Rita in the foyer during which Clint nibbled his own fingers and sucked the tips as if he'd just finished eating a plate of his favorite ribs.

"Hello, Rich," Clint said, still not looking up.

"Can I go on back, man?" Rich asked without bothering to introduce Beau, who was looking at Clint like he was a freak in a circus act.

Clint stopped nibbling long enough to point at the dull sil-

ver doors behind him. The door had black and yellow duct
tape stripped across it and a sign on posterboard that said AU-
THORIZED PERSONNEL. Rich pushed the door in, then glanced
over his shoulder at Beau. His red mustache worked up and
down over his lip as he swallowed.

"You aren't going to blow on me, man, are you?" Rich
asked him.

"Fuck you, Rich," Beau said, but his voice was weak, watery.

Rich grinned at him. He then walked into the autopsy
suite and held the door open for Beau. The room had two
aluminum tables fitted with faucets to help wash fluids away.
A rollaway cart filled with hand tools Rich had seen in action a couple of times stood between the two tables. Rita sat
in a swivel chair at a desk against the opposite wall. Because
the front of the desk was against the wall, all they could see
was her thin back. One of the autopsy tables held a body
covered in a blue cotton cloth. Rich casually lifted the blanket as he passed the table.

"Who's the new guy?" he said. "Anybody we need to be
concerned with?"

Rita, who was wearing a gray plastic apron that made her
look thin as a pencil, swiveled around to look at them at the
sound of Rich's voice.

"No, Rich," she said matter-of-factly as she stood. "Some
people do die of natural causes."

"Now, I wouldn't know about that, would I?" he answered. "Why are you doing an autopsy, then, if you think it
was natural causes?"

Rita chuckled. *"Think* is the operative word there," she
responded. "Besides, he died unattended, no physician present, and the family, as always, is looking for answers."

He smiled and walked toward her. Beau followed slug-
gishly behind him. Rita folded her arms across her chest.

"Rich," she laughed, "where have you been, anyway? I've
been paging you all morning."

Rich shrugged as Kendra's face floated in his mind.

"Out," he said. "I forgot my pager this morning. Don't you have my cell phone number?"

Rita smiled slightly, shook her head. "So you forget your pager on the one day I needed to talk to you, and I don't rate high enough to have your cell phone number?" she asked with a teasing light in her eyes. "Should I take that personally?"

Rich stared at her for several seconds. "You know something, Rita," he said, "if Dinah ever dumps me—"

"It would probably be the best thing she ever did," Rita said, still laughing.

"I see you are in a better mood than you were a couple of days ago," he answered.

"Let's just say it's not been as busy," she countered. "And my mother left town."

Before Rich could respond, Beau cleared his throat.

"How are you, Beau?" Rita said, the easiness gone from her voice.

"Fair to middlin'," Beau replied with what Rich thought was a much-rehearsed smile.

"Why don't you both sit down." Rita pointed to two small chairs near a metal desk. "Let me take this thing off. I was just about to start the autopsy on Mr. Lucky over there."

Rich and Beau sat down in two plastic orange chairs near Rita's desk. Beau looked like he was sitting in a chair from a kindergarten class, his meaty hands folded in his lap. Rita had swapped her gray plastic apron for a white lab coat. She now carried a thick manila file folder.

"What did you need, Rita?" Rich asked. "I need to get back to the office."

She held up a hand. "Just a sec," she said. "I need to get situated." After plopping into the swivel chair, she scooted up to them. She opened the file on her lap before speaking again.

"Violet Hamilton . . ." she said absently.

Rich felt every single nerve he had stand at attention as her voice trailed off. Violet Hamilton. Again. What could it be this time?

"They don't give you a lot of room to work, do they?" Beau asked her.

He seemed more comfortable now, even though the tiny chair he sat in made him look like a giant.

Rita laughed. "Usually the desk is big enough for me. I don't get a lot of upright people in here"—she motioned at Rich—"except for a couple of observers like Rich every now and then."

"What about Violet Hamilton?" Rich broke in. "Is that her file?"

"Yepper," Rita said.

"What's going on, Rita?" Rich asked, unable to keep the dread out of his voice.

Rita stopped flipping through the files and gave Rich a long, questioning look. They had known each other for over ten years, and it was clear by the slant of Rita's mouth that she was about to tell him something that she knew he very much didn't want to hear.

"I heard that you've been ordered to investigate the Violet Hamilton case as a murder."

"And where did you hear that?" Rich asked.

"Rumor mill."

"Rumor mill, my ass," Rich said. "I bet Grady couldn't wait to call and tell you that I fucked up."

Rita sighed and looked at him. Rich could tell she was exasperated and amused. They both knew Grady, the cop who thought Rich had betrayed the old sheriff for his ambition. Rich knew Rita when she used to be a morgue attendant like Clint. She worked alternate schedules so she could get her medical degree in pathology and was named medical examiner when the previous one retired. Like Rich, she had also been friends with Grady, and it was obvious that she remained friendly with the old cop.

"He didn't say you fucked up, Rich," Rita said. "He was just giving me a heads-up and told me that I might want to pull the Violet Hamilton file."

"That old man hates me," Rich breathed, thinking about

the look that had passed between him and Grady on the way from Freehold's office.

"Rich," Rita soothed, placing a bony hand on his knee. "Forget about Grady, okay?"

Rich didn't miss Beau's glance at Rita's thin hand lingering on his knee. The big man frowned under his mustache. But before Rich could speak, Rita snatched her hand away. All business now, she started rifling through the folder.

"Okay," she said. "Officially, Violet Hamilton died of a drug overdose. I mean that's the cause I listed on the death certificate."

"Did Kendra pick up the body yet?" Rich asked before he knew he was going to ask it.

Rita stopped. The room fell silent, and Rita regarded him with a look that told him that she knew him all too well. "Yes," she said finally.

Because he felt a need to justify the question, he said in a rush, "Because if you need to conduct another autopsy—"

Rita shrugged her thin shoulders. "I don't need to conduct another autopsy," she said. "It's what I told you."

"Bad dope?" Rich asked.

"Yes."

"Then why in the hell have you been beeping me all morning?"

Rita stopped and pulled off her gold wire-framed glasses. She rubbed her eyes for a minute. "I don't think this one is as simple as that, Rich," she admitted.

Rich jumped up and started pacing the floor. Rita said nothing. He walked to the gurney burdened with the body of the man who had died of natural causes; Mr. Lucky, Rita had called him. Rich leaned his palms against the table and looked at the tips of his shiny shoes.

"Don't lean against that, Rich," Rita said. "Please."

Rich didn't move. "You told me a couple of days ago and just now that it was an overdose," he said each word distinctly.

"What I told you was that her symptoms were consistent with what is commonly known as a drug overdose."

"What do you mean, 'commonly known'?" Beau asked now, not taking his eyes from her.

She turned to him and continued in a matter-of-fact voice. "An overdose implies that she died because she had too much heroin, but the fact is that there wasn't enough in the mixture she ingested."

"How do you mean?" Beau continued.

"Some experts believe that rarely does an addict die of too much heroin. What happens in overdose cases is that addicts are usually responding to the adulterated materials in the drug."

Beau said nothing. He looked at Rich, then Rita. His face was a question mark.

"What she is saying, sharp guy, is that she died from what was mixed in with the heroin. Did you miss that day of class at the academy? So what was it, Doc?" Rich asked.

"What was what?" Rita said absently.

"The substance in the heroin."

"Why, quinine, Rich," she replied. "What did you think it was?"

Rita sometimes had the annoying habit of relating a piece of information that was so weighty that it seemed a proclamation from the pope. But she did it in such a casual way, it sounded as if she were talking about the weekend weather forecast. Rich knew when it was about to happen. She would go over the facts again and then announce something so totally fucked up that it would keep him in paperwork for a week.

"What's quinine?" Beau asked.

Rita barked a laugh. "Wow, it seems as if you missed more than one day at the academy."

"It's a drug used to treat malaria," Rich answered. "A lot of dealers cut heroin with quinine because it increases the rush. Because both heroin and quinine are bitter, the junkie usually can't tell how much quinine is in the heroin just by tasting it."

"Here it is," Rita said, pulling a piece of paper from the

folder. Rich saw only the back of it, sharp and crisp as a new spring afternoon.

"Rita," Rich said. "You told me it was a heroin overdose."

"No, I didn't," Rita replied, her voice unemotional. "I told you what we found was consistent with what is commonly known as a heroin overdose. You, Rich, as you always did since the first day I met you, jumped to conclusions. I told you we hadn't gotten the toxicology report back on the substance in the syringe yet."

"What do you mean, you hadn't gotten the toxicology report back yet?"

Rita shrugged her shoulders. "I mean we hadn't gotten it back yet, Rich. It got lost twice, and I kept getting the runaround from the lab. I finally had to go down there and stand on the supervisor's desk to get my hands on it. You'd think it was gold or something. . . ." she trailed off.

"Wait, back up," Beau said, leaning forward. The chair creaked under his weight. "I'm still on 'no one dies of a heroin overdose.' Explain that to me."

Rita smiled. "I'll let you in on a little secret, big guy," she said. "I've yet to see any kind of study that would suggest someone has died after ingesting too much heroin."

"Then why do people say that?"

"Say what?" Rita asked, her large, drooping eyes serious. "Drug overdose?"

She leaned back in her chair and smiled. "Let's say we take a lesson from your partner here. We see a body with a needle sticking out of its arm, we examine the substance in the syringe and find an illegal and known-to-be-dangerous substance, and we find evidence of the substance in tissue and fecal matter. We are going to say heroin overdose because it sure is a damn sight better than saying I don't know."

Beau shook his head, and blew air out of his mouth. "I still don't get it."

"Look," Rita said patiently. "In the 1940s, when addicts started dropping dead for no apparent reasons, rather than say 'I don't know,' coroners wrote down 'overdose.' It's still done today."

"Can we cut the history lesson?" Rich said.

"Wait, Rich," Beau responded. "If people are dying because of something in the dope, like this quinine or something, why don't we tell people to just stay away from drugs mixed with that shit? If we did that, a lot less people would die, right?"

Rich looked at him as if he had just dropped his pants, but Rita responded casually. "Yeah, and if wishes were horses . . ."

"Beggars would ride, right?" Rich broke in. "Meaning who wants to make heroin safe for a bunch of strung-out addicts? Rita, you were trying to make a point earlier."

"The point I was trying to make with this little piece of paper right here?" she asked him, and snapped the paper toward him.

"Rita."

"Okay, the point I was trying to make is that the substance we found in the syringe was over ninety-percent quinine."

"Oh, Jesus," Rich stood up from the table and walked over to the silver doors. He placed his hands on them as if about to leave. "So what does that mean, Rita?" he said.

"Well, it means I'm going to change my official finding to death from quinine poisoning."

"So you are saying she was murdered?" Beau asked.

"I'm not saying anything," Rita countered. "My job is to figure out what killed her. It's your job to figure out how it happened."

"Rita, you told me it was bad dope," Rich said again.

"It was," she said. "I just didn't know how bad."

"Do me a favor, Rita," Rich said. "Just keep it to yourself for a while, okay?" If it was murder, he didn't want the person who gave Violet the dope to think they thought it was something else besides an overdose.

"Rich, if there is bad dope, shouldn't we let someone know so they can warn people?" Beau asked.

Rich folded his arms across his chest and thought for a moment. "No," he said finally. "If there is some dope like that going around, we would have more trouble on our hands than just Violet Hamilton."

Rita nodded and turned back to her desk. "If you will excuse me," she murmured, "I have work . . ."

"No problem," Rich said and motioned to Beau. Walking back through the silver doors was like returning to reality. Clint, the self-made cannibal, sat at his desk sucking his middle finger like it was a juicy piece of sausage.

The white lines on the asphalt in the parking lot of the morgue looked wet, just painted. Gregory stood uneasily beside his BMW, the khaki slacks he wore hanging from his waist like a full skirt. He shuffled from one foot to the other with both hands jammed in his pockets. He avoided eye contact as they approached.

"What's with him?" Beau asked.

"I don't know," Rich answered.

It could have been Gregory's uneasiness at just being in the morgue's parking lot. But he had to admit that his friend had been acting strange ever since they'd found Violet Hamilton's body. Rich put his sunglasses on, reached into his pocket, and brought out a box of green Tic-Tacs. He held it out to Gregory, who only shook his head.

"What happened in there, old man?" Gregory asked.

Beau, who had taken the box from Rich and shaken out half the contents into his hand before slapping them into his mouth, responded. "Hell if I know. I'm still trying to sort it out."

Gregory gave him a closed-lipped smile. "Rita on one again," he said. "Sometimes I need a road map to figure her out." His New England accent added sharpness to his words. A slight breeze lifted Gregory's hair from his shoulder and blew it around his face. He tucked a strand behind his ear and smiled a smile that didn't reach his eyes.

"She sounds like a damn lawyer," Beau said. He swallowed the last of the candy, then hawked a glob of spit onto the shiny black asphalt.

"Jesus, man," Rich said and wiped at his sports jacket.

"What do you want me to do?" Beau responded. "Swallow it?"

"You're disgusting, Blair. You know that?" Rich said.

Beau shook his head and rolled his eyes. "Sorry, I don't mean to offend you girls."

"Well," Gregory interrupted, his voice mild. Rich thought it was deliberately so. "Anybody want to fill me in on what went on in there?"

"Rita said it was quinine poisoning. Somebody meant to take her out," Rich answered.

No one spoke for a moment. Rich saw Gregory use the palm of his hand to push back the strands now blowing all about his face. They watched a hearse labor along like a lazy black animal through the empty parking lot, the sun cutting diamonds of light into its dark surface.

"I see," Gregory said finally. "So it looks like we have a good old-fashioned murder on our hands, eh?"

"I guess," Rich tightened his mouth and stared at Gregory.

"What are you thinking, old man?" Gregory asked him.

Rich didn't respond right away. He didn't want to tell Gregory what he was thinking. He was thinking how this murder was bringing up every unpleasant memory he ever had growing up, including a few that he had after becoming an adult. And he was thinking that Kendra was right. He had missed something, had let himself miss something, to get it finished, done with. The whole thing had clouded his judgment.

The worst part was that it was making him think about Gregory, his long disappearances and his secretiveness. Where was he the night that Violet Hamilton died? What did he do on those weekends that he didn't come home?

"Say it, Rich." Gregory's voice was soft, but challenging.

Rich didn't drop his gaze, but let it go. "I'm thinking we should go after the guy who gave her the dope."

"So, we pick up Smalls, right?" Beau jumped in eagerly.

"No," Rich answered. "We aren't ready for that, not yet. I want to talk to Jiffy again, and I want to find out exactly where Violet Hamilton's supply came from. Nine'll get you ten that this is going to be hard as hell to pin on Smalls."

"So we talk to the old man again?" Gregory asked.

Rich nodded. "When did forensics say they would have the whiskey back, Gregory? We need those prints."

Gregory sat on the BMW's bumper and folded his arms before answering Rich. "I don't know," he said. "I instructed Beau to check them into evidence."

"So forensics doesn't have them yet? They're still in evidence?" Rich asked, as a nasty feeling traveled down his throat.

"Well . . ." Beau scuffed a big boot against the asphalt, making an unpleasant scraping sound in the stillness of the morning. "I ain't exactly got around to that yet."

"What?" Rich replied, planting his hands on his hips. "That's the first thing you should have done."

"Well, with all the other stuff happening, it just slipped my mind."

Rich turned to Gregory. "Did you know about this, Gregory?"

Gregory took a deep breath; his thin chest heaved. "Not really," he responded.

"This is insane, Gregory," Rich said quietly. "Where are the glasses? And the whiskey?"

Beau pointed to the back of the white Monte Carlo. Rich dropped his head, then brought his face up. He spoke to Beau but didn't look at him. Instead he kept his eyes on Gregory. "Check the glasses and the bottle into evidence, then get them over to forensics," he said. "Please."

All three of them remained silent as Gregory opened the trunk and handed Beau the glasses and whiskey, still in crumpled paper bags.

CHAPTER 12

R ich instructed Beau to drive Gregory's BMW back to the station and get the evidence checked into forensics. Rich's ear hurt like hell. It felt like someone had taken a match, struck until it sizzled, and then held the burning flame to his ear. The top of it, now folded over like an envelope, stung as he thought about the night he had come within a hair's width of meeting some of Dunhill's deceased residents. He had nearly lost his entire ear in a knife fight with a perp several years ago over less than an ounce of weed. It was the perp's third strike, and he didn't want to go to jail. Rich was furious, and it took two cops to pull him from the dumb son-of-a-bitch. The incident left Rich with the top of his left ear missing, and an occasional pain that made him want to drop to his knees.

But the pain only happened when he felt he had gotten hold of a case he couldn't win or clear. Gregory, ever logical, told him that it was all in his imagination. That his doubt and uncertainty were manifesting into physical pain. Bullshit. His ear hurt like hell, simple as that.

Rich turned and climbed into the driver's seat of the white Monte Carlo. He didn't start the engine until he heard the passenger door open and a creak of leather as Gregory sat beside him. Rich glanced at the shotgun between the seats and resisted the urge to snatch it up and pound Gregory over the head with it. He couldn't believe the man had forgotten to make sure that Beau had checked the whiskey and glasses into evidence. It was not like Gregory to be so sloppy. Not like him at all.

Rich nosed the car out of the morgue's parking lot. To get to The Pit, Rich had to go through a part of Dunhill the media considered under rebirth. Houses in the throes of restoration by yuppies and buppies existed side by side with broken-down Victorians. Sunshine sprinkled from the late April sky like rain. The day was going to be a hot one—the third in a row since the end of winter despite occasional bouts of frost. With one hand clutching the steering wheel, Rich shrugged out of his suit jacket until he wore only a holster and white T-shirt. Gregory helped him but kept his own jacket on. Rich screwed the lever for the air conditioner all the way up. The fan was deafening in the silence.

For the first time, Rich recognized on a conscious level that spring had finally come. Flowers threatened everywhere, their bright pink and orange heads pushing up through cracks in sidewalks, sticking relentlessly out of crevasses in crumbling walls. And people gave into it. They plunged their hands into the dark moist earth to plant pansies and marigolds and azaleas. A barefoot man with his white torso bared to the sun mowed his small strip of grass. Two houses down, a woman in a pair of jeans and a T-shirt shoveled dirt into neat little piles, stepping carefully around pansies still in their store-bought cartons.

Rich hated spring because people got like this—all giddy and careless. They forgot to be on their guard, forgot about all the cruelty in the world. Even in a town like Dunhill where people died as often as people in other places got the flu.

Rich moved the car into the left lane to turn onto Factory Drive, a long stretch of road that started with houses and ended up in factories now abandoned. Though he didn't turn to look at it, he couldn't help but think about the house on his right, the house on the corner of Factory and Ninth. The narrow Victorian with the long, skinny steps was the house he grew up in. When he lived there with his parents and brothers, the stair rail was a constant source of splinters, and the gray paint was always cracked and peeled.

Now the couple who owned it were painting it a cheerful pink. They had long ago replaced the wooden stairs with wrought iron ones and nailed bright blue cornices to the porch. Rich saw them sometimes as he drove past. They were a young couple with a toddler, and they looked happy, content.

When the green arrow appeared, he turned left, driving the car deeper into The Pit. He called this place zombie-land because the dead still walked. At least, that was the way he thought of them, like the walking dead. People littered the streets like bugs. If they had something to hide, they moved into the shadows when they saw the Monte Carlo slide among them like a splash of light. And those who had nothing to hide would glare balefully as it rolled along the narrow streets, sinking in and out of potholes like a ship on the ocean.

"Didn't you grow up in that house back there, Rich?" Gregory asked.

Rich turned to him. He expected to see pity in Gregory's gray eyes. But instead, his eyes were unreadable. But Rich was so sure Gregory wanted to say something to him that he could almost hear the words. He waited. But when Gregory spoke again, Rich knew the words that eventually came weren't what his partner had on his mind.

"What do you think when you drive through here, Rich?"

At first, Rich didn't answer. He turned his attention back to the street and barely slowed down when a stray dog with a sore on its rump as big as a baseball trotted across the street. He resisted the urge to press on the gas.

"Why are you asking me that, man?"

"I'm just curious, I guess." Gregory shrugged. "I've always been curious, but I didn't want to pry."

"Then don't," Rich said shortly, still annoyed at him for the fiasco that morning.

If they did happen to catch someone for Violet Hamilton's murder and the person was able to get ahold of a lawyer with even a little sense, the lawyer would seize on the fact that they had ridden around with the evidence in the back of the Monte Carlo for days. The chain of custody had been broken.

Rich doubled-parked the Monte Carlo next to The Elite Hotel and flicked on both the sirens and the flashers. He shrugged back into his sports jacket and stepped out of the car. Old Shirley Sherman, a.k.a. Jiffy Pop, looked wearily at them from behind the clerk's counter when they walked inside. A twisted strand of greasy gray-blond hair fell over his left eye. His grimy fingers clutched the pages of the *Dunhill Review* as they approached. Rich walked up to the counter and leaned on it. Gregory stood beside Rich, patiently waiting for him to begin.

"Jiffy," Rich said. "We got to talk, man."

All pretense of being the friendly old man who had known Rich when he was *one of them Marvel boys* had disappeared from Jiffy's face. Now Rich knew that to Jiffy he was just one thing, a cop who wanted answers.

"Ain't got nothin' to say, Mr. Policeman," Jiffy said, stretching out the "O" sound in policeman so that his mouth opened wide enough to reveal what was left of his rotting back teeth. "Done said it all."

"Jiffy," Rich began, gently taking the paper from him. He folded the newspaper neatly and placed it on the left side of the counter. "I think you may have left something out the other day. Right, my man?" As he said the last, he turned to Gregory, who nodded in agreement, his face the picture of gentleness.

"Are you sure you remembered to tell us everything, Mr. Sherman?" Gregory asked, his voice low and respectful.

"I done tole you all I'm gone tell you," Jiffy said, reaching around for the paper Rich had taken from him.

Rich placed his hand over Jiffy's and pushed it onto the counter. Jiffy's hand felt rough as sandpaper, and Rich felt one of Jiffy's fingernails scratch his palm. It took all of his determination to keep his hand clamped over Jiffy's.

"Let's go somewhere to talk, Jiffy," Rich said, a warning under his friendly voice.

"Why should I talk to you?" Jiffy asked, whiny and defiant.

"Gregory," Rich said, without taking his eyes from Jiffy, "isn't it illegal to rent rooms by the hour?"

"Last time I checked," Gregory said.

Jiffy pulled his hand from beneath Rich's and gummed his lower lip. His furtive silver eyes glided from Gregory and back to Rich. He was clearly sizing up the situation. Rich could see the wheels turn behind the old-timer's flashing eyes.

"Who gone watch this here counter?"

Rich looked around the lobby. An old whore stood by the double doors paralyzed in fright. Rich had noticed her when he walked in but had ignored her. Her purple spandex skirt was so short that it exposed every inch of her varicose vein–covered legs. She backed inch by inch to the door as Rich's gaze rested on her.

"Hey, you." Rich curled an index finger at her. "Come over here."

"Her?" Jiffy yelled. "No way. She ain't even a payin' customer. She does her business in the alley like an old cat. The winos pay her in Boonesberry Farm."

"Don't worry about it, man." Rich started toward the whore, but Gregory placed a restraining hand on his arm.

"Leave her alone, Rich," he warned.

"Why?" Rich asked, jerking his arm away. "You a customer?"

"Can't you see she's scared witless?" Gregory asked quietly.

"I don't want to arrest her," Rich said, irritated. "I just want her to watch the counter while we talk to good ole Jiff here."

The old woman inched herself forward now. She slid her feet over the floor on her purple platforms as if they were too heavy to pick up. "I can't be locked up," she explained. "My nerves real bad in them closed-up places."

"And the alley is not closed up?" Rich asked, raising one clean eyebrow.

He heard Gregory blow out a puff of air and knew that he was annoyed. Gregory thought he knew more about these people than Rich did. But he didn't. Gregory didn't have a single clue.

"Just stand behind the counter and tell people Jiffy will be back in a minute. You don't have to do anything. Come on, Jiff, man," Rich said.

Jiffy shuffled from behind the counter. He still wore the same flip-flops and clothes that he had worn on the morning Violet Hamilton died.

"Anywhere we can talk in private, Jiffy?" Rich asked.

"The onliest place is in there," Jiffy said. "All my other rooms is occupied."

Jiffy pointed to a darkened hallway. Rich put his hand inside his jacket and flicked up the snap on his holster. His ear still burned. *Better to be safe than sorry,* he thought.

Rich heard moaning and the creak of bedsprings through the doors of the rooms they passed. From one, he heard music and a man singing Bob Marley's "Castles in the Sky" one word at a time. High-pitched squeals of "castles" and "sky" followed them down the hallway. Jiffy shuffled to a stop as they came to a single door with a missing doorknob.

"We can talk in here," Jiffy said. "I ain't anxious to have my customers see me talk to no police. This long drink of water here just needs to step aside."

Gregory moved away, and Rich noticed him casually reach into his jacket to release his holster snap. For all of his bleeding heart, Rich knew that Gregory had a spark of common sense that had kept him from becoming target practice during his long thirteen years on the force.

Jiffy stuck his hand through the hole in the door and

pulled it open. He walked in without looking to see if Gregory and Rich followed. They were in a broom closet about twice the size of an old-time phone booth. The ceiling was so low, they had to duck down to enter the room. Dirty string mops and brooms and aluminum buckets were piled in the corners. There was a stepladder, three cans of Lysol, and a bottle of Clorox bleach with the top missing. The bleachy smell of the room coupled with the damp smell of the mops made Rich's eyes water. He fought the urge to cough.

"What ya'll wanting?" Jiffy asked him, pulling up his shoulders and placing his hands on his hips.

"You said Violet Hamilton was alone the night before she died—" Rich began.

"No I didn't," Jiffy countered in a voice that sounded contrary and ornery. "I ain't said nothing of the sort."

Rich moved closer to Jiffy until the smell stopped him. "You said—"

"I ain't said nothin' of the sort," Jiffy repeated. "I ain't said it 'cause you ain't asked me, Richard T. Marvel."

Before Rich could respond, he felt Gregory's hand on his shoulder in light warning. "Well, Mr. Sherman," Gregory said in a gentle voice. "We are asking you now. Was there anybody with Violet the night she died?"

Rich turned away from both of them and took a step or two to the opposite wall. He knew that Gregory would have a better time getting something out of Jiffy. He couldn't believe that he hadn't asked Jiffy that. He had made an assumption that it was a drug overdose and therefore wasn't worth investigating the way he would have investigated a case of someone who'd been stabbed or shot. He had jumped to an immediate conclusion, something that someone in his line of work should never do.

And Kendra Hamilton was right. He had jumped to conclusions because he wanted the investigation done and over with. He wanted to get on with his Sunday and go to church with his soon-to-be father-in-law and his fiancée. He wanted his Easter Sunday surrounded by women in big hats and dresses covered in gaudy flowers instead of a man like Jiffy who smelled like an army of alligators.

Gregory's soothing voice cut into Rich's thoughts. "Think hard, now," Gregory said to Jiffy.

Jiffy dropped his hands to his sides and looked down at the floor. He stuck his red bottom lip out in a mockery of concentration. Rich knew, as Gregory probably knew, too, that the man was simply trying to decide if he was going to help them or not.

"Let's see if I can recollect," Jiffy brought his yellow nails up to his chin and scratched. Then suddenly he stopped scratching and snapped his fingers as if a light had clicked on under that greasy head of his.

"There was this one man, but I don't know if he was for Violet, but I remembers him though 'cause he was actin' like some kind of weirdo."

"Weirdo?" Rich raised an eyebrow and looked pointedly at Jiffy.

"Yep," Jiffy said. "Like a psycho. You know them psychos that don't know how to dress quite right? That's what makes me remember him. His clothes wasn't matching up in no kind of way."

Rich looked at Jiffy from the tips of his curled toenails to the tip of his greasy blond head.

"I *knows* what you thinking, Richard T. Marvel," Jiffy said. "You thinkin' how can I tell if someone wasn't dressed right. But look at me. I gots on cheap clothes, but they cheap all over. I got on cheap shower shoes and cheap pants I bought at the Salvation Army. I tries to stretch 'em and make 'em last longer by not washin' 'em a lot. I have a cheap shirt that I treats the same way. But it all goes together, you see . . ."

Rich made a move to cut him off, but Gregory held up a hand to him in warning. Rich knew his partner long enough to know that Gregory wanted Jiffy to talk because he thought the funny old man was on to something.

". . . but this guy"—Jiffy pointed a yellow fingernail at

Rich—"wasn't matching like that. He had on this wool watch cap pulled down over his head and some big ole dark sunglasses. A wool cap, as hot as it was on the Saturday 'fo Easter. That's the first thing that struck me funny."

"What was the second thing?" Gregory soothed him on.

"The second was he had on jeans, 'ceptin they wasn't faded. They was pretty clean, and looked brand-new."

"But what wasn't matching?" Rich asked, the exasperation gone from his voice. When Jiffy had started talking, Rich had felt all the fight leave him. He imagined that the distant flushing sound he heard was his career going down the toilet.

Jiffy lifted up one foot and pointed to it. "His shoes, that's what. They wan't matching fo' this neighborhood, and they wan't matching for what he was wearing."

"And why is that?" Gregory asked gently.

They waited in silence for Jiffy to answer. Rich noticed a pile of dirty magazines he hadn't noticed before. They were stacked neatly halfway up the wall as if waiting patiently for the recycle bin. Rich knew from his years working vice that they were hard-core porn.

"Because they was them shiny leather shoes I see in them movies sometimes, you know? Them shoes men wear when they in them fancy pants."

"Dress shoes?" Rich asked.

Jiffy nodded his head, slowly at first, then faster in a little rocking rhythm.

"Dress shoes like you'd see them rich kids wear to a prom or something. 'Ceptin they were more expensive 'cause I could see lights shining in 'em from way across the room."

"So you didn't see him up close?" Rich asked.

"No sir, he didn't come up to the desk. And I didn't see his face."

"Was he white or black?" Gregory asked.

Jiffy shook his head.

"Hispanic?" he pressed on.

"I couldn't see his face," Jiffy repeated.

"But you could see his shoes?" Rich asked derisively.

"I tole you they was real shiny," Jiffy said, giving Rich a defiant look. "Besides, he had that damn wool cap pulled over his head till it touched his jacket. And he had his head hunched down in the collar of his jacket like this." Jiffy hunched, pulling his neck into his shoulders. He turned to Gregory and then to Rich, his shoulders and neck stiff, his bottom lip stuck out.

"Jacket?" Rich asked. "You didn't say anything about a jacket."

"Well," Jiffy said, "I'm saying it now. He had on a thin windbreaker."

"But you didn't say anything about a windbreaker before," Rich reminded him again.

"Look," Jiffy exploded. "If ya'll ain't gone believe nothing I say, then why you asking me? He had on a windbreaker, I tell you. It wasn't zipped."

"Did you notice how tall he was?" Rich asked, exasperated.

"Tall?" Jiffy said in confusion.

"Yeah, tall, man. Tall," Rich said. "How far up off the ground?"

Jiffy shook his head. "I dunno." He shrugged. "Maybe a little taller than me." He stopped and pointed to Gregory. "Or as tall as that one."

Rich sighed, and rubbed both palms over his head. He tilted his neck backward as far as it would go.

"Did you see anybody else she might have been with that night?" Rich heard Gregory ask.

"Just Cassady," Jiffy confirmed.

"Who is Cassady?" Rich said, more surprised than ever.

"Friend of hers," Jiffy explained.

"When was she there?"

"The first time or the second time?" Jiffy asked.

"You mean she was there two times?" Rich asked, recognizing that his voice had an unbelieving squeak in it.

"Yep."

"Both times, Jiffy." Gregory broke in smoothly.

"I dunno." Jiffy shrugged his shoulders. "I'm not sure about the second time. But the first time I guess it was 'round eight Saturday night. At least that's when I heard 'em. Around eight."

"Heard them?" Rich asked, incredulous.

"Yep," Jiffy said. "They was fightin'."

"Oh, jeez," Rich said and stuck his hands in the pockets of his slacks.

"What were they fighting about?" Gregory asked.

"I dunno." Jiffy shrugged again. "I just tole them to quit the screamin' or get out. They was disturbin' my paying customers."

"So you saw Violet Hamilton around eight that night?" Gregory confirmed.

"That's what I said, man! Ain't you hearing good?"

Rich touched his own throat, looking at Jiffy intently. He knew that it was a long shot, but he asked anyway. "Was Violet wearing a cross?"

"Yep," he said. "She was. I told her that she should be giving that to me fo' my rent."

"When did you see the man in the watch cap?" Gregory asked him.

"I dunno," Jiffy said, then thought hard. "I guess it must have been after nine or so. But I reckon I'm not that sure."

"And Cassady, the second time she showed up, was it before or after that other guy?" Rich asked.

The old man stroked his chin, considering. "After," he said finally. "I think it was after."

"Okay, Jiffy," Rich breathed. "Okay. Does this Cassady have a last name?"

"Yep," Jiffy said.

"Well, what is it?" Rich asked.

Jiffy looked surprised. "Well, I don't know it."

"But you just said she has a last name."

"Everybody has a last name, Mr. Policeman, even trash like me."

Rich saw a little flick of intelligence he hadn't noticed be-

fore behind the man's silver eyes. For the first time, he saw
Jiffy as a person. Maybe a person he thought was scum, but a
person, regardless. And for the first time, Rich realized that
Jiffy knew what he, Rich, thought of him. For some reason,
Rich felt embarrassed.

"If you ask me—" Jiffy started.

"Well, we are not asking you," Rich snapped to cover his
embarrassment.

"But of course we are," Gregory soothed. "Go on, Jiffy."

"If you ask me, you need to be checkin' out that daughter,
Kendra Hamilton. They wan't getting along that good."

"Why is that?" Gregory asked.

"Because. Violet was hounding her for drugs all the time,
showing up at the clinic and out at the hospital, too, 'barrassing her. She's a doctor, you know."

"Yeah, we know," Rich said and sighed.

"Anyway, I hear sometime Violet showed up looking or
asking for drugs or money, 'barrassing Kendra real bad.
They fought over it some over here. I heard 'em."

"What does this Cassady look like," Rich said, dismissing
Jiffy's statement about Kendra. He reached in his coat pocket
and grabbed a notebook. He flipped it open.

"She's in her mid-twenties. Fat. White. Stringy brown
hair. Big tits."

Rich stopped writing. Jiffy was standing so close to him
that the tip of his pencil hit Jiffy in the nose a couple of
times.

"She take drugs, too?" he asked, though he already knew.

"Yep." Jiffy nodded. "Big junkie, just like most of 'em."

They stared at each other, Rich and Jiffy, understanding
that they thought alike when it came to the people of The Pit.
A slow smile spread across Jiffy's face, and he said something so softly, Rich wondered if he had really heard it. But
he didn't question the faint feeling that went through him, a
feeling like he was looking into a mirror and not liking what
he saw. Jiffy had said, "You and me, Rich Marvel, you and
me ain't so different."

April

April Hart, still captive and chanting her name as if it would save her life, thought about how she came to California. A year or so after she dropped out of school, April Hart had walked along Pecan Row, dreaming of those malls in Houston, places she had only heard about. They sold things people really didn't need—perfumed candles and coffee mugs with their kids' faces plastered all over them. They were nothing like the General Store in Red River. Mr. Harrison, the owner, was only interested in selling things like sacks of flour and tractor blades.

That day, as she walked along Pecan Row, she had no idea that her life was about to change, even when she saw a man get off the Greyhound Bus near Red River's lone bus station at the end of Pecan Row. But when the man strolled over to her as if he had come to buy the town, right down to the last chicken coop, she knew something was about to happen. He didn't waste any time, that's what she remembered most about him, that he didn't waste a microsecond of time. He did everything fast, like a rattler who had already made its mind up to strike.

He stepped right in front of her, blocking her path. He crouched down and framed her face with his long, bloodless fingers. He told her that she looked like a model and could be a model like the girls in Los Angeles. He had this weird off-world accent. She didn't know what it was, but she knew that he wasn't from Red River or Texas, probably not even from America.

He asked her how old she was and gasped in surprise when she told him. Most of the models in L.A. were thirteen—exactly her age. Then he gave her a bus ticket and told her to meet him later that night. They would go to Hollywood. Her dreams of getting away from the suffocating coolness of Red River would come true.

For some reason, the man she had met on Pecan Row was not at the bus station that night, but she had his ticket. She climbed on that Greyhound, and it took her all the way to L.A., just like he said it would. When she stepped from the bus and into the Los Angeles bus terminal, she felt as lost as an egg fallen from its nest. People were everywhere. They bumped into her, stepped on her toes, turned to stare at her. They pointed and laughed at the way she just stood there, not sure what to do or which way to go. They had noticed the pure country bumpkin look of her. Her stomach knotted; her throat went bone dry.

She didn't know where to go, so she started walking. It wasn't until she got almost outside the bus terminal that she saw a man with skin like browned butter. He smiled at her, not a crooked or small smile, but a full-toothed smile that lulled her into trust. And when he asked her if she was hungry, she simply told him yes.

That was two full years ago, her first step toward here, where she was now. April Hart crossed her arms on the hard hill of her pregnant belly. She kept them wrist-side down, refused to turn them over. She knew that if she did, she would see blue tracks like freeways running up both arms. She pulled her bare feet onto the bunk and rested her head between her knees. Man, did she stink. She had that sweet, meaty smell, the smell that she had become so familiar with when she lived on the streets. Usually, when she started smelling like this, she would look for a john who would want to spend the night. She would only charge him the price of a hotel room for the sex he wanted.

Afterwards, as the john slept with one eye open and one hand on his wallet, she would run a tub full of water so hot that she would have to sink into it an inch at a time.

If she were lucky, there would be a tiny bottle of shampoo at the hotel. She'd pour the entire bottle into the water and wait until the sweet smelling water was high enough to come up to her chin.

She would close her eyes and just stay there. Sometimes all night or until the john just kicked her out, whichever came first.

But if she could, she would stay until the bubbles popped and the water turned to glass, exposing her thin white body and the needle tracks on her arms. She would stay until the water turned as cold as the Savior's—that's what he called himself—as cold as the eyes of the man now holding her prisoner.

A branch scraped against the window of the garden shed. April knew that it belonged to a morning-glory flower called "My Blue Heaven." There were three things April knew about, despite leaving school so early. She knew and loved numbers. Because of that, she knew exactly how long she had been in captivity. Today was April 25th, just two days after Easter. The man had been holding her for almost five months.

The second thing she knew was animals because it was her job to slop the hogs and feed the chickens on their farm in Red River. Lastly, she knew her plants. She knew the flower pushing through the mud-stained window was a morning glory, and it gave her confidence she didn't know she had. After all, she had escaped it, hadn't she? She had escaped Red River.

It was the coldness, April thought, the coldness that drove her away from Red River. The coldness and the sameness. She remembered a patch of water that sat in a triangle formed by a fallen tree and a rock. What was strange about that water was that it never got warm. Not ever. Not even when the sun beat down on it all day long.

She had taken a drink of that water one day, and the coldness burned right through a hole in an open tooth and settled on her brain. It sat there like a thought, the thought of leaving. It was that day that she saw the man get off the Greyhound, saw him bounce over to her with the promise of a new future in his eyes. Providence. That was what Nana would have called it. The hand of Providence.

CHAPTER 13

Kendra Hamilton sat on the table in Exam Room One with an open newspaper spread on her lap. She tried to push thoughts of Rich and their conversation of yesterday morning away. But no matter how she tried, she couldn't. She had brought the picture of April Hart to the Courtroom Bar & Grill that morning because she was going to ask Rich to help find the missing girl. She had also brought April's medical records. April Hart had been almost three months pregnant when she visited the free clinic earlier that year.

Kendra had a fair number of pregnant teenagers in the clinic and didn't remember April Hart by name. She only remembered that the girl had been in when she pulled her chart. April's eyes were as blue as the ocean, and she had needle tracks running up her arms. She didn't take the news that she was pregnant well but in the end had promised Kendra that she would be in at least once a month and that she would trade the heroin for regular doses of methadone. But Kendra hadn't seen her since that first visit. In fact, she had forgotten all about her until Nana Hart showed up on the free clinic's doorstep.

Kendra thought Rich would be willing to help her and had planned to ask him that morning. But one look into his depthless brown eyes and she couldn't. She saw clearly his dislike for her; anger radiated from him like heat. She couldn't believe for one moment that he would help her more than he had to with anything.

After that, she did for April what she had told Rich to do for her mother. She began asking questions around the neighborhood, starting with Ray Ray, but he returned her questions with a raised eyebrow and a blank stare. No, he hadn't seen April Hart, didn't know her from Eve. Kendra then went to all the junkie hangouts with April's picture, asking if anyone had seen her, all the time reminded of how she used to search for Violet when she was alive. The other junkies either didn't know or wouldn't tell her about April. She remembered the taunt from the crow woman at the homeless shelter on J Street. It was the same woman who had been in the clinic the Sunday Kendra was notified of her mother's death. The old woman answered the question while her deep-set crow eyes glittered black light. "Why you worried about one ole white girl," she had said, "when plenty of black girls go missing in The Pit all the time? Ain't nobody try and find them befo' they turn up dead." It was then that Kendra realized in some ways she had become as alien as Rich had in The Pit's community.

She thought about all of this as she sat tucked away in Exam Room One with the *Dunhill Review* in her lap. Feeling as if she hadn't sat down for two days—her feet ached from toenail to ankle—she reread the article she had already read twice but had not comprehended. It was a blurb in the right-hand corner on the second to the last page of the *Dunhill Review*. Three overdoses had been reported in Dunhill County in the last two months. One, the paper said, was the mother of prominent area doctor Kendra Hamilton.

She looked up from the article, the smell of newsprint in her nostrils. Any other county and the news of these deaths would be on the six o'clock news, or at least closer to the front of the paper. Reporters would be warning of bad dope, and health agencies would be telling junkies to be careful.

James Freehold won the sheriff's election by claiming that the previous sheriff didn't care that Dunhill's poorest residents were dying of poverty and crime. But it now became apparent to Kendra that Sheriff Freehold didn't give a shit either, unless someone forced him to.

Three people dead in less than two months, and until her mother, Sheriff Freehold did nothing. What if there was something to these deaths other than a campaign issue? A fragment of the old crow woman's statement floated in her mind: *Girls go missing all the time, and ain't nobody tried finding them befo' they turned up dead.* She didn't say women or men or boys, she had said, "Girls go missing all the time." Why did that happen? Kendra shook her head and jumped from the table. It didn't mean anything, only that she was tired and needed to get some rest instead of chasing ghosts.

She folded the newspaper and went out into the waiting room. The faint growling in her stomach told her that it was going on noon, but there would be no lunch or rest for her today. Two of The Pit's prostitutes were waiting for their semi-annual checkups, and a teenage mother holding an infant in nothing but a diaper waited for her well-baby checkup. The mother, pregnant again, wore a tube top beneath a pair of overalls. Her big stomach was hard as an artichoke and bulged out of the sides of her overalls. Looking at the chart, Kendra noticed that the teenager was nearly eight months' pregnant. She sat on a bench with her back against the wall, her bulging belly bouncing up and down to the beat playing in her earphones. Kendra looked down at the chart again. The girl was fifteen years old.

"Doctor, I think he's getting worse."

Kendra looked at Maria. The fact that she called her Doctor and not Kendra was not lost on her. Maria had accused her of being distant since her mother's death, and Ray Ray showing up like he did didn't help matters.

The patient she referred to was a little eight-year-old with huge eyes and a big name. Ezekiel Nathaniel Rutherford came in with his mother, Doris, and was suffering from a mild asthma attack. The attack could have been handled at home if Doris could afford the inhalers, and Maria had tried giving him an inhaler when he first arrived. But just being in the clinic seemed to have panicked the boy more. The muscles in his neck bulged as he struggled to breathe. Kendra could hear him wheezing from across the room.

Kendra walked over to him and looked into his eyes. She rubbed an index finger across his cheek, which was as soft and red as a rose petal. Doris had tried to handle the attack by rubbing Vick's Vapor Rub on the boy's chest to help him breathe. But that was as useless as putting butter on a burn. It was a good thing that Doris had brought him in when she did.

"Come on now, Ezekiel," Kendra said. "Take some deep breaths. You're going to have to be brave."

The boy nodded without taking his eyes from hers, and his breaths came a little easier. She stood up and walked away. Maria followed.

"He needs to be in a hospital; you know that don't you?" Maria said.

"I know," Kendra said. Though she had calmed his breathing for now, she knew it was a good chance that he might get worse. He needed a nebulizer treatment, the smoke-and-mist machine that would help him breathe. But people—especially mothers—in The Pit feared, sometimes with and sometimes without reason, taking their kids to the emergency rooms. They feared that some doctor might deem them unworthy and take their kids away. Or make it as hard as hell for them to keep them.

"Kendra . . ." Maria started.

Kendra didn't miss the worried look on her face. And Kendra knew that only half of Maria's worry was for Ezekiel. The other half was for her. Since the day Kendra learned of her mother's death, she hadn't spoken of it. She'd acted to Maria as if nothing had happened. Kendra didn't want compassion; she simply wanted to find her mother's killer. Compassion and sympathy could come later.

"I need you to call Dr. Willis at Doctor's. See if we can get an 'unofficial treatment' for Ezekiel, and if he can scrounge up some inhalers."

"Sure," Maria responded quickly. And then, "Are you doing okay?"

"I'm doing fine, Maria," Kendra responded with a polite smile. Maria didn't smile back. Kendra knew that she was not convinced.

"You really should take some time off, Kendra," she warned. "You are not doing anyone any good by dragging yourself to work."

"Look, Maria," Kendra said, and forced herself to look into her eyes. "I'm fine. I need to work."

A silver bell chimed. Both Kendra and Maria looked toward the door. Detectives Richard T. Marvel and Gregory Atfield walked into the clinic. Detective Atfield hesitated just inside the door. He surveyed each patient in the room, his eyes lingering on Ezekiel as he labored to breathe. Rich, on the other hand, ignored everyone. Everyone but Kendra. He made a beeline straight for her. Kendra suddenly felt a little sick to the stomach. She told herself that it was a déjà vu feeling of when she had learned of Violet's death.

"Doc," Detective Marvel said. "Do you have a few minutes so we can talk?"

Even though it sounded like a question, Kendra knew that it wasn't. It was a summons. Rich wore an expensive sports jacket with ridiculous suede patches on the sleeves. His cleanly shaved face was set in seriousness, all business. He was handsome and sure of himself, smelling and looking as clean as the razor that had cut him this morning.

And for some reason, Kendra hated him and his confidence. She wanted him to be unsure for once, to stammer over his words. She felt her face get hot at the unwarranted emotion. She recognized it as jealousy, and wanted to lose that emotion as soon as possible. She and Rich had grown up on the same streets, and during that time he had barely deigned to talk to her. She remembered him and his brothers walking to school. They followed their mother to the bus stop like a passel of brown baby ducks. Rich lifted a velvet eyebrow in the face of her silence. But Kendra ignored him. She wanted to be sure her voice wouldn't shake when she spoke.

"Maria," she said. "Doctor Willis for—"

"I'm on it," Maria responded.

"What else do I have?" Kendra asked, glad that her voice was guarded but even. Maria looked at the sign-in sheet, and then looked at the patients in the room. One of the prostitutes was looking Rich up and down with a gleam in her eye that suggested she would like to eat him for breakfast. The other one used her acrylic red nails as a mirror to adjust her blond wig. The teenage mother was oblivious to everything except the rap music blaring in her ears. Her belly bounced like a beach ball on the water.

"Believe me, they'll hold," Maria said, smiling at Rich. "Take all the time you need."

But before Kendra could speak, Doris rushed over to them. "Doctor," she said, "you have to do something about my boy. He still ain't breathing good."

Kendra walked over to Ezekiel. Doris was right. Ezekiel now struggled more than ever. His fingernails were turning blue.

"Maria," Kendra called. "We need to get him in an exam room. Sit him up and get him some oxygen at—"

"I know, I know," Maria said. "I got it, Kendra. I've been a nurse almost as long as you've been alive. I got it."

Maria helped Ezekiel past Rich and Gregory, snatching the cordless phone from her desk on her way to Exam Room Two.

"What she doing?" Doris asked. "She ain't calling no ambulance, is she? The last time I took him to the emergency they wanted to take him away because I didn't have enough money for them inhalers."

Doris still didn't get it. She still did not realize how much trouble her son was in. Kendra put her arm around the woman's shoulders and walked away from both Gregory and

Rich. She could feel the heat of Rich's eyes on her back. In a low voice she told the woman that Maria had called another doctor, a friend, at Doctor's Hospital.

"We can't go to no hospital," Doris said again, waving her hands at her. "The last time—"

Kendra squeezed the woman's arm. She threw a glance over her shoulder at Rich and Gregory. Gregory pretended to be engrossed in an AIDS pamphlet. But she could tell that Rich intently listened to every word.

"Look," she said quietly to Doris. "If we can't get him on the smoke-and-mist machine, he's going to get worse. Dr. Willis will pick him up in an ambulance and get him a treatment at the hospital."

"He won't put his name down in the emergency room?"

Kendra grimly shook her head. "He's going to help this time, Doris. He will take care of him and get you some inhalers. Maria will put you in touch with a social worker . . ." Doris started to pull away, but Kendra held on tighter. "She doesn't have to know what happened. We are going to just get you some Medicaid help so this doesn't happen again."

"He's not going to check him in, is he?" the woman asked, rubbing her hands together.

Kendra shook her head again and guided Doris to the second exam room. When she returned to the waiting room, she ignored the disapproving slant of Rich's mouth. Instead, she led him and Gregory to Exam Room One without a word. The day was hot, unseasonably so, and the little room felt like a small oven. After they were all inside, Kendra went to the door and held it open with one hand. She was looking around for something to stop it with when Rich spoke.

"You may want to leave it closed," he said. "I want to make sure this is private."

Kendra looked at him, then shrugged her shoulders. After the door swung shut, she walked back to the exam table. She held her body still under Rich's intense gaze.

"Do you think you are really helping these people?" he asked her.

"Shut up," she responded without hesitation. She wanted to slap him, arrogant bastard.

Gregory folded himself into the chair she usually occupied when treating patients. He had taken his jacket off and had laid it on the end of the exam table.

"Can you two at least be civil to one another?" Gregory asked in a tired voice. Rich seemed to consider something for a moment or two, then he held up his hands in mock surrender. Perspiration beads had broken out on his brown forehead.

"Please, Detective," Kendra said. "You may take off your jacket. I wouldn't want you to be cooked alive."

Rich searched her face and then smiled with his mouth closed. "Glad to hear it, Doc," he responded.

The first thing she noticed was how physically fit he was. His stomach was flat and tight, his shoulders broad and well-defined. He obviously worked out, and Kendra was not surprised. Vain men like him, especially cops, probably lived in the gym.

The second thing she noticed was the gun in his shoulder holster. Unlike Gregory, he wore a leather holster for his weapon. She could see the rough, textured surface of the upper barrel. A pang of fear went through her, and she suddenly felt sick and dizzy. She realized that she had gone simply from grudgingly admiring the man's body to being plunged into the nightmare of her brother's death, of watching Adam being shot down by a cop's bullet on the streets of The Pit.

"You okay, Doc?" she heard Rich's voice as if from a distance.

"Can I get you some water?" Gregory had stood up.

Over Gregory's voice, she heard blood drops splatter like heavy rain. And she heard someone's voice, her own, screaming no, no, no. Luke called it post-traumatic stress syndrome. Whatever it was, it seemed to hit her at the most inopportune moments. Adam. She gave her head a shake to destroy the memories.

"What is it?" Rich asked.

Even though he held both alarm and annoyance in his voice, it was the annoyance she seized on and used to find her pride.

"Nothing," she said, steadier now. "I hate guns, that's all. And your holster's unsnapped."

Rich leaned back against the sink. Relaxed now, he crossed his arms. "Oh come on, Doc," he said jokingly. "We are not going to shoot you."

"What do you want?" she asked, not smiling and wanting them both to leave.

"Do you know who your mother's supplier was?" Rich clipped each word from his mouth.

"What?" Kendra folded her arms across her chest and stared hard at him.

"You heard me," Rich answered curtly.

"You are the detective," she said. "You tell me."

"Look, Doc," he snapped. "I don't have time for games. Who was your mother's supplier?"

"Who do you think?"

She saw his jaw clench. He took in a deep breath through his nose. "Look, ultimately we know it's probably Raymond Smalls. But it's likely she got the drugs from someone working for him, or maybe even somewhere out of the neighborhood. We need to know who."

"So you think you can find that out by coming in here and questioning me like some common drive-by?" Kendra recognized that she had asked the question without an ounce of respect in her voice.

Rich raised an index finger to point in her face, but Gregory placed a hand over his.

"Your mother died from quinine poisoning," Gregory said. "There was enough quinine in that dime bag of heroin to kill an ox. We need to know where she received her regular supply. It may have been poisoned on purpose."

"That's impossible," Kendra responded without thinking. "If my mother got the heroin from her regular supplier, there was no way it would have been poisoned."

"And why is that?" Rich asked, his muscled arms folded across his chest.

Kendra looked at him, suddenly at a loss for words.

"I . . . I just know it, that's all," she said.

"Great," Rich said, stepping close to her, so close she could smell his aftershave. "That's what we can tell the D.A. if he asks us why we didn't bust the supplier for murder. We will tell him that he couldn't have poisoned Violet Hamilton because you just know, that's all."

"Rich," Gregory put a warning hand on Rich's arm and forced him to take a step backward. Gregory turned to Kendra. "Just tell us, Dr. Hamilton, and we will be on our way."

"Look," Kendra said. "If my mother was poisoned, then someone other than her supplier *forced* her to take the poisoned dope. I know you think that she was just a dumb junkie, but she wasn't stupid enough to take drugs from someone she didn't know."

Rich chuckled, but the sound was devoid of humor.

"Do you hear what you are saying?" Rich's eyes bored into hers. "Listen to yourself." He tapped the sides of his head with his forefingers. "You are saying that your mother wasn't stupid; but she spent her entire life chasing a heroin-filled syringe around. Isn't that the essence of stupidity?"

Kendra's eyes filled with tears as Violet's face appeared before her. "My mother," she said without taking her eyes from Rich, "was sick. Do you understand that, Detective Marvel? She had a disease." She continued over Rich's snort of disbelief and took a step toward him. "You ever do anything that wasn't good for you because you couldn't help it? Like smoke? Drink coffee? Get drunk on a Sunday night when you had to go to work the next day?"

"Sure I did," he answered her. "But your mother had a long string of I-can't-help-its. At least mine were not lifelong obsessions."

"Come on, you two," Gregory stated. "This is getting us nowhere."

But Kendra ignored him, and Rich showed no signs of having heard him.

"And what about your ambition?" she asked Rich. "What about the reason you moved to homicide, and got yourself engaged to a judge's daughter? Isn't your ambition your one big I-can't-help-it?"

Rich smiled handsomely. "Why Dr. Hamilton," he said sweetly. "I didn't think you noticed."

Kendra took a step back as if she had been slapped. She hadn't realized her heart had been beating rapidly until it slowed to normal. Her throat constricted with anger and embarrassment.

"Don't be ridiculous," she said, hurling the words at him.

Gregory had stepped in between them, but Kendra hadn't noticed that. He held both hands palms up in a placating gesture. "No matter what you two feel toward each other," he said. "No matter what's happened in the past, we have business to do here. Rich, please."

Kendra saw Rich set his face back into that impassive stone state she knew. The anger and cruelty blew away from his face like sand in the wind. "As always, Gregory, you get to the heart of the matter," he said. "Back to the original question . . ."

"No," Kendra cut him off, her voice flat.

"Can you at least wait until I ask the question?"

"You've asked it already, you don't have to ask it again. I don't know where my mother got that dime bag full of quinine."

Rich nodded and leaned against the sink with his arms folded. Kendra could tell he was trying to keep his annoyance under control.

Then Gregory said, "But that wasn't quite the question, was it? Do you know who your mother's regular supplier was?"

She could barely breathe for the heat in the room, and she felt sweat around the collar of her polo shirt. "That's not going to help you," she answered.

Rich sighed sharply, obviously disgusted. Gregory deftly changed the line of questioning. "Did your mother have any friends?" he asked.

"She knew people," Kendra said, looking up and raking stray hair behind her ear. "People she got high with."

Though she tried to concentrate only on Gregory, her gaze was drawn to Rich. She noticed he was studying her as if trying to remember every line and curve of her face. His stare made her feel like she was under a microscope; it was powerful and coldly objective.

"What about this Cassady," he asked her now.

"What about her?" Kendra countered.

"Look, Dr. Hamilton," Gregory said. "I know this is difficult for you, but we are not the enemy. We are just trying to find out who killed your mother. That is what you want, isn't it?"

Kendra looked down at her feet. He was right, of course. That was what she wanted. She was letting her resentment of Rich and her hatred of cops in general get in the way of what needed to be done.

"I'm sorry," she said and sighed. Her voice sounded tired even to her own ears. She wondered how she must have sounded to them. Bitter. She probably sounded bitter, unreasonable. "I didn't know Cassady well. I only knew my mother hung around with her more than she did other junkies. They were like a set, you know, like . . ."

"Lovers?" Rich asked.

For the first time, Kendra felt a smile tug at her lips.

"You do strike me as the type that would think that, Detective Marvel," she said with a chuckle. "Two women can be friends without being lesbian lovers. What I was going to say was that they were like really close friends, best friends. They were like joined at the hip, I hear."

"You hear?" Rich asked. "You mean you didn't know?"

"No," Kendra said. "I really didn't. Cassady and I . . ." She stopped, gathered her thoughts before continuing. "We didn't see eye to eye on a lot of things where it concerned my mother. I knew she was using my mother for the drugs. She mostly disappeared when I was around."

"So where did you hear this from?" Gregory asked.

"You know, the usual sources. From Jiffy, and . . ." she stopped.

"And who?" Rich asked, his voice as soft as down.

Kendra shook her head. "It doesn't matter, does it?"

"I'm afraid everything matters," Gregory said. "No matter how small you may think it is."

Kendra chewed on her bottom lip, tasting the strawberry Chap Stick she always wore. "Ray Ray," she said finally.

Rich's laugh was dry. "Yeah, sure," he said. "A drug dealer is always the usual source of information about our mothers."

Kendra simply glared at him, wishing she could turn her gaze into daggers to send smack into his big fat mouth.

"Do you think Cassady had anything to do with your mother's death?" Gregory asked.

"Cassady? Absolutely not. She loved my mother, however misguided."

"Maybe Cassady gave her the dope that killed her," Rich persisted.

Kendra looked slowly from Gregory, then back to Rich. Gregory didn't seem surprised that Rich had come back to this vein of questioning. But she was. A little. She thought they had given up trying to find out where her mother got her drugs.

"That's impossible, Rich," Kendra said, not realizing she had used his first name.

"Why is that impossible?" he said, leaning against the sink. Kendra saw that he was clearly suspicious. "Maybe she had a supply problem. She got low, and Cassady was there—"

"It's impossible because it is, that's all," Kendra said, avoiding his eyes. "My mother never had a supply problem."

Rich stood up, dropping all pretenses of being casual. Kendra didn't know exactly what his intent was as he advanced toward her in the tiny room, but she had the feeling that if Gregory Atfield hadn't put his bony hand on Rich's chest, Richard Marvel would have grabbed her in an effort to force the truth from her.

"Come on, Rich," he said. "Dr. Ham . . ."

A knock accompanied by Maria's voice interrupted them. "Dr. Hamilton," she said. "Dr. Willis and the ambulance are here."

Less than six minutes had passed since Maria had made the phone call for Ezekiel, but to Kendra it seemed like hours. "Okay," she said toward the door. Then, looking up at Rich, who blocked her path to the door in the tiny room, she asked, "Is there anything else?"

"We will let you know if we have any more questions," Gregory said, giving her a noncommittal smile.

"I have one," Rich said, still standing inches in front of her. "How did you get along with your mother?"

Kendra felt a small bomb go off in her head, clearly a warning. "Why do you ask?" she said softly.

"There's some who say you wanted her out of the way, that she was embarrassing the hell out of you. You thought she was a royal pain in the ass, is that right?"

"Did Jiffy tell you that?" she asked him in that same soft tone.

Rich didn't answer, just shrugged with his face full of stone.

She caught his eyes with her own, and looked at him. She noticed the small scar on his cheek, his brown eyes, which revealed nothing. Nevertheless, she tried to catch a glimpse of the person behind that hard face, but came up empty.

"You know, Detective Marvel, I'm really sorry for you, living in the world you live in," she responded.

As she stepped around him, she felt a strong hand encircle her upper arm. She looked down at Rich's hand, then at his face. "Your mother own any jewelry?" he asked her.

It wasn't the question she expected, but she pulled away anyway. "She owned a small cross that I wouldn't exactly call jewelry. It was a funny-looking thing with a bit of diamond dust hanging off the end."

"Where is it now?"

"If you didn't find it on her, it could only mean that someone took it. She wouldn't have parted with it voluntarily. Not for anything."

"Not even for a fix?"

"Not for anything," Kendra repeated firmly. "Now if there isn't anything else, I have an eight-year-old boy in my waiting room struggling for breath."

Rich looked into her eyes for several seconds longer. For some reason, she thought he was about to say something else. But in the end, he just let her go, and she felt more alone than she had since hearing the news that Violet had died.

CHAPTER 14

Kendra woke in the middle of the night in her apartment. But it really wasn't her apartment yet, not fully. She still slept on an air mattress, and the place barely had any furniture. Luke Bertrand owned the building, and he let her stay rent-free until she could find a permanent place of her own. But she really wasn't thinking about that now.

Instead, she wondered why she awoke shaking in the dead of night. She dropped her hand to her sweat-slicked thigh. Bright spots floated in front of her as she blinked, trying to become accustomed to the darkness.

After Gregory and Rich left the clinic earlier that day, she switched entirely into automatic. She got Ezekiel, the boy with asthma, sent off with Dr. Willis. She treated the two prostitutes and gave the well-baby checkup, telling the mother to stay away from drugs and alcohol, especially since she breast fed. Lastly, she called Doctor's and told them that they would have to find someone else to man the clinic the next couple days because she had some personal business to handle. After the last patient walked out of The Pit's clinic, she drove to her apartment, walked the three flights of stairs, made a bowl of Campbell's soup, and went to bed.

Now she sat on her air mattress, her breath scraping the inside of her throat like sandpaper. And things had finally settled down to where she was forced to notice them. The clock blinked a steady twelve-zero-zero, she heard the drip-drop of the bathroom faucet. She could almost see the water form into a crystal teardrop before plopping into the sink. She heard a door squeak open in the hallway, and the footsteps of someone walking across the floor above her.

She wound her hands through her hair, trying to remember what had her so spooked. She squeezed her eyes shut and let her body drop back onto the mattress. She was on her fifth deep breath when she remembered the dream. Except it really wasn't a dream, but a memory of the first time she saw someone die.

Kendra was five, with clear brown eyes and a bushy ponytail. She lived at The Elite with Violet, who would sometimes forget to come home for days at a time. In those days, patrons were allowed to stay for weeks, sometimes months. But not every room had a private bathroom. They had to share the facilities with other occupants. One of Kendra's first memories was of walking that graffiti-covered hallway to the bathroom. She was so afraid of that long walk that she would hold her bladder until she thought it would burst. It wasn't the drug dealers or prostitutes that scared her, but the drunks crumpled against the wall.

One old man, who seemed more sober than the others, followed her with his eyes down the long hallway every time she went to the bathroom. Sometimes he made comments, things like, "You gotta go, little girl?" or "You want me to take you to the potty?" She would keep her eyes focused on the greasy bathroom door at the end of the hall, and except for the terror boiling in her stomach, things usually turned out okay.

But that summer when she was five, she had been alone for two days. She made up horrors in her five-year-old mind that made the trip to the bathroom almost impossible.

Almost, because there came a point when she simply couldn't hold it anymore. She had no choice but to slide back the deadbolt and close the door behind her.

She let go of the doorknob and balled up her empty hands by her sides. She took a step forward. The wino, the one who seemed sober, was sitting in the hallway. He wore a dirty jacket and had one hand flung across his knee. He grinned and leered. "Come on, little girl. I ain't gone bother you." Kendra took a step backward, meaning to run back into the room. But the tickle between her legs told her she would make a mess if she didn't get to the bathroom soon. Needing to trust him, she began the walk down the hallway.

True to his promise, the wino sank back against the wall. He even began singing, a casual humming that made her feel slightly better. But only slightly. She took a step forward. He didn't move, sat still as sandstone. She took several more steps forward. He didn't drop a note. Instead, he continued singing, "Skip to my lou, skip to my lou, skip to my lou, my darling." She walked faster, calculating that it would take only three more steps to be past him and out of his reach.

But as she stepped around him, he snaked out a yellow hand and grabbed her around the waist. She screamed and kicked, but he still managed to stand up. She pounded her feet against the wall until her shoes flew off and her feet stung, but she knew no one would come. She and Violet had heard screams many times in that hallway, and always, Violet would tell her not to open the door, to get down. Some fool may have a gun.

The wino smashed her face inside his jacket, and Kendra smelled pee and vomit. He pinned her arms against her sides and laughed as he bounced her against him like a rag doll. It was when she started to cry that she felt hard floor beneath her. She opened the eyes she didn't know she had closed and saw a man standing there. The wino backed against the wall like a beetle.

"I wan't gone do nothing, man," the wino said. "I was just

funning her, tha's all. She walk around here like a scared chicken all the time."

The man smiled at the wino, easily. She had seen him a couple of times before because he was not one of Violet's regular johns. He had eyes that twinkled all the time, especially at her.

Now, she saw him simply reach down and close a black hand completely around the wino's neck whose eyes bulged as he tried to find his breath.

"You will know not to mess with what's mine," the man said to the wino as he choked the life out of him.

Kendra could not look away no matter how hard she tried. She watched until pee ran down the old wino's leg. She watched until his body stopped twitching, and he went still and limp like a sleeping baby.

As the man turned his eyes on her, she scrambled backward against the wall, and felt something wet. She had stepped in the wino's urine with her bare feet.

"Get back in the room," the man said to her.

And she did, running and stumbling the few steps back to the room she shared with Violet. Fear had overcome her need to go to the bathroom. When she had to go pee in the future, everyone left her alone. And the wino who always seemed a little sober? Well, he simply wasn't there anymore. He only existed on occasion, when she would dream about the incident, creating more detail than she could have remembered and feeling guilty at having been the instrument of someone's death.

Now, over twenty-five years later, Kendra pressed her fingers to her face. It was cold, clammy with the memory. She tried to remember the face of the man who saved her, but she couldn't. Only the eyes were complete, dark brown, almost black and sparkling with pinpoints of light that assured her that she would always have someone watching over her.

Kendra pushed the sheet back from her damp body and padded into the kitchen. She got a glass out of the cupboard and ran tap water into it until it was full. She drank the tepid water in one swallow. As she gasped for air, she thought about April Hart. No one had been watching over her, or those other girls who had "gone missing before they turned up dead." She thought about the old crow woman's words and Freehold's campaign promise. How many missing girls had there really been? And how many had passed through the doors of the free clinic only to walk out again, forever, their memories forgotten and replaced by other helpless souls being treated at the clinic? "Did you check your records to see if April ever came to the clinic?" Guilt coursed through her as she remembered Nana Hart's question. No she hadn't checked, and probably wouldn't have if Nana Hart hadn't flown all the way from Texas to ask for help. As Kendra dressed in jeans and T-shirt, she silently promised Nana Hart that she would not forget again. Nor would she wait. Kendra didn't care how early it was; she would go to the clinic in search of other girls who may have passed her way before they went missing.

Kendra had forgotten how frightening this time of night could be in The Pit. It was a little before four in the morning. The bars had long ago closed, and it was late even for the hoodlums. Those who did occupy the street at this hour would be the desperates, the junkies who didn't score and the whores who didn't make their quota for the night.

She had once felt a part of this, but she had been away too long and cursed the impulse that had brought her down here. She drove past two prostitutes in tight skirts and heels as high as skyscrapers on the corner just before the clinic. They eyed her black two-door Acura until they caught sight of her, and then they turned and ducked down an alley like black ghosts.

Kendra parked next to the clinic, cut the ignition, and sat in the car with her lights on. The silence, the stagnant stillness, on Main Street constricted her breath, made her heart beat double time. A sense of being watched climbed over her. She twisted around and looked out the rear window. Darkness and shadows scrambled behind her; every single streetlamp was a broken useless eye.

Breathing hard now, she reached in the glove compartment and pulled out a tube of mace. She shoved it in her pocket and reached for the flashlight as well but decided against it at the last minute. If someone did lurk in the shadows and hadn't noticed her yet, she didn't want to shine a spotlight on herself. *Look at me! Rob me, rape me, let Richard T. Marvel off the hook!*

The thought of Rich got her going. "I don't want you playing detective." She remembered his angry words at breakfast the other morning. "Well, fuck you," she breathed now as she switched off the headlights. Even the sound of the lights clicking off seemed loud in the surrounding silence. She made sure that she had the key to the clinic ready when she stepped from the car.

And there it was again, that feeling of being watched. She shook it away and walked quickly to the front door. Her tennis shoes bounced softly against the pavement, and she heard crickets bleat in the cool morning air. The metal door handle felt solid and a little cold, reminding her that this was real—that she was actually in one of the most dangerous neighborhoods in Dunhill at four o'clock in the morning.

Her hand shook as she brought the key to the lock, and the jangling sound startled her so that she dropped them. She cursed softly, and bent down to retrieve them. When she stood up, the keys hanging limply from her hand, she was face to face with one of The Pit's residents. He wore a black rag tied around his head and a satin jacket with a Nike swoosh over the left breast pocket. His small eyes glittered in the darkness as he watched her, summed her up.

"Hi, Doc," he finally said in a gruff voice. "I didn't know that was you."

Kendra gripped the mace in her jacket pocket, thinking about all the good it would do as her eyes fell on the handle of a gun tucked into his jeans.

She tried to laugh, sound casual and self-assured, but she knew her voice shook.

"Yes," she said forcefully, "it is me. And you are?"

"Don't worry 'bout who I am," he said.

Before she could protest, he took the keys from her hand and opened the door to the clinic. He held it open for her, keeping his eyes on hers. "What you doing down here this time of night?" He lifted his chin a little as he said this to her.

"I had some work to do," Kendra responded. "Who are you?"

"I said don't worry 'bout it," he answered again. "You just need to be careful. Ray Ray wouldn't want you gettin' yourself hurt by doing something stupid. You shouldn't be out at this time of night, anyway."

Kendra nodded her head, finally understanding, as he unlocked the front door for her. Ray Ray. Clinics like these usually got robbed two or three times a month. The Pit's clinic had rarely been robbed, and had never been robbed since she had been back in town. Rumor had it that Raymond Smalls kept watch over it because of their relationship.

The man nodded at her again, then turned and left. Inside, Kendra flicked on the lights, then made sure all the blinds were closed before going to the clinic's metal filing cabinets. She didn't know what she was looking for, not really. She went to the first file drawer, and tried to pull it open. It was locked. Maria. She should have known. She rummaged through Maria's desk and found the key under some old *Redbook* magazines.

Kendra turned the stiff lock and pulled the drawer open. There weren't many files, and she didn't expect many. Half of the patients treated at the clinic refused to give any information about themselves. If Kendra insisted, they would leave, telling her that they didn't need her jive bullshit for an aspirin. Those that needed the treatment desperately often gave false names. As she ran her fingers along the tabs, she noticed a Lizzy Borden, a Maya Angelou, and a Dorothy Dandridge—and that was only in the first file drawer, the A thru M's. Ignoring the obviously fictitious names, she sorted through all three file cabinets until she had a pile of files she could look at in more detail.

"A lot of girls gone missing from here," she heard the smoky voice of the old woman in her ear. *Young girls,* Kendra thought, *I'm looking for young girls, young and pregnant, like April.* She soon discovered that the clinic files went back only five years, and after she sorted through them, she had file folders for thirty girls. Most of them had been seen by Dr. Willis when he ran the clinic before she came back to Dunhill. She had seen only three of them herself, including April.

She had seen one girl during her first week at the clinic—a Rochelle Smith. And Kendra knew that Smith was probably not Rochelle's real last name. The other girl, Kitten Taylor, she saw a few weeks after. She had seen both of them only once. After the initial diagnosis, neither one of them had bothered to return. Kendra sat in Maria's chair, drumming her fingers against the desk, thinking of what she could do. Had any one of these girls "gone missing"? She could call them, but they probably didn't stay in one place long enough for that to work. Besides, no phone numbers. She could go to the public library, see if she could find any newspaper articles of girls reported missing, and cross-reference the names. But she doubted that the *Dunhill Review* would bother to run an article even if the girls were reported missing.

Reported missing. As the words tumbled over in her mind, she realized their full import, and it became clear to her what she must do. It was time she paid a visit to an old friend.

CHAPTER 15

Kendra passed a curious Dr. Willis on her way out of The Pit's free clinic three hours after Ray Ray's hoodlum unlocked the door for her. Dr. Willis was a tall, thin black man who wore his hair in an afro that looked like a smoky black halo around his thin head.

"I thought you were taking a couple of days off?" he said, eyeing her curiously as she juggled the files in her arms and tried to grab for the door at the same time.

"I did," she said, a little breathless, "but I had some last-minute paperwork I had to catch up on. I hope you don't mind, but I took some copies."

Dr. Willis helped her with the door. "You could have taken the originals for all the good those damn things do me in this hellhole. Why didn't you let Maria do that for you? You don't need to be worried with this now."

Kendra smiled, shook her head. "This was something I had to do for myself. How is Ezekiel?"

He shook his head, as if trying to catch up with her sudden change of subject. "Oh, he's fine," he said. "Perked right up after two nebulizer treatments. I gave the mother a bunch of samples, told her to come back if she needs more. Seemed grateful."

"Hey, thanks a lot, Carl," she said. "I really appreciate it."

"No worries." He shrugged. "Do you need any help with those?"

She told him no and carried the files to her car. The streets were still and deserted except for a few people standing outside the BART station around the corner from The Elite. An old wino with gray, leathery skin and a comb stuck in his nappy hair eyed her as she stepped into the Acura. She put the files in the backseat, knowing what she had to do. But instead of doing it, she pointed her car in the direction of the Dunhill County Library.

As much as he meant to her, Kendra didn't want to go see that old friend—not just yet. The price she would have to pay for seeing him would be to walk into a place where she hadn't been since her brother Adam was killed. The library might be able to afford her the answers she needed. She knew that it was just a long shot, but she had to try. If these girls did indeed disappear—instead of just forgoing prenatal care, which wouldn't have been so unusual—maybe some news of their disappearance would be in the *Dunhill Review.* If she found something, anything at all, she would go see that old friend. *If not, then what?* Then she would know that the old crow with the beady eyes and white head rag was wrong. These girls had not disappeared, and had nothing to do with April Hart.

The library had always been surreal to Kendra, like someone had superimposed the now crumbled facade over the ornate structure that once existed. Two crumbling columns flanked either side of a heavy mahogany double door. The once rich wood had faded to a muted brown, and Plexiglas had been used to replace broken panes in the door. Long cracks fissured the marble stairs.

But if she looked hard enough, Kendra could remember the structure as it had once looked—ornate and inviting. When she was a girl, she spent countless hours in the Dunhill County Library reading everything she could get her hands on while her mother slept in one of the study carrels. She shook away the memory and checked her watch. The library had just opened.

The place was still a refuge for Dunhill homeless. An old woman with lank gray hair slept on two encyclopedias in a study carrel. A Safeway shopping cart piled high with trash bags filled with clothes and soda cans stood beside her. A yellow dog, its fur matted to its skin, stared at her from the woman's side. Kendra noticed that the woman had it leashed to her wrist with a piece of rope. A sour smell, coming from either the dog or the woman, hung in the air.

"She says it's her seeing-eye dog." The voice was hard, the words enunciated perfectly as if the speaker had chiseled each one from the marble steps out front.

Kendra turned toward the voice and came face to face with the librarian, an old wrinkled woman with skin as dry as powder. She had worked at the library for at least thirty years, had been there when Kendra was a girl. But each time Kendra came in, the old librarian treated her as if it were her first time seeing her.

"We don't normally allow dogs in here," the woman continued, peering over round glasses with lenses as thick as microscope lenses. "But I didn't feel like a fight this morning. Besides, she said it was her seeing-eye dog."

"Okay," Kendra said, not really wanting to get into a conversation about the homeless woman now snoring peacefully.

"How can I help you?" the librarian asked.

"I need to see some back issues of the *Dunhill Review*," Kendra said.

"How far back?"

Kendra thought back to the first girl Dr. Willis had seen—Lorna Jones. She had come into the clinic, had been told that she was pregnant, and had not visited again. That was . . .

"Five years," Kendra said aloud. "I need to see at least five years back."

The woman nodded as if understanding exactly what Kendra needed. "Ah," she said, holding up a forefinger as wrinkled as a stick of beef jerky. "We'll have to set you up on one of the microfiche machines. I'm afraid we haven't gotten everything computerized yet. We are spending most of our funds on trying to keep the place from being closed down. This way, please."

She led Kendra into a room with a table and a machine that looked like a deformed television. After showing her how to work the knobs and dials, the librarian stacked slick microfiche files on the table and left.

Two hours of flipping through the microfiche yielded nothing except aching eyes and a burning headache. There were plenty of articles on fatal accidents involving cars or hunting rifles and in one case a runaway chainsaw, more articles on fundraisers thrown by Luke Bertrand and his high-society friends, electoral races, and page after page of obituaries that had Kendra almost believing that the town was cursed.

But The Pit, the neighborhood where the girls had last been seen, was barely mentioned at all. She released the current fiche with a click and slapped in another one, thinking about the names on the files she had taken from the clinic. She surprised herself by memorizing all of them: Lorna Jones, Rochelle Smith, Kitten Taylor, and Beth Rinehart. They all sounded made-up—Smith and Jones, for example. And she knew that Kitten couldn't possibly be a real name. Beth Rinehart, though, that sounded real enough. She might not be able to find any newspaper articles on the other girls, but maybe she would find something on Beth Rinehart, if there was anything to be found.

She looked at the dwindling pile of microfiche. There were only three left, and Kendra was about to give up hope when she placed the next-to-last fiche in the machine. The headlines raced past: *Wealthy Couple Perish in Plane Crash; Luke Bertrand Receives Dunhill County Man of the Year Award; Local Sheriff's Policy Under Attack Again.* Next came the society pages, and then the obituaries again. She was about to pull the fiche out when something told her to go back to that last article. She moved the knob again until she came to the article titled *Local Sheriff's Policy Under Attack Again.* It was a full-page article on the prior sheriff of Dunhill, Bill Conner, complete with pictures and crime statistic charts depicting the rise in crime since the sheriff had taken office. She read the first few lines:

> *Deputies rally around local Sheriff Bill Conner as his political rivals attack his policies on Pit crime. Conner's critics claim that he is concentrating too much on crime prevention, and not on finding those responsible for increased homicides and robberies in the area. Bill Conners defends his record saying . . .*

Kendra stopped reading, not knowing what had made her go back to this article. She moved the microfiche sideways, then up and down, scanning the entire page. She shook her head, swallowed, and thought that exhaustion was finally getting to her, that she was hallucinating. She reached to take the fiche out and then stopped.

There it was, a small article, less than two paragraphs long, at the bottom right-hand corner of the same page as the article on the prior sheriff. It was obviously meant to complement the article on the embattled sheriff, and to act as a filler for white space the editor didn't know what to do with. The headline read, *Parents Say Disappeared Girl Was Murdered.* Kendra continued to read:

> *In an interview yesterday, Keith and Elizabeth Rinehart, parents of Beth Rinehart, said that their daughter has obviously met with foul play. The couple admits that their fifteen-year-old daughter ran away from home and became involved in drugs but say that they maintained a close relationship with her. Elizabeth Rinehart reported her daughter missing three months ago when she failed to appear for an appointment at a rehab center. "Beth had just found out that she was pregnant, and wanted to do right by the baby," Rinehart*

says. She accuses the sheriff's department of "standing by and doing nothing while Beth is missing." Spokesman for the sheriff, Calvin Sykes, says that they have no reason to believe Rinehart met with foul play and that the girl is no longer believed to be in the area. "The sheriff's department is handling this case as a runaway and is giving it due diligence," Sykes says.

The article then went on to say a couple of other things about the Rineharts before it ended. Kendra's heart beat fast. She looked at the last microfiche, then convinced the librarian to let her use the front desk computer, the only computer with an internet connection in the whole place. At first, the librarian refused, but in the end, she capitulated. Her need to be helpful had won out. Kendra tried to find mention of Beth Rinehart's disappearance or reappearance online, but could not. The article in the paper was it. That was all Beth Rinehart's disappearance merited, fifteen years of life crammed into a space no bigger than a Post-it note.

Kendra sat for long time in the black Acura Raymond Smalls had lent her when she got back in town. She'd had it for almost a year now, and he hadn't asked for it back. Neither one of them had ever mentioned it, and now, parked in a visitor's space in front of the sheriff's department, she wondered about it. She wondered when Raymond would ask for the car back. Nerves. That was why she thought of it now. She was nervous about going to the police in a car that belonged to a known drug dealer, even if the policeman she planned on talking to was an old friend. But she knew deep down that wasn't the real reason for her nerves. It was that if Raymond knew she was here, he would be furious with her. She could almost see the wind of anger in his bright, dark eyes. He'd think that she was a traitor.

"Come on, girl," she said aloud, "you are being ridiculous. Just go and do what you have to do."

Without knowing why, she pulled the rearview mirror down and got a good look at the face of Kendra Hamilton. Not beautiful, but pretty enough. That is what Luke always told her: *you are pretty enough.* But pretty enough for what? He would never say. Luke and Raymond, the two men in her life. One who treated her with the obsession of a father and the other with that of a husband if she chose . . . chose what? She didn't know, and she certainly didn't want to think about it now.

She pushed the rearview mirror back up and looked down on the pile of files in the passenger seat. She flipped through them until she came to Beth Rinehart's. She took the file and placed the copy she had made of the article on top of the medical record. As she stepped from the car and gazed at the newly remodeled sheriff's department, her throat contracted in a spasm of pain brought on by emotion.

Just as Violet refused to step foot in hospitals, Kendra felt the same way about the sheriff's department. But Kendra's fear was based on a single event, which Luke euphemistically referred to as *the accident.* So maybe the cop who shot her brother, the cop with the still wet pimples and itchy trigger finger, thought he was doing the right thing at the time. But an accident? No. Never. More like a negligence brought on by the cop's assumptions about Adam's color.

Violet was so distraught and so obviously high when Adam was shot that the cop's partner arrested her just to shut her up. And Kendra, seventeen at the time, was taken down to the station as well. Every time she passed the sheriff's department, she remembered gray asphalt, chocolate skin, and sun sparkling in a pool of blood as thick as syrup. She remembered cops trying to get her to talk, nudging her Keds with the tips of their shiny patent leather shoes in frustration at her silence.

She knew that she wouldn't be here now if it weren't for the kindness of one cop who realized what she had been going through long before Adam died. He let her rave and cry against him until it almost healed her. It was his help that she sought now.

The front office of the sheriff's department was wide, unnaturally bright. The cop behind the high desk just inside the front door barely gave her a second look. Swallowing, she slid around the desk, hoping that he wouldn't notice her. Relief washed over her as she heard the voice of Officer Grady.

"Girl, you look like hell on a rampage," he said. Officer Lindstrom Grady took both of her hands in his as she approached. She knew that Grady was right, especially if she looked like she felt. Her stomach boiled in protest. The only thing she had eaten in two days was a can of Campbell's soup. Her eyes felt as dry as marbles in their sockets.

"Hello, Grady," she said. "Thanks for seeing me."

He smiled as he assessed her. Officer Grady was the only cop Kendra had known personally. He used to walk the beat in The Pit—when cops still walked the beat in that part of town. When she was on the streets with her mother, he would make it a point to search them out, always with a gift—a blanket or a pair of jeans his children no longer needed. And when Adam was killed, Grady made a point to let her know what was going on with the internal investigation even though it didn't win him any points with his fellow officers.

He folded his arms across his chest, still regarding her. "I'm not going to like what you're about to ask me, am I?" he said, his voice gruff and quiet.

She glanced around the room, noticing one or two uniformed cops eyeing them curiously. "Can we go somewhere—" she started, but he cut her off before she finished.

"Of course, of course," he responded.

She followed him down a corridor into a tiny room furnished with a metal table and three metal chairs. White paint covered the walls and ceiling. Even the door was painted that same blinding white. When the door shut, it disappeared into the surrounding walls.

"I ain't gonna like this, am I?" Grady asked again.

"I'm afraid not," she said. "Can I sit down, Grady?" She did not think twice about the use of his last name. He had always been Grady to her and to everyone. Lindstrom, the formal-sounding first name, did not fit him. It was a name he did not wear well.

"Yeah, yeah," he said. "I don't even know why you asking."

He pulled out a chair, which was lower than she expected. She sat down too hard, and a twinge of pain traveled up her leg. Grady remained standing, his arms folded across his chest and his lips in a full-blown frown now. Kendra looked up at him. His badge glowed like newly polished gold in the white room. She again thought of the men in her life, how she had a knack for not trusting the right people. Instead, she gravitated toward complicated people. Luke was so private that she had rarely been in his home, though she had known him practically all of her life. And Raymond? Well, he had his own problems. And now Grady.

"Kendra . . ." Grady began, his voice impatient.

"Yeah, well," she replied, more to her own thoughts than to his question.

Grady pulled out a chair and sat beside her. He took the file she had been holding and placed it on the table. He stilled her trembling hands with his own before he spoke.

"When was the last time you got a good night's sleep?" he asked.

His question surprised her, but it also put her at ease. She answered with a laugh.

"About two years ago," she joked, "the night before I came back to Dunhill."

Grady said nothing, just stared at her, his lips pursed.

"What's this all about, Kendra? Why you come down here?"

"A woman came to see me the day after my mother died . . ." She didn't know why, but she stopped. Then she continued.

"Nana Hart." Now she laughed wryly. "She said that everyone calls her Nana Hart." Grady said nothing, just waited. Kendra continued. "She said that I treated her granddaughter, April Hart, and that she disappeared several months ago. She asked me to help find her."

"And why didn't you send her to the police?"

Kendra swallowed, paused before answering. "Her granddaughter is a junkie, Grady. And a whore. Nana Hart said that she had called the sheriff's department, only to be laughed at."

Grady sighed and sat up. He placed his hands over his eyes and shook his head.

"You want me to see what I can—"

"No, no." Kendra shook her head. "I've been asking some questions, but no one has seen her. But that's not why I'm coming to you."

"So you running around playing cop? Is that what you tellin' me? Have you even buried your mother yet?"

"Grady, please," Kendra said. "Not now." She didn't want to think about what he had just said. She opened the file on the table, then handed Grady the article on Beth Rinehart. Confusion rippled over the officer's face as he read it. When he finally looked up, he said only one word.

"So?"

"Well, I think that this girl's disappearance may be related to April's. I mean, she was pregnant when she disappeared, just like April was."

Grady paused, his face displaying myriad emotions. It finally settled on one that told Kendra he would humor her, for now at least.

"So what, Kendra? So what if she was pregnant? This Beth girl disappeared almost three years ago. What has that got to do with this here April Hart?"

"When I started asking questions around The Pit," Kendra explained, "I found out that a lot of girls, pregnant ones, turn up missing all the time. . . ."

Grady's chair scraped loudly against the cement floor as he stood up. "No, no, no," he said. "You don't know what you talkin' about, girl. That girl wan't pregnant."

"You know about this?" she asked.

"Of course I know about it," Grady said. "I was one of the uniforms assigned to the case. This girl wan't pregnant."

"You remember Beth Rinehart?"

Grady continued as if she hadn't spoken. "This girl's family dragged Bill Conner's name through the mud over this goddamn hooker. They ranted and raved, wrote their congressmen and whatnot. It's what gave that political prostitute that's sheriff right now the idea that he could challenge Bill Connors on this and win. Of course I remember."

"But what makes you say that she wasn't pregnant. I have her medical records here. She was seen at the clinic—"

He held up his hand to stop the words flowing from her mouth. "Because we found her body about two months after this article was written. The girl had overdosed on heroin and she wasn't pregnant and there weren't no baby around, either."

"So Beth Rinehart is dead?"

"Dead, and been dead almost three years."

"But, Grady," Kendra said, "her parents insisted in this article that Beth was pregnant, that she was ready to turn her life around because of the baby. . . ."

Grady shook his head. "Oh, Kendra," he said. "You lived with a junkie all your life. You know what kind of lies they tell so they can get money or get back in with they folks so they can take from 'em. This girl weren't no different."

"Oh," Kendra breathed. She didn't know what to say next. She had come here hoping that Grady would tell her what had happened to Beth Rinehart, hoping that she could find her and talk to her just to prove to herself that girls weren't *disappearing* in The Pit. People just didn't disappear like that without anyone noticing—or caring.

"Can I see the police file?" she asked.

Grady drew back at her question. "What?" he said, as if he

hadn't heard her correctly. "See the police file? Have you lost your mind?"

"Grady, come on," she pleaded, "I need to see for myself that—"

"That what?" he challenged. "That Bill Conners was doing his job back then? That we was doing our job? You know me better than that, don't you, Kendra? I busted my ass for the people in The Pit. Why do you think I'm still in this uniform? Why do you think that I'm not a detective like that Richard Marvel by now?"

Kendra licked her lips and opened her mouth to apologize. But nothing came out, because what she wanted to tell him was that busting his ass for people in The Pit had nothing to do with why he wasn't a detective. Lindstrom Grady had joined the sheriff's department as a rookie almost thirty years ago. He didn't go to college, barely passed his GED exams. Even though the younger cops he showed the ropes respected him, they always surpassed him because of two things: education and will. Instead of education, Grady had instinct, which allowed him to be a successful cop, and if he did have will, it had been hampered by one thing and one thing only, and that was loyalty to Bill Conners.

"Now if you want me to look into finding that April Hart, I will," he said. "But I ain't gone let you become obsessed with smoke because you trying to keep from grieving for you mother's death."

"That's not true, Grady," Kendra said.

He reached out and pulled her chin up, forcing her to look into his face. "I've known you for a long time, Kendra. And I know when you tryin' to run away from something. You need to go home, get some rest, and stop thinking about all of this."

"All I need is an address, Grady," she said. "I don't need to look at the whole file. Just an address, that's all."

Grady sighed, let his hand fall to his knee. "Whose address?"

"The parents," Kendra replied. "All I need to do is talk to them, find out what happened to the baby. . . ."

"I told you that there weren't no baby!" Grady said again, this time agitation and annoyance in his voice.

"Then it wouldn't do any harm to let me talk to them," Kendra said.

"No harm 'ceptin' to get them all stirred up," Grady said.

"I promise I won't," Kendra said. "Please, trust me, Grady." She made her eyes wide and pleading as she looked at him. The silence in the room stretched to the blinding white walls.

He gave one final sigh. "Okay," he said. "I guess you could always get it from somewheres else besides here."

"There is one more thing."

Grady threw both hands into the air. "Of course there is."

She scribbled four names at the top of the article Grady had just read and pushed it to him. "Could you tell me if these girls were ever reported missing?"

Grady scanned the names. "I guess there ain't no harm in it." He stopped and pointed a finger at her. "Promise me you'll get some rest after, though, hear?"

"I promise," she said, trying not to let the satisfaction she felt show on her face.

He walked out of the room, closing the door behind him until it disappeared into the sea of white walls. Kendra stood up but had to quickly sit down again. The twinge of pain in her leg had transformed into a full-fledged cramp.

Kendra didn't understand why Grady would say that Beth Rinehart wasn't pregnant. Her medical records showed that she most certainly was. She ran her hand over that particular report to see who treated her. Dr. Willis. He was as meticulous as a prize-winning chef when it came to his medical records even though he did contend that they weren't worth a damn. He wouldn't have made a mistake, and he certainly wouldn't have written the entry into the wrong record.

She whipped around at the sound of the door opening. The smile died on her lips when she came face to face with

Richard T. Marvel. His face was set in stone as usual, but his eyes betrayed him. He was angry as hell.

"Expecting someone else?" he asked, his voice edged in sarcasm.

She opened her mouth to speak but changed her mind. He leaned one shoe against the door and folded his muscled arms across his chest. Rich was dressed entirely in black—black jeans, black belt, and a black T-shirt that was too small for him. *Probably on purpose*, she thought. Rich Marvel wouldn't miss a chance to show off the body he had obviously worked so hard for. He still had his shoulder holster on, and the gun she had seen at the clinic protruded recklessly from the holder. Once again, he didn't have the safety strap fastened. Kendra caught her breath, thinking that she not only had to get used to hanging around cops, now she had to get used to guns as well. Violet's death seemed to have changed everything.

The walls closed around her, and suddenly Kendra found it hard to breathe. She was more afraid for Grady than she was for herself. She didn't want him to lose his job. And if Rich found out that Grady was helping her, his job would be on the line. Her heart beat faster, in anger, she told herself. Rich stood at the door, waiting for her answer as if he owned the damn place.

She lifted her head. "As a matter of fact, I *was* expecting someone else."

Rich languidly strolled over to her, his serious face belying his casual movements. "May I ask who?" he said, lifting an eyebrow.

"It's none of your business, Rich," Kendra said. "What are you doing here, anyway?"

He took the seat next to her and scooted so close that she could smell the woody scent of his cologne. He put his face near hers, clearly meaning to intimidate. "So are we on a first-name basis now?" he asked.

Instead of moving away from him as she wanted to do,

she cocked her head and smiled sweetly. "What would you like me to call you?" she asked. "Detective Asshole?"

He pulled back, surprise and anger flickering in his eyes. Without answering, he reached for the file folder on the table. Kendra placed a flat palm over it. She didn't take her eyes from him.

"This is a personal matter," she told him.

They stared at each other for several seconds, though it seemed like minutes. Kendra couldn't pull her eyes away from his. An unwanted flush crept up her face as they stared at each other. He finally broke the silence between them.

"In answer to your earlier question, I work here. The question is what are you doing here, Dr. Hamilton?" His voice had lost the earlier sarcasm. "If this has something to do with your mother's death . . ."

"It has nothing to do with that," she said. "Nothing at all. I told you that this is a personal matter. I'm here to see an old friend."

He nodded but said nothing. Instead he leaned back in his chair and brought his palm up to his face. He rubbed his smooth chin, ran his fingers over his mouth while regarding her steadily, as if he were engaged in dissecting the lie she had just told. To cover her fidgeting under his intent gaze, she picked up Beth Rinehart's file and went to stand up.

But she had forgotten about the cramp. To keep from falling, she caught herself on the edge of the table. But Rich was up in an instant, one hand moved around her waist, the other at her elbow. She looked up into his face, not knowing what she would find there. She saw concern, but anger spoke next.

"Look at you," he said. "You are a mess. You're lying to me; you've been lying from the start. And you show up here still lying your ass off. I'm going to find out, Kendra. You might as well tell me now."

Her shoulder grazed his solid chest, his arm felt like a snake of fire around her waist. Her heartbeat quickened again, and a thrill of fear ran through her as an unfamiliar emotion claimed her.

"Take your hands off of me," she said through clenched teeth.

"You will fall," was his immediate response.

"I would rather fall," she shot back. "Now back off."

"What's going on in here?" Grady's rough voice shattered the tension that had filled the room the moment Rich walked in the door. Rich chuckled as he let Kendra go.

"I should have known you were involved in this somehow, Grady," Rich said. "You mind telling me what's going on?"

Kendra glanced at Grady, her eyes pleading. Grady didn't respond, just looked at Rich with eyes filled with hatred. He held the article she had given him earlier in his wrinkled fingers. It was folded in half, and she guessed he had written the addresses and the information she needed on the other side.

"I do mind," Grady was saying. "Especially since it ain't none of your business."

Rich sighed tiredly. "How did I know you were going to say that?" he asked. "But you better watch yourself, Grady." As he said this, his hand snaked out and grabbed Kendra's chin.

"Take your hand off of her!" Grady ran over to him and grabbed his arm. But Rich ignored him and stared at Kendra for a long time. Kendra swallowed, unable to pull away.

"Because I'm telling you she's hiding something." He pushed her chin roughly from him.

"You go to hell," Kendra said when she got her voice back. She didn't shout, her voice was level, and cool. "Do you hear me? You go straight to hell."

Rich paused at the door and turned to her. His words spilled into the quiet room like a sudden frost.

"I don't know if I'll ever be able to prove it, but I believe, Dr. Hamilton, that you already have a head start."

* * *

The Rineharts lived in a middle-class neighborhood on a court where the houses were identical to each other except in color. The developer had used wood, not stucco, and had painted each one of them in pastels—shell pink, pale lime, and soft beige. The Rineharts' two-story was pink. White shutters framed the front window like lace. Children watched Kendra curiously as she stepped from the Acura. As a matter of fact, there were more children here than Kendra had expected. They skated or scooted up and down the court on rollerblades and skateboards. It must have been Beth's mother, Elizabeth Rinehart, who answered the door. She was a pear-shaped woman with mottled pink skin.

"Yes?" she said, a little rudely. A stained apron with bright flowers covered a pair of stretch pants. She busily dried her hands on a dish towel as she waited for an answer.

Kendra hadn't called beforehand because she didn't want to risk rejection. She remembered Grady's warning not to get the Rineharts all stirred up and had developed a plausible lie on the way over here. But one look at Elizabeth Rinehart's no-nonsense face blasted the lie from her mind.

"Mrs. Rinehart?" Kendra asked.

"Yes," the older woman answered. "Who are you?"

"I'm Dr. Kendra Hamilton. I work at the free clinic in The Pit."

The quick movements of Elizabeth Rinehart's hands stopped as if she had been frozen in time. She nodded, slowly, and gripped the door frame. "The Pit, did you say?" she said. "What do you want with me?"

"I know your daughter disappeared some years back," Kendra said. "And I wanted to—"

"She didn't disappear," Mrs. Rinehart said. "She overdosed. My daughter was a drug addict, Dr. Hamilton. What can I do for you?"

Kendra swallowed. She hadn't expected Beth's mother to be so cold. But what had she expected? Tears at the mention of her daughter? Had she expected to be welcomed with open arms?

"I was hoping that I could ask you a few questions," Kendra said.

"Why? What questions could you possibly have for me?"

Just as Kendra was about to respond, a baseball whizzed by her head. The ball knocked over a potted plant in a wrought-iron holder. Dark dirt spilled on the cement porch. Elizabeth Rinehart pushed passed Kendra and leaned her bulging stomach over the railing.

"Billy Settle," she shrieked, "if you hit one more baseball into this house, I swear . . ." She stopped and shook her fist at the boy holding a bat. He wouldn't look at them, just stared at the asphalt. She sighed.

"I guess you better come on in," she said. "No tellin' what will happen to you outside with those hoodlums."

Two words struck Kendra as she entered the Rineharts' formal living room—barren and blue. Thick white carpet stretched over the wide floor. Elizabeth pointed Kendra to a couch with robin's-egg blue upholstery covered in white flowers. The couch, with its straight, high back, was as uncomfortable as it looked, definitely not a couch for sitting back and relaxing. As Kendra shifted on the short pillows, she noticed an oval cherry wood coffee table and caught a glimpse of her own face in its gloss. The only other furnishing was a phone table next to the door. An 8 x 10 photograph framed in sparkling silver was its only decoration. A girl of about ten, in pigtails and braces, stared at her with mischief in her eyes.

"Is that Beth?" Kendra asked, pointing to the picture.

"Can I get you something to drink?"

Kendra shook her head.

"Why are you here?" Elizabeth lifted her head up quickly as if to punctuate the question.

"I'm looking for someone, Mrs. Rinehart."

"Go on."

"I think that this person's disappearance, the person I'm looking for, is related to Beth's, but there is one thing . . ."

Kendra stopped at the bitter laughter coming from Mrs. Rinehart. "Haven't you heard what happened to my daughter, Dr. Hamilton? She overdosed. End of story. She wasn't missing, probably never was."

"What happened to the baby, Mrs. Rinehart?"

That question stopped the woman's bitter laughter. She straightened, took a deep breath, and threw the dish towel over her shoulder. She sat down heavily in a chair opposite Kendra and put both palms on her dimpled knees.

"The police think she lied to me about being pregnant, do you know that?" She stared at Kendra, waiting for an answer. Kendra nodded.

"I thought so, too, for a long time," she continued. "I thought that was just one more lie I could pile on top of the others. Though I'd heard from her, I hadn't seen her. She sent email, we talked on the phone. I never had any proof. When they found her two weeks after she disappeared, she wasn't pregnant, wasn't pregnant at all."

"So you never believed that she was?"

Elizabeth leaned back in her chair. She held up a finger. "I'm not saying that she wasn't pregnant, but I'm not saying that she didn't lie to me, either."

"How do you mean?" Kendra asked.

"I'm guessing if you worked at the clinic, you looked at my daughter's medical records?"

Kendra nodded. She leaned toward Kendra and caught her eyes with her own. Kendra smelled the distinct odor of vodka on the woman's breath. She drew back, sickened. Elizabeth noticed her distaste and smiled with teeth as small and sharp as a rodent's.

"Look closer," she said.

"Mrs. Rinehart, please . . ." Kendra began. "I don't want to play games. . . ."

"I don't like playing games any more than you do," Elizabeth cut her off. "But what did you expect? That you'd come here and I'd give you all the answers like a present? No one helped me when my Beth disappeared; they didn't hand me anything, either. Why should I hand it to you?"

"Mrs. Rinehart," Kendra said, disgusted by the woman's uncaring attitude. "A girl's life might be in danger."

"Then why aren't the police here asking me these questions? I'll tell you why, because they don't give a damn. Does this girl have someone who cares about her?"

"Yes, as a matter of fact she does."

"Well, you do me a favor and tell them for me that it doesn't matter, especially when the person you care about is not worth the *spit* in your mouth. Beth took from me from the moment she came into this world until the very moment we put her in the grave—she's still taking from me today, even though she's dead. And when she was alive, she lied every chance she got, stole things that have been in my family for years for a fix. And what did I get in return? Heartache." She stood up. "Tell them not to waste their time."

Kendra stood up, too, and looked at the woman. She wished that she could feel the disgust that she knew she should be feeling, but she didn't feel disgust at all. She understood, and it scared her.

"You know what I'm talking about, don't you?" Elizabeth's voice had lost that bitter edge and had turned soft. "I read the papers, Dr. Hamilton, and having no children and a husband who'd rather stay at work than come home, I find that I have time to read them cover to cover. You know what I'm talking about, don't you? Your mother was the same way."

"I think I'd better go," Kendra said. "I'm sorry that I came."

Kendra started toward the door, but Elizabeth stopped her with a hand on her elbow.

"Wait here a minute," she said.

She left, and when she returned she had a gold chain weaved in her fingers. She handed it to Kendra. It was a cross, pointed at the bottom with a piece of diamond dust hanging on the end. And it was exactly like the cross Violet wore, the one that was missing when she was found.

"Where did you get this?" Kendra asked.

"It isn't your mother's," the other woman answered grimly. "It belonged to Beth, except I have no idea where she got it. There was a picture of you and your mother along with that article, and I noticed something hanging around her neck. For some reason, it got me to thinking, so I took a magnifying glass to the picture. I still couldn't tell what it was, but it looked like a necklace or something. I bet it was a cross. Am I right?"

Kendra couldn't believe her ears. She took a deep breath to steady her nerves.

"Do you know what this is about?" Kendra asked.

"I sure don't," Elizabeth replied. "But after Beth died, I started a support group for families whose daughters lost their lives through heroin." She stopped, sighed. "It worked for a while, but as you can probably tell I found more comfort in alcohol than talking. Two girls who'd overdosed just like my Beth did had these crosses around their necks when they were found. The families had no idea where they had gotten them, either."

Kendra turned the cross over in her hand, thinking. "It could be from a pimp or something like that. Maybe he used these things to mark his girls. It's not that unusual."

"That's what I thought," Elizabeth Rinehart said, her voice suddenly agreeable. But then she cocked her pink face to the side and regarded Kendra steadily before asking, "So what was your mother doing with one?"

CHAPTER 16

When Kendra opened her eyes the next morning and stared at the blank ceiling of her apartment, she convinced herself that the events of the previous day were part of an ugly dream. The fantasy lasted until she dressed and went into the kitchen.

She thought about calling Dr. Willis, to find out if he needed anything while he covered for her at the clinic, but before she reached for the phone, something caught her attention.

The cross that Mrs. Rinehart gave her lay coiled on the counter. She picked it up and weaved the thin chain through her fingers, thinking that if she pulled on it hard enough, it would break. The cross was identical to the one her mother carried. And for the life of her, she couldn't remember how Violet had come by it.

She didn't have a lot of time to think about it—not today anyway. Today she had to pick up her mother's ashes from the Place of Peace Funeral Home. She thought about what she should do with the information she had learned. Rich helping her was out of the question. He already thought that she was hiding something and would only think she was trying to distract him from the case. Luke was a choice, but in the end what could he do? What about the sheriff, James Freehold? She could go to him and tell him what she had found; she could get him to reopen the cases. But why would he do that? All she had was a flimsy dime-store cross as common as dust. She really had no new evidence. In the end, she knew that she had to handle this herself. She was on her own.

She felt lonelier than she had ever been as she drove to Turlock to pick up her mother's ashes. In the course of ridding herself of one addict, the woman who'd raised her, she was willfully searching for another, a person she had met only once and didn't remember. She had simply traded one burden for another. It was enough to make her question her judgment.

She had chosen Turlock to take care of her mother's remains because it was far away from the chaos of Dunhill. The streets were wide, the sidewalks white and clean. Trees lined both sides of the street, their young leaves quivering in the still air. Japanese maples grew from the planters dividing the street. The burgundy leaves reminded Kendra of old blood.

She parked the car and jaywalked across the street, barely noticing the gold Lexus parked at the curb right in front of her. Then Luke Bertrand lifted himself from the leather driver's seat and stepped out of the car. With his presence, the wide streets of Turlock suddenly became a little narrower. She hadn't told him she was coming here today. As far as she knew, he didn't know about this place.

Luke reached out and grabbed both of her hands in his before she could speak. She looked down at his hands and was reminded of his age. Although he sometimes could be mistaken for a man of forty, Luke's hands, veined and somewhat wrinkled, revealed his age.

"Hello, Kendra," he said.

His voice dripped sympathy. He smiled warmly, using every muscle in his face. Luke's charm was easy, practiced. He had a way of making people feel that they were the only ones on earth for him. And that he, Luke Bertrand, had been put there by God to make their path smoother.

"Luke, how did . . ." she started in confusion.

"Maria," he stated. "I called the clinic today, and she told me you were doing this arduous task alone, by yourself. Kendra, why didn't you tell me?"

Because you suffocate me, she wanted to say. *You've always suffocated me.* She just wanted to retrieve her mother's ashes, sit for a while in the comforting quietness of the funeral home, and leave. She wanted to remember Violet the way she had always imagined her—not the way that Luke knew her.

But now, here was Luke Bertrand, reminding her of how Violet had really been, constantly on a heroin high, scratching her face and neck and arms until she bled. Kendra remembered why she and Luke had fought. It was her way of claiming her independence from him. But she had never told him that. She never told him that he was as oppressive and smothering as heat in an oven. And instead of telling him that today, she felt herself smile. And lie.

"I didn't want to bother you, Luke. I know how busy you are."

"Kendra," he said. "I'm never too busy to help you, especially when you so obviously need me."

But I don't need you, she thought, but quickly tucked the thought away. Luke was only trying to help, after all. He took her elbow and guided her to the door. The pressure he exerted on her elbow gave her an unreasonable feeling of being trapped. A little wildly, Kendra looked back at the Lexus parked in a no-parking zone. Luke's cat, Jupiter, sat on the dashboard, returning her stare with blue eyes that looked like ice chips.

Well, at least it was only Luke, Kendra thought. *Thank God Ray Ray wasn't—*

"Kendra," a voice said before she could finish the thought.

Raymond Smalls jogged across the street to catch up with them. He was dressed more appropriately for a funeral than either one of them. He wore a black, closely cut Armani suit with small notches in the collar. His silk black and white tie was tied into a large knot, and except for the two-carat diamond earring glinting in his left ear, he could have passed for a rather successful if flamboyant accountant.

He and Luke didn't speak to each other. Ray Ray kept his gaze focused on Kendra. Sensing trouble, and not wanting any, Kendra squeezed Luke's arm in warning. Luke didn't acknowledge it.

"Ray Ray," Kendra breathed. "How did you know I was here?"

Ray Ray's full lips curved into a cool smile. "I have my sources," he said. "You forget. I keep my ear to the street."

"Oh," Kendra said. "I guess you can come in. I'm not really having a service."

"I understand," Ray Ray said. He turned his gaze to Luke. "Though you and I have some fundamental disagreements, Mr. Bertrand, it seems we do have something in common." He gestured toward Kendra.

Kendra looked at Ray Ray, then back at Luke. She noticed how much they were alike. Ray Ray, at five eight, was maybe an inch shorter than Luke. They both had the same dark skin coloring, the same face that could be cold and brutal sometimes. And they both had a way of exuding charm when it was necessary, and especially when it suited them.

At first Kendra thought Luke wasn't going to answer. But then he smiled, his eyes twinkling in guarded amusement.

"I say we do," he replied, and walked toward Ray Ray with a hand outstretched. Ray Ray took it, and they shook for a long time, like they were old friends.

"Kendra, my dear," he said. "Don't let this surprise you. I've always said that we can catch more flies with honey than vinegar. And we can bring more lambs back to the fold with nourishment and encouragement than with chastising and criticism."

Kendra blinked in surprise. She had never heard Luke

make a religious reference in her life. She had thought that he was like her, a bit on the agnostic side, only believing in God when she really needed it or was really pissed off and needed someone to blame. Now here he was, if not straight out quoting a Bible verse, preaching like he meant it.

Luke and Ray Ray flanked both sides of her as she walked into the Place of Peace. The light inside was dim, and she heard rather than felt the cool hum of an air conditioner. A sallow man with bulging eyes sailed over to them. He acknowledged Kendra first by using his oversized hands to swallow her small ones.

"Everything went just as expected," he said with quiet enthusiasm, respect infused in every word.

The man was the funeral home's director, and his name was Mr. Edwards. When Kendra had contacted him about cremating her mother, he told her everything she wanted to know in a voice that reminded her of Bert from Sesame Street. Now, if she looked at him hard enough, she could even see some resemblance in his bushy eyebrows and long head.

Kendra wondered briefly what he would have said if everything had not gone as expected. What would he say to her then? Would he have said that her mother's ashes had gotten mixed up somehow with a veteran's and were now on their way to Arlington for a full military funeral with a twenty-one gun salute? Would he use the same tone?

Or what if they had misplaced her mother's ashes? Would he have come to her and said, *I'm so sorry, Dr. Hamilton, but your mother was cremated by the cremation society on the same day as the gardeners were scheduled. And, unfortunately . . . how should I put this? She was placed in a sprayer and used as fertilizer on the Queen Anne's tea roses in the garden.*

"Is there something wrong, Doctor?" Mr. Edwards asked.

Kendra cleared her throat, embarrassed. She hadn't realized she had chuckled aloud until he spoke. "I'm sorry. I guess . . ." she started.

"I know," the sallow man said knowingly. "These are very trying times, and sometimes we respond unexpectedly to grief and stress. I was asking about your companions."

"Oh, yes," Kendra said. "This is Raymond Smalls, a friend."

He and Ray Ray shook hands, then she introduced him to Luke Bertrand.

"Ah," he said, his long face glowing recognition. "I don't think we have met, but I know you by reputation. I must say, it is a pleasure."

"The same," Luke responded.

"Please," Mr. Edwards continued. "Have a seat, and I will retrieve the deceased."

Luke sat down in one of the red velvet chairs trimmed in white wood. But both Raymond and Kendra stared after the retreating man.

"Retrieve the deceased?" Raymond said. "That man is very, very strange."

"Not strange," Luke contradicted. "But unusual in a spiritual and respectful sort of a way. Remember, in the end, we will all have to see someone like that. Let's all hope they are as respectful as he is."

"If I have to see someone like that," Raymond responded, "I'm glad I'll be doing it with my eyes closed."

"Kendra, please sit." Luke patted the chair next to him.

Kendra sat. Raymond paced back and forth in the tiny waiting area. He kept both hands in his pockets. Kendra guessed it was probably because he was afraid to touch anything in the room with his bare hands.

"For someone who has chosen a career bathed in as much risk as yours, Mr. Smalls, you certainly seem uncomfortable around death."

Raymond stopped pacing long enough to flash Luke a look. "What happened with all that honey and vinegar shit?" he asked.

Luke lifted a hand, pretending as if he meant to appease. "Sometimes truth works just as well."

Raymond's face hardened. He stared at Luke with eyes that could melt stone. "I see," he said. "So you want to talk truth now, old man? Let's talk truth."

Kendra turned, looked at Luke, and waited. What in the hell was Ray Ray talking about. Before Luke could respond, Mr. Edwards returned with Violet's urn, and she forgot what she had just witnessed. The urn was low and flat and had three short legs that resembled shark's fins. It reminded Kendra of a whirling vortex of wind. The company who made the urn called it Peace in the Storm. And if Violet deserved one thing, it was peace. They all stood up. Mr. Edwards carefully placed the urn in Kendra's hands.

"I'll get you a box . . ." he began, but Kendra shook her head.

"There's no need," she said.

"Can I help you with the disposition of the ashes? Or do you plan to keep them?"

"No," she responded. "I'm going to scatter them. I'll take care of it myself."

"Oh, but, you must understand, there are certain rules and regulations—"

"She said," Ray Ray broke in, "that she will take care of it."

Mr. Edwards looked at Ray Ray a moment before responding. His eyes focused on the earring in Ray Ray's ear, and his face changed as if he finally understood something.

"Ah, I see. There is a small matter of payment . . ."

Before he could finish, Raymond pulled out a money clip. "How much?" Kendra moved to open her purse, told Raymond to put his money away. But he would not hear of it, refused, mumbling something about the least he could do.

"The least for what?" she asked.

"Just let me do this, okay?" he asked. "I want out of here and don't feel like arguing with you Kendra."

Kendra did not feel like arguing either. She decided to let it pass, vowing that she would take care of it later. Now was not the time or the place.

Mr. Edwards' eyes bulged more as he stared at the thick wad of bills. He then looked into Raymond's impassive face.

"Twenty-six hundred and twenty-four dollars," he stammered.

Raymond peeled away twenty seven crisp one-hundred dollar bills and stuffed them into Mr. Edwards' hand. The man stood looking at it for almost a full minute. "Is this real?" he finally asked.

"Are those really Violet Hamilton's ashes?" Raymond asked, a quirky smile on his face.

Kendra looked at Ray Ray in surprise. He had known what she was thinking after all. Even though they had known each other since early childhood, it surprised her sometimes that he could read her so well. How could their lives have taken such different paths?

"Why of course," the man gasped.

"Then that's real," Raymond responded. "Kendra, are you ready to go?"

"I'll get change," Mr. Edwards said, not moving.

"No," Raymond smiled. "Keep it as a tip for not getting things mixed up. Kendra?" Ray Ray looked at her. "Can we . . ."

"Yes, of course." She turned to Mr. Edwards. "Thank you."

Mr. Edwards smiled at her, his palm still open, the hundred-dollar bills spilling from his hand.

Luke cleared his throat. "It's been a pleasure," he said and extended his hand.

Mr. Edwards assembled the bills into a neat stack and put them into his coat pocket rather quickly. He smiled back at Luke and shook his hand. Kendra noticed that Luke's shoulders were rigid with disapproval. She hoped that he wouldn't make a scene with Ray Ray. But when they walked outside, she found she needn't have worried. Luke wouldn't have time to make a scene, because Richard T. Marvel was outside, leaning against her black Acura like he owned it.

For one crazy moment, Kendra thought that Rich might have come to say good-bye, or pay his respects. But then she noticed the way he leaned against her car, the sole of one shoe planted squarely against the driver side door. He had his hands in his pockets and stared at Kendra, Luke, and Raymond as if he had caught them doing something illegal.

Kendra hugged Violet's ashes close to her with both hands, as if she were trying to hide them from Rich. He was wearing a tight pair of faded jeans and a blindingly white T-shirt. Kendra surmised he probably bought the jeans that way—faded. He didn't strike her as the kind of person who would wear clothes that became old and faded with wear. He had a look of uncompromising perfection about him. Raymond squeezed her elbow.

Luke stopped in midstep when he saw Rich. He squinted in his direction, then smiled and held up a palm in acknowledgment. Kendra noticed that Rich didn't respond right away. Instead he folded his arms across his chest before finally returning Luke's acknowledgment with a begrudging smile. Luke leaned over and kissed Kendra on the cheek before climbing into his Lexus.

When Ray Ray and Kendra reached Rich, Ray Ray spoke first.

"Detective," he said cordially, "What a shame you have to work on such a beautiful day."

"I'm not working," Rich replied. "What are you doing, Smalls? Checking on your handiwork?"

The easy smile left Ray Ray's face. He nodded to Rich.

"I don't think this is a place for us to do battle. We are not on our own home turf," Raymond said.

Rich gazed at his surroundings, the antique shops with flowers on the windowsill. A young couple glanced curiously at them as they passed. Kendra thought how they must look to them. She must have seemed a little crazy, standing so close to Ray Ray, clutching an urn. She looked up only to find Rich looking at her, a question in his face.

"Detective," she said, trying and failing to make her voice cool.

His eyes flicked to her chest. "Nice cross," he said without missing a beat.

Kendra's hand flew to her chest. She touched the cross she had placed around her neck that morning. She had done it thinking that the best place to keep it without losing it would be around her neck. How stupid.

"Oh," she said truthfully. "I forgot I had it."

"Is that the one your mother's missing? Is there something you want to tell me?"

She saw the anger behind the casual lift of his eyebrow and tried to steady her voice. It felt as if bees had lodged themselves in her throat.

"No," she said. "It's not hers. A friend gave it to me. What are you doing here, anyway?"

"I think the question is, Kendra, which one of us is he following?" Ray Ray cut in. "Come on, Marvel, which one of us has the tail, huh?"

Rich remained silent.

"I don't understand . . ." Kendra began, but Ray Ray cut her off again.

"Detective Marvel obviously followed one of us up here. Which one?"

"Since you are so smart, Smalls, why don't you tell me?" Rich said.

"Okay," he said. "It couldn't be Kendra. She's the victim, right?"

Rich kept his eyes focused on Ray Ray. "Some say."

"And Luke, the only reason you would be following him is to lick the dirt from his footprints. So that leaves me, doesn't it?"

"Well," Rich said with a chuckle, "You might not be as dumb as you look."

Kendra had had enough when she noticed Ray Ray struggle to keep his face still. The bees in her throat vanished, and when she spoke, her voice was filled with anger.

"Look, Detective," she started.

"Call me Rich," he said in a taunting tone aimed at Ray Ray. "You have before."

Kendra ignored the bait, but Ray Ray curled his fists at his sides. He took a menacing step forward. She stopped Ray Ray with a hand on his arm.

"Whatever," she snapped at Rich. "I don't care who you followed, you shouldn't be here screwing this up for me."

Rich straightened and stepped closer to her. "Screwing what up?" he said. "Allowing you to run around with dope dealers while I'm trying to find out who killed your mother?"

Kendra lost all pretense of trying to be civil. She was so angry she barely realized what was being said, except later she would apply the words *arrogant* and *asshole* to the memory of his attitude. Ray Ray was saying something as well, but she couldn't hear him. They continued to shout over each other, but finally stopped as a thick silence surrounded the two of them when the last words registered. She had said, *You are supposed to be helping me,* and he had said, *Maybe it was you I was following.*

Her shoulders dropped. She was stunned. Was she really a suspect? Luke's car stopped beside them, the motor of the gold Lexus purring like a cat. The tinted window glided down, and Luke Bertrand peered out at them.

"Kendra. Rich," Luke pleaded and then looked at Raymond. "Please. This can be done on any day. Kendra, you say good-bye to your mother only once."

She let go of some of her anger at Luke's words. Of course, he was right. They shouldn't be doing this here; not now.

"Do you mind?" she said to Rich, not looking at him.

"Of course not," he said. He kicked off from her Acura and pointed at Raymond. "Don't think I'll forget about you, Smalls," he said. "No matter how this turns out, you are still on my most-wanted list."

"Hey, man," Raymond said, laughing. "I'm on everybody's most-wanted list."

"I'll be watching you," Rich responded as he walked back to his own car.

"You do that," Raymond shouted after him.

Luke did not leave until both Raymond and Rich had driven away. After they left, Kendra watched the Lexus glide away, saw the gold roof gleam in the sun.

April

April Hart counted until she fell asleep. Her dream returned her to the Los Angeles Denny's where a man with skin the color of browned butter watched her eat two breakfasts in a row. Through the clinking of silverware, he watched her. He did not eat at all, and his eyes never left her face. He asked her if she had any place to stay. She told him no. He said she could stay with him until she got on her feet. She had nodded, looking at his skin, his curly black hair, and his brown eyes flecked with gold. She looked, too, at the fat gold chain around his left wrist, a wrist so thin she saw a knob of bone sticking out of it. Maybe he was the only one she could trust, she had thought back then. How could she know then that he was the pimp who would eventually turn her out?

A rustling at the door of the garden shed startled her awake. She sat straight up when she heard the wooden door opening. She thought it was him, the lunatic who kept her here. Now was her chance to tell him like she'd been planning to that he had simply gotten things all mixed up, that this was no way to help her and her baby.

But it was only Sage, standing in the only light April would see that day. Sage was the man's helper, his assistant.

She sometimes brought April's daily supply of methadone and her breakfast. Today Sage held a brown paper bag in one hand and the butcher knife in the other. The knife was sharp and clean. A drop of morning sunlight fell from its tip like liquid silver.

As April watched Sage, a girl of her own age, she wondered briefly if Sage had ever felt fear. Sage was a black girl, as thin and smooth as a shadow. Her head was shaped so perfectly it reminded April of an egg. Her thin lips never smiled, and her slanted eyes never held one speck of kindness. Or fear—of April or anything, for that matter. For all of her thinness, Sage was strong and well-fed, and stood a good four inches taller than April. She was not a person April would want to fight even if she weren't eight months pregnant and scared as hell.

Sage threw the crumpled paper bag on the dirt floor and pointed at it silently. Though she kept the knife pointed toward the ground, April saw that she held the handle tight. The girl's fingertips were bright red. April went to the bag and picked it up. In it she found a banana, spotted and brown, a stale bagel, a carton of milk, and a little package of cream cheese. Two little white pills wrapped in plastic wrap were there, too. April swallowed them both with a big swig of milk. Sage watched her, her slanted eyes narrowing as if she were watching a dumb but dangerous animal.

"You've got to help me," April whispered to her. But she knew that it was useless. She whispered this to Sage every time she saw her. But the girl would just stare back silent as death.

"What does he want from me?" April pressed on, wiping the milk from her mouth with the back of her hand. Sage didn't answer. April started to wonder if Sage was a mute, like the boy who lived on the small farm next to the one she shared with her grandmother. Leroy couldn't talk, but he could laugh in a strange little way that sounded like strangled hiccups. Leroy went to a special school that taught him to sign. Sometimes April would go over to his house, and they would sit and listen to old vinyl records that belonged to his mother. Diana Ross and the Supremes. Martha and the Vandellas. April would try to dance while Leroy hiccupped strange laughs that sounded like choking.

April even knew a few signs herself, but she knew that they would do no good here. She had heard the man call to Sage on that first terrible morning, call to her in his preacher's voice. Sage could hear and she could talk. She just did not want to talk to April.

CHAPTER 17

Rich cursed himself the entire way back from Turlock to Dunhill County. He *had* actually been following Kendra Hamilton. Before he started the tail, he had tried to find out from Grady what she had wanted at the sheriff's department, cajoling at first and then threatening when the policeman remained as silent as a taxidermied black bear. Rich wanted to know what Kendra Hamilton was hiding. And now he did. Shit. Raymond Smalls. He took a deep breath and looked out the car window. Rolling hills raced by. Metal windmills churned their arms steadily, like unfriendly giants.

And then there was that cross. Where in the hell did she get that damned thing? She had told him that it was hers, and that could very well be true. Rich remembered seeing necklaces that women sometimes wore—two halves of the same heart. It could have been something like that between Kendra and her mother, but Kendra didn't strike him as the type. What friend gave it to her? Raymond? That damned drug dealer, who had nerve enough to have his arm around Kendra's waist while her mother was dead, probably from the dope that he had sold to her?

It didn't really surprise him that Kendra Hamilton knew Raymond Smalls. What surprised him was that she still hung out with him. He had known Raymond Smalls himself growing up in The Pit. All three of them went to the same school.

He switched lanes and curled a fisted hand under his chin, gripping the steering wheel so tightly with his other hand that it hurt. He tried to remember if Kendra and Raymond had been friends in high school. They probably had been. He had not been friends with either one of them. His mother would have killed him if he had looked at them sideways. Whether or not he knew for sure if Smalls and Kendra were friends in high school, he did know the rumors about the two of them in The Pit. They said that Raymond Smalls was obsessed with Kendra Hamilton, in love with her, actually.

But even if it weren't for his mother, Rich probably still would not have had anything to do with them. Kendra and Raymond were loners, occupying the dim halls of their high school like shadows. They didn't seem to need or want anything or anybody. The fact that Raymond Smalls actually noticed him enough to save his ass was a miracle.

Rich remembered now that it was the usual fight. Three boys in stocking caps, shirts open and scrawny chests bared, couldn't find the usual satisfaction in just kicking his ass. This time, one of them pulled a pocket knife with a three-inch blade. He accused Rich of thinking that he was better than everyone else. *The sad part,* Rich thought grimacing, *was that I actually thought I was—and still do, as a matter of fact, at least better than some of the trash that litter The Pit.* Rich remembered how the boy used his forearm to press him against the chain-link fence. Even as he thought about the event now years later, he could still feel the crisscross pattern of pain against his head.

Rich struggled to stay conscious as the boy pressed the tip of the pocket knife beneath his chin. He felt warm blood trickle along his neck. When the other two boys saw the knife, they vanished. They were okay with a little push and shove, but they didn't want to be involved in a murder. Rich didn't know what would have happened if Smalls hadn't appeared. Smalls had a reputation as a drug dealer even then, and when he told the boy to leave Rich alone, he did. It took all of Rich's strength and pride to look Smalls in the face after the boy had left. Rich remembered how Smalls had looked back at him. His face was as empty as a blank line.

"Thanks, man," Rich mumbled, trying to thank Smalls anyway.

Smalls gazed at Rich as if he had just reversed the fate of a bug. "Nothing personal, small fry," he replied before walking away without once looking back.

Both Gregory and Beau looked up expectantly as Rich sat at his desk and swung around in his swivel chair. He ignored them. Instead, he picked up an envelope lying on his desk and turned it over in his hand. He knew what it was, knew it by the absence of the return address. But he didn't read it; he wasn't in the mood. He simply picked up the envelope and threw it in the bottom drawer, where it landed on top of the other crazy letters some lunatic was sending him. He shut the drawer on the entire lot without thinking twice.

He closed his eyes and massaged his temples with his middle fingers. He didn't open his eyes, not even when he smelled Beau's cheap cologne hovering over his desk like a personal stink cloud. Finally, Rich opened his eyes to see Beau's red face beaming at him. Rich let him wait, closed his eyes again. Giant arms from the windmills he had seen along the Altamont flickered in the darkness.

"I guess I shouldn't ask how it went," Gregory said.

Rich dropped his hand to his thigh and looked at his partner's long face. File folders and photographs covered Gregory's desk.

"It was like a fucking high school reunion," Rich said. "What's that shit on your desk?"

Gregory lifted his elbows. "Oh, this," he said. "Just something I'm looking into. It could be nothing."

"What do you mean by a high school reunion? Where did she go?" Beau asked, returning to his desk. Rich ignored the disappointment running through Beau's voice. Obviously, Beau was bursting to tell him something. But that didn't stop him from picking up a sandwich about four inches thick and taking an enormous bite.

Rich sighed. "Turlock. She picked up her mother's ashes."

"Ashes?" Beau grunted around his sandwich.

"Yes, she had her cremated."

"Humph," Beau answered. "That's convenient."

"What's that supposed to mean, Blair?" Rich asked.

Beau chomped and took a swig of a Yoohoo on his desk before answering.

"Well, if we ever want the body again, we couldn't have it."

Rich rolled his eyes toward the ceiling, but Gregory followed up on Beau's comment. His voice thoughtful, he said, "So if Dr. Hamilton had something to do with the murder, and she wanted to hide evidence, she would cremate the body. . . ."

"Don't be stupid," Rich said, an unreasonable anger welling up in his belly. "She couldn't hide anything if she wanted to. We have the autopsy reports, including toxicology. We've gotten everything we needed from that damn body. Shit, we told her to take the damn thing. Besides, there is nothing to hide."

His own words surprised the hell out of him. Of course, he did think that she was hiding something, but he had always been comforted by the fact that Gregory and Beau hadn't suspected it. Now that they did, it caused an unreasonable unease in him.

"But if Sandbourne wanted to take another look. . . ." Gregory interrupted.

Rich let his feet drop to the floor. He leaned on his desk and looked at Gregory. "Have you ever known Rita Sandbourne wanting to take another look? At anything? What? Are you trying to say we consider Kendra a suspect?"

Gregory raised a blond eyebrow. "Don't you consider her a suspect, Rich?" he said finally. "Isn't that why you followed her? You said yourself that she's hiding something. Remember that day in her office?"

"It may not be that she's hiding something so much as she might be protecting someone."

"Well, maybe the person she is protecting is herself," Gregory suggested quietly.

Rich held back the urge to fling his pencil holder at Gregory. Instead he placed his elbows on his desk so hard that the sting traveled all the way to his fingertips. He put his head in his hands. Except for Beau's chomping on the sandwich, there was a complete and utter silence. Rich took a deep breath. He tried to push the reason he was so upset into the recesses of his mind. His own voice sounded far away when he spoke. He thought if he heard that voice on someone else, he wouldn't believe it, either.

"If she's hiding someone, it doesn't have to be the fact that she killed her," he said. "Besides, that doesn't make sense. Why would she come to us?"

"It makes perfect sense, Richy boy," Beau answered.

Rich looked at him. Beau laid the sandwich directly on his desk. White mayonnaise hung on his red stringy mustache. Wiping his hand vigorously on a napkin, he began.

"Do you know what a Tiffany lamp is?" he asked them, looking from one to the other. Gregory just smiled, but Rich looked at him in utter confusion.

"A Tiffany lamp," Beau continued, "you know? Those lamps that have all the different colored glass? Real fancy, makes you want to put on a tie every time you see one."

"Your point, Beau?" Rich said.

"Well, my dad collected them. He had, I think, maybe three or four. Not those fakes you see in JC Penney's, but the real thing. Some of them he got from relatives that kicked the bucket. Anyway, there was this one he loved. It had dragonflies all around the bottom of the shade. And one day it got broken."

"Got broken?" Rich questioned, now knowing where Beau was going with the story.

"Yep, sure did, it got broken," he confirmed. "I went to my mom first. I told her that the lamp was in a million pieces on the living room floor and we had better find out what happened to it before Dad came home. I told her that I had just walked in and saw it and I didn't have anything to do with it."

"Did she believe you?" Gregory asked in a mildly amused voice.

"Yep," he said. "She did."

"What about your dad?" Rich asked.

"He kicked my ass." Beau picked up the sandwich and went to work again.

"So you are saying that Kendra came to us so we wouldn't suspect her," Rich questioned.

"I'm just saying that we need to look at all the possibilities, and in my book, I think Dr. Kendra Hamilton is one of them," Beau answered.

"That doesn't make any damn sense, Blair," Rich said, knowing that it did. It made perfect sense.

"What did you mean by high school reunion?" Gregory asked.

"Oh," Rich said. He stood up and stuck his hands in his jean pockets. "Luke Bertrand was there, and Raymond Smalls."

"That may not mean anything. She's very close to Luke, and you told me once before that you both knew Smalls in high school. It's not unusual that they would all three be at her mother's funeral."

Rich ran his hand over his head. "Except it wasn't a funeral. They just picked up the ashes and left."

Beau grunted. "It means that she's got access to the dope, maybe even got the dope that killed her mother from Smalls."

"It still doesn't mean anything," Gregory reasoned, his quiet gray gaze on Beau.

Rich got the feeling that Gregory was trying to calm him down. To get away from the feeling that he needed to be calmed down, Rich quickly changed the subject.

"Beau, what did forensics say about the glasses, the whiskey?" he asked. "Do we have the prints yet?"

"They haven't gotten back to me."

"What are you waiting for? Call them, then. Shit," Rich snapped.

"I have been!" Beau said. "They're giving me the run-around, man."

Gregory stood up and walked over to the whiteboard. "I just keep thinking of what Jiffy said." He leaned against the board.

"What are you getting at?" Rich asked.

"We know Violet Hamilton died between eight and eleven-thirty that night," Gregory answered smoothly. "Cassady and the murderer, if they are not one and the same, may have been the last people to see her alive."

Rich stood up and used a black marker to write "8:00 PM" on the top half of the board. He wrote "11:00 PM" on the bottom before scribbling the name "Cassady" beside "8:00 PM."

"What are you doing?" Beau asked.

"What does it look like?"

"Like you're trying to do some half-ass timeline," Beau answered.

"When did Jiffy first see the man go up to Violet's room?" Rich asked.

"Hey, I read the interview notes on your desk, man," Beau contradicted. "We don't know if he actually went to Hamilton's room."

Rich closed his eyes.

"He's right," Gregory said. "Just because Shirley "Jiffy" Sherman saw a strange man in the lobby of The Elite doesn't mean he actually went to Violet Hamilton's room."

Rich wrote the words "unidentified male" next to the "9:30 PM" anyway.

"Okay, I'll buy in," Gregory conceded. "What about the second time Cassady showed up?"

Rich cocked his head in Beau's direction.

"About ten-thirty," Beau said. "What can I say? I have a photographic memory."

"Anything else you remember while you were snooping around my desk?"

"Nope," Beau said and shook his head. "Everything else was as boring as hell."

On the whiteboard, Rich wrote the name "Cassady" next to "10:30 PM."

"What about the cross?" Gregory asked.

"I'm betting that this Cassady took it," Rich said. "I'm also betting that she may have gotten a look at who was with Violet Hamilton that night."

"So, are we still looking for the cross?" Beau asked.

"Yep," Rich confirmed. "I think we are, because if we find the cross, we find Cassady. We need to find out if she can put the man in the watch cap in Violet's room. . . ."

As Rich stopped speaking, he remembered the cross Kendra had on that morning. She could have easily taken it for a trophy after killing her mother. Maybe the cross she wore belonged to her mother after all.

"Why don't you ask her?" Beau said.

Rich whipped around to see Beau staring at him with a smug smile on his face.

"What the hell you talking about, Blair?" At first, Rich thought that Beau had somehow read his mind, that he was talking about Kendra.

"We found her," Beau said. "Cassady Moon. I've been trying to tell you, but I couldn't get a word in edgewise because you wouldn't shut your trap. She's down the rabbit hole."

"You got anything else you want to tell me, cowboy?" Rich asked.

Beau nodded, a gleam in his eye, and then told him something that made Rich's whole day. Almost.

* * *

They nicknamed the interrogation room the rabbit hole because the file cabinets placed at an angle in each corner of the room made it look almost circular. Plus, the room was located downstairs in the basement, but the two-way mirror was on the same level as the homicide squad room. Observers actually looked down on the suspects.

If Cassady knew that Rich was watching her, she didn't seem to give a damn. She was about twenty, maybe twenty-one. Except for her enormous breasts, which bulged from her torso like two torpedoes, she was shaped like a cube. Her hair, brown and full of grease, lay against her pasty face. She wore a tight black T-shirt and gray leggings that outlined every ridge and bubble on her gelatinous ass. Her tennis shoes didn't have strings, nor did she wear socks. Purple sores covered her ankles.

Cassady sniffed around the locked door of the interrogation room, jiggled at the handle, then threw her heavy body against the locked door. When she saw that she wasn't going anywhere, she pulled a chair below the two-way and stood on it. Pressing her round face against the glass, she used her breath to fog the mirror over. It was as if she were trying to hide herself from the people she knew were watching her from the other side.

Her face, up close against the glass, scared Rich. She had a tiny, misshapen mouth and ratlike teeth stained a tobacco brown. Her black pupils were so large that Rich couldn't see the whites. Her eyes were two pitted holes in her face.

"Lovely, isn't she?" Gregory said wryly.

"Caught her trying to pawn that piece-of-shit cross," Beau said as if he had just won the lotto.

Rich dropped his head and swallowed as relief washed over him. So Kendra hadn't been lying about the cross. It belonged to her, not Violet. But still . . .

"Do you want to do the honors, or shall I?" Gregory interrupted his thoughts.

Rich heaved a sigh. No, he didn't want to do the honors,

but he would anyway. "Just watch, man, and come save me if she tries to claw my eyes out."

Cassady watched Rich warily as he sat across from her at the table in the rabbit hole. Rich smiled and set a glass of water in front of her. She stared at it as if she didn't know what it was.

"That's for you," Rich said. "Go ahead and drink up."

"I ain't got nuthin' to say," she said. Her tongue darted against her top lip. She was thirsty, no doubt about that. Though he didn't ask, he knew that she had probably been locked in here for hours. "I told that cowboy I ain't had nuthin' to say. That priest, too." She spoke as if her throat were filled with gravel and water.

Rich leaned over the table, filled his eyes with kindness. "Did they let you go to the bathroom?" he asked. "I can let you go if you need to."

She stared at him a long time. She sniffed the air, darted her head to the corner. Rich followed her gaze and noticed the puddle. He didn't smell it until he saw it. But that wasn't the worst part. The worst part was the picture forming in his mind of her pulling her gray leggings from her fat ass and peeing in the corner like an animal. He looked back at her. She smiled.

"I don't need nobody to let me go to the bathroom," she said in that wet, raspy voice. "I can take care of most things myself."

"I see that," Rich said, fighting to keep his voice even. "Did the two detectives tell you why you were here?"

"The big one said he found some shit on me," she said. "But he a liar."

Rich nodded. Beau had indeed found something on her—heroin. He had gone over personally and gotten Rita Sandbourne to test it, and they found it was the same quinine-heroine mixture that had killed Violet Hamilton.

"Did you know Violet Hamilton?" he asked her.

Her thick eyelids dropped over the eye-pits in her face.

She then looked up at the ceiling. "I ain't got nothin' to say," she repeated.

"You know her daughter?" he asked.

She looked at him directly then. Hate gleamed in her black eyes.

"I ain't got—"

"I know, I know," Rich said. *"You ain't got nuthin' to say."* He stood up to leave. "Can I get you anything else before I go?" he asked. "Something to eat? A bedpan?"

"What?" she stammered. "Where you going?"

Rich looked at her, fixed an innocent expression on his face, thinking what a waste of flesh and bone this woman was. "Well, I'm going to arrange for you to be formally charged," he said. "Don't tell me that you haven't been through this before."

"I did, I have," she said, flustered for the first time. "What for? I ain't done nuthin'."

"What for?" Rich mimicked her voice. "Why, murder. That's what for."

Cassady stood up. Her breast thumped against her chest. "I ain't killed nobody! I want a lawyer."

"That's fine," Rich said in a mild voice. "We'll get you a lawyer. I'll call the public defender's office, and they'll send somebody over right away. And if I'm guessing right, it will probably be someone right out of law school. I'll bet he'll have such a heavy caseload that he will think nothing of sleeping right through yours. You see, you are not worth anything to him or society. He'll probably hold the cell door open for you."

Cassady blinked. Red stained her fat face. She looked as if he had just slapped her. "If I tell you what I know," she said. "I don't want nobody arresting me for the dope. For no murder, either."

Rich stroked his chin with his fingers, pretended to consider the deal.

"Okay," he said finally. He sat down. She sat down in the chair opposite, not taking her eyes from him.

"What do you want to know?" she said.

"Let's talk about the night Violet Hamilton died," he said. "That's where you got the cross, didn't you?"

She nodded. "I came by earlier that night. I needed a fix, and I knew that she had stuff coming. But the bitch didn't want to share, so I took off."

"About what time was that?" Rich asked.

She stared at him blankly. Rich sighed. "Okay," he said. "Did you see anybody when you were there that night?"

She shook her head.

"Nobody?" he pressed. "Not a soul?"

"Just Jiffy, man," she said. "I swear, that's it."

"Why did you go back?" Rich asked.

"I didn't—" the look on his face stopped her. "Okay, I did. I went back later on that night. I needed a fix real bad, man. I had some stuff, but someone swiped it from me. But she was already pretty sick. I think she might have been dead."

"So you just robbed her dead body and left?" Rich asked without trying to disguise the disgust in his voice.

She didn't turn away, held his gaze with a noncommittal look on her pasty face. "I tole you," she said. "She was a bitch."

"Then why did you hang around her?" he asked.

"It was a job," she answered him.

He looked up, confused. "A job? What the hell do you mean a job?"

"I got my dope for free by keeping an eye on her, and keeping her from getting herself into trouble."

"Someone paid you to keep an eye on Violet Hamilton?" Rich asked. "Who?"

"Smitty," she said. "I think he works for Raymond Smalls."

"Then what in the hell did you need dope from Violet for?" Rich asked. Cassady didn't respond for several seconds, then, licking her lips, she said, "I got a business on the side. I try to make a little profit."

"Oh I see," Rich said. "You sell the stuff you get from

Raymond Smalls and this Smitty, but take care of your own problem by using Violet."

She didn't say anything, didn't try and defend herself. Only shrugged.

Rich leaned back in his chair. Raymond Smalls, that name again. But why would he want someone to keep an eye on Violet? Unless it was for Ken—

"Kendra Hamilton," she was saying. "He wanted me to keep Violet away from Kendra Hamilton, to let him know when she was bothering her."

Suddenly it all made sense. Raymond Smalls was obsessed with Kendra Hamilton. He had paid Cassady to watch Violet, then killed her when she got out of control. But he didn't like the way this was coming together. It was just too easy.

"Where did you get the dope you had today?" he asked.

She looked at him as if he were stupid.

"Why, the same place I always get it," she said. "Smitty. They still pays me to do little things now and then."

"So, now that Violet's gone," he said, "you'll have to keep that dope for yourself, huh?"

"I guess I do," Cassady responded.

Rich leaned across the table, looked her into her moon-shaped eyeless face.

"Well, I've got something to tell you, watch girl." Cassady said nothing. Her tongue darted over her lips. Rich went on. "I think you were about to get fired."

"Fired?" Cassady asked, confusion bathing her wet voice.

"Yeah, fired," Rich explained. "That dope you had today—" he stopped.

She stared at him, nodded slowly.

"It was poison," he said. "It would have dropped you in your tracks just like the worthless piece of shit you are."

"Process her out," Rich said before he had gotten back to his desk.

"Process her out?!" Beau exclaimed. "She had the dope that killed Violet Hamilton hidden down her crotch."

Rich walked over to Beau and looked at him with a face that he hoped would calm him down. "That animal in there didn't kill Violet Hamilton. She was simply the messenger, the errand girl. You saw her face when I told her that the dope was poisoned. She had no idea."

"What the fuck you talkin' about? She had both motive and opportunity." Beau stood up and shouted at him across his desk. "You heard her say that she hated Violet Hamilton. She used her for the extra dope."

"What about the man at The Elite?" Rich asked. "You remember him? The man with the shoes."

A struggle passed across Beau's face, then Beau shrugged. "Coincidence," he said.

Rich snorted, looked at Gregory, and waited for him to educate Beau. Gregory's silence surprised him. Rich turned to Beau.

"Look," Rich said, "the way Violet Hamilton was killed was too calculated. It meant something to the person who killed her. It was too subtle."

"So what are you saying?" Beau still protested. "Let that Moon bitch go? She did it, man. We could make this bust and this shit will be all over. We can then get back to the business of what this department was set up to do, investigating murders people care about, okay?"

It amazed Rich how Beau could twist situations to make them fit his own needs, and somehow make wrong sound right. But Beau Blair simply echoed the thoughts playing like distant drum music in his own head. This entire Violet Hamilton thing could all be over with the arrest of Cassady Moon for her murder. And it might also be a way for them to finally get Raymond Smalls.

Rich turned his back on Beau and walked over to the two-way mirror. He walked slowly, both thumbs hooked into the belt loops of his jeans. He looked down on Cassady, who still sat at the table, her black eyes turned upward toward the mirror, her fat palms flat on the wooden table. Who would defend her if they did arrest her, and more importantly, who would miss her? Her face said it all. No one. He touched the mirror with a forefinger as he actually considered Beau's suggestion, but the cold glass reminded him of something.

"Yes," he said slowly, as if speaking to himself. "You are right. We could arrest this Cassady, and it will probably all be over. Everyone will go home happy. But if we do that, Blair . . ." At this point, Rich stopped and turned to Beau. "If we do that, we will be giving a break to one big-ass fish."

"You mean Raymond Smalls," Gregory said. Rich nodded.

"Bullshit," Beau said. "That's narcotics' business, not ours, Rich. Besides, she could rat on Smalls; we could bring him in based on what she got to say."

"Who would believe her, Blair?"

"But—"

"Process her out," Rich said again. "Put a tail on her. If she looks like she's going to fly, we'll pick her up."

"But—"

Exasperation and anger shot through him at Beau's protest. He whipped around and fired the next few words from his mouth like bullets. "You got a problem with that, Blair?"

Beau didn't respond, just mumbled something.

"I can't hear you," Rich said, with a hand cupped around his bad ear.

"I said, no. No," Beau boomed, "I don't have a problem with it, not at all. I'm happy as a freaking clam, man."

Rich walked to his desk and started putting his jacket on. As he punched his fist through the sleeves, Gregory asked him where he was going.

"Where do you think?" Rich responded, annoyed. "We need to talk to Raymond Smalls, find this Smitty—"

Gregory cut him off. "We can't do it tonight, Rich."

"Why not?" Rich asked. "We have to go tonight."

Gregory and Beau looked at him as if he had suddenly sprouted two heads. Finally, Beau broke the silence.

"He forgot," he said matter-of-factly.

"Yes, I think so," Gregory confirmed.

"Forgot about what," Rich said. He looked from one to the other of them, puzzled.

"Your fiancée's party," Gregory said.

"Ah, shit," Rich said as it all came back to him. Dinah and her father, Judge Webster, were throwing a charity event tonight. It wasn't for charity really, just an excuse for Dinah to throw a high-society party. She had been talking about it for weeks. She probably mentioned once or twice what it was for, some boys', or girls', club or some shit like that.

Rich saw a black tux in a clear plastic bag hanging behind Gregory's desk. His own was at home, somewhere. Dinah had bought him a tux when they started getting serious. Maybe he could get out of it. He looked at Beau for support.

"We can't let a party get in the way of this, man. I especially don't want Cassady running around. We need to get to Raymond Smalls first—"

"Then put her on ice for tonight, old man," Gregory broke in easily.

Rich regarded him for a long time. "So you agree with Beau?" he asked, feeling betrayed.

Gregory shrugged. "Maybe."

"It's an easy way out, and you know it, Atfield," Rich accused.

"I thought that was what you wanted, Marvel." Gregory assessed him coldly, an old challenge in his thin face. Rich looked away first.

"Okay," he said tiredly. "Put Cassady on ice for tonight." He turned to Beau. "You going?"

"Well, uh, yeah," Beau said, avoiding Rich's eyes. He began rearranging file folders on his desk, picking up the pencil cup and putting it down again in the exact same spot. For the first time, Rich noticed that the porn magazines had disappeared some days ago.

"With who?" Rich asked. "You are not going alone, are you?"

"No," Beau answered.

"Well who?" This time it was Gregory asking the question.

"Rita Sandbourne," he mumbled.

"Who?" Gregory said again. "I don't think I heard you correctly. Did you say Dr. Rita Sandbourne?"

Beau kept quiet. Rich let out a long whistle. He walked over and sat on the edge of Beau's desk. Gregory leaned on the wall, next to the door.

"She's at least ten years older than you," Gregory said with a laugh.

"So?"

"How did you manage that?" Rich asked.

"I managed it," Beau said. He glared at them both.

"I'd imagine that he managed it with a fair amount of begging." Gregory laughed again.

"How *did* you ever manage to land a date with a doctor," Rich chuckled.

Suddenly the embarrassment left Beau's face. His beady blue eyes sparkled. "I don't know," he answered. "But come see me when you're ready for some pointers."

Rich sat up. "What does that mean?" he asked, as a wave of fire traveled up his face. He glanced at Gregory, but his partner's face was noncommittal.

"Nothing." Beau waved the question away.

"No," Rich challenged. "What does that mean?"

"Dr. Hamilton, Rich," Beau said. "It's obvious that you have the hots for her."

"Don't be ridiculous, Beau," Rich exploded. "I'm engaged to Dinah."

"That don't mean anything," Beau said complacently.

"Rich," Gregory said, chuckling. "You'd better get a move on it. You need to pick Dinah up at three in the city, remember? Then you have to get ready."

"What are you, my personal Palm Pilot?" Rich said angrily to him.

"No, I'm not," Gregory explained. "But I do not want you

to get in trouble with Dinah anymore. If you do, you won't be marrying anybody, and I can't stand those late-night arguments you two seem to get in. You're not the only one who needs sleep, you know."

As he said all this, he ushered Rich to the door. Beau's sing-song voice followed them.

"Tell you what my friend, you got a problem. That's why it's so hard for you to believe that the lady might have something to do with this. I'm surprised you just don't let it all end with Cassady."

"Beau," Gregory warned. "Cool it."

Rich started back in the door, but Gregory stopped him. "Leave it alone, old man," he said. "You go on, now. I have something I'm working on here. I'll be there, probably around eight or nine."

"Rich," Beau said. He stood just beyond Gregory's left shoulder, his small blue eyes like two bright beads staring at Rich unblinking. When he spoke, his voice was serious. "Just because Violet Hamilton had some visitors that night," he said. "It don't mean that she got the dope from one of them."

Rich said nothing. He didn't feel like explaining to Beau how wrong he was. Rich remembered the vomit in the corner of the hotel room where Violet died. It was dry but still had a wet sheen on top. Violet was going through withdrawal symptoms before Cassady and the man in the watch cap appeared on the scene. She was desperate. One of them had the dime bag that killed her.

He walked out into the parking lot. The day had cooled, and a slight wind had come along and swept some of the clouds from the sky. Things were looking clearer, but that didn't make him feel better. That didn't make him feel any better at all.

CHAPTER 18

She smelled good, Dinah did. She smelled almost better than she looked when she walked into the Starlight Hotel hanging on to Richard T. Marvel's tuxedoed arm. Rich examined her from the top of her head to the tip of her perfect toenails, painted a shimmering gold. She wore a sequined spaghetti-strapped number that dipped so low in the back that it almost showed the crack of her ass. Butterfly hair clips studded with diamonds swept both sides of her glossy hair into a cascade of large curls that swung against her neck. She returned his gaze as if reading his thoughts, then winked and smiled.

She was perfect. He had a woman who could make love as good as she looked. She was prosperous; she had connections. Half his ticket was written just by being with her. Yes, he was lucky. Lucky as hell, except he didn't feel it. He felt as if he were working from some predefined script.

The theme of tonight's party was "starry starry night." Someone had strung the ceiling with white cotton to resemble clouds and hung Christmas lights small as pinpricks from the ceiling. A simulated moon, big and round as a satellite, hung in one corner. At least it provided enough light so the guests wouldn't have to squint all night in the dark.

Those same pinpricks of light hung on baby trees—real ones. They were alive, but whoever decorated the ballroom for this party had stripped them of their leaves and sprayed the limbs with white paint. White roses, the edges of their petals worn yellow like parchment paper, filled floor vases placed around the room. Women fluttered among them like misplaced swans, all trying to outdo each other in their designer dresses and whisper-thin wraps.

Rich spotted Beau and Rita by the bar. Beau wore a tux, but even from where he stood, Rich could see the silver points shine on the tip of his snakeskin cowboy boots. Rita had on a black backless dress that stretched around her thin body and flooded to the floor in folds. Beau raised his shot glass. Rich answered with a grin and started toward them. Dinah stopped him with a hand on his arm.

"Please, darling," she said. "This way."

She guided him to a circular table in the very center of the room. Judge Webster, his big face shaped like the ace of spades, turned his mouth up in what was supposed to be a welcoming smile. He reached out and shook Rich's hand with both of his.

"Glad to see that you could make it this time, Rich," he stated. "We missed you at church last week."

Without waiting for a reply, he turned to his daughter and kissed her on the cheek. He then introduced Rich to the others at the table. There was a senator and his daughter, a CEO of a major software company and his wife, and a superior court judge. Sheriff Freehold and his wife also sat at Judge Webster's table. The bouncy blonde was at least twenty years younger than her husband.

"But you two know each other, of course," Judge Webster said.

Rich chuckled and shook Sheriff Freehold's hand. His wife stood up and wagged fingers in such a way that Rich could not help but notice the rock on her hand and the diamond bracelet jiggling up and down on her wrist. Rich wondered whose pockets Freehold was picking to get enough to buy his wife a bracelet like that.

Judge Webster sat down, politely questioned Rich about his day and his activities, and then dismissed him. Rich knew how Judge Webster felt about him. And to tell the truth, if he were Judge Webster, he would probably feel the same way. Rich had blown countless appointments and social engagements with the father of his soon-to-be wife. And it must have killed the old man to see his daughter, who graduated top of her class at Berkeley, marry someone raised in The Pit.

The conversation turned to politics, and Rich's attention drifted away from the table and out to the crowd, which consisted mostly of politicians and prominent businessmen. The politicians were there because they wanted to show supporters that they were not soft on crime. The businessmen were there to curry favor with the politicians. A few washed-up actors and musicians floated around the room acting as if they were still the stars they had been a few years ago. They pretended not to be grateful for the free publicity that they needed in order to boost their disappeared careers.

Rich's mouth felt dry. He took a sip of the scotch-and-water Judge Webster had ordered for him without asking what he wanted. He hated scotch but drank it anyway while turning his thoughts away from the party. When Rich was growing up in The Pit, his dream wasn't to live in a three-bedroom, two-bath house in suburbia. No, he'd dreamed of having an estate with a lawn so wide you couldn't see the house from the street. The house itself would have at least eight bedrooms, and each one would be filled with a son or a daughter. He looked at Dinah, who conversed easily with the senator while managing to throw a few smiles to the senator's wife. Rich realized as he watched her that Dinah's dreams didn't play into any of his fantasies. She was his reality now. At least she did want children, or so she had told him.

As he scanned the room again, wishing he could somehow speed up time and get the hell out of here so he could go question Smalls, he realized that someone was missing from the party. Just as the thought entered his mind, Luke Bertrand, wearing an Armani tux, walked through the door with Kendra Hamilton on his arm.

Kendra wore a pale rosy dress that stopped just above her ankles. The dress was plain, strapless, and cut in a neat straight line just above her breasts. Her rich brown skin glowed against the pale fabric. Her face was almost bare of makeup except for some frosty brown gloss. Unlike Dinah's hair, Kendra's did not behave. She had pinned it up in a loose bun, and corkscrews of curls escaped and fell around her neck and face. She kept adjusting the sheer shawl hanging loosely around her shoulders and pushing her hair back. She looked completely out of place, and he could tell by the fake smile plastered on her face that she was absolutely bored. *Funeral in the morning and partying at night,* Rich thought. Kendra Hamilton didn't strike him as the grief-stricken daughter.

Suddenly Rich caught a whiff of scotch. He looked away from Kendra and right into the face of Judge Webster. "Who is that?" the judge asked him.

Rich swallowed, feeling vaguely guilty for staring so long at Kendra. "You mean the woman with Luke Bertrand?" He tried to make his voice sound innocent. The judge regarded him silently for a moment while sounds of the party continued around them.

"Yes," he said finally.

"Kendra Hamilton." Rich answered. He swallowed a mouthful of scotch. It burned like acid all the way down his throat. "She works for Luke at the free clinic in The Pit."

"Oh," the judge answered as he sat back in his chair. "I thought you were going to tell me that she was Luke's lady friend or something. I was beginning to think it was about time."

Rich smiled but didn't join in the judge's laughter. To his knowledge, and obviously to Judge Webster's, no one had ever seen Luke Bertrand with a *lady friend.* He either kept his affairs very private or he didn't have them.

Dinah touched his sleeve. He looked at her, and she

winked at him. Obviously, she had not seen him staring at Kendra as if he wanted to eat her up. Dinah smiled one of her best-friends smiles. He raised his glass to her, thinking how pleased she must be to see him sitting there with his mouth shut like a good boy.

As Rich set his glass on the table, Luke Bertrand sailed over to their table. Kendra followed, reluctantly, her eyes smoky in the dusky light. Everyone started to stand, but Luke waved them back down. But Dinah and Judge Webster stood fully. Rich followed suit.

Judge Webster and Luke laughed, shook hands. They melded all four of their hands together and exchanged a few words. Luke half-jokingly asked the judge about making a donation to the clinic and the judge committed to a five-figure sum. Luke then smoothly turned to the senator and CEO and received similar commitments.

"You know, Dr. Hamilton had to practically turn away an asthmatic child the other day because we don't have the proper equipment or medicine," he explained. "Your donations will go a long way, believe me, gentlemen. If we don't protect the children, who will?"

Rich's head snapped up at Luke's last words. They sounded familiar somehow, but he couldn't put his finger on why. The others all murmured things like "Glad to help" and "Anything we can do," but Rich barely noticed. He kept staring down at the ice melting in his scotch-and-water to keep from staring at Kendra. Out of the corner of his eye, he saw her fidget nervously with the shawl again. As Luke introduced her, she stretched her mouth into a bright smile and nodded.

"And this is Dinah Webster," Luke finally said. "Judge Webster's daughter."

Dinah faced her fully then, still standing. She towered over Kendra in her three-inch heels. She looked her up and down, assessing her as one would an enemy. Dinah's behavior reminded Rich that she was not stupid. She had noticed Rich's earlier stare. When Dinah's eyes reached Kendra's bewildered face, she gave a tight, polite smile.

"My dear," Dinah said. "What an interesting ensemble. Where on earth did you come by it?"

Rich recognized a thread of disquiet running through Dinah's cordial voice. He knew that Dinah felt threatened. Kendra didn't answer right away but stared at Dinah for several seconds, letting her eyes wander over her perfect hair and rest on the diamond butterflies pinned there.

"Macy's," Kendra responded without an ounce of embarrassment in her voice.

Dinah lifted an eyebrow before taking a sip of red wine in the silence that followed. The senator's wife spoke up, her voice matter-of-fact.

"I don't blame you," she huffed. "You see this thing I'm wearing?" she waved her hand over the pale blue silk dress. "Dillard's." She leaned over her husband to get a good look at Kendra. "On sale. I don't see the sense in spending ten thousand dollars on some one-of-a-kind designer disaster that falls apart the first time you wear it. The money's put to better use at your clinic. Have a seat and tell me a little more about it."

Rich didn't have to look at Dinah to tell that there was an angry glint in her green eyes. He felt a little sorry for her.

"Rich," the senator's wife said, "you've been lovely. But why don't you let the doctor sit down so we can chat."

"By all means," Rich said as he stood.

As Kendra sat down, Luke took Rich by the arm and walked him away from table. Luke didn't say much to Rich. He just tipped his glass and smiled at the party guests. Then he said, "How are you coming on the investigation?"

Rich took a good look at Luke. For a man of sixty or more, he looked young. His face reminded Rich of a dark, smooth wood, like mahogany. Whether he dyed it or not, his hair was as black as shoe polish except for the diamonds of light dancing in it. Luke had stopped in a corner next to one of the tall vases. He leaned against the wall and stuck one hand in his pocket. He still didn't look Rich directly in the eye, but Rich had the feeling that Luke Bertrand knew he was being studied.

What did anyone in Dunhill *really* know about Luke, anyway? Despite throwing parties and raising money and being the local hero, he was a very private man. He rarely talked about his past. What was known was that he grew up fatherless. His mother had worked for the man who later adopted him and sent him to medical school. The old man had left Luke enough money to lead a lifestyle that fit him so perfectly everyone thought that he was born to it. Still, Luke Bertrand knew junkies and had become so close to the likes of Violet Hamilton that her death was actually on his radarscope.

"What's on your mind, son?" Luke asked.

"How long did you know Violet Hamilton, Luke?" The question surprised even Rich. He hadn't known he was going to ask it until the words popped out of his mouth.

Luke gazed at Rich, his face unreadable. Then he smiled and shrugged. "I've known her longer than I've known you and your family, Rich," he said.

But that doesn't really answer the question, Rich thought. He knew that Luke noticed the emotions warring in his face. For a minute, Rich thought about letting it go, moving on to something else, some small talk that would return them to the mentor relationship that had existed between them since Rich was sixteen years old.

"So, if you knew us both so long, why did you feel that you had to go to Freehold to ask my help?"

Luke laughed. "Come on Rich," he said, patting him on the shoulder. "I know how stubborn you can be sometimes. How judgmental. Your mind was already made up. If I had asked you, you would have humored me for a couple of days and then let it go."

"So you thought with Freehold breathing down my neck . . ."

"And freedom from your other cases," Luke pointed out. "Don't forget that. I wanted this taken seriously, for Kendra's sake. She would not have been satisfied with some cursory investigation."

"But you still didn't answer my quesion." There, he had done it again. Surprised even himself. "How long have you known Violet Hamilton?"

Luke answered without hesitation. "I've known—" He stopped, began again. "I *knew* Violet Hamilton for over twenty-five years. She was a prostitute, a whore, a junkie who used to come to the free clinic in The Pit. I tried to help her."

Rich pretended to consider Luke's words for a minute or two. Cursing himself, he plunged in with both feet. "A lot of prostitutes, whores, and junkies have been treated at that clinic over the years. What made you want to help that particular one?"

"Some things are personal, Rich. No matter how well you know a person, there are some aspects of their life that should remain private. Don't you think?"

Rich didn't like the look on Bertrand's face. And it surprised him that he thought of him that way, not a person, but as a last name. Bertrand. A suspect.

"Am I a suspect, Detective Marvel?" Luke asked in a soft voice.

"Come on Luke." Rich laughed in spite of his churning stomach. "You know the drill. The first place you start in any investigation is with close friends and acquaintances. They are all suspects." The churning in Rich's stomach grew worse. He had put on his best *I'm-your-friend* voice, a voice he had used with countless suspects over the years. Though it sounded genuine, it was as fake as a Hollywood snowstorm.

Luke laughed in return. "Yes, I know that," he said. "It's just a little startling coming from you, Rich. You are like a son to me."

"Hey"—Rich held up both palms—"I'm just doing my job. I know it's messed up sometimes."

"No problem. I understand." Luke took a sip of his drink. The whiskey left a wet sheen on his lips. "I don't know why I took a special interest in Violet Hamilton. It wasn't sexual, if that is what you are thinking." Luke's eyes bored into his. Rich turned away. "But there was something about Violet that cried out for help. And, God help me, I thought she could be helped." Luke stopped, heaved out a long sigh. "But I guess it was the child more than anything. Kendra. I wanted to help the child as I had been helped. No telling what would have happened to me if my benefactor hadn't come along."

"But your mother wasn't a junkie," Rich countered.

"No," Luke responded. "She scrubbed toilets. Your point, Detective?"

Rich ignored the chill Luke's tone had sent up his spine. "Where were you the night Violet died?" he asked instead.

"I was raising money for Big Brothers and Sisters at this very hotel, Rich," Luke answered easily. "I can produce about three hundred of the Bay Area's wealthiest to testify to my whereabouts in a court of law."

Neither one of them spoke for a moment. Then Luke, the old Luke, returned. "So," he said. "I'm guessing by this line of questioning that you found something more than just a simple overdose?"

Before Rich could respond, an eager young man in a tuxedo and black hi-top tennis shoes bounced over to them. He thrust a CD into Luke's hands and babbled about how it was his first jazz CD and how pleased he would be if Mr. Bertrand would help him promote it. Luke smiled, then clamped the young man on the shoulder. Rich barely heard the murmured words of encouragement. As the boy left, Luke turned to Rich and said in a voice as smooth as cream, "I hate jazz." After a pause, he added. "We'll have to continue this conversation another time, Rich. After all, I can't neglect my date."

As Luke strolled away, Rich felt the need for a drink to kill the churning in his stomach. A drink he liked. He walked over to the bartender, a man of about twenty-five with dreadlocks like blond caterpillars attached to his head.

"I need a beer," Rich said. "What do you have on tap?"

"Samuel Adams," the bartender smiled. Without waiting for Rich to confirm, he began to fill a glass. "Looks like you know the big man," he said as he slid the glass toward Rich.

"Yeah," Rich said dryly. "Lucky me."

"Lucky you?" the bartender responded. "Lucky *me*. If it wasn't for Luke Bertrand, I wouldn't have gotten this gig tonight, man. He told the management that I did such a good job that they hired me special for tonight." He leaned toward Rich, his eyes bulging like a fish. "These cats tip crazy, man."

"You worked for Luke before?" Rich asked.

"Yeah, last weekend. I made two thousand dollars in tips alone. I found hundred-dollar bills in my tip bowl." He laughed, shook his blond dreadlocks out of his face. He picked up a white cloth and started wiping the lacquered counter.

Rich laughed, too. "Seems some folks just don't know what to do with their money."

"That's fine with me, man. Yes sir, fine with me."

"So, did the old man stay at the party all night?"

The bartender wiped the counter around Rich's Samuel Adams. He gave Rich a few big nods. "Yep, sure did. He even stayed long enough to get a little ass-candy, if you know what I mean." The bartender winked at him.

"No, I don't. Tell me," Rich said, smiling.

The bartender stopped wiping the counter. His face turned serious. "I've said enough already," he said. "I don't want to stop getting gigs like this because of a big mouth."

"Come on," Rich said. "You're among friends. I ain't like those people out there, man. You won't get a hundred-dollar tip from me 'cause I ain't got it."

The bartender studied him for a while, then leaned against the bar. He lowered his voice to a whisper. "He took a bottle of whiskey from me, some expensive shit, strong, to meet some old broad in one of the rooms upstairs. An old chick with blue hair and sagging tits." He shook his head. "An old man like that."

"Whiskey?" Rich said. "Do you know what kind it was?"

"Not really. I wasn't payin' that much attention. I just know it was one of those bottles that Mr. Bertrand said should just sit on the counter to impress people. It wasn't meant to be served."

"Did he take any glasses?" Rich asked.

The bartender shrugged. "I don't remember," he said.

"About what time was this?"

The bartender looked at Rich for a couple of minutes. "Why you so full of questions, my man?"

"I said," Rich repeated, "about what time did Luke Bertrand get the whiskey."

The bartender nodded, understanding. "Cop? Luke Bertrand in trouble?"

Rich said nothing.

"About eight-thirty, nine o'clock, I guess." All tones of friendliness had left the bartender's voice.

"How long was he gone?" Rich asked.

"Don't remember," he mumbled, his voice sullen, unfriendly.

"You sure you don't remember?" Rich asked.

"I'm sure." The bartender didn't look at him, stared down at Rich's glass still half full of beer. "You mind?"

Rich smiled, "Of course not," he said. He drained the glass and set it down on the bar. The bartender scooped it up.

"Thanks, man," Rich said.

The bartender didn't respond. Instead he turned his back and plunged Rich's glass into a sink filled with soapy water.

The room tilted, or so it seemed to Rich later that night. The room tilted, and the music continued to play, but it seemed to be coming from the ball of tension buried in his gut as he held Kendra Hamilton on the dance floor. As she swayed stiffly, staring at her feet as if afraid she would trip, he went over in his mind how this had happened. One minute he had been watching Luke and Kendra on the dance floor, and the next he was dancing this tight little box step with Kendra. Luke had waltzed her over to their table and simply traded. He'd pulled Dinah by her wrists and said to Rich, "I'll take this one if you will take Kendra."

Dinah had stood up and followed Luke to the dance floor. "Come on, darling," she said to Rich over her shoulder. "You are not going to let this sly old fox show you up, are you?"

He grimaced and said no. As he approached Kendra, she gave him a tight smile.

"You don't have to, you know," she said.

"Are you kidding," he turned the grimace into a grin. "I'd be charmed."

At first, he thought it would be funny. He wondered how it felt for her to dance with someone she had obviously hated. And then again, maybe she would let something slip, reveal what she was hiding. He held up his hands, and she put her hands in them like they were a couple of dead fish.

Then, before he knew it, they were doing this weird little box-step thing. One step forward, one step to the side, and one step backward. It was when she suddenly took two steps forward, and slid her hand around his neck that the room swayed. She stood on tiptoes and looked over his shoulder, then leaned back and looked into his face.

"She doesn't seem to be your type," she said as her eyes pierced his.

"Oh?" he said, distracted. It took a couple of seconds for her words to reach his brain. He had been distracted by the slope of her breast touching his chest. He looked over his shoulder and saw why she had crept closer. She had done it to get a better look at Dinah, who was laughing and chatting with Luke as if she'd known him her whole life.

"And what type do you think that might be?" he asked, annoyed.

"Docile," she said. "You wouldn't have the patience for someone with a will of her own."

Rich chuckled then, pressed his palm into the rough silk of her dress. No longer paying attention to her feet, she stumbled slightly into him and immediately stiffened. She no longer smelled of antiseptic, but of soap as sweet as flowers. He let go of her hand and placed two fingers against the pulse beating rapidly against the brown skin of her neck.

"Thought so," he murmured as she jerked away from him. He smiled. "Looks like you got me all figured out."

Pushing away from him, she tilted her head so she could look at him. "I'd bet that there isn't anyone who has you figured out yet, Rich," she said. "Not even yourself. Not even your girlfriend who's shooting daggers at us right now."

"Maybe she hasn't figured me out," he said with a shrug, "but she has other strong points."

"Oh?" she said with a raised eyebrow. "Like what?"

He answered her with silence as three beats of the music slipped by. Then, "She lets me lead."

Her laughter surprised him. It lit up her face and made her eyes sparkle. He felt different with her in his arms, but he couldn't put his finger on just how. Not yet.

"Maybe she isn't as smart as she looks," she said, still laughing.

"What are you doing here tonight, anyway?" he asked.

"Luke dragged me."

"Ahh," he sighed, pulling her closer and ignoring the fact that she stiffened against him once again. "Good old Luke Bertrand. He seems to have his hands into everything, doesn't he?"

She examined him quizzically. "What are you getting at?" she asked, the annoyance back in her voice.

"Tell me, how much do you really know about Luke?"

"I've known him almost all my life," she said.

He gave her a little shake. "I'm not asking you how long you've known him, I'm asking how *much* do you know about him."

"What do you mean, how much do I know?" Her laughter was nervous. "I know a lot. He's not from Dunhill, but he's lived here for a good part of his life—"

His soft laughter stopped her cold. "You can read all that stuff in the society pages," he said. "Where are his parents?

Who's he seeing? Have you ever met anyone that he's dating? How does he make his money, Kendra?"

"Stop it!" she spat. "I don't like it."

He regarded her while the music played around them. "You've thought about this before, haven't you?" he challenged.

"You know, you've got nerve, Richard T. Marvel," she said. "After all Luke's done for you, you have the nerve to, to . . ." she stopped.

Rich didn't say anything for a while, just watched the confusion in her face. Then finally, softly, "To what?"

"I don't know," she said. "What is it exactly that you are trying to do? Implicate my friends to make me regret bringing my mother's murder to your attention?"

He shrugged. "You can think that if you want. Okay, question number two. What in the hell were you doing with Officer Grady yesterday?"

He felt her arms go slack. He had to press her fully against him to keep her from turning away. And he didn't find the situation unpleasant. It wasn't unpleasant at all.

"Stop it," she hissed. "Your girlfriend is watching."

He raised an eyebrow. "I don't care. I'm not doing anything wrong; I don't have anything to feel guilty about. What about you, Kendra? You have something you feel guilty about?"

"I didn't come here to be interrogated by you," she answered.

"Then what did you come here for? You knew that I'd be here, didn't you? And don't give me that shit about Luke dragging you. You came here to see me, didn't you?"

He'd struck a nerve. He saw the truth glimmering in her eyes. *My God,* he wanted to say to her, *you feel it, too.* But he couldn't get the words out because he didn't fully know himself what he meant. He only felt the length of her body pressed against his and heat radiating from it like unfiltered sun.

"I don't know what you are talking about," she said, using

both elbows to put distance between them once again. "Instead of browbeating me, you should be telling me about my mother. Have you found anything yet?"

He searched her face for a while, debating whether or not to tell her about Cassady Moon. How easy would it be for him to end it all with her arrest and the announcement that the thing he had interrogated earlier had been responsible for Violet's death. But he knew that Cassady was not the answer. And on some level other than professional, he did not want the perpetual dance he seemed to always be in with Kendra Hamilton to end.

"Did you get everything taken care of today?" he asked instead of answering her question.

"I asked you a question," she responded.

"No," he said flatly. "We don't have anything concrete yet."

He didn't say anything for a while, just let the music play. When it became clear that she wasn't going to break the silence, he asked her the question again, this time gentling his voice. "Did you get everything taken care of today?"

"Why are you being so attentive all of a sudden?"

He sighed. "We don't have to be enemies, you know."

"I know," she said seriously. "But you don't seem to know that yourself, showing up like that at the funeral home, making a scene." He saw her swallow on the last words before answering his question. "Yes, I got everything taken care of. I sprinkled my mother's ashes near the Sacramento River."

"Alone?" he asked before he could help himself. He didn't realize how close they had been dancing until she stepped back so she could look at him.

"What has that got to do with anything?" she asked him.

"I was just curious to know if Smalls was there."

"And if I said yes?" she countered.

"I'd say that was kind of ironic, wouldn't you? He may be responsible for Violet's death."

"I don't believe that," she said.

"He's a drug dealer."

"I know that. But he's also my friend. Ray Ray and I grew up together. He stood by me when no one else would, not even Luke. I'm just not going to turn my back on him because—"

"Because he deals dope?" Rich finished for her. "I would sure like to get a look at your rule book, lady."

Kendra looked at him, then smiled—a saccharine smile.

"There is a good reason why I went my way and you went yours," she said. "And if you did get a peek at my rule book, you would see one of them is not turning my back on my people."

Rich returned her smile. "You know, I have the same rule," he said. "But it changes when the people stop being people and start being predators."

Kendra stopped, and it wasn't because the music had stopped. Dinah was standing there with her hands on her sequined hips.

"You don't mind if I have him back, do you?" she asked without looking at Kendra.

Rich watched Kendra's face melt into a mask of sympathy. "I'm sorry," she said. Dinah immediately moved to step between them, but Kendra stopped Dinah by placing a hand on her bare arm. "I do mind. I need to talk to him for a minute. Privately."

First surprise, then fury moved over Dinah's face. "I don't understand . . ." she began.

"It's a business matter," Kendra broke in smoothly, as if she were speaking to a child.

Dinah turned to face Rich. "Can't this be done some other time?" she asked. "Must you do this now?"

Rich started to say something, but Kendra cut in. "I'm sorry," she said. "But this can't keep."

"We won't be long," Rich said, taking Kendra by the elbow and guiding her off the dance floor before Dinah could protest.

* * *

Kendra pulled her sheer wrap closer and hugged her bare arms as Rich stared at her. The room they'd managed to find unlocked was a small sitting room with red velvet furniture trimmed in swirls of dark wood. Rich tried to find overhead lights, but there weren't any. Before sitting down, he snapped on two Tiffany lamps, and he was reminded of Beau's earlier story. The glass shades greedily picked up the light from the meager bulbs. Pink and red and blue jewels of light scattered across the floor. Rich sat on the arm of a velvet sofa the color of blood. He folded his arms and waited.

"First"—Kendra said, holding out a forefinger—"let's get something straight, Detective Marvel. I came to *talk* to you, not *see* you. I have no interest in *seeing* you."

Rich drove down his annoyance at the use of his title, wanting to point out how easily she had shifted into using his first name before. But he didn't say a word. He needed her comfortable now.

"Okay, okay, I understand," he said, holding up his hands in a placating gesture. "What is it that you wanted to *talk* to me about?"

She walked into the darkened room and sat beside him, twisting to look into his face. Her shawl slipped from her shoulders and landed softly on the velvet sofa. The dim light in the room enriched her eyes, made them seem almost liquid, and her brown skin sparkled like dew. He sculpted his face into an emotionless mask and waited.

"I don't know where to begin," she said.

Rich sighed, annoyed. "Kendra, I don't have time for games. Just tell me what's going on."

"It's about the cross I had on yesterday," she said. "I lied . . ."

Rich laughed. "No . . . You? Lie?"

She placed a hand over his to silence him. "Rich, please," she said. "Let me finish before you jump to judgment."

He stared at her hand. She quickly moved it back and swallowed. He looked into her face a long time before responding. "Go ahead," he said at last.

"A friend didn't give it to me . . ." she started.

Kendra then told him some shit about looking for a girl named April Hart, finding files of missing girls at the clinic. Grady had helped her find the address of one of the girls' families. Rich knew that he was being blinded by his hatred of the old man, but when she mentioned Grady's name, he discounted the entire story.

"How did I know that old man would be involved in this?" he said dryly.

She stopped talking and looked at him. "I don't understand."

"I told you to stay out of this, didn't I?" he asked. "But you just couldn't, could you? Now you are in here telling me some bullshit story about missing junkies. . . ."

She drew back at the anger in his voice. "You don't believe me, do you?" she asked.

"Why should I? Tell me one reason why I should?" he asked. "You have been lying since this investigation started."

"Why would I make this up?" she asked him, standing up.

He stared at her again. "Let's say you didn't make this up. Why would you tell me?"

She stared back at him, the look on her face incredulous. "Because the cross that Beth Rinehart's mother gave to me is the same cross my mother had. Something is going on here, Rich. You've got to see it. I mean . . ." She stopped when he snorted. "Why would I lie to you?" she asked him again.

He folded his arms across his chest and regarded her in the half-light. "Hmmm," he said. "I can think of a lot of reasons. The number one reason is to call attention away from yourself. The other reason is make the cops look like idiots by chasing ghosts. Everyone knows how you feel about the sheriff's department."

Kendra picked up the sheer wrap from the sofa and drew it over her arms. "You were wrong about something tonight, Detective Marvel," she said, her voice as hard as stones.

"And what was that?" he answered.

"I don't have you all figured out; I didn't realize how incredibly blind you really are."

Rich ignored Dinah's questioning look when he returned to the party. As Dinah slipped into his arms, he watched Kendra walk over to Luke's table.

"That must have been an intense conversation," Dinah said to him, leading him to the dance floor. "I hope you saved a dance for me."

He rested his hands on her waist. The sequins felt like fish scales. As they moved to the music, Rich knew what had been different with Kendra. When he first took her in his arms, he realized what the last few months had been like for him. He had been walking around with a scowl etched on his face and an ache of tiredness between his eyes. The closer he got to his dreams, the promotion, and the marriage to Dinah, the more tired he became.

When he first started with this police force, he'd focused on helping people. Lately it seemed that he had been more focused on catching people. Both his job and Dinah had become a giant vacuum sucking the life right out of him. When Kendra had stepped closer to him, he had felt something give way. Maybe he was reminded of the old neighborhood. Despite the hardship, there were some good times growing up. He was more like his old self again. The tiredness fled from between his eyes like dust. Now Dinah had brought all the stress of his ambition back.

"Well?" Dinah said now.

"Well, what?" He looked into her green eyes.

"What were you two talking about?"

Rich shrugged. "Nothing much. Mutual acquaintances, old times."

"Old times?" Dinah asked. "Do you know you both danced right through two entire songs?"

Rich took a breath. No, he hadn't known that.

"And then that conversation that you had to have *pri-*

vately," Dinah went on. "Rich, you must know how that looked."

"It didn't look like anything, Dinah," Rich said. "That was just business. Everyone knows that I'm in charge of her mother's murder investigation."

Dinah let go of him as the music abruptly stopped. She looked at Rich then, contempt on her face.

"I would advise you, Richard T. Marvel," she said, "that you not, for one minute, mistake me for being stupid. Not if you ever want to marry me, or should I say my money?"

She left him standing like an idiot on the dance floor. She walked quickly toward the exit door. Pretty soon, he knew that he would have hell to pay.

CHAPTER 19

Richard T. Marvel was dreaming, a fact that graced his mind for only a fleeting second. He was afraid in the dream. Rich knew that he was usually afraid even while awake. Over the years, he had been able to push that fear aside. But the fear was different in the dream. He couldn't control it. It wrapped its invisible hands around his throat and squeezed until he could no longer breathe.

He was wearing the designer jacket Dinah had brought back from New York. Except for the spotlight pooling around him, he was surrounded by darkness. He was running from something, but the weird part was that he remained completely still. He looked to his left and to his right but saw nothing beyond the light except total darkness. When he twisted his head to look behind him, he saw a brick wall with red oversize bricks the color of rusted blood. The wall blocked his path. He was trapped.

Cold sweat sprouted on his forehead and under his arms. His breath rushed from his throat in hot gasps. His chest ached with the effort of it. He tried crying out, but his tongue refused to form words. His lips would not move.

Rich swiped his hand over his mouth. The garnet from his college ring cut him on the lip, drawing a bead of blood. Just at the point that he thought he would go completely crazy from the empty darkness, the dark alley filled with faces. Floating, disembodied faces, white as moons, laughing. He could see teeth shining in the darkness. The women had clean, made-up faces. They were all beautiful. Every single one of them.

They all had plastic surgery, he heard a whisper in his ear. *They can do that, you know? Have plastic surgery and live in fancy houses. They can hang out with people, you know what I mean, Rich? With people like Dinah.*

What are you talking about, man? Rich asked in his dream.

He had recognized the voice, but not the tone. It taunted and patronized. Rich backed up until he stood plastered against the brick wall. He noticed that the brick wall had no temperature. It was neither hot nor cold. It was just there, like a part of his body. A perfect ninety-eight point six degrees, like the back of another human being.

Gregory stepped from the darkness. It wasn't the Gregory he knew. This Gregory had on a designer suit. His shoes shone like mirrors. His hair glowed gold in the darkness. He had that well-fed look of the rich, confident, and successful. Gregory stepped toward Rich as if reading his thoughts.

Do you know who I am, Richard? You think you can step into my world, as I stepped into yours? Even Dinah can't get you that. Gregory emerged from the darkness as he spoke. His jacket became a little less designer and a little more Salvation Army. The silk shirt he wore turned into a T-shirt.

What's going on? Rich asked. And then the faces, the disembodied faces, howled with laughter.

What do you think, old man? Gregory asked him. His partner stood close, and Rich smelled Old Spice cologne. The scent was so strong that it stung Rich's nose. He touched Gregory's face. It was cold.

Get away from me, man, Rich said. *You are not who I thought you were. I don't know who you are.*

Gregory raised an eyebrow. *It's not that you don't know*

who I am, dear Richard, he said. *It's that you don't know who you are.* And Gregory clipped out the words in that accent of someone who had been raised all over the world. Someone not like him.

Rich didn't know what woke him up. He just knew that both eyes opened at the same time. One minute he slept, the next he was fully awake and watching the silver moon floating outside his bedroom window. He stayed still for a minute or two, staring at the moon and thinking of absolutely nothing. But there was an uneasy feeling in his stomach, teasing him, trying to make him remember something he didn't want to remember.

Dinah's honey-colored face entered his mind for a moment. He heard voices, his own and hers, filled with anger and accusations. He pushed the sounds away, and Dinah became nothing in his mind, insignificant as dust floating in a funnel of sunlight. Even though her body had been as stiff as a two-by-four in his arms on the dance floor, Kendra Hamilton had seemed more real to him than Dinah had earlier that evening. Part of him, that teasing part, asked for an explanation. But he ignored it.

Instead, he propped himself up on his pillows and laced his fingers behind his head. The breeze of the air conditioner cooled his naked chest. Thoughts, the ones he could deal with, returned one by one. He remembered Jiffy's words about those damn shiny shoes, not to mention that ridiculous disguise. The man had worn a wool watch cap and a windbreaker, as hot as it was the night Violet Hamilton died. He wanted to be noticed. Maybe he thought he was doing good and wanted congratulations.

Rich remembered Luke Bertrand at the party earlier, his shoes glittering in the low light. Expensive shoes. Worse, he remembered the bartender telling him about the whiskey. *Shit,* he thought. He did it. Luke Bertrand did it. But did he? So what if he grabbed a bottle of whiskey and two glasses from the bar? The bartender said he met a lady friend in one of the rooms. That would be easy enough to check. And if it turned out not to be true, that Luke met no one, it would have been easy for him to leave the party, catch the BART train to The Elite Hotel, give Violet the dope, and return to the party like nothing happened. But Luke Bertrand did not have a motive. However, maybe he knew something. Maybe he was covering for someone. Kendra Hamilton or Raymond Smalls. He obviously knew them both. The funeral proved that.

Rich thought about all three of them, Luke, Kendra, and Smalls, streaming from the funeral parlor in Turlock. He remembered Freehold during the election campaign calling Bill Conner Boweless Bill because of all the drug deaths in The Pit. And he heard Beau's voice: *If there is bad dope going around, shouldn't we warn people?* And Rich's own words floated back to him: *Then there would be more than one death on their hands.* It took Kendra Hamilton, an outsider who hated cops and who only wanted to find out who killed her mother, to actually connect the drug deaths in The Pit. Rich peered at the red numbers glowing on the clock on his nightstand. It was three-thirty in the morning.

Half an hour later, he found himself at Kendra Hamilton's apartment door. Two lights were out in the hallway, and he could barely see in the dim light. Kendra answered his straight five minutes of knocking with sleep-rimmed eyes and tousled hair.

"What? You just answer the door without asking who it is first?"

She blinked at him through the open sliver of the door and then put an open palm on her face.

"What are you doing here?" she asked sleepily.

"Where is it?" he answered instead as he grabbed the doorknob.

"What are you talking about?" she said, yawning.

"Look," he responded. "Don't get cute with me. I don't have time for you to be cute." He knew he was being unreasonable, but the very sight of her irritated the hell out of him.

A woman in pink curlers stuck her head out of the next

apartment door and peered at them. Kendra swallowed before opening the door wider. She put her hand on Rich's chest and grabbed his shirt. She pulled him inside. "Come in," she said. "I don't want you to give my neighbors a reason for gossip."

He obeyed but didn't go beyond the wood-floor entryway. She faced him with her head cocked to the side. He could see that she was almost fully awake now. She wore a short pale blue silk robe, unbelted. She hadn't bothered to tie it shut, and he could see hard nipples outlined against the tight white tank she wore with a pair of bikini panties. His eyes traveled back to her face, and he didn't see what he expected. The look on her face wasn't coy or sly; instead she wore a look of pure contempt. It was a look that told him that he was behaving in a way that she expected. And it pissed him off. She folded her hands across her chest and waited.

He took a step or two into the entryway, but she didn't move. Just stood there with that look on her face.

"You think you know why I'm here, Doc?" he asked.

Her face angered him, the way she stood there judging him. He pulled back his jacket, placed a hand on his hip. Her eyes flickered to his holster and back to his face. He saw mirrored in her face the same reckless anger that he felt.

"I thought you said you didn't want to play games," she hissed. "And now you want to play twenty questions? You came here, Rich, to see me. How in the hell am I supposed to know what you want?"

He willed his face still. Her robe was still open, and she hadn't bothered to shut it. He stayed just inside the door, his feet planted squarely on the hardwood floor. She stood about two feet away from him, not bothering to hide the contempt smoking in her eyes. It said that she knew him, that she had known men like him, and that usually they were after only one thing: sex. But she probably wouldn't say sex. She would say power, wouldn't she? Growing up with a whore for a mother, this woman probably didn't have a healthy view of relationships between men and women.

He evaluated her for a minute more, while she stood there and waited. Finally, he spoke. "You think you know me, don't you?" he said.

"Shit, Rich." She sighed. Then, her voice soft and tired, she said, "It's too damn early in the morning for psycho-analysis. Just tell me why you are here or leave. Get the hell out of my apartment."

He looked down at his feet, pushed down the anger bubbling in his throat. He studied the shiny tips of his shoes, attempting with all his might to listen to the warning voice playing at the back of his head. *Get the files and go,* it said.

"I need," he started slowly, "those files you told me about at the party. And I need the cross." He still didn't look at her, just studied how the hallway light shone on his shoes.

"Why?" she asked him. "Why do you want them?"

He brought his head back up to look at her. The words, *Why do you think?* jumped to his lips, but he didn't say them. Again, he heeded that warning voice in his head. He didn't need an argument with her, especially with the electricity flowing between them right now. He felt as if they were connected by a lightning bolt. But if she felt the same thing, she hid it well. Her poker face was perfect, and if it wasn't for that tell-tale pulse beating in her neck, he would have been fooled.

"Evidence, Kendra." He made his voice patient. "I need them."

"So you can what?" she asked. "So you can bury them like you bury everything else for your precious sheriff's department. You are so full of shit, Rich. You know that's not why you came—"

He stopped her next words with a warning finger. "You had better be careful, girl."

She did something totally unexpected. She slapped his finger away. The anger in her eyes had spread to the rest of her face. "Don't "girl" me, Marvel," she said. "I'm not your girl. Yours or anybody else's."

It would have been funny if he hadn't been so angry, so

sick of it all. Sick of her pretending and sick of her self-righteous attitude. He closed the distance between them in two long steps. She took a quick step back. He quickly slid a hand inside her robe and crushed her body against him. She twisted her hands up to push him away, but he seized her by the wrists. Her hands were so small that he could hold them behind her back with one of his own. He used his other hand to hold her face toward his. Her skin was as soft as it looked, and he stroked the side of her face with his thumb. He ignored the alarm bells clanging in his head. They both breathed heavily, and he could see fear drive out the anger on her face.

"Let me go," she said through ground teeth.

And he saw that she meant it. She wanted him to let her go, even though he could feel her hips arch slightly into his and her lips move almost imperceptibility toward his.

"You are so damned self-righteous, aren't you?" He leaned his face into her roughly coiled hair. He let go of her face and her hands, and plunged both of his hands into her thick hair. She didn't move back when he kissed her bottom lip briefly. She smelled of sleep and soap.

"Rich," she said against his chin. "Let me go." Her voice was calm and hard despite the fear he had seen on her face.

"Why?" he asked. "You want me as much as I want you, yet you treat me like a leper."

She moved her head back, placed a firm hand on his chest. When he looked into her eyes, he saw that her face had closed again. Her next words stopped him cold.

"You are engaged," she said. "You have a commitment. And then there is one more thing."

He stepped away from her then, closer to the door. He ran his hand over his hair and looked at her. "What's that?"

She waited until he faced her. With that same poker face, she found his eyes with her own before she started speaking.

"I don't like you," she said. "I don't like you at all. You are arrogant, judgmental, not to mention vain—"

He cut her off. "You said *one* more thing."

"—and I don't trust you," she finished as if he hadn't spoken.

He wished he could convince himself that his feelings for her had cooled because of her words, but they hadn't. He knew that hers hadn't, either. She just had better control than he did.

"You have no choice but to trust me now," he said as he held her eyes. "And your lack of trust doesn't detract from the fact that you *do* want me."

She shrugged. "Think what you want," she said. "But want has little to do with need."

He held his arm up, then dropped it in defeat. "Just get me the files and the cross," he said quietly. "If there is something to them, I'll find it."

She turned on her heel and went into a back room that was most likely her bedroom. Rich cursed himself as she left. His entire future was at stake and this woman was to blame. She not only had gotten him into an impossible situation, she now threatened his marriage to the only woman who could catapult him into the life he had wanted since he was a kid in The Pit.

She returned and gave him the envelope that she had had at the Courtroom Bar & Grill the other morning. She told him that the cross was in there with the other files. He opened the door, and she followed him with her hand on the knob, intending to close it behind him. But he turned around quickly before she could. Their faces almost touched.

"Tell me this, Kendra Hamilton," he said. "Has there ever been a man that you did trust? Besides Luke Bertrand?"

She dropped her eyes, clutched the edge of the door with both hands.

"Good night, Rich," she said, shutting the door and abandoning him in the darkened hallway.

CHAPTER 20

THE SAVIOR

about Violet Hamilton's death. I need to know why

Gregory Atfield sat hunched over a pile of file folders in the homicide squad room when Rich walked in. The light from his desk lamp made his skin glow. His crumpled white shirt was rolled up at the sleeves. Behind him, Rich noticed the tuxedo, clean and pressed and still in its clear plastic bag.

"Looks like you missed the festivities last night," Rich said dryly.

Gregory looked up from the mess on his desk.

"What? Oh, yes," he said and looked at his watch. "It's early. What are you doing here?"

Rich strolled into the room and sat down behind his desk. He studied his partner. Gregory looked like the absent-minded professor. His blond hair, almost platinum, fell over his lined forehead. And he had a faraway look in his eyes, as if he were deep in thought about something else. But Rich knew that Gregory was anything but the absent-minded professor. Gregory could turn that shit on when he needed it. Then, when it was no longer useful to him, he would shut it off like a water pump. Rich wondered if Gregory already knew what Rich suspected.

"Gregory," he began, "I need to know what you know

about Violet Hamilton's death. I need to know why you psyched out on me at the scene."

Just as he expected, Gregory dropped the absent-minded professor act. He sat up, placed his hand on his chin. He studied Rich in a way that made Rich think of how he must have handled an unruly servant when he was growing up rich and privileged in New England. Rich returned his gaze without blinking.

"Be straight with me, man," Rich said.

Gregory looked away and leaned back in his chair. He crossed his hands over his nonexistent belly.

"And what if I told you that it was my personal life, that it was really none of your business?" he asked mildly.

Anger and impatience crept over Rich. That was the second time in twenty-four hours that someone had told him that something was personal when refusing to answer his questions about Violet Hamilton. It made him realize how close this case hit home.

"Come on," Rich said. "Don't be stupid. You know why I'm asking this; I need to know that I can trust you."

"Do you really think I had anything to do with Violet Hamilton's death?" Gregory asked.

"No," Rich answered. "I don't. But you obviously knew her. I need to know how and why."

"Do you think you can handle it, Rich?" Gregory asked. His voice had a slight tease to it, which did little to put Rich at ease. It reminded him of the dream. He had a feeling that he was not going to like what Gregory was about to say.

Gregory walked over to Rich and sat on the edge of his desk. He folded his arms over his chest and stared with gray, unblinking eyes. Rich adjusted himself nervously in his seat.

"When I was younger, about fifteen, sixteen, I used to be what my family called a doper. You do know what a doper is, don't you, Rich?"

Rich felt his breath come shallow in his throat, but he didn't say anything. He just waited for Gregory to continue.

"You see, I know when you grow up, you want to be just

like me, or at least part of the same world I came from. But what you've failed to understand is that that world is fraught with some of the same problems as yours, albeit we experience those same problems surrounded by imported crystal and expensive cigars."

Rich stood up. "Don't patronize me, man," he said.

"I don't mean to patronize you," Gregory answered. "I'm just telling you how it was. I could tell you that my parents' constant bickering drove me to dope. But the fact is, I tasted it, I liked it, and I decided to do it again." He stopped abruptly and studied Rich. Rich said nothing.

"And again," he started, but Rich turned away from him. "And again," Gregory continued softly, following him so he could look into his face.

"Okay, I got it," Rich said. "Did you ever get caught?"

Gregory's face went white. He drew a large hand across his brow. "Yes, I did. A friend and I got caught together. Some reprobate sold us some bad dope, and we overdosed on a beach in New England. It was winter, and the water was like ice. It was a miracle that anyone found us."

"How did you ever get into the academy?" Rich asked him.

"Are you kidding?" Gregory laughed. "My old man is rich, remember?"

Rich tried to keep the feeling of betrayal from his eyes. "So what you are telling me is that you are a heroin addict?" he asked.

Gregory laughed. "Come on, Rich," he said. "Do I act like a heroin addict? Do you ever see me go off in a nod; scratch the hell out of my face? Do you see tracks on my arms?" He held out his white arms to Rich. "I said *used to be a doper*, Rich," he explained. "Not that I still am one."

"How did you clean up?"

"Fear," Gregory said. "My friend and I never touched heroin again after that night. He went to the grave, and I went to rehab."

"Why didn't you ever tell me?"

"Because I valued your friendship and I didn't want to lose it. You can be very judgmental sometimes, old man," Gregory explained.

Rich stuck his hands in his pockets. "Yeah, I know," he said. "I'm working on that. But what has this got to do with Violet Hamilton?"

Gregory walked back over to his desk and sat down hard. One of the file folders slipped from the desk and fluttered to the floor. "I saw her on the day she died," he said.

"What?" Rich asked, hating how his voice rose to almost a squeak.

Gregory put a palm up to stop him. "Listen to me for a minute, will you?"

Rich turned his back to him and brought his fingers up to his head in a gesture of disbelief. He willed his mouth silent. Gregory went on.

"I'm a counselor at one of the drug rehab centers," he said. "That's why I disappear sometimes. I keep quiet my specific qualifications, though, as much as I can. I had a long conversation with Violet Hamilton that day. She had been coming into the center on and off for the past couple of weeks. She was begging for methadone, but we don't give that medication out unless they agree to participate in the program." He stopped and swallowed.

"Go on," Rich prompted.

"Well," Gregory said with a sigh, "on that last day she came in, I could tell she was beginning to experience some withdrawals. We had a long conversation about her addiction, and she promised to go home that night and think about joining the program, but instead—"

"She found a fix," Rich said. "You know that she probably just wanted the methadone to stretch out her usual supply."

"I know that," Gregory said, running his hands through his hair. "But I was hoping that she would be one of the ones we could save."

Rich turned to Gregory and studied his still face. "That it?" he asked.

"No," Gregory said. "One more thing?"

"Oh God," Rich groaned.

"It's not that bad," Gregory said. "I know Kendra as well. She came to pick up her mother at the center once. We didn't speak then. I don't think she recognized me the other day at the clinic."

"And you didn't think that this had any bearing on the case?" Rich asked him, disgusted. "You stood here last night and let Beau say that Violet may have gotten the dope before that night. What's wrong with you, man?"

Gregory ran his hands through his hair. He didn't look at Rich. "You are a good detective, Rich. I knew that you would figure it out. Besides, I told you why I didn't tell you . . ."

Rich held up his hand to stop him. He turned away. The walls were closing in on him. He would have given anything just to get the hell out of there, go home, get in bed, and put his head under the covers. But he knew he couldn't. This confirmed for him that Violet Hamilton got the bad heroin the night she died. And who had motive? He saw Raymond, Luke, and Kendra walk out of that funeral parlor again. His instincts told him two things—that he had to look no farther than those three to find out what happened. And that there was something more going on here.

Instead of running for the door like he wanted to, Rich handed the envelope that he had gotten from Kendra to his partner and told him what he was thinking. He told him in a calm voice stripped of emotion, but filled with the trust he knew he had to place in Gregory if they were ever going to find out who killed Violet Hamilton. And why.

Gregory and Rich did not notice the sun bleeding through the grime on the windows. Beau came in late, around ten. Both Gregory and Rich only grunted at him, not looking up from the papers they studied.

"What's this?" Beau indicated the pile on his desk.

Rich, who had been bending over Gregory's shoulder, finally looked at Beau. Rich grinned. "Merry Christmas, man," he said. "What did you and Rita have for breakfast?"

"Very funny. I'm bustin' a gut, asshole," Beau said. "What am I supposed to do with this?"

Rich rubbed his hand across his face, stretched and yawned. Though it was only ten in the morning, it felt more like late evening in spite of what the sun proclaimed outside. He saw letters, numbers, and dates float around him. He and Gregory had been studying the files that Gregory had piled on his desk the first day in homicide and the files from Kendra Hamilton. What was funny as hell was that Gregory had piled them on his desk out of sheer boredom, not because of the empty promise Freehold had given to the voters. Freehold had promised to explain the drug deaths in The Pit, to really care about them, and to actually do something about them. *You don't know how right you were,* Rich thought now as he sat behind his desk.

Based on the cross, Rich and Gregory started looking at the personal effects of the women who had overdosed. All together, the twenty or so overdoses in the past two years didn't seem all that significant. But then they started noticing similarities in a few cases. In the personal effects of four of the girls, there had been crosses. They had also just recently given birth. All had been notorious prostitutes and heroin addicts. Digging further, Rich discovered five other drug overdose deaths with similar circumstances going back twenty years. The crosses were there in two of them, and they had all been pregnant. Three of them had given birth, but there was not a baby in sight. All had been poor. They had no family. *Or,* Rich thought, *the family that they had didn't care about them or had no choice but to let them go.*

Then there was Beth Rinehart. The medical files and the autopsy didn't match. The file he had gotten from Kendra said that the girl had been pregnant. But the autopsy file was not complete. Pieces were missing.

Beau asked again what was going on. Rich barely heard him. He grabbed the baseball from his desk, squeezed it as hard as he could. He imagined that the leather oozed between his fingers. He brought it up to his chin and let his thoughts run deeper. He remembered the young and pregnant teenager in the free clinic in The Pit when they went to question Kendra that second time. He guessed that these girls, at least some of them, must have been seen by someone in the clinic. The very same clinic owned by Mr. Smooth, Mr. Popular, Mr. Shiny Shoes himself—Lucas Cornelius Bertrand. And the same clinic that Kendra Hamilton worked in.

"This is giving me a damned headache," Gregory said from across the room.

His voice sounded as dry and hot as Rich felt. Rich swung his feet from the top of his desk. Still holding the baseball, he got a glass of cold water from the fountain. He could almost hear the train engine running in his head, part of the background now. It was coming up with something, he knew. But just now it didn't need his conscious thought.

"One of you girls mind telling me what's going on here," Beau asked. He wagged his big head from one side to the other, reminding Rich again of a big sheepdog.

Gregory placed his red fingertips over his eyes, then lifted his index finger tiredly toward the water fountain. Rich obediently put water into a new Styrofoam cup and walked it over to Gregory before sitting back at his desk. Gregory drank, then recounted the entire thing to Beau.

Rich didn't listen. Instead, he threw the baseball up in the air. He watched it spiral upward, the red stitches turning over and over in the air. Then he watched it spiral back down again until it fell solidly in his hand with a hard slap.

"Who investigated the Beth Rinehart disappearance?" he asked, throwing the ball up in the air again. He heard Gregory rustling through the paperwork on his desk.

"Officer Lindstrom Grady."

Rich snorted. "I should have known. Who was the detective assigned to the case?"

More rustling, then Gregory spoke. "None other than Detective James Freehold."

Rich turned to stare at Gregory. "You gotta be shitting me," he said.

Gregory shook his head. "No, Rich," he said. "It's right here." He rose and gave the file to Rich, who flipped through it and saw Freehold's elaborate signature on the police report, right next to Lindstrom Grady's.

"So where the hell is the rest of the autopsy?" Rich questioned.

"I don't know . . ." Gregory started to answer.

But Beau interrupted him. "So does this mean that we are off the Violet Hamilton case?" he questioned.

"Not necessarily," Gregory said. Rich could tell he was working to keep the exasperation out of his voice. "Remember, she had a cross, too."

"But that doesn't mean it was the same cross," Beau reasoned. "A lot of whores wear crosses."

Rich threw the ball up and watched red stitching and white leather bleed together as the ball spiraled upward. So it was Sheriff Freehold himself who had investigated the Beth Rinehart disappearance? What did it mean?

But Beau was right about the cross, of course. He was obviously smarter than he looked. Rich threw the ball up again, the wheels in his mind turning and turning.

"And she wasn't pregnant? I mean that would have had to have been like the second coming of Christ or something, right? She was too damned old."

Gregory sighed. "Beau, we've already been through this. I don't feel like recounting it again."

"So do you think we have a serial killer?" Beau pressed. "Wouldn't we have caught on to that before now?"

"All of these homicides"—Gregory stopped, corrected himself. "I mean overdoses, were handled by different officers. Some of them are not in any of the computer databases, so it could be possible that we simply missed the similarities."

Or covered up the similarities, Rich thought. *But why?*

"But a serial killer who was getting off like this, I mean

getting away with it, and only nine bodies. Shouldn't there be more—"

Slap. The ball stung Rich's palm. He let his chair drop to the floor. The sound startled both Beau and Gregory. They whipped toward him. Beau, that damned hothead, had his hand on his holster.

"Missing persons," Rich said. His voice scratched the inside of his throat. "We need to be looking at missing persons. Pregnant girls, drug addicts in the last twenty years. Not just cases where we have bodies."

Beau snorted. "Do you know how much time that would take? There isn't enough space in here to even put files for all the people reported missing in this county alone. Those damn things would probably fill a bus," he said.

"Do you know how to use that thing?" Rich pointed at the computer on Beau's desk. Beau grinned that big ole Texas-boy grin that at first had so annoyed Rich but now was a joy to see.

"Does a bear shit in the woods?" he answered. Then he scratched his balding red head. "But I thought your girl-friend Gregory over there said that not everything is on the computers?"

"Nowadays they should be, nitwit," Gregory said with only a hint of exasperation in his voice. "Bill Conners started having everything logged into a database before he got booted out of office. You may have some luck."

"See what you can dig up in the last ten years or so," Rich said. "And then I want you to do some checking on these files, especially the one on April Hart. She may still be alive somewhere out there. She's recent."

"Checking what?" Beau picked up the file with his thick hands. He thumbed through a couple of pages.

"See if you can find out what happened to the babies," Rich explained. "And Beth Rinehart. See if you and Rita can dig up the rest of the autopsy report."

"Anything else?" Beau asked. "You want me to find out the whereabouts of Jimmy Hoffa?"

Rich ignored the sarcasm. "Luke Bertrand threw a party last Saturday," he said, not looking at Beau. "I want a guest list from that party, down to the bathroom attendant. I want to find out what kind of booze he served."

"Booze?" Beau asked.

"Yeah, booze. Get me a list," Rich said. "Any news from forensics about that whiskey?"

Beau didn't answer for a moment or two, and Rich could see by his face that he was putting two and two together.

"I haven't heard anything," Beau finally answered. "I've been calling, but they keep saying they're really busy."

"Then you go down there, Blair, and stay until you get what you need, you hear me? We are already behind the eight ball on that one."

"Yeah, I hear you," Beau answered. "But—"

"But what?" Rich snapped.

"What should I tell the sheriff if he asks me why I'm doing all this shit? Or if he asks me about the Violet Hamilton case?" he asked.

Later, when it was too late, Rich realized that he should have stopped Beau right there. Should have found out what in the hell he was talking about. But he was in a hurry. Adrenaline raced through him. He put the baseball back into the golden glove holder. He grabbed his jacket from the back of the chair. He didn't look over at Gregory, to make sure he was getting ready to go. He knew that he was.

Before they left, he grabbed a brown envelope that contained pictures of nine dead girls. He also grabbed the envelope that Kendra Hamilton had given him. Finally, he looked at Beau, who stared at both of them as if he had never seen them before.

"Tell him that this *is* the Violet Hamilton case," Rich said. They left the squad room, closing the door on Beau's confused round face.

CHAPTER 21

Tess & Terry's Coffeehouse was located on that famous border between The Pit and The View. It was a narrow slice of building in a row of ice-cream colored Victorian houses marching uphill in aspiration of somewhere better than their current location. As Rich pointed the white Monte Carlo up the hilly street, he noticed houses slump as the hill descended before petering out into weeds pitted with gravel.

The coffeehouse had the inglorious honor of being the third house from the top, the very place where the slope started to descend into nothingness. Terry and Tess Miner, the new owners, had painted the coffeehouse a cheerful pale blue, the trim an optimistic pink. They had rototilled the weedy grass under and replaced the two narrow swatches of lawn on either side of the walk with Kentucky bluegrass. Along the sidewalk and fence they had planted yellow and purple lilies with long leaves that looked like knife blades.

Rich nosed the car to the opposite side of the street. He looked away from the row houses and saw the chain-link fence following the line of Victorians uphill. Beyond the fence there was a field that couldn't decide whether it wanted to be weeds or grass or gravel. Beyond that were the railroad tracks. The tracks looked ghostly to Rich, rusty and unused.

Though, as Rich was well aware, a train had not blasted through Dunhill on its way to Northern California since the late sixties, the crumbling tracks still served a purpose, and he was aware of that, too. The reason Tess & Terry's was considered to be in the poorest part of Dunhill was because it was located to the east of the railroad tracks. When people argued about which part of Dunhill County they lived in, old-timers would ask one question: "To the east or west of the railroad tracks?" And the answer would always decide it. Maybe that was why Rich and his brothers were so fascinated with trains growing up. They had always wondered what life was like at the other end or on the other side of those damn tracks.

"Lots of renovation going on here," Gregory commented.

"Yeah," Rich said, sighing. "Looks like it." But Rich didn't mention that it wouldn't do any good. It would still be The Pit no matter how many flowers were planted, no matter how many cans of Kelly Moore paint were used to cover the rotted wood of these Victorians.

"Are you ready?" Gregory asked him.

Rich didn't speak, only nodded. An hour earlier, he had threatened to take his informant Peanut and squeeze his skinny butt between his fingers until it made peanut butter if he didn't give up the whereabouts of Raymond Smalls. Peanut had believed him without hesitation and had told Rich and Gregory in an unwavering voice about Tess & Terry's Coffeehouse on the border of The Pit and The View.

"Rich . . ." Gregory prompted.

Rich sighed deeply and opened the driver's side door. Gregory followed suit. They walked up to the thin screen door of Tess & Terry's. They both knew it did indeed belong to Tess and Terry Miner because when Peanut told them about the place, Rich had called Beau. He'd asked him to get his fat fingers working on an exact address and anything else he knew about the property. Before they had traveled two blocks north, they had their answers. Rich knew more about the little coffeehouse and its supposed owners than he did his own apartment building. Beau had hung up only to call back moments later.

"What, Blair?" Rich said into his cell phone.

"Oh," Beau said, his voice fat with satisfaction. "I forgot to tell you, I have the guest list from the party Bertrand threw the night Violet Hamilton died. Big Brothers and Sisters or some shit, right?"

Rich snorted. "That was fast."

"Well," Beau said and chuckled. "I wish I could say it was good detective work, but it was mostly luck. I have an aunt who writes one of those society columns for the *Review*. She gave me the official list."

Rich sent a sidelong glance to Gregory, who watched him intently from the passenger's seat.

"Any shockers?" Rich asked. He knew that there were. Otherwise Beau wouldn't be calling him.

"No," Beau said. "Not about the list itself. Aunt Nora said that it was pretty run-of-the-mill. But it was who wasn't on the official list but happened to be there. That's the kicker."

"What do you mean?"

"Raymond Smalls," Beau said. Rich could almost see him leaning back in his chair and propping his feet on his desk.

"Shit."

"Yep," Beau said. "That's what I thought, too."

Now, standing at the cracker-thin screen door of Tess & Terry's, he thought about what Beau told him. The bartender said that Luke asked for the whiskey and the glasses at the party. Could he have mistaken Smalls for Luke? They were both the same height, and build. They both had the same coloring. If the ballroom at The Starlight Hotel was as dark as it was the night of the party he attended, then the bartender could have made a mistake.

But the bartender told him that he knew Luke, recognized him as he stood across the room chatting it up with Rich. And what in the hell was Raymond Smalls doing there anyway? He still hadn't told Gregory about his suspicions of Luke Bertrand, hadn't told him any of it. Part of him didn't want to tell Gregory what he suspected. In a way, he knew that he was trying to find something that would prove him wrong.

"Rich," Gregory said again, and Rich realized he had been standing still, staring at the screen door.

"You all right, old man?" Gregory asked him.

"Yeah," Rich said. "I'm fine."

Inside, the place was air-conditioned cool in spite of the open front door. Rich and Gregory stepped down onto a thick maroon carpet. The coffeehouse was thin but deep. Except for the area behind the coffee bar, bookshelves stretched from floor to ceiling. A gold espresso machine gleamed in the subdued light. The shop had merchandise for sale as well—novelty coffee cups and dark green T-shirts with cutesy sayings like I'M STRUNG OUT ON COFFEE. One T-shirt had an intravenous line with a bag of coffee beans as the IV bag. The words JUST HOOK ME UP were scribbled beneath it.

Gregory walked over and touched one of the volumes on the built-in bookshelves. Rich figured that the books must have been pretty heavy reading. The bindings were thick, the titles written in gold lettering.

The place was empty, except for one person. Rich noticed him the minute the screen door banged behind them. It was Raymond Smalls in a pair of jeans and a silk shirt buttoned up all the way to his neck. He dangled a cigarette from one hand and held a book open on his lap with the other. A white woman, a green cotton apron tied low on her skinny waist, hurried over to them.

"Two . . ." she said absently, scooping up two menus stacked on the bar. She was about to say something else but stopped when she noticed their faces. Rich didn't smile, and he knew that Gregory didn't, either. Though his steps were soft, Gregory walked around Tess & Terry's like he owned the place.

"You must be Tess," Rich said.

"Ummm, you guys want menus or not? We offer fifty-six varieties of coffee," she said.

Her tone was a little less friendly. Rich casually placed his hands in his pockets, which caused his holster to be in full view. She stiffened. The red blotches crawling up her neck confirmed his suspicions about the coffeehouse.

"So if you are Tess," he said slowly, "then where can we find Terry, your husband?"

The red blotches appeared in two rough patches on her cheeks. "I don't have a husband," Tess said. "Terry is my partner."

"Female?" Rich guessed.

Tess flicked her black hair out of her face. Her brown eyes sparkled with defiance.

"So?" she challenged.

"We are not here to eat," Gregory said. "We are just here to—"

"We don't sell food," she interrupted him. "Coffee, that's all you can get here. Fifty-six varieties." The words flew from her mouth as if she was trying to hurry them up so they could get the hell out. She didn't want them there.

"—just to talk to someone," Gregory continued as if he hadn't heard her. He waved his long fingers at Raymond Smalls, who had not so much as flicked his cigarette in acknowledgement of their presence.

"I don't like cops bothering my customers," Tess said.

Rich had to admit she was brave. Her voice sounded almost bold, but then there was this little tremor that reminded Rich of bubbles in a backed-up toilet. He leaned forward until he was inches from her.

"Tess," he said, smiling into her face. "You don't want to do this, do you? You don't want to piss me off."

"I don't know what you're talking about," she countered.

Rich stepped closer to her. She didn't back up. "You know damn well what I'm talking about." Even to his own ears, his words sounded as sharp as cut glass. He was tired of playing games. She stood there for a full ten seconds tapping her sandaled toe on the carpet. Finally, she swung away from them with her nose in the air.

Smalls sat in a fat armchair at a table so small it barely had room for his ashtray and coffee cup.

"Mr. Smalls," Gregory said.

"Gentlemen," Smalls replied and then took a drag on his cigarette. He still did not look up from his book. Rich pulled another chair over to the table. Gregory did the same.

"I don't recall telling you that you could be seated," Smalls said.

"I don't recall us asking," Rich answered.

This time Raymond Smalls did look up. He gave Rich the full force of his black eyes. Both their color and their shape reminded Rich of two tiny cannon balls. Rich could almost feel the arctic air emanate from him. How Kendra Hamilton didn't feel it, he would never know.

"This how you clean your money now, Smalls?" Rich waved his hand around Tess & Terry's.

Smalls touched the cigarette to the amber glass ashtray until the ash fell off. Rich knew that he wasn't going to get any answers to that question from him. Besides, that wasn't his fight right now. Rich stretched over and sniffed the coffee next to Smalls.

"Isn't it a little early in the morning for that shit?" he asked. "What is in there, anyway? Whiskey?"

"I find I have an affinity for it," Smalls said. "It's not illegal *yet*, is it, Detective?"

Rich laughed. "Like you care, Smalls."

"We were a little surprised to find you here, Mr. Smalls," Gregory broke in, his voice mild.

Smalls turned his two tiny cannons to Gregory. "What did you expect?" he replied. "To find me in a club with hip-hop playing in the background, surrounded by my homies and my bitches?"

Gregory returned Smalls's stare steadily before answering. "Yes," he said.

Raymond laughed. It wasn't a joyful sound. "Not all drug dealers are gangsters, Detective Atfield. Some are businessmen."

"I stand corrected," Gregory said, his voice noncommittal.

Rich wasn't quite sure if the tinge of respect he heard in Gregory's voice was feigned.

"May I ask what you are reading?" Gregory pointed at the book now laying facedown on the table.

Raymond shrugged and told him to go ahead. Gregory picked it up.

"Descartes," Gregory read. *"Médiations de Prima Philosphia. Meditations on First Philosophy."*

"Day who?" Rich asked.

"Descartes," Raymond began. "He—"

"—is considered the father of modern philosophy," Gregory finished for Raymond. "He argued the existence of the soul."

Rich looked at Raymond Smalls and remembered something his grandmother used to say to him. *Boy, if you continue to act up, your soul is going to start bleeding pure evil.* He, Rich, had read Descartes, but hadn't touched it since college. Instead, Rich relied on his grandmother's wisdom. As he looked at Smalls, that was what he thought of, a man bleeding pure evil.

"Man," he said to Smalls now. "You don't have to worry about all that shit. Your soul is going straight to hell."

Raymond laughed. "As usual, you seem to miss the point." He laid his hand on the book. "Although I do enjoy chatting with you, can we please get to the reason as to why you are here?"

Rich quietly and deliberately swept the tabletop free of the coffee cup and ashtray and even the Descartes book— what did Gregory call it? *Mediations on First Philosophy*— to the floor. Smalls didn't respond to the thuds as the items fell, or the black coffee soaking into the maroon carpet like oil.

Without speaking, Rich opened the envelope he had carried into Tess & Terry's. He took out the photos of the nine dead junkies. He dealt them out one after the other on the empty table. He waited ten seconds between each. He wanted

Smalls to get a good look at the death scenes, the bodies contorted in pain and the foam escaping from the mouths like final cries for help.

"And what is this?" Raymond asked. He had absolutely no expression in his voice. His face remained as vacant as a vacuum. There was nothing there. Absolutely nothing.

"I was hoping that it would be a walk down memory lane for you, Smalls," Rich said. "Do you recognize any of these women?"

"They don't look like women. They seem mostly to be girls."

"Do you recognize any of them?" Rich repeated.

"No," Raymond answered. "I don't. Why?"

"They're dead," Rich stated.

Raymond breathed impatiently. "I can see that."

"Bad dope," Rich responded. "Yours, Smalls?"

"Absolutely not," Smalls said, the words whipping out of his mouth. "I'm a businessman. How long do you think I would remain successful if I pushed bad products?"

Rich shrugged. "Why should you care? Maybe somebody in your organization made a mistake, cut in too much quinine or fucked up the mix. You had to get rid of it somehow. So what if you lost a few junkies in the process."

Smalls looked at Gregory, then looked again at Rich.

"It's not my product," he told them levelly.

"Then whose? All these happened in your territory. If it's not yours, then whose is it? The tooth fairy's?"

Smalls fired his eyes at Rich. Ever since that day Raymond Smalls had saved his life, neither of them had ever mentioned it. Rich sometimes questioned if it had really happened. But now, looking at Smalls, he knew that it did. The other man's eyes said it. They held the same threat that they had held that day on the school's playground. But instead of being directed at some hoodlum, the threat this time was directed at Rich.

"You had better check your boy," Smalls said to Gregory, without so much as sending a sidelong glance Gregory's way.

Rich laughed even though there was something akin to fear in his stomach under Smalls's stare.

"Look, Smalls," Rich said. "Don't try that shit on me. I'm not fourteen years old about to get my ass kicked, and we are not on some playground. Do you know a Cassady Moon?"

"No."

"She knows you," Rich retorted. "Says you paid her to keep an eye on Violet Hamilton." Rich leaned in close to Smalls. "Now why would you do something like that, man?" he asked as if he were talking to a favorite brother who had just bet on the wrong football team.

"I don't know what you are talking about," Raymond answered smoothly.

Sarcasm edged Rich's laugh. "Man," he said. "You sound just like your girlfriend. *I don't know what you are talking about,*" Rich mimicked. "What, you two practice your lines together?"

Smalls lifted an eyebrow. "My girlfriend?"

"Yeah, you know," Rich leaned back in his chair and crossed his ankles. "The doc. Kendra Hamilton. She the reason you wanted to keep Violet Hamilton in check? That why you gave her the dope that killed her?"

Rich had to give it to Smalls. He seemed unaffected at his words. "Gentlemen," he said, "do I need to contact an attorney?"

Rich shook a finger at him, casually. "Yeah, I was over there this morning, at your girlfriend's place," he taunted. "Must have been around four or so. I can understand why you'd murder for that sweet little ass."

The skin hardened around Smalls's eyes. He glared at Rich, who knew that the only thing keeping Smalls from jumping out of his seat and strangling him was the control he had cultivated over the years. But his hand shook slightly as he picked up the cigarette and took a long drag.

"I told you that I don't know any Cassady Moon, nor do I know what you are talking about. If you would like to continue this line of questioning, you can contact my attorney.

Now"—he placed the cigarette back in the ashtray—"is there anything else?"

"Yes," Rich said. "There is one thing. I need to know your secret, Smalls."

"Secret?"

"Yeah," Rich said. "How does scum like you get invited to a high society party at the Starlight Hotel?"

A slight smile flickered on Smalls's face. "I don't see what that has to do with anything," he finally said.

"How well do you know Luke Bertrand?" Rich asked.

"As well as most," he replied. "As well as you do, I suppose, Rich."

Rich didn't respond. It would have been useless. He was a little surprised that Smalls didn't seem surprised by that particular line of questioning. Rich scooped up the pictures and placed them back in the envelope.

He thought of the process to cook heroin. Junkies heated it on a spoon until the part they injected or snorted ran as clear as the truth he now sought. He wished that he could do that to perps like Raymond Smalls. He wished he could strip him naked, take a lighter, and hold it to his ass until he told the truth.

Smalls opened his book and started reading. He looked cool and calm. Unconcerned.

"Mr. Smalls," Gregory said. "Don't leave town. Please."

"I wouldn't think of it," Raymond answered without looking up from his book.

Rich and Gregory stood and started for the door. Tess was nowhere in sight. Before stepping out into the sunlight, Rich glanced over his shoulder. Raymond no longer read but instead stared out of the window with that same practiced look of unconcern on his face. But Rich could see that Smalls's black hands twitched as he laid Descartes' *Meditations on First Philosophy* facedown on the table.

April

Somewhere way down deep in her mind, April Hart knew that she was dreaming. She did that a lot lately, slept and dreamt. Because basically, that was all she could do. She had two choices, either stay awake and cry or fall asleep and dream. So the part of her that could have kept her awake let her be. It didn't force her to remember that she slept locked in a garden shed and cared for by the twin of Satan himself.

Some nights she continued a dream or memory that she had had the last time she slept. She remembered the last dream about the pimp who had been so nice at first before finally turning her out. But she didn't like that dream. She liked the dream she was having now better, because it was a dream of home. Of victory.

She knew it was a dream because it was more real to her than the memory that caused it. The day was brighter, the sun hotter, the gravel sharper beneath her bare feet. Her Nana, her grandmother, stood on the front porch, a fat wrinkled hand clutching the railing and just asking for a splinter. And she was laughing at April, laughing and calling her a fool for picking a fight with a chicken.

April had been after this particular chicken for about a week now. As if sensing what she meant to do, longed to do, the clucking thing wouldn't come within a yard of her. April easily recognized that chicken out of the dozen or so chickens her grandmother kept on their subsistence farm. At least, that's what the social worker who had initially placed April with Nana called their farm. "Because you are only a subsistence farmer, and have no real means of income Nana Hart, the state may have a hard time permanently placing April with you. It's quite possible she could go back to her father." April did not want to live with her father. The man was a drunk, the earliest memories of him tainted by the smell of alcohol. April remembered the woman standing on the porch where Nana was now. That day, the woman wore a silk shirt with patches of sweat under each arm, and looked as if she owned the place.

April shook all thoughts of the bubble-headed woman from her mind. She wanted that chicken. She wanted that chicken like nobody's business. Tonight she was going to have that chicken, and Nana would make soup as hearty as her laugh. The chicken goosenecked one more time and headed for a post to hide behind. A sound, a very small sound, escaped from its knowing chicken neck. It was as if the thing knew that its life depended on silence. And it did. Because the minute April laid her hands on those snowy dream-retouched feathers, she was going to wring that frail neck.

The other animals, including a rooster with dull red feathers, seemed to make room for April Hart and the chicken she was after. They parted, moved to the sidelines as if they were watching some kind of boxing match. Suddenly April just stopped, just stood still. The chicken, its moist neck hooking in and out, moved behind the post. The whole barnyard went silent. The pig Nana was raising for the fair, the cow they kept for milk were as still as statues.

"Well, I'll be . . ." April heard Nana's voice from the porch floating down to her. "Girl, what have you got against that particular chicken?"

Though April didn't answer, she went over the reasons in her mind. That chicken, with the snow white feathers and perfect red bill, just might as well be the very reason why she would no longer be allowed to stay with Nana. That day the social worker with the sweat patches under her arms stood on their front porch and told Nana that the country was no place for April. How would she get to school? There was no transportation. And since Nana had only graduated fifth grade, she certainly would not be able to homeschool her.

But Nana, her voice as soothing as butter, convinced Miss Pretty Pants to at least think about the situation. Or that's what April heard her say through the screen door as she sat listening. "I'll certainly think about the situation, Nana Hart." When April heard the social worker stand up, she stepped away from the screen door. Miss Pretty Pants walked out onto the porch as April stood by the railing, her head down and her blond curls raking over her shoulders. "My, she is such a pretty child. And she does look happy here," the woman said before turning back to Nana. "I can't promise anything, but I will try." She looked at April and smiled again.

Then it happened. That chicken, big as you please, marched up and pecked April so hard on her leg that it immediately spurted blood. April yelped. Since this wasn't the first time that the chicken had pecked her, April forgot everything. She forgot the promise in the social worker's voice and the hopeful look on Nana's face.

She dove after the chicken, chased it down the steps. But her foot caught in the last step and April fell face first in the dirt with her arms sprawled full out. She heard the screen door bang as Nana ran from the house. She heard the social worker gasp. Nana hurried down the steps, her weight making uneven thumping sounds on the bleached wood. "Child, are you all right?" she asked. The social worker was beside her, and the look on her face told April everything. The look said that this farm, Nana's farm, was no place for a child.

Now April crouched and carefully placed one foot in front of the other at an angle so her steps wouldn't make a sound. She walked like one of those Indians in those old

black-and-white westerns she and Leroy watched sometimes. And it was that damned chicken's fault, the chicken
that clucked behind the roll of chickenwire, hiding from her
in fear of its life.

CHAPTER 22

Kendra Hamilton lay in her bed for a minute, not realizing that it was still dark outside and not hearing the steady knocking at her apartment door. She lay there for a minute longer, not fully awake. It took about five seconds longer for her to realize that someone was at the door knocking with all the patience of the pope.

She swung her legs over the side of the air mattress she slept on. The room swayed for a minute or two when she stood up. She waited until it steadied before moving toward the door. She turned on every light she passed as she did so. Thinking about what happened the last time she had opened the door too hastily, she pressed her eye to the peephole but could see nothing. Someone had obstructed it in some way, probably a hand. The knocking had stopped with the first light she turned on. Whoever was out there knew that she was awake and at the door, probably trying to decide whether or not to open it. Then she heard Raymond Smalls's voice.

"Kendra," he said. "It's Ray Ray. Please open the door."

She didn't. Something told her not to, to flick out the lights and go back to bed.

"Raymond, my God, do you know what time it is?" Even

as she said the words, she realized that she didn't, either. But her fear told her it was early, very early in the morning.

"Kendra," he insisted again. "Please open the door."

Again, she heard the warning voice. *Turn around; leave it alone, Kendra.* But then she remembered the boy she knew growing up. Not the man, not the notorious drug dealer, but the boy she'd played with, dreamt with in The Pit. She remembered her words to Rich the other night, her words about not turning her back on her people. Ray Ray obviously needed her help.

She pulled the deadbolt back slowly, as if she were still making up her mind. She twisted the knob, but before she could open the door, Raymond pushed in. He fell against her. Blood, still warm, soaked through the cloth of the tank top she slept in.

"Oh my God," she said. "Ray Ray?" But it wasn't Raymond's blood, after all.

"I'm okay." Smalls stepped all the way in and closed the door behind him. A slim thread of urgency tinged his voice, but other than that he was completely calm. Confused, she looked at him standing there, complete and whole. He wore a pair of dark blue jeans. Blood stenciled a pattern up the left side of his white suede jacket. As she watched him, he grabbed the man who had fallen against her and gently pulled him from her chest.

"Where can we put him?" he asked.

She knew then what he wanted. "Holy shit, Raymond!" she said, feeling her eyes growing larger in her face. "What happened?"

Raymond's full lips twisted into a smile. "Occupational hazard," he said. "Where can I put him?"

She looked at the man now draped on his side. Blood trickled from his shoulder in a steady stream. His face looked clammy, and he shivered. Obviously, he was in shock and needed help badly. But even that thought did not make her move.

"Are you out of your mind, Raymond?" she said. "Have you finally lost every single marble in your head?"

"Kendra," Ray Ray said in a warning voice, "We don't have time for this."

"Just who do you think I am?" she continued. "One of your flunkies to clean up your messes?"

"I thought you were my friend," he said. "We don't have time for this."

"What happened?" she asked. "Who is he?"

"You can't know what happened, and you don't need to know who he is to treat him," he responded in a tired voice.

She walked up to the man. He was about a foot shorter than Raymond. His short hair looked like charcoal against the lumps on his head. She could hear his teeth clatter as she stood there studying him.

"He needs a doctor," she said.

"You are a doctor," Ray Ray replied.

"No," she shook her head. "I mean he needs a doctor in an emergency room. A hospital, Ray—"

"No," Ray Ray cut her off. "No hospitals. No emergency rooms."

Kendra brought her fingers up to her eyes and rubbed. Her head felt as if it would simply pop off her neck at any second. When she spoke again, her voice gurgled. It sounded as if she had her head submerged in a bucket of water.

"I could lose my license," she explained, still rubbing her eyes.

"That's never stopped you before," he replied.

She looked up as she recognized that tone in his voice. It was that icy tone he had used with others but never with her. He was right, of course. It had never stopped her before. But this was different, and she told him so. She did treat an occasional non-life-threatening knife wound; or fix someone up whose face looked like it had been through a meat grinder without reporting it to the police.

And her mother . . . but she shook that thought away. The fact was, on occasion she had provided treatment to people who might otherwise have received none. And for the most part, they had begged her not to go to the police.

"I could lose my license," she repeated.

Ray Ray didn't answer. As his eyes raked her face, she became aware of how she was dressed, in a tank top and a little pair of bikini panties. She folded her arms over her breasts, looked away. For some reason, she thought about Rich holding her in this very spot the other morning. She could still feel his hands around her waist, on her back. As Ray Ray stood there, with the bleeding man hanging from him like a defective limb, she imagined that he could see it, too. She saw in his eyes that she had failed him. He had expected her help without question.

A door slammed in the hallway. With the sound came the sudden feeling that she and Raymond Smalls had been involved in a war as real as one where soldiers in flak jackets carried Uzis on their shoulders. And she felt that she had sold out to the other side. She took a deep breath. Hating herself, she knew that there was one last thing she had to do for him before they retreated to opposite sides.

"Bring him into my bedroom," she said.

Ray Ray half dragged, half carried the man into the bedroom. Kendra helped lower him onto the tangled covers. She grabbed some quilts from a laundry basket in the corner of the room and tucked them around the person she had named in her mind *unidentified male.*

She left to get her medical kit and got a look at herself in the bathroom mirror. It stopped her for a second or two. She had pulled her hair back into an elastic band before going to bed. Blood stained one side of her cheek. Her tank top was soaked with it, making her breast look heavy. Her eyes looked haunted and bitter. She touched the blood on her face. It felt sticky, warm. It seemed as if Ray Ray, like Violet, wanted to drown her in the blood of The Pit. Well she didn't let it happen with Violet and she certainly would not let it happen with Raymond Smalls. She scrubbed the blood away from her hands so hard they hurt.

When she returned to the bedroom, she threw a plaid shirt over her sleeping clothes. She felt Ray Ray's eyes on her as she removed the blankets and cut the man's shirt. She rummaged in her first-aid kit until she found a pair of latex gloves. Kendra had a habit of keeping her medical bag pretty well-stocked. Besides the normal stuff, gauze bandages, alcohol, iodine, she carried catheters, saline fluid, fentanyl, antibiotics, everything she thought would be needed in emergencies.

"Sir," she said. "You need to sit up."

Ray Ray walked over to the bed and placed a knee on it. He helped Kendra raise the man into a sitting position. Blood matted the sparse, kinky hair on his chest. There was a small entry wound in his shoulder, a gunshot wound. She looked at his back and saw that the bullet had traveled straight through.

"It looks like it went straight through," she said, not expecting an answer from Ray Ray. It didn't matter anyway, because he didn't give her one. His eyes fell over her like a dark cloak.

She cleaned the wound and pressed a gauze pad against it. The man screamed and gripped the side of her air mattress. His teeth clamped together in pain. Red soaked through the first gauze pad. Leaving the pad in place, she put another pad over it. She looked at Ray Ray.

"Is he a friend of yours?" she asked.

"No, an employee," he said briefly.

She snorted. "I'm surprised you didn't leave him," she said. "Isn't that what you guys usually do?"

"So is that what I am to you now? One of those guys?" She knew he waited for an answer. But she didn't give him one. "That's not my style, Kendra," he said finally.

A few red spots seeped through the second gauze pad. Kendra didn't ask the next question, though she wanted to. And that was why didn't he just do what had to be done himself. She looked at his suede jacket. Except for the blood-stains, it was spotless. *Doing the dirty work isn't his style, either*, she thought.

When she was satisfied that the bleeding had stopped, she bandaged the wound. She started an IV, explaining to Raymond that he would have to keep the man on a saline solution for one or two days and showed him how to change the bag.

"Do you know if he's allergic to anything?" she asked.

Ray Ray simply raised an eyebrow.

"Never mind," she said. She filled a syringe with fentanyl and turned the man on his side. Ray Ray held his shoulder as Kendra plunged the needle into his thigh. Then she looked at Raymond hard in the eyes.

"You are going to help me clean up this shit," she said. "And you owe me another air mattress."

"No problem," he said smoothly.

"Ray Ray, don't expect—"

"I don't," he cut in. "And I won't, not anything from you, not anymore."

She pulled her eyes away from him, and they both gently laid the man on his back. Together they managed to get him to the living room and sit him on the couch. They both stripped sheets from the air mattress, stuffing them into two plastic garbage bags. She put the extra medical supplies in a plastic Safeway grocery bag and tied the handles into a firm knot. Kendra felt as if she were doing something dirty. They didn't speak throughout the entire operation.

She helped Ray Ray and the man into a silver Mercedes parked in the back of the apartment building near the fire escape. After they got the man settled, Ray Ray put the plastic garbage bags in the trunk. Kendra didn't walk around to see what else might be in there.

"What are you going to do with those?" she asked.

"Don't worry about it," he said. "I'll take care of it. Do you need any more help cleaning up?"

She shook her head, not looking at him.

"Thank you for your help," he said.

She folded her arms over her chest. "You are welcome," she said, but still could not bring herself to look at him.

The next day a young boy with huge pants hanging from his ass came to the door with a new air mattress. In the old days, which ironically were just yesterday, Ray Ray would have delivered it personally. She and the boy silently stuffed the blood-stained mattress into a garbage bag.

And after the boy had left, she scrubbed the hardwood floors in the living room on her hands and knees. The water was so hot, it burned her hands and turned her fingertips a bright pink.

CHAPTER 23

Two days after Raymond Smalls appeared at her apartment with a bleeding man on his arm, Kendra pulled into a parking space of Martin Luther King Elementary School. The school was a red brick one-story structure located on a slab of concrete about an acre wide. When she had gone to school there, it was minus the eight-foot chain-link fence now crowned by swirls of barbed wire. Armed guards, mostly off-duty cops, were now a permanent fixture at the elementary school. They were there to keep the drug dealers, people like Ray Ray, away.

She hadn't heard from Raymond Smalls since that night, hadn't really expected to hear from him. But that didn't stop her from wondering what in the hell he had gotten himself into this time. Who was on the other end of the gun that shot the man she treated? She told herself that it didn't involve her; she didn't have anything to do with it. But she knew that she did and jumped every time the doors to the clinic opened, half expecting to see Rich with an *I-told-you-so* look on his face. But so far, nothing. It looked like she was going to get away with it.

She looked at her watch and saw that she was already ten minutes late for Career Day. Her third-grade teacher,

Mrs. Robinson, had convinced her to talk to her class about being a physician.

The guard in the foyer, a red-headed freckle-faced cop in his mid-twenties, asked her to lift her arms. He passed a wand in front of her, then the sides and back. Another cop went through her purse. He was courteous but effective, which surprised Kendra. It was a real search and would have been funny if it wasn't so necessary.

"State your business, please," the red-headed cop said.

"I'm Dr. Hamilton," Kendra said. She tried a smile but it died on her lips. "Mrs. Robinson asked me to come in and talk to her third-grade class for Career Day."

The other cop, the one who had searched her bag, ran his finger along a clipboard. "Oh, yeah," he said. "Here we go." He was friendlier than the red-headed cop, and even gave her a little wink. "Sorry about all this," he explained. "We had a few people lately pretending to be on official business. We are just trying to be extra cautious."

"No problem," Kendra said. "Can I go up now?"

"Sure," he said, returning the purse.

Kendra walked up a short flight of stairs to the second floor. Even though the halls were empty, she imagined that she could hear the shouts and whoops of the other kids who had gone to school with her here. She felt them push around her as they loped up the steps. Except for Ray Ray, she didn't have any friends back then. She was afraid that the other kids would make fun of her because of Violet. But Ray Ray had always been there. And now she felt as if she had betrayed him.

Only her reflection in the narrow glass of the metal door at the top of the stairs brought her back to the present. She wasn't that little girl anymore, and Raymond Smalls was not the boy she knew. She ran her hand against the satin of her white blouse. Mrs. Robinson asked that she wear something professional, something that would impress the children. Kendra didn't own a skirt or blouse and had to buy the outfit, including pumps and panty hose, the day before. She could already feel the blister forming on her little toe and visualized the shoes in the Dumpster before the day was through.

She pushed open the metal door. The air conditioner struggled in the thick silence. The school was not as bad as some she had seen in other areas of the country, and not near as bad as those in Washington D.C. Luke Bertrand had raised a lot of money for Martin Luther King Elementary. His money had repaired the gaping holes in the walls and painted over the graffiti. His fundraising kept the toilets flushing and toilet paper in the bathrooms.

Walking fast with her head down, she concentrated on the patterned echoes of her high heels clicking along the polished floor. She was amazed to realize that she was walking these hallways in the same manner as she had years before as a student. Head down, eyes on the floor. How easy it was for her to slip back into those old patterns. She lifted her head only to see a figure approach from the opposite end of the hallway. It took her a minute or two to recognize Richard Marvel. His soft-soled shoes didn't make a sound on the slick floor.

She quickly ducked her head, pretending not to see him. She stopped by the door of Mrs. Robinson's room. She smelled him before she saw him. His cologne was almost overpowering. He stopped in what seemed inches from her, but when she looked up she saw that he stood a polite distance away. He searched her face.

"Doc," he said, nodding to her without smiling.

"Detective," she said, returning the greeting just as formally.

"What's this," he waved his hand to indicate the hallway. "A walk down memory lane?"

"I could ask you the same thing."

He inclined his head. "I'm here because Mrs. Robinson asked me . . ."

"Career Day?" she inquired.

"Yes," he said, and studied her. "Something like that."

They stopped speaking. A security guard walked by, inclined his head to Rich.

"Me too," she said.

Just then the door opened and Mrs. Robinson stood there. Her face was wrinkled, but her black eyes were as piercing as Kendra remembered. Mrs. Robinson noticed Rich first, laughed and hugged him. With one arm still around Rich, she grabbed Kendra's hand and shook it.

"I'm so glad you both could come," she said, smiling. Before either of them could speak, she continued. "It's about eleven-fifteen now. The children start leaving for lunch at twelve, so we don't have a lot of time, you know."

Kendra tried to break in, but Mrs. Robinson held up a finger to hush her. "Rich, you'll go first. Then Kendra. Now, the kids already know that you are a policeman, and they promised not to act up. I asked them to keep an open mind. Just be friendly. Answer all the questions that you can."

Mrs. Robinson turned back into the room, then turned abruptly around and looked at them both. "Come on," she chided. "What are you waiting for?"

Kendra and Rich walked into Mrs. Robinson's third-grade elementary class. The kids, most of them Black or Hispanic, were quiet for the most part, but Kendra heard a suppressed giggle. It abruptly stopped with one look from Mrs. Robinson. Kendra noticed that her old teacher kept the same paddle that she'd had on her desk when Kendra went to school. It wasn't that she ever used it, and legally she couldn't. But Mrs. Robinson was the type of person who would make the children *think* that she would use it. She now walked to the front of the class and began speaking without preliminaries.

"Detective Marvel is going to speak first," she said. "He is going to tell us how he became a police officer. Then you may ask questions. You may first stand up beside your desk, state your name, then ask your question. Do you understand?"

There was some head nodding and yes ma'aming.

"After Detective Marvel finishes, Dr. Hamilton will speak. How many of you already know Dr. Hamilton?" she asked.

Over half of the class raised their hands. Kendra smiled.

Thank God for The Pit's free clinic. She had seen a lot of them there.

Mrs. Robinson nodded. "I thought so. Would you believe that both Detective Marvel and Dr. Hamilton sat in this exact same class?"

"Man," someone said. "That must have been about a hundred years ago."

Everyone laughed. Kendra saw one boy in a Power Ranger T-shirt fall sideways out of his chair with laughter. Kendra caught Rich's eyes, smiled, and bit her lip. He looked at her as if deciding something, then smiled a little himself. Mrs. Robinson picked up the paddle and rapped it on her desk.

"Quiet," she said in a voice that could still make Kendra jump.

"Richard," she guided Rich to the front of the class. "You may begin."

Kendra noticed Rich walked a little stiffly to the front of the room. She looked at the children in the classroom. Some rested their heads on their desks. One boy, already an earring in his ear, looked at him as if he wanted to punch him. A girl with two pink ribbons on her pigtails didn't look at him at all. Rich sat on the edge of the desk and cleared his throat. Mrs. Robinson walked over to Kendra, motioning for her to sit down.

Rich studied the students for a moment. Kendra could tell by his hesitation that he sensed their mistrust. But still, he smiled easily, and Kendra was struck again by how handsome he was. His smooth brown skin crinkled around his eyes when he smiled; the smile seemed genuine.

"Instead of me getting up here talking," he said, placing his fingers against his chest. "Why don't y'all just ask some questions."

Nothing. Only silence greeted him. Kendra looked at the pictures lining the walls for this classroom. Mrs. Robinson had pictures of Martin Luther King and Malcolm X shaking hands. A sign saying RESPECT YOURSELF hung on the closed front door. She was reading a poster of the timetable on the wall and feeling a little sorry for Rich when a small boy with a skinny barrel chest stood up. He wore glasses so large they almost covered his face.

"Sir . . ." It was the boy in the Power Ranger shirt.

"No, no, no," Mrs. Robinson cut off his tentative voice. "What did we forget?"

"Oh," said the little boy, and scratched behind his ear. "Ronnie Watson," he said in a low voice. His eyes were focused on the floor.

"What?" Rich said. "I can't hear you, man."

The little boy looked up. "Ronnie Watson!" he yelled. A couple of the kids giggled. "What made you want to be a cop?"

Rich seemed to take his time thinking about that. "Well," he said. "I didn't always want to be a cop. Can anyone guess what I wanted to be?"

"A drug dealer," said a boy from the very back row.

The class collapsed in laughter. The boy exchanged high fives with his desk mate. Kendra noticed he had tattoos on each finger of both hands. She was too far away to read what they said. Rich held up a hand to stop Mrs. Robinson from getting up. He was laughing, too.

"No, not quite," Rich said, still laughing a little. "I thought I did, when I was about your age. But as I got older, I came to realize that what I really wanted was all the shit that they had."

The class sat up and took notice at the word *shit*. Kendra hazarded a glance at Mrs. Robinson. She pursed her lips together but said nothing.

"But what I really wanted to be was a baseball player."

"Like Sammy Sosa?" Ronnie asked.

"No." Rich wagged his head from side to side with a chuckle. "More like Reggie Jackson."

"Were you any good?" the boy with the tattoos on his fingers challenged.

Rich studied the boy before answering. "What did Mrs. Robinson say, little man?"

The boy stood up and balanced his tattooed knuckles on his desk. He placed one knee on his chair. "Marcus Jackson," he said, with only a touch of sullenness in his voice. Then, "Were you any good at it?" he repeated.

Rich shrugged his shoulders. "I was good enough to get a scholarship to college."

"What happened?" Marcus pressed.

Kendra could tell that Rich had expected the question, so she was surprised that he hesitated before answering. He looked down at the floor, then looked up.

"When I was seventeen," he began matter-of-factly, "I got shot. It was a drive-by. They thought I was someone else."

"Where did you get shot?" Marcus asked.

"Here," Rich reached down and indicated the back of his knee. "Right in the knee. The bullet went in the back and came right out through the front. The whole thing had to be reconstructed."

"How did you get shot in the back of the knee?" Marcus pressed. "Was you runnin'?"

"Yes." Rich nodded. "Yes, I was. I saw this long dark Oldsmobile, I saw semiautomatics sticking out the window, and I ran."

"Man, they probably shot you 'cause you was running," Marcus said, disgusted.

Rich shrugged. "Maybe you're right. I never thought of it that way. How many of you have ever been shot or have known someone who has been shot?"

Everyone's hands went up. Mrs. Robinson's hand went up. But Kendra kept her hands folded tightly on her lap. She felt tears sting her eyes. She looked up and saw Rich regarding her curiously.

"Okay," he said softly, still looking at her. "Go ahead and put your hands down. So most of you know what a bullet can do. I couldn't play baseball anymore."

The boy in the Power Ranger shirt stood up. "But didn't you hate cops when you were little?" he asked.

Rich waited before answering. Then, finally, "Yes," he said.

"When I was little, I hated cops just like you all did and probably still do. But as I got older, I understood that it was only some cops that I hated. You know, the dishonest ones. . . ."

"The ones that stop you when you ain't doing nothin'," Marcus said and folded his arms across his chest.

Rich ignored him. "I see you like the Power Rangers, Ronnie," he commented.

"Yeah, baby," Ronnie exclaimed. He jumped into a kung fu stance, his barrel chest puffed out. The entire class laughed again.

Rich laughed with them. "Well, what do those Power Rangers do?"

"Fight bad guys!" Ronnie said from his kung fu pose.

"Yes, that's what they do, and that's what I decided I wanted to do. When I realized that I couldn't play baseball, I decided I wanted to put away the bad guys who would do shit like what happened to me."

Marcus stood up and then sat back down. "Did you still go to college?" he asked.

"Yes, Marcus, I did," Rich said. "I was sick for a while, but after I got well I went to that same college."

"How did you pay for it?"

"Well, a lot of people felt real bad about what happened to me," Rich explained. "The other students collected some money for me. People in the neighborhood gave what little they could. That put me through school, books and everything, for about a year. After that, I worked my way through college."

"Doing what?" It was Marcus again. Kendra noticed that though he slumped in his chair with both hands tucked under his armpits, he listened intently.

"The question is what didn't I do." Rich chuckled. "I worked at McDonald's, washed dishes, swept floors, cleaned toilets. Anything somebody would give me money for."

"Toilets?" Marcus said. "Wasn't you 'shamed of that?"

"Nope," Rich said, without elaborating. "After college, I went to the academy and here I am."

"Did *you* ever shoot anybody," said a small, shaky voice from the back of the room. The little girl crouched so far down in her desk, only her little pointed nose was visible. Kendra hoped Rich wouldn't make her stand up. He didn't. Instead he got up from the desk and walked in the silence toward the little girl. He stopped beside her desk and kneeled down on one knee.

"What's your name?" he asked.

"Stephanie," she whispered.

"Well, Stephanie," he said, his voice grim. "I did. I didn't want to, but I had to or they were going to hurt other people."

"Did they die?" she whispered. She put tiny hands on the desk and hoisted herself up until she could look down at Rich.

"A couple of them did," he said.

"Oh," she breathed. "Were you sorry?"

Rich's answer was immediate. "Yes. Yes, I was."

"Did you ever shoot anybody by accident?" Stephanie asked in that same whispered voice.

Kendra felt Rich's gaze on her, but she didn't look up. Instead she fiddled with the clasp of her thin handbag, hoping that this entire thing would come to an end. Then she heard his voice.

"No, I don't think so, Stephanie," he answered.

"Oh," she breathed again. "A cop shot my daddy by accident, so I just wondered," she said, shrugging her shoulders.

"Did he die?" Rich asked as if they were the only two people in the room.

Her eyes grew huge. She nodded.

"I'm sorry," he told her.

She smiled a little but said nothing.

"Oh my goodness," Mrs. Robinson exclaimed, standing up as the lunch bell pierced the quiet. "It's already lunchtime. Dr. Hamilton, Kendra, I hope you can come back another day. I hadn't expected Rich to take that long." She turned her attention toward the children. "Go and line up for lunch, kids," she said. "I'll walk you to the cafeteria in a minute."

Kendra felt relief wash over her as the children crowded out of the door. She hadn't realized how nervous she was about talking to a bunch of eight-year-olds.

"But you didn't get a chance to speak," Mrs. Robinson was saying over Kendra's thanks for inviting her.

"Oh no," Kendra said. "I'm just glad to have had the opportunity to be here. Besides, Rich did a fine job."

"Oh, yes, he did, didn't he?" Mrs. Robinson beamed. Turning to Rich, she said, "I think you may even have gotten through to that Marcus. He's been a hard nut to crack. Would you be willing to do some one-on-one work with him, Rich?"

"Sure," Rich said absently.

"And, Kendra," Mrs. Robinson said. "Would you mind speaking at a later date?"

"Sure," Kendra used Rich's line while making a mental note to check Caller ID for the next several months before picking up the phone. Maybe by that time, Mrs. Robinson would have forgotten about this. She could not imagine being grilled as Rich had been just now. She looked at him and found his eyes all over her.

"See you kids," Mrs. Robinson said and hugged both of them briefly before hurrying from the room. Voices of excited laughing and hungry children floated into the room.

After Mrs. Robinson left, Kendra turned to pick up her purse laying on the chair. But she was stopped cold by Rich's eyes on her.

"What?" she asked him in exasperation. "Why do you keep staring at me?"

Rich raised an eyebrow. "I didn't know I was staring," he said.

"Well, you are." She snatched up her purse. "And it's bugging the hell out of me."

"I'm sorry," he said. "Your brother was shot to death by a law enforcement officer?" he asked her.

She whipped around. "His name was Adam and there was nothing lawful about the way he was shot down," she said.

"Anyway, do me a favor, and keep his name out of your filthy mouth."

"I just didn't notice you raising your hand—" he continued.

"What, you going to psychoanalyze me now?" she challenged. "Well, if you are, you should know that I'm not eight years old, and I'm impervious to that cop bullshit you just pulled on those children."

Incredibly, Rich laughed. "Come on, Doc," he said. "You think I was faking all of that?"

She didn't answer, just looked at him with a face filled with suspicion.

"I love kids," he said. "I get along well with kids. I don't *pretend* to like them—I really do."

"Well," she conceded. "They seem to like you, too."

"Somebody has to, right?" He held up his hands to her in a conciliatory gesture, and Kendra realized he was teasing her. "Look, this isn't going the way I wanted it to. . . ."

"The way you wanted it to?" Kendra asked in surprise. "You knew that I was going to be here?"

"Yes, I did. I did," he acknowledged. "Mrs. Robinson said that you would when she asked me."

Kendra ignored the little thrill of excitement that went through her. She ignored it because she didn't like it.

"You find out any more about my mother's death?" she asked him in a businesslike tone. She didn't like this new personal thing between them.

"I'll tell you over lunch."

"What?" Kendra asked.

He walked up to her and stood so close she had to tilt her head to look into his face. She wanted to take a step backward, but something held her to the spot. He put a hand on one of her forearms and gently pulled it to her side. Then he did the same with the other one. Now she was standing in front of him with her arms unfolded. He held both of her wrists in his hands. She told herself that surprise was the only reason she couldn't move.

"Look, Kendra," he said in a soft voice. "We have to eat, right? Let's call a truce until after this investigation. When it's over, you can go back to hating cops, okay?"

Kendra looked down, disturbed by his proximity and the sheer masculine smell of him. She had to fight the urge to step into him and call more than a truce. His hands still encircled her wrists, which burned all the way up to her breasts. She didn't look at him but instead looked at a spot over his left shoulder.

"Okay," she said. She could tell by his sharp intake of breath that he was as surprised by her agreement.

"But just lunch, though," she said.

He smiled. "Okay, just lunch. You can hate me after lunch."

CHAPTER 24

Standing in the parking lot of Martin Luther King Elementary, they contemplated and dismissed three restaurants. Kendra didn't want anyone to see them sitting together at the Courtroom Bar & Grill, especially remembering how Rich's fiancée had stared at her, jealousy plain in her green eyes.

Rich suggested Fat Burgers, but Kendra told him that she didn't eat burgers. And Denny's, about a block from the school, was a favorite hangout for junkies and drug dealers. Anyway, Kendra didn't like the way Rich Marvel was acting. He was standing too close, like he had a right to. And he was pushing her into this lunch. She didn't like to be pushed.

"We can always go back to my place," he said after a long pause.

She raised an eyebrow. In the distance, she heard kids spilling into the playground. Their screams of laughter and yelps of pleasure made her think of her own schooldays— days she'd had to play by herself because people like Richard T. Marvel didn't think she was good enough to associate with.

"I don't think that's appropriate," she told him, trying to make her voice sound stiff and formal.

"Appropriate," Rich said, laughing easily. "What's appropriate got to do with anything dealing with this case? Why, Doc"—he dropped his voice and stepped slightly closer—"I didn't think you were the type who cared about what was appropriate."

The lump in her throat made Kendra impatient. She put her hand on his chest. It felt hard and muscled. She pushed him away and walked around to the driver's side of the Acura, saying, "That's enough. I don't know what your game is, but I've had enough." She found her keys and opened the car door.

"I don't have a game," he said, watching her. "Do you hear what I said? I don't have a game. Look, I just want to give you an update about your mother."

Maybe it was the tone of his voice, the pleading, not-so-sure tone of his voice, that stopped her. She sighed. "Okay," she said. "Maybe we can go back to the clinic—"

"No," he cut her off. His eyes were unreadable. "How about we go back to the station, my office, and I'll give you an update. That way, it's all business, and you don't have to be scared."

Kendra slammed the door. Her heels clicked furiously on the parking lot pavement as she walked over to Rich. "I'm not 'scared' of anything," she said, "especially you, Richard T. Marvel."

"Okay," he said, calmly, his voice quiet. *"Uncomfortable.* We can go to my office so you won't feel *uncomfortable.* You know, so you won't have to explain to your cop-hating sisterhood that you were fraternizing."

Kendra sighed and rolled her eyes upward toward the blue sky. "If you are trying to gain my cooperation, Detective, that's not the way. Didn't they teach you that in the academy?"

"I know," he said. "I seem to be forgetting a lot of things they taught me in the academy when it comes to you."

Kendra didn't look at him, just let the silence fold around them. She then looked him straight in the eyes. "I'm going to pretend you didn't say that, Detective Marvel."

"Figured you would," he replied. "My office?" he repeated.

She stared at his face. His handsome features had assumed a serious look—as if he were thinking only about business.

"I can be there in about forty-five minutes," she said. "I need to stop by the clinic first."

"No problem," he said turning away and not saying good-bye.

She watched the sun spin diamonds on the windshield of the Monte Carlo as he drove away. She wished the apprehension that she felt could be driven away just as easily.

Kendra got lost inside the Dunhill County Sheriff's Department three times before finding Rich's office. She had been walking back and forth on the polished linoleum floor of the new addition when she saw Grady, who directed her to homicide.

Rich stood up when she walked in. He was alone at a desk neater than the other two in the office. There was only a file folder, a pencil holder, and a pad of yellow legal paper on the dark wood.

Rich had changed his clothes since that morning. Instead of a shirt and tie, he now wore a tight gray T-shirt. He still had on his shoulder holster, but it was empty. No gun in sight. Kendra wondered briefly if it was missing on her account.

"Where is everyone?" she asked, looking around. She didn't sit down. For some reason, he hadn't asked her to yet. It was as if he wanted to make her feel uncomfortable, despite his earlier assurances.

Rich chuckled, a friendly, affable sound. "Out investigating. Where do you think?"

"Who's taking care of the homicide department?" Kendra asked, her eyes raking his face quizzically.

"Department?" he asked. "What department? Freehold closed down the store so we could concentrate on your mother's problem."

Kendra stared at him. Her face felt still.

"Why is it," she asked conversationally, "that cops, especially homicide cops, seem to speak of death that way?"

"What way?" he asked.

"Like it's some sort of temporary problem that you can fix. I remember when my brother died. The cop told us that he was in the wrong place at the wrong time, like he would have the opportunity to be someplace else again. The fact of the matter is that he was in the wrong place at the wrong time for the last time. No one seemed to get that."

Rich smiled at her. "You getting philosophical on me, Doc?"

"I'm sorry," Kendra smiled sweetly, suddenly feeling a little evil. "I forgot who I was talking to for a minute."

Rich laughed. "What, you think I'm some sort of dumb jock?"

"I don't think anything, Detective," she said, shrugging her shoulders.

"Because I'm not, you know. I read Plato, Aristotle, all that shit in high school and college. Even that Descartes your asshole boyfriend reads."

"He's not my boyfriend," Kendra said.

"And if you ask me," Rich continued as if she hadn't spoken, "it's a bunch of crap."

"I'm not asking you," Kendra said.

"People so hung up on philosophy, people like your boyfriend Raymond Smalls, need to just pick up a Bible from time to time. That's what I say."

She didn't answer him, tried to hold back the smile tugging at her lips. Rich ducked behind his desk and grabbed some crumpled paper bags.

"What's that?" Kendra asked.

"What's that?" Rich repeated, pointing at the bags. "What do you mean what's that? It's lunch."

"Whose lunch?"

Rich stopped for a minute and stared at her. "Our lunch," he said. "Remember, I said I was going to buy you lunch."

"What is it?"

Rich pulled out two oblong objects wrapped in foil.

"Hot dogs. Got 'em from Costco on the way back."

"I don't eat hotdogs," Kendra said. She sat down, crossed her legs.

"What do you mean you don't eat hotdogs?"

"I mean I don't eat them. You never know what's in them."

"Oh I know what's in them," Rich said. He unwrapped one of the foil packages. "Sauerkraut, relishes, mustard." He held it out to her.

"No," Kendra protested.

She felt her stomach turn over. The smell was making her sick. When she was younger, she read Upton Sinclair's *The Jungle,* and ever since then she couldn't stand processed food. The thought of hot dogs was enough to make her stomach heave.

"Really, no," she repeated.

He wasn't listening. Instead, he shoved the stinking packet two inches from her nose. She smelled boiled meat and mustard and pushed his hand away.

Rich looked at her. His feelings seemed genuinely hurt.

"I was just trying to be nice."

"Well, don't," Kendra snapped.

"What?" Rich said. "Don't be nice? Now you're asking me not to be nice?"

Kendra leaned both elbows on the desk. She placed her face in her hands. "You said you had some updates on the investigation?"

"Uh huh," Rich said. He shoved half of the hot dog into his mouth.

"Do you have to eat that now?"

Rich wiped his hand on a napkin. "Now I can't eat?" he asked, pointing at the torn-open package.

"It's making me sick," she explained.

Rich screwed up his face, confused. "What are you, pregnant? Whose is it? Ray Ray's?"

"That's it," Kendra said. "I've had enough. I'll get my updates from Detective Atfield."

"No, no, no," Rich said, laughing. "I'm kidding, I'll stop." He stood up as he spoke and reached across the desk to grab her wrist. "Please, sit down."

She didn't want to, but she sat down. She rubbed her throat. "What's up with the investigation," she asked, studiously avoiding his gaze. "Did you find anything out about April Hart?"

He shrugged, wiped his hands on a napkin, and then threw it in a garbage can six feet away. Three points, perfect shot. She looked at him. Perfect. That's what he thought of himself, she was sure. He nodded his head, took a long draw on his soda before he answered.

"You know she was a whore," he said matter-of-factly. "We thought she was one of Raymond Smalls's girls, but it turns out that she wasn't. Some jackass pimp from down South. Swears he doesn't know what happened to her." He stopped, looked at her.

"We got a few leads on Beth Rinehart," he finally stated.

"Like what?" she asked.

He shook his head and took another long drink of his soda. "Nothing I want to get into right now."

"Wait a minute," Kendra said. "That's not fair. I gave you Beth Rinehart. The least you can do is—"

He held up his hand to cut her off. "Police business now," he said. "You find out anything relevant since we talked last?"

Kendra dropped her eyes. *That depends,* she thought. *Is what happened with Raymond Smalls relevant?* But she kept her mouth shut. When she looked up, she found Rich looking at her with disgust on his face.

"You ever get tired of lying?" he asked her.

"What about my mother's case?" she said.

"We have a suspect," he said, regarding her steadily.

"Who?"

"Cassady Moon."

She laughed. "Come on, Rich. You know that can't be."

He regarded her curiously, leaned back in his chair. "Why can't it be?" he asked.

"She doesn't have the heart. Besides, she loved my mother."

"She hated your mother," Rich put in. "And you had the nerve to call me blind. The only reason she hung around her was that Smalls was giving her dope to keep her out of your way. Did you know that, Dr. Hamilton?"

"I don't believe it."

He shrugged. "Believe what you want."

Kendra looked around, pretending that she was comfortable with the silence. She noticed that the room, except for the files piled haphazardly on the other two desks, did not look like the homicide team spent a lot of time there. Sharp yellow pencils and pens with their caps still on stood neatly in the pencil cups. There were no pictures on the grease-stained walls. All of the garbage cans were nearly empty.

"The place just doesn't look lived in, does it?" Rich asked her, his fingers interlaced on top of his desk.

Surprised, Kendra stared at him. Sometimes it surprised her how astute Richard T. Marvel was. Under that handsome exterior and that easygoing manner he didn't miss a thing. Nothing slipped past him. She turned away from him, growing a little uneasy under his appraisal.

"No, no, it doesn't," she confirmed. "You and the other detectives don't spend much time back here?" she asked.

He leaned back in his swivel chair, and placed a foot on his desk. He laced his hands behind his head. He seemed relaxed and gave the impression that he wanted to talk to her, really talk to her.

"We used to," he said. "I mean, you know we haven't been a separate team for that long. Homicides used to be investigated by patrol. But when we first started, we were cooking. Gregory had pulled a bunch of these cold cases. His desk"—he pointed toward Detective Atfield's desk—"used to be so covered with files that once he couldn't find his lunch for two days. But now those files on his desk are just from your mother's case."

"And you and Detective Blair?" Kendra asked.

"Me"—Rich shrugged—"I had a few things I was working on, but I was organized. Beau, though"—he pointed toward Beau's desk—"didn't have a lot by himself since he was a rookie."

"What happened?" Kendra asked.

Rich took his feet from the desk and leaned forward to look at her. "What happened?" he repeated the question.

"Yes, what happened to all the work?"

"What happened," Rich said. She didn't miss the exasperation in his voice. "What happened was that your mother died, that's what happened."

"I don't . . ." Kendra started.

"The sheriff reassigned the other cases," Rich said, "so we could concentrate on this one."

"Why did he do that?" Kendra asked.

"Partly because Luke Bertrand told him to." Rich brushed some crumbs off his desk and into the garbage can. "But I think the other was that he needs a scapegoat. One of his campaign promises was to clean up The Pit, find out why so many people are dying down there. One way to prove that he's serious is to put three detectives on this one case. And once we fail—and we will fail, Kendra, unless we give him Cassady Moon—he'll serve us up."

"You don't really believe that . . ." she started, but he cut her off before she could finish.

"I do believe that," he said, almost laughing. "This county is not big enough to have a homicide division, and he knows it. He's looking for an excuse to reverse that decision. With your mother's death, he's able to find a reason to do that and suck up to Luke Bertrand at the same time."

Kendra considered his words as they hung on the air like mist. He put the trash can back on the thinly carpeted floor. It made a hollow clanging sound. When the sound stopped, the room seemed quieter than it had been before.

"You don't have to give him a reason," Kendra finally spoke. She was surprised at how soft her voice sounded. "He won't have a reason if you find out who killed my mother."

He said nothing, and Kendra felt compelled to speak again. "Please don't just go through the motions," she whispered, not caring if he thought she was begging. "Please."

"I'm trying—" Rich began, but now Kendra interrupted.

"No," she denied. "No, you are not trying. You are sitting in judgment, wondering why you should care about a junkie. You are bitter and cynical and intolerant. I suppose I know why. It's because of what you've had to deal with, isn't it? Being a cop, working with people in The Pit, wondering why we all didn't turn out to be as perfect as you." She kept her voice level, though she could feel a volcano of anger erupting in her stomach. "The reason why you think you will fail is because you are not trying," she continued. "And you are not trying because you don't care. You don't know how to make yourself care, and I'm sorry for you. Do you have an update for me, or did you just get me here to make me feel guilty for caring about my mother?"

He remained silent, not looking at her. She could tell by the bend of his head, the muscle jumping in his jaw that she had made him angry. She had made him very angry, but he was trying to control himself. When he didn't answer her, she stood up. She pulled her purse strap over her shoulder, and folded her arms around her waist. She wanted to say something else but couldn't find the words. Instead, she did what she should have done two seconds after she'd walked in and sat behind his uncluttered desk. She stood up and walked out.

CHAPTER 25

"Make me care," he said to her, one hand leaned against the door frame of her apartment. He held the other hand on his hip. He looked comfortable, but uncomfortable, too. Kendra realized why his stance struck her as unnatural. It was so obviously rehearsed. She wondered how long he had been standing outside her door. She thought about closing it, but he must have read her face. He simply moved his body until he had one foot inside her apartment.

"Look," he cajoled, "truce, okay? I'm really going out on a limb here. I really want to understand."

She believed he was going out on a limb, but not about understanding. He had the look of a man who had decided to do something and felt he needed to do it quickly before he changed his mind.

After she'd left the station earlier that day, she'd come home and thought about exercising. She'd changed into a pair of black leggings and a white T-shirt that hugged her body like a second skin. She'd pulled her unruly hair into a rubber band, though tight curls floated about her face and neck.

But instead of doing the ritual forty-five minutes on the StairMaster, she called Maria and asked her to come over and watch *Imitation of Life* and participate in a mud facial.

Kendra had had a hard time being alone in the apartment since Ray Ray and the man she'd treated invaded her space that night. She kept seeing blood spatters on the wall, imagining what terrors Raymond had inflicted before knocking on her door.

Worse, she'd had nightmares about the condition of the man she treated. What if she missed something? What if his injuries were more serious than she'd thought? Her calls to Ray Ray had gone unreturned. She was officially, in his eyes, no longer part of his circle of friends. For some reason, she couldn't muster up enough feeling to care. That bothered her most of all.

Maria had told her that she would think about coming over to watch the movie, saying, "If I'm there, I'm there. Don't do anything special for me." After she hung up the phone, Kendra grabbed a bowl of vanilla ice-cream, turned off all the overhead lights, lit a couple a candles, and switched on a lamp.

She'd thought it was Maria knocking at the door and had flung it open without asking who it was, a dumb mistake considering what had happened the other night. *But even dumber,* she thought now, *considering who was standing there saying, "make me care."* She looked at the wooden foyer, wondering if she imagined the slight spot next to the baseboard. Her heart pounded, and she told herself that it was nerves, because of what had gone on here the other night. She tried to screw up enough courage to tell him to take a walk. But before she could speak, he touched the cold metal spoon sticking out of her bowl.

"You have enough for me?" he asked.

"Where's Dinah, Rich."

He shrugged. "Hell if I know. She hasn't returned any of my calls since the party."

"That's not good," she said.

"Nope it's not," he agreed, then repeated, "So you have enough for me?"

She sighed and looked up, and found herself staring directly into his eyes. He was so close, she could smell him. She stepped back quickly and turned her back to him. Though she couldn't see him, she felt his eyes all over her.

"I don't have a lot of time," she said spinning smoothly around on the hardwood floors to look at him. Rich didn't answer; instead he was looking at his surroundings as if he were casing the joint. She looked around, too. At first she thought he saw some evidence of the other night. She looked at the hardwood floor again, but it was scrubbed clean. She had a new air mattress and another sofa she had picked up at a garage sale. There was absolutely nothing for him to find. Then she saw for the first time what he probably saw.

Kendra lived in a two-story apartment complex somewhere on the border of The Pit and The View. It depended on who you asked as to what part of town the building actually fell into. The people of the Pit said it was part of The View, the good side of town. The people of The View said, with their noses in the air, that the barely restored stucco, vomit brown 1950s building fell squarely in The Pit. It was, after all, literally on the wrong side of the tracks.

Kendra's one-bedroom apartment was in the northeast corner of the second floor. The small foyer emptied into the living room. The hardwood floors looked cold and a little antiseptic. Kendra had placed a thin, fragile-looking throw rug near the door, but it did nothing to warm the place up. A three-pillowed couch upholstered in dark cotton sat off to one side of the room. It would have been the perfect size if there had been more furniture.

But the only other furniture in the wide room was a circular bamboo chair with a black cushion, and a TV stand with metal rails, the kind found in old folks' homes. The TV itself was a Magnavox, at least fifteen years old. Maria would complain when they watched *Imitation of Life* that Lana Turner looked green.

She watched Rich now, as he let his gaze wander around the nearly empty room. "What?" she asked him. "You act like you've never been here before. What are you staring at?"

"Nothing," he said. He wouldn't look at her. What was he? Embarrassed?

"No," she said, annoyed. "I'm curious. What?"

"All this stuff just looks old, that's all," he explained. "Like you bought it at the Salvation Army. It's like you never left The Pit."

She felt her face flame. "Look," she said. "I don't know how long I'm staying. This stuff is just temporary until I decide what to do." She blew out both candles. The smell of cooling candle wax and dying flame filled the room.

"I can tell you don't plan on staying long," he said. "There are no pictures on the wall; this place is almost empty. It's like you're just camping out."

"Detective," she said. "Did you come here to comment on my decorating skills?"

"No," he said, looking for a place to sit down. "But do you have something to drink?"

"Like what?"

"Beer?" he queried.

"I don't have any beer," she said.

"Wine?"

"No wine."

"What do you have?"

"I don't drink, Detective Marvel."

"Really?" he raised an eyebrow. "Nothing? Not even a beer?"

"No, nothing," she said. "Especially not beer. I have ice water and carrot juice."

"I'll take the ice water," he said.

Kendra walked into the kitchen and put the bowl of ice-cream into the sink. She would flush it down the disposal later. She couldn't eat it. Her stomach felt jumpy; her heart beat a mile a minute. She opened the refrigerator and put ice into a plastic tumbler.

"I hope you don't mind water from the tap?" she asked from the kitchen.

"No, I don't," he said.

She walked back to the living room and handed him the plastic cup. He took it from her, touching her fingers. She pulled her hand away too quickly. She was sure that he noticed. She was also sure that he had touched her fingers on purpose. He looked around the room for a place to sit.

"You know," she told him. "I don't know why it should be so difficult. You don't have that many choices."

He chuckled and said, "True." He sat down on the edge of the bamboo circular chair. Kendra curled up on the end of the sofa.

"Detective Marvel . . ." His look stopped her. "Rich," she started again. "I don't have a lot of time. Do you mind telling me what this is all about?"

He looked at her then—her bare feet curled beneath her, her exercise clothes, and her hair, which was a mess though she had tried the best she could to pull it back. His gaze slid to the videotape on top of the Magnavox. She had all night and he knew it. But instead of commenting on it, Rich took a long swallow of his water.

"So why don't you think you will be hanging around that long?" he said finally.

"What?" she asked.

"You said earlier that all this stuff is just temporary, that you don't know how long you will stick around."

"Oh," she said. "I promised Luke that I would work in the clinic until he found someone to replace me. And the assignment at Doctor's is just about up. I was filling in for a doctor on sabbatical."

"And then what?" he asked.

She shrugged. "I don't know. I haven't decided that part yet."

He nodded, not speaking.

"Rich," Kendra started softly, but he cut in before she could finish.

"You know, you were right about something today," he said.

She didn't speak, just waited for him to continue.

"I am having a hard time caring about this case. Usually, you know, that's what gets me going, gets me motivated. . . ." he stopped.

Kendra rubbed her hand over the smooth fabric of her leggings. She felt a lump in her throat, but she pushed it down.

"What do you want me to do, Rich?" she asked him. "Justify my mother's existence so you can get off your ass and find out who killed her?"

He didn't respond to the bite of sarcasm in her voice. Instead, he looked at her, his clear brown eyes straightforward and direct. It was as if he had come to seek answers.

"Why do you care so much about your mother? After what she put you through?"

Kendra thought about her answer a long time before speaking. For some reason, she needed to be honest with him, to give him an answer devoid of anger and the pent-up resentment she had been feeling toward cops since she was in diapers. She desperately needed him to understand. When she answered, her words came out halting and uncoordinated.

"When my mother died . . ." She stopped, swallowed, and started again. "I mean after you and Detective At . . . I mean Gregory, told me she had passed, I felt relieved," she stopped. The appalling word, *relief,* the word she had been running from since she found out, didn't sound so terrible spoken aloud. But, still, she didn't dare look at Rich's face. She was afraid of what she might find there. She started again.

"I did. I felt glad. But right after that, I thought . . ." She stopped again.

"You thought what?" he prodded gently. His voice came from only inches away. She hadn't noticed that he had gotten up from the chair and had sat down on the sofa beside her.

"I mean I thought," she said, picking at the fabric of her leggings, "I thought that everything I had ever hoped for, I mean for her and for me, had died with her. Until then I never lost hope that she could get well, that we could have a real relationship."

She looked up at him now and pushed the hair off her forehead. Still holding it back, she went on. "I know I'm not making any sense. And I know that if *I* was relieved when she died, I would have a hard time finding someone who cared about what happened to her."

"Why were you relieved?" Rich asked her.

She let her hair fall back around her face.

"Oh, come on, Rich." She smiled wryly. "I'm sure you already know that. Didn't Jiffy tell you?"

"Kendra," Rich sighed, exasperated. "I'm asking *you*, okay? Look, can we put all this petty bullshit aside and just talk like adults?"

"Okay." She nodded. "My mother came up to the clinic a lot asking for drugs. She would even come to the emergency room at the hospital sometimes when I did a rotation there, strung out and raising hell. Look"—she let her hand fall against her knee—"you probably know most of this." She paused before continuing. "But that's just a drop in the bucket compared to what went on with my mother. She was in pain. All her life. She had been on drugs since she was sixteen years old; she didn't know how to live without them and would do anything to get them. She had been in so many rehab programs, I couldn't find one—not one, Rich—that would take her anymore. She was killing herself by inches already. When I. . . . when I found out that it had finally happened, I felt relieved that her pain was over. I felt relieved for me."

Another apartment's door slammed down the hall, and Kendra put her hand to her mouth before finishing. "I felt relieved that I would not have to worry about her, about what gutter or hospital or jail or morgue she was in. Does that give me motive? Make me a suspect?" she asked, turning to him.

He didn't answer her. She gave a little hysterical chuckle. She knew damn well that it did. She turned away from him, picked out a place on the hardwood floor and stared at it.

"After that initial feeling of relief," she said, "her face"— Kendra spread her fingers in front of her face—"just floated in front of me. And I could feel her, I could smell her. And I remembered the good times, you know, those two or three weeks when she was sober, after she got out of rehab. Sometimes she would really try. After my brother Adam was killed, she stayed drug-free for two entire years."

"That's a long time," Rich conceded, his voice encouraging her to continue.

"It *is* a long time." She looked at him intensely. "It is. Even if she was maintained on methadone. She was able to work. She had this one job at Denny's, and I swear, Rich,"—she stopped and leaned closer to him—"she almost did it, almost had it beaten. Sometimes, in the summer when I didn't have school, she would let me sit in the corner and read. Sometimes she would slip me a coke. And for just a minute or two, I felt normal, with my own *normal* mother, not someone else's mother in one of those foster homes. But *my* mother, who loved me." She stopped abruptly, lost in the memories.

"She had dreams, too, Rich," she continued. "She talked all the time about moving to Sacramento, to the country. She talked about this one rehab center all the time. It was this two-story farmhouse in Sacramento with a river running behind it. She talked all the time about how the street had no traffic, how it was quiet as a cemetery. She would tell me that there were wild pheasants and geese and how the deer would walk right up to the back door when the apricots were out."

Kendra could almost feel the downy skin of an apricot, see it colored in yellow and orange like a sunset. She fell silent. In her mind, she heard the river rushing past the back door, whispering promises that never would come true now that Violet was dead.

"What happened?" Rich said, breaking the silence.

"What?" She blinked back into the present and stared at him for a moment as if she had forgotten that he was there. "Oh," she said, waving a hand at him casually. "She ran into some junkie friend at Denny's and fell back into the life again."

She remembered how Violet had kept it together for a few weeks after that first high. She remembered Violet crying at night when she thought Kendra was sleeping. Kendra touched her own face now to make sure that it was still cool and dry. She didn't want to cry in front of Rich. But the more she tried to hold her emotions in, the more they threatened to escape. She waited until she could trust her own voice again.

"When she died, I knew that she would never have that chance to live in that house by the river, and I had lost my chance to . . ." She stopped. She took a deep breath, tried to swallow back the tears. And she would have been able to do it if Rich hadn't put his arm around her shoulders and pulled her to his chest.

At first Kendra felt and heard nothing except the sobs escaping from her. She rarely cried, not while she was awake anyway. The tears came sometimes while she slept. Some mornings she would awaken before the sun came up with a headache and tears bathing her face, the remnants of some horrible nightmare.

And now, as her sobs faded slowly, she became aware of her circumstances. She sobbed in the arms of a cop, exposing a weakness that she rarely exposed to anyone. She opened her eyes and her sobs began to dwindle. She heard Rich's soothing voice, murmuring over and over the words, "It will be all right." She gave one or two final sniffles, placed her hands flat on Rich's muscled chest to push away.

But his arms tightened around her. Suddenly, her nose filled with the scent of him. His cologne made her think of green, grassy meadows covered with yellow flowers. She realized that her face was pressed into his strong neck. She felt something course through her veins with the onslaught of a sudden thunderstorm. For a moment, she wondered what it was. Then her cloudy brain recognized it as desire. She remembered feeling that way only once before, a long time ago in medical school when her virginity became an annoyance and a distraction. Two of her girlfriends, she barely remembered their names now, teased her unmercifully. They told her stories about what she was missing. She asked a close friend, a man she trusted but didn't love, to show her what all the fuss was about. She did feel a flame of desire, but it was quick as a sparkle of sunlight. The rest of the session with that boy had been clinical and mechanical and downright messy. They didn't look each other in the eyes when it was over and avoided each other for days afterward.

After that, Kendra had a couple of what some would call boyfriends, but they were really more friendships than anything. Sex was just a necessary and unappealing accompaniment. It was what all couples did because society expected it. Kendra had never been particularly impressed with the sexual experience. But, then, she had never shared anything with these other men as she had with Rich. She had just told him things she had never told anyone Not Maria. Not Ray Ray. Not Luke, and certainly not Violet Hamilton, her mother.

Kendra felt her nipples harden against her white shirt. She knew that if she pulled away now, he would know how badly she wanted him. But if she stayed in his arms like this, she would end up doing something crazy. She attempted once again to struggle upward. She didn't care what he saw. She just wanted to get away from him, so she could put her confused mind in order again.

But he only held her tighter, wouldn't let her go. She felt his hand, the one that had been stroking her back, her neck, her hair as she'd been crying, drop to her waist. She made her body still, wondered briefly if he wanted her, too. He put several fingers under her white shirt, and the feel of him on her bare skin made her breath catch. With two fingers hanging on to the end of her shirt, he pressed his hand into her side.

He began moving her shirt slowly upward. Kendra swallowed. Part of her brain ordered her to tell him to stop; but that other part, that needy part she hated scattered those thoughts. All she could hear was the pounding of her heart and all she could feel was his body against hers. It was the flash of his gold badge inside his jacket that brought her back to her senses, made her remember who he was. Who she was. She pushed him away, more forcefully this time.

"Look," she said, wiping the tears from under both eyes with her fingers. "I don't need this. And you don't have to feel sorry for me."

Rich let out a breath of annoyance. He reached down and tilted her face upward with his free hand. The other hand still grasped her side, just below her breast. The intensity on his face startled her. He was still perfect and handsome, but out of control. Storm clouds rolled behind his brown eyes, his nostrils flared as he struggled to control his constricted breath. Kendra's own breath caught in her throat. He seemed to hesitate for a couple of seconds; then, still staring into her eyes, he slowly moved his face to hers.

Kendra's own mouth parted, and she heard him groan before their mouths touched. His hand, the one that had been holding up her T-shirt, continued suddenly upward and over the slope of her breast. All hesitation gone now, he dragged his lips down her neck. Tentatively at first, Kendra put her arms around his neck. Maybe he was afraid she would change her mind, because he maneuvered quickly until he crouched over her. He kissed her until she lay back on the sofa.

When his weight suddenly left her, she opened her eyes. She saw him shrug out of his jacket. She struggled onto her elbows, but he covered her mouth before she could speak. She felt flames of sensation rush over her. His mouth was warm, and he kissed with only his lips, then suddenly plunging his tongue into her mouth. It took all of her concentration to keep up, to respond in kind. It was as if he were deliberately trying to keep her off balance, trying to make her forget what they were doing. And worse, that he was about to be married to another woman.

Kendra felt cool air wash over her skin as he pulled her white T-shirt over her head. She shivered, moved her hands upward to cover her exposed breasts. But Rich caught her wrists before they reached her chest. He raised her arms above her head, and laid his entire weight against her. She felt his erection press against her thigh, and knew there was no turning back. He whispered her name in her ear, trailed kisses along her neck. She brought her hands to his hips, but he stopped her. She didn't know why until she heard the snap of the shoulder holster.

It was the thought of that gun that brought her fully back to reality. *What was she thinking?* She moved to roll from beneath him, but he stopped her.

"Look," he said. "I don't know what this means, Kendra." His voice was thick, his eyes pleading. She detected no deception or slyness in his face. "But we both want this. Just let go for once, and we'll figure it out after."

Kendra stared back at him, her mind confused, her body humming with desire. She didn't know what to think. He reached above her head, and she heard the gun settle on top of the wooden end table. He didn't move on top of her, just looked in her face and waited. She pulled her wrists from his hand and placed them inside his shirt, caressed his muscled chest in answer.

Later she realized that Richard T. Marvel had not come to her apartment that night to talk about her mother. He hadn't wanted to talk about her mother at all.

April

April Hart had been asleep for sixteen hours straight. But she only admitted that fact—the fact that she was sleeping—to a part of herself. The other part, the best and biggest part of her, still crouched in her Nana's barnyard, after a chicken that had probably ruined her life for good.

The thing now scampered next to a fencepost, flapping its wings from its body as if it were trying to escape in flight. April stood still. Calling on every ounce of patience inside her, she stayed that way for what seemed like ages. She stayed that way so long that the other animals went about their business. Other chickens pecked at the feed scattered on the ground. The pig dropped with a splat into the mud and stuck all four hooves in the air. Nana even turned and went back into the house, shaking her heavy head as she did so.

Then finally, the chicken stepped cautiously from behind the fencepost. April would have sworn that it saw her out of its beady little side-eye. It kept that eye on her as it pecked idly at some feed. April stayed still, crouching with both palms over the ground. The chicken came to her, pecked idly around her feet. She didn't move. It stopped, too, and stared at the curious girl, the statue who was only minutes before trying to wring its neck.

As it turned to go, April dove for it. She landed square on top of the bird. Several bones snapped in the small chicken body. The chicken cackled in pain. April stood up and grabbed its neck. She jerked her hand around. The small little body went one way and its chicken head went another.

That chicken had the most feathers out of all the chickens she had ever plucked. She plucked steadily for what seemed like hours, and feathers fell around her like snow. Nana made chicken soup that night. The meat was tough and stringy, and it didn't taste good at all. But to April it was the best chicken soup she had ever tasted.

It was the taste that awakened her finally, or the remembered taste. Because what actually woke her was the phlegm in the back of her throat. For a minute, she didn't know where she was. She was sitting up on a small bed with her back against the wall. There were fresh bandages on her wrists now. There must have been something in the food that made her sleep for Sage to be able to bandage her wrists without waking her. April stared at the bandages for several seconds. They were fresh and clean, snow white. The color reminded her of all of those damn snow white feathers falling around her feet like victory.

CHAPTER 26

Richard T. Marvel believed he had gone completely crazy, lost his mind. That was his excuse for his behavior the night before. But the pure and simple fact was that he had simply given in during a weak moment. He hadn't been able to stop thinking about Kendra Hamilton since that night of the party.

He avoided his own face in Kendra's mirror. All of his life, he had done the right thing. His integrity was more valuable to him than money, more valuable than his own life. He had always been the one to shake his head at someone else's transgression, quick to judge and condemn.

And now he had acted like he had the morals of an alley cat. He bent down to the sink and splashed cold water on his face. He finally looked in the mirror as he slid his hands down. But he didn't see himself. Instead, he saw Dinah, her green eyes flashing accusingly. He groaned, clutched both sides of the sink and stood there for a minute until his stomach stopped churning.

He had awakened earlier on that damned air mattress. His back felt like someone had danced the Latin boogie on it in high heels all night long. Guilty relief shot through him when he saw that Kendra was gone. At least he would have a chance to think.

She had left a note and key for him on the small counter in the kitchen. Rich read the note three times, confusion ripping through him. Despite the night they had just shared, the note was short and impersonal. It just told him to please lock up and put the key in the planter outside. He looked around the tiny kitchen for something else, but he didn't know what. Then he noticed two pieces of crumpled paper laying in the bottom of the empty wastebasket. He bent down, picked them up and smoothed them out on the counter. Only one was complete and personal. *God Rich,* it started, *I don't know what happened last night, but we must both be careful not to read anything into it. I'm sorry I'm not there, but I had to work an early shift in the ER. Listen, Rich, you really don't have to call me if you don't want to.* Rich swallowed. Ignoring the warning voice in his head, he folded the note carefully and put it into his jacket pocket. He liked this note better, much better.

He picked up the silver key and started toward the door, but another thought stopped him. He was alone in a suspect's apartment. And she was a suspect, regardless of what he had told Beau and Gregory. As a doctor, she had access to quinine. Heroin she could have gotten from her buddy Raymond Smalls. And last night? She had admitted that she had been relieved when her mother died. Was her making love to him a smoke screen, another one of her endless deceptions? No matter how he tried, he couldn't push that thought away.

Before he knew fully what he was doing, he began searching the place. Casually at first. He opened one of the kitchen cabinets to find two plates and a chipped coffee cup. Except for a can of chickpeas, there was no food. He opened the refrigerator to find only a box of soy milk, a bottle of carrot juice, and an apple. Kendra Hamilton lived like a monk.

He walked out into the living room and stood in the middle of the floor. His eyes crawled over the walls, the brown hardwood floors. He didn't know what he was looking for and felt like an asshole for doing what he was doing, but he couldn't help it. *Put it in with my list of other sins,* he thought.

Near the door he noticed a light spot on the hardwood floors. He walked over to it and ran a hand over the surface. Someone had scrubbed too hard there. Along the baseboard, he noticed a dark thick line. His mind told him that it was blood, but another thought replaced the first one too quickly. It could be anything. She may have spilled a coke or a cup of black coffee. Except it was obvious that she didn't drink either.

He stood up and walked back into the bedroom. He saw the box for the air mattress pushed in one corner of the room. It struck him then that it was brand new. What had she been sleeping on before? He lifted the flap on the box and found something that looked like a toolbox slanted inside. He hesitated a moment before pulling out the toolbox and opening it. It was just filled with medical supplies—rubber gloves, bandages, syringes. But the funny thing was that many of the packages had been ripped open.

He flicked on the light switch located beside the sliding door of the closet. Kendra didn't have a lot of clothes. Two pair of jeans, a couple of T-shirts, and a skirt hung from the wooden pole. The pink dress and shawl she wore at the party lay crumpled on the floor.

As he was turning away, he saw a steel box leaning against the back wall of the closet. It was one of those gray and white fireproof affairs people used to store important documents like birth certificates and marriage licenses.

Cursing the impulse that made him do it, he stooped down and slid the box out of the closet. It grated noisily against the floor, accompanying his guilt like some weird background music. He half thought that Kendra would have left the key sticking out of the lock, like most people did.

But instead the silver lock gleamed blankly up at him, returning his steady gaze with a challenge. He ran his thumb over the lock. It felt smooth and cold. He could pick it easily and was going to. But something stopped him. A soft voice he recognized as his own whispered in his ear. *Open it.*

He shook his head. The words scattered like seeds on the wind. Making more noise than necessary, he resolutely slid the lockbox back into the closet. He leaned it against the wall, positioned it just like he found it. He was about to close the door and then one thought: *Fuck it.* He reached for the lockbox, but the piercing ring of his cell phone stopped him.

He listened hard to what Peanut was telling him as he locked Kendra's apartment door behind him and walked to his Firebird. Raymond Smalls had resurfaced in what Peanut called his country house.

"Country house?" Rich asked as he jangled the keys from his pocket and opened the driver's door.

He had been looking for Smalls for a couple of days now. Rich had floated April Hart's picture with some old friends in narcotics. As he had told Kendra the previous day, April used to whore for this pimp named Judah in Los Angeles. They happened to pick up Judah in Dunhill County and had shown him April's picture. Judah had laughed, said that he sold her to one of Raymond Smalls's pimps about a year ago.

"Yeah," Peanut said. "He got some bitchin' pad right outside The Point."

Rich checked his watch after getting directions from Peanut. He thought about going home to change and bringing Gregory along for backup. But he quickly changed his mind. He couldn't miss the chance of talking to Smalls. If he had somehow gotten word that the cops were looking for him, Smalls wouldn't chance sticking around a second time. He would disappear like smoke.

Smalls's country house was indeed set in the country. But it was not a house; it was a cabin built with thick, heavy logs and a stone front porch. The cabin sat in the middle of grass so green and pure that it looked good enough to eat. Flaming pink oleanders and honeysuckle surrounded the grass, making the place look like something from a picture postcard instead of a vacation getaway for a notorious drug dealer.

Rich looked around for a car but didn't see one. He stepped onto the stone porch and found the door slightly ajar. For the second time that day, he felt his integrity compromised. No car, door open. He could say that he thought Smalls was in trouble, in danger. He could walk right in, and no telling what he would find. When he was in narcotics, Rich had spent years trying to get his hands on Raymond Smalls. But no one could touch him. Still, there were simply some things that Rich was not willing to do.

He walked down the steps and stood on the last one with his hands in his pockets. The morning air was perfect, cool, just the right temperature. He could smell sweet honeysuckle and could hear birds calling to each other in the pure blue sky. Not one cloud floated in that blanket of blue. The sky was unbearably clear.

It wasn't until he felt a breath of air in his throat and the accelerated beat of his heart that he realized he was going to search Smalls's place. Shit, for all he knew, the man was in trouble. He was about to turn back to the door when he heard something on the edge of the yard.

Curious, he left the last step and went out into the yard. At that point, Rich was taken back to a moment of terror in his life that he had never forgotten, that still haunted him to this day. It took his brain a second to register the rottweiler hurtling toward him. The dog was put together so perfectly, so deliberately, that it looked as if it had just jumped out of an artist's canvas still wet with paint. Glistening black fur stretched over the muscles now rising and falling in easy effort.

Rich couldn't hear a damn thing. He couldn't remember what commands to give his body to make it run. All he could do was watch the animal race toward him with his teeth bared and pearls of spittle flying from its mouth.

Rich reached for his Beretta, but it was way too late. The

dog leapt up and clamped his forearm between his strong jowls. Rich felt as if he had stuck his arm into a bear trap. The Beretta flew from his hand and thudded on the soft blanket of grass. Rich stumbled backward. A wet growl rumbled from the rottweiler's throat, and Rich smelled sweet shampoo. The dog didn't smell like a dog at all.

"Thor, heel." The voice was deep and a little amused.

Rich felt the pressure leave his arm. He didn't stand, simply sat on the ground waiting for the ball of fear to leave his stomach. Each breath caused his entire chest to heave. He looked at his arm and saw that his jacket sleeve had been ripped off. There was a gash in his forearm that stung like hell, but he didn't think he needed stitches. He must have sat there a long time, because when he looked up, he saw Raymond Smalls shove a dish towel into his face. Rich took it and pressed it against his bleeding forearm.

"You have to forgive Thor," Raymond Smalls said. "Sometimes he gets a little over zealous, especially around strangers. I hope he didn't hurt you."

Rich stood up unsteadily. Thor sat next to Smalls, every one of its healthy muscles tensed. It glared at Rich with eyes of obsidian. Rich swallowed, realizing that the dog would spring with just the slightest indication from Smalls.

"What can I do for you, Detective?"

Rich ignored the question. Needing a moment to catch his breath, he reached down and picked up his Beretta. He placed it in his holster but left the snap open. He realized how stupid he had been to come out here without backup. Hell, the only person who knew that he was even here was Peanut. And there was not another house around for at least ten miles.

"To what do I owe this pleasure, Detective?"

Rich's mind buzzed in confusion. He was acutely aware of Thor sitting on its haunches next to Raymond with a look in its eyes that said it wanted to eat Rich alive, piece by piece.

Smalls shifted on his feet. "Can I get you a drink of water?" he asked. "Maybe that will make you feel better."

Rich shook his head. He walked over to the stone steps and sat down. Smalls walked over to him and leaned against the post, watching Rich with eyes that were unreadable.

"I need to ask you a few questions, Smalls," Rich finally managed.

"You have my complete and undivided attention, Detective," Raymond answered with an amused lilt to his voice.

"We picked up a pimp the other day; think his name was Judah or some shit." Rich pointed a finger at him. "He says he knows you."

Smalls gave Rich a small shake of the head. He still didn't understand.

Rich went on. "He said that he sold you a girl once. A girl from the country. April Hart. You know her?"

Rich watched Raymond Smalls's face. It didn't change, not by one crinkle.

"No," he said.

"Grandmother real worried about her, man. She flew here all the way from Texas to find her."

"That's too bad," Smalls replied without missing a beat.

Rich sighed. He knew he wasn't getting anywhere. He tried another tactic.

"There's one more thing," Rich said.

"I'm at your disposal," Raymond responded with a thin-lipped smile.

"Are you in love with Kendra Hamilton?" Rich cursed the question the minute it left his lips. He hadn't meant to put it so bluntly. The fact was that the dog had thrown him off-kilter.

"No, Rich," Smalls responded with a raised eyebrow. "Are you?"

Rich said nothing. Smalls sighed and sat beside him on the porch steps. The dog stayed at the mouth of the steps, staring at both of them as it licked its lips with a thick red tongue.

"Are you going to tell me why you asked that, or leave me and Thor guessing all day?"

"Tell me something, Smalls," Rich said. "Did you really pay that piece of shit Cassady Moon to keep an eye on Violet?"

"Let's say for speculation's sake that I did," Smalls responded finally. "So what?"

"I believe whoever killed Violet Hamilton was doing it for Kendra's sake. It's someone who is obsessed with her."

Raymond Smalls laughed out loud. It sounded like music in the still morning. "And you are thinking that person was me?"

"Was it?"

"Absolutely not." Raymond's face went still. He tugged at the diamond in his ear. "Besides, I'm a businessman. I do what's necessary to remain profitable, not for emotional reasons."

This time Rich laughed. "Bullshit, Smalls."

"Bullshit?"

"Yeah, bullshit. You keep that up if you want. But everyone in The Pit knows you've been trying to get into Kendra Hamilton's pants since you were fourteen. And everybody knows what that piece of shit you wear in your ear is about."

Rich knew he was stepping on dangerous ground, but he couldn't help it. He wanted Smalls to know that he wasn't as smart as he thought he was.

"And what is it about?" Smalls now asked softly.

"It was a ring when you bought it first," Rich said. When Smalls didn't answer, Rich continued. "Am I right? You bought that ring right when you started making it big because you were going to ask Kendra Hamilton to marry you. What happened, Smalls? Did she say no, or did you chicken out? Did you even have the guts to ask her?"

The careful cool Raymond Smalls always kept in his face shattered like ice. He grabbed Rich's lapel jacket and pushed him against the porch railing. Thor jumped and went for Rich's ankle, but Smalls held up a hand to stop him. Rich would have knocked his hand away, and gone for his gun but knew he would be dog food before he could get a shot off.

"I never took you to be a stupid man, Richard *T.* Marvel," Smalls now said softly. "But the last month or so, I have to say that I've changed my opinion of you. You are all talk, all spit and shine, but no substance. You don't see anything that's not painfully obvious. It's no coincidence that you are being found out for the fraud that you are."

"Don't do anything stupid, Raymond." Rich breathed.

Smalls's eyebrow lifted. "Oh, so it's Raymond now. Are we friends?"

He jerked Rich back and forth when he said this last. Thor stood up and paced in front of the steps. The dog finally placed a paw on the step and stuck its muzzle an inch from Rich's face. Its lip quivered upward as it growled.

"If we are friends, let me give you a piece of advice. You are looking too far from home for Violet Hamilton's murderer."

"Did you kill Violet Hamilton?" Rich asked him.

Smalls looked into Rich's eyes, and Rich winced. For the first time he saw something behind Smalls's eyes, something that the man had spent the better part of his life trying to hide. Anger flamed in them, anger as pure and as hot as hell.

"Listen to what I'm saying," Smalls said softly. "Too far away from home. Much too far," he repeated.

He let Rich's lapel go, and Rich tottered against the porch railing. Smalls stood up abruptly.

"Come, Thor," he said.

The rottweiler whimpered.

"Thor," Smalls commanded again.

Rich stood up, both of his legs feeling like rubber bands. He stepped out onto the carpet of grass. The closer he got to his Firebird, the calmer he felt. Raymond Smalls was crazy. He'd killed Violet Hamilton because he was obsessed with Kendra Hamilton. But did he? *Look closer to home,* he had said. What did he mean by that? *Kendra? Luke?*

Rich placed his hand close to his weapon. He could feel two sets of eyes on his back. He knew that Raymond Smalls might try something, might not let him get out of there alive.

"Rich."

Rich spun around. Raymond looked at him curiously, his head tilted to one side. "Living out in the country as I do, I sometimes neglect to lock my door."

"Good for you," Rich retorted, a line of tired anger shooting through him.

"I really hope you did not make yourself at home," Raymond said.

Rich grinned, shrugged. "Maybe I did, maybe I didn . . ."

Before he finished speaking, he saw Thor's body release. The dog rushed toward Rich with ferocious glee, his eyes shining with anticipated satisfaction.

This time, Rich's body knew exactly what to do. He pulled the Berretta from its holster but before he could fire, he heard Raymond's sharp voice. "Thor heel." The dog stopped almost in mid-air and his paws fell heavily onto the green grass.

Rich looked up, the gun still drawn. He and Raymond stared at each other. Rich knew what Raymond meant to communicate by that hard stare. Raymond was telling him, through Thor, that Rich was at his mercy. Raymond could kill him—or have him killed—anytime he wanted. When Raymond was sure Rich got his message, he chuckled, shook his head slightly. Then he turned and walked through the open door of his country house.

Raymond Smalls had let him walk away. Rich wasn't really surprised. Smalls had sicced Thor on him because he was angry at the thought of Rich prowling around his house when he wasn't there. But the man wasn't a fool. Even he couldn't run away from the death of a police officer. Sheriff Freehold would never allow it. Rich wasn't a fool, either. He knew that he wouldn't get anywhere if he tried to pull Smalls in for the attack. Besides a dog that wanted to kill him, Rich really had no proof. Smalls, with his platinum gold lawyers, would squirm his way out of it.

Blood flowed freely from the wound in Rich's arm. He took a look at it again, debating whether to take a trip to Doctor's. He was about to start the car when his cell phone rang again. This time it was Sheriff Freehold, not Tammy his secretary, but the man himself.

"Where the hell have you been, Marvel?" he asked before Rich could even croak out a hello.

"What do you mean?" Rich snapped. He no longer cared that the man held his career in his meaty palms. His arm stung, and he craved sleep.

"I've been trying to get in touch with you all night. Where have you been?"

Rich ignored the question. "How can I help you, Sheriff?"

"Oh, so now we are all respectful, huh?"

Rich didn't answer. He let the silence stand.

"Well," Freehold said finally. "I hear we got a murderer in Violet Hamilton's case."

Rich swore under his breath. Where did Freehold hear that? It had to be Grady. That old cop had worked for the sheriff's department so long he probably knew about the arrest before Rich did. Rich forced a chuckle

"Don't call Channel Ten quite yet, Sheriff," he said. "Cassady Moon is just a material witness. She's not a suspect."

Sheriff Freehold grunted, then changed the subject.

"There are a couple of corpses in the Elephant's Graveyard I need you to take a look at."

"I don't . . ."

"I know the patrol division usually handles this, but Sandy's got his hands full out there. We could use some experience on this. Looks like a drug hit."

Rich knew Detective Sanders and had recently heard that the man had been promoted to a team lead. Rich's head began to pound. There was something else going on here, something Freehold hadn't told him yet.

Rich rubbed his tired eyes. "Sheriff, you can't expect me to drop the Violet Hamilton case and jump over to—"

"There isn't a Violet Hamilton case anymore. It's cleared. You made an arrest, remember?"

Rich's blood turned to ice. "You care to explain this to me?"

"Cassady Moon has just been charged. The Violet Hamilton case is closed. Get your ass over to the Elephant's Graveyard. Now."

"That's bullshi . . ." Rich stopped.

The line was dead. Sheriff Freehold had hung up.

CHAPTER 27

He went home after talking to Sheriff Freehold. He showered quickly, bandaged his wound, and tried reaching Kendra. When he received no answer, he dressed in a fresh pair of jeans and a sports coat and tried to call her again. Still no answer. He took the note she had written him that morning and stuffed it in his breast pocket. He left his apartment and drove to the squad room to pick up Beau for the drive out to the Elephant's Graveyard.

Gregory didn't want to come along. He opted to stay in the office to continue his work on the Violet Hamilton case. He had both crosses weaved through his bone-thin fingers. He was calling drugstores and dime stores to figure out where they could have possibly come from. Rich didn't tell him about his conversation with Sheriff Freehold. Rich had no intention of dropping the case. Based on what Beau had found lurking in the sheriff's department databases, Rich knew that all the cases were linked, that they might even have a serial killer on their hands.

Beau was able to locate the files for over a hundred unresolved missing-person cases in the last ten years. He immediately discounted the seventy or so men. That left thirty females. Out of those thirty, twelve had not been of childbearing years. Beau then took the remaining eighteen and cross-referenced them with the files from other counties, and learned that fifteen of the women had turned up in other places. Some in jail, some gone home to their families. That left three women of childbearing years still missing in Dunhill County. All three of these women had been seen at The Pit's free clinic and were in the files Kendra had given them. It helped that these three women had given their real names when they went to the clinic for treatment. They all had been pregnant. Beau contacted their families, who didn't give him much in the way of their whereabouts.

"They gave me a big fat zero, dude," Beau had said.

"Did you find out anything more about April Hart," Rich asked.

"Only what you found," Beau grunted. "I found out from a friend in investigations that a grandmother wearing a steel-colored wig and an Aunt Bea dress reported the girl missing. She's from the good old state of Texas."

"What does that have to do with anything?" Rich asked, amused in spite of himself.

"She was raised on a farm, Rich, so far out in the hot Texas countryside I'm sure the armadillos were bused in. How could she get messed up in something like this? I think her grandma is sniffing up the wrong tree looking for her out here in Dunhill."

"Except Judah placed her in Dunhill, remember? Raymond Smalls?"

Beau snorted a laugh. "Look," he said. "I know how you boys depend on informants, but I ain't there yet. This Judah could be just tellin' you what you want to hear to keep his ass out of jail."

"You get hold of the grandmother?" Rich changed the subject. He wanted to tell Beau that the look on Raymond Smalls's face when he'd questioned him about April Hart placed her right here in Dunhill. Grandma was indeed barking up the right tree.

"Yep. And Grandma told me the same thing she told your

doc. The last time she heard from her she was down South, in Los Angeles or somewhere. She said the girl wasn't on drugs or anything. Then nothing from her for eleven months."

"What about Beth Rinehart?" Rich asked. "Were you able to find the missing pages from the autopsy report?"

"Yep. Sounds like a screwup in paperwork or somethin'," Beau answered slowly.

Rich glanced over at Beau and saw his mouth work up and down. Rich could tell that he was bothered and trying to justify something to himself.

"Anyway." Beau sighed. "Rita keeps a set of her own files, a copy of each one of the autopsy reports in case they get lost somewhere. We found Beth Rinehart's. She wasn't pregnant when they found her, but she had just had a baby."

"Shit," Rich whispered.

Gregory let out a low whistle.

"Yeah, shit," Beau echoed. "And if you don't like that, you sure as hell ain't gonna like the fact that I still can't get anything out of forensics. They said they are just way behind, maybe two or three weeks before they could have something for us."

Rich said nothing. He was not surprised. He would have asked the sheriff to run some interference, but to him, the case had been closed. Sheriff Freehold wanted the Violet Hamilton case over and done with.

As he and Beau drove to the crime scene, Rich remembered how much he hated outdoor crime scenes. Weather, animals, both two-legged and four-legged, had all kinds of chances to fuck with the evidence. But he hated something even more than outdoor crime scenes—he hated it when the crime involved a part of town known as the Elephant's Graveyard.

"The Elephant's Graveyard?" Beau asked him. "What in the Sam hill is that?"

Rich didn't answer, still thinking about what Beau had said back at homicide.

"Hey, asshole, I'm talking to you."

Beau's voice and the smell of salami interrupted Rich's thoughts. He steered the Monte Carlo along the stretch of highway, watching the trees whip by as he answered Beau.

"The Elephant's Graveyard, Beau, my man, is where washed-up drug dealers come to die."

"Oh," Beau said.

Rich could tell that Beau still didn't understand. He slowed the car to a stop and parked in a dirt area on the side of the road. The place was a commute corridor for people who knew the area well enough to take the back roads in and out of the Bay Area. It didn't look like anything special. Yellow weeds, more gravel than dirt. People drove by here every day, not knowing what existed in the ditch below this two-lane road.

Rich slammed the car door and stood beside the car for a minute. He could feel sweat under his armpits, and his jeans had started to stick to his legs. He closed his eyes, put both hands on his lower back and stretched. He heard a bird calling—it sounded like a crow—and water trickling in the valley below. Or at least that was what he chose to hear. He ignored the quiet hum of voices floating up to him and the smell of exhaust from the vehicles zooming along the road behind him. He opened his eyes. The crow he had heard earlier glided across the sky, laying its wings on the heavy air like he owned it. Beautiful for probably the only time in its life.

The double doors on the coroner's wagon were flung open, ready to be fed. But Rita Sandbourne was nowhere in sight. Sheriff Freehold had told Rich that there were two victims, a young female along with an older male.

"What's the hell wrong with you, man?" Beau asked.

Rich stretched one more time before answering. He bent all the way over until the blood rushed to his head.

"My back is killing me," he responded. He didn't say anything about his arm, only checked quickly to make sure that he hadn't bled through his bandages.

"Oh," Beau said. "Maybe you should let Doc Hamilton on top next time."

Rich made an effort to keep his face still. "Did I ever tell you what an asshole you are, Blair?"

"Many times."

"Good, just checking," Rich said. He took a deep breath, quickly changed the subject. "Don't you just love that smell?"

"The smell of what?" Beau asked.

"A real murder scene, not some nebulous *I-wonder-if-somebody-did-it-on-purpose drug overdose,* but a real live crime scene with bullets and victims and perps. . . ."

"Why are you so ornery? What *is* wrong with you, man?" Beau asked again from behind him.

Rich had started to walk toward Officer Franklin, who was guarding the path to the valley floor beneath them.

"What do you mean?" Rich asked over his shoulder. "Two people are dead. What in the hell do you think is wrong with me?"

"You been walking around for the last three or four days with that sour-ass look on your face. Ever—since—" He stopped suddenly, then his broad red face broke into a smile. "Ever since your girlfriend's party."

Rich didn't like the grin on Beau's face. "Look, man," Rich explained. "I'm stressed. I got a wedding to plan, and my career's going to shit."

"No, you are not stressed, Rich," he said. "You are conflicted. When are you going to tell that pretty little thing of yours that you got eyes for the good doctor?"

"I don't know what you're talking about, man," Rich said.

Rich did know what he was talking about. He couldn't get Kendra Hamilton off his mind, and he had to admit that he had been what Beau called sour lately. He had been sour right up until the time that he walked up to Kendra's door and said, "Make me—"

"Yes, you do," Beau boomed from behind him. "I seen

you two dancing. I thought that—what's her name?" Beau asked.

He ignored Beau's bait. He wouldn't get into a discussion about his love life with Beau Blair. He was thinking about what he had found in Kendra's apartment, the lockbox, the stain on the floor. She was hiding something. He was sure of it. But what?

"Hey," Beau interrupted his thoughts again. "I said what was her name?"

"Whose name?" Rich snapped.

"Your fiancée?"

"Dinah, Beau." Rich sighed. "Dinah."

"Yeah, Dinah," Beau nodded. "I thought she was going to scratch Kendra Hamilton's eyes out that night."

Rich didn't answer. Instead he thought about how in the hell he was going to get rid of Beau today. He didn't feel like his nonsense.

"Detectives," Officer Franklin said, the brim of his head cover slick and shiny. "I'm sorry I can't let you down there. I have strict orders from Detective—"

"Hey Marvel," a voice cut him off. "Get your ass down here."

Rich recognized the voice immediately, Detective James Sanders. He could see only the man's torso and balding head. Even in this heat, Sandy wore a tweed wool jacket with a white shirt and a fat seventies-looking polyester tie. His ears stuck out from the sides of his narrow face like two tiny flags.

He worked with Detective Sanders, nicknamed Sandy because of his brushed yellow skin as well as his name, in narcotics. They weren't great friends, but sometimes Rich had a beer with him and his wife after work.

"Come on, big man," Rich said to Beau.

He pretended he didn't notice Beau's hesitation. Instead, two thoughts entered Rich's mind as he looked down the steep hill below. Thought number one was how in the hell would they get the bodies out of here? And thought number two was how in the hell was he going to navigate the steep hillside gracefully enough not to slip and slide to Sandy's feet like a big lump of melted chocolate?

"Ain't there another way down?" Beau asked.

"Nope," Rich answered. "One way in and out of a crime scene. You should know that, Blair. You don't want to disturb any evidence, do you?"

"How about not wanting to fall on my ass?" Beau complained.

Rich stopped and turned around to face Beau. "If you do fall," he said, "just fall around me, would you?"

"Yeah," Beau said, hitching up his Wranglers. "Doc Hamilton wouldn't want anything to happen to that pretty face of yours."

Rich took a step forward, but stopped when he heard Sandy's voice again.

"Marvel?" Sandy yelled. "You coming?"

"Okay, okay, I'm coming," Rich answered.

He turned sideways and slid the first few steps. Then he regained his footing and inched down the hillside. Beau grunted and cursed behind him. Eventually they made it to the bottom of the hill. A narrow band of land hugged a shallow creek. Brown, muddy water trickled over flat rocks and beer bottles. Rich watched the water weave itself over and under the rusted spokes of a bicycle tire. Yellow weeds covered the hillside in some places. In others, bushes clung to the soil by their very roots. Thin trees struggled out of the ground and leaned like crooked fingers toward the muggy sky.

Rich looked around him and saw six uniformed officers combing the scene. Paper bags and yellow markers grew among the weeds like they were indigenous to the area. Instead of shaking hands, Sandy gave both Rich and Beau pairs of latex gloves.

"Just in case you want to get closer." He grinned at them. Addressing Rich, he asked, "Who's the big guy?" and pointed at Beau, who had his eyes fixed on the bodies. At first Rich thought it was because Rita was stooped over one of them. But then Rich noticed Beau's eyes. They were wide and wet, and Rich knew it wasn't from the heat.

"That's my partner," Rich said. "Beau Blair."

"Hi," Beau croaked, splaying gloved fingers at Sandy.

Sandy regarded Beau for a moment. "My wife's telling me you been hacking into the computers?"

"You must have the wrong person." Beau grinned. He had regained his composure.

"Wrong person, shit," Sandy said. "You left your finger-prints all over the fucking place."

"Good going, Blair," Rich said disgustingly.

"If you need something, why don't you just ask, Rich?" Sandy questioned.

"I want to keep it quiet for a while," Rich explained. "If you know what I mean, man."

Sandy looked at him for a moment or two and nodded in a way that told Rich he knew exactly what he meant. Besides, Sandy owed him some favors.

"What we got?" Rich asked abruptly.

"Ah, looks like a drug hit," Sandy said. "The man's been tortured."

He pointed to a man, sprawled on his back, with a shock of black hair. Blood matted the hair into thick ropes which flopped over the dead man's forehead. Rich guessed he prob-ably had a bullet under that Elvis Presley do. Both arms were thrown above his head, his hands disappearing into the water.

"Somebody cut off the fingers of his right hand, probably before they killed him," Sandy continued.

"What about the girl?" Rich asked.

About three feet from him, a young girl was curled into a fetal position near the base of a tree. She was blond, bare-foot, and almost as tiny as Rita, who was now examining the body.

Rita, wearing a tight T-shirt and a pair of navy blue jeans

on her pencil-like body, stood up and sauntered over to them. She said hello to Rich but simply nodded at Beau.

"They've been dead a couple of days," she explained. "The male's not a dump job."

"What?" Rich said. Usually, dealers killed their victims elsewhere before dumping their bodies here.

"He was killed here," Sandy said. "Somebody wanted him to think long and hard about his fuckup. They let him bleed to death here."

"Bleed to death?" Rich asked, confused.

"It looks like they cut the arterial vein in his thigh before they pushed him down the hill," Rita said.

Sandy pointed toward some bent weeds. Rich could see yellow markers curving up the hill.

"But you never gonna believe this," Sandy chuckled. "The son-of-a-bitch had a gun down his pants, a tiny one no bigger than this." He held out his thumb and index fingers to demonstrate. "He got a shot off. He hit somebody, because there is blood spatter on some plants near the top of the hill. And if that ain't enough, I've got somebody up there digging a bullet out of that tree."

He pointed to a sickly redwood near the top of the hill. It was a surprise that the damn thing hadn't shattered in two when the bullet hit.

"So you're looking for somebody wounded," Rich said. "You checking hospitals?"

"Got somebody on it now, for all the good it'll do me."

Rich nodded. People like that usually didn't get patched up in hospitals. If the wound was bad enough, he and Sandy would most likely be looking at another corpse in a couple of days.

"And the girl? Was she killed here, too?"

Sandy shook his head and sighed. "Nope," he said. "She was done clean, a shot to the back of the head. And there is something else, Rich."

"What?" Rich said, even though he had a sneaking suspicion.

"She's only fourteen years old," he explained.

"What?"

Sandy handed him a Ziploc bag. Rich took it and pressed the plastic against the laminated card inside. It was a blue and white Oakland High School student ID. The name on it said Emily Smythe. A girl in black lipstick and an earring in her eyebrow smiled at him.

"We found ID on him, too," Sandy said. "His name is Gerald Smythe. I'm guessing daughter, not wife."

"Oh, Jesus." Disgust and anger filled Rich. Smythe. Smitty. He was Cassady's Smitty, her supplier.

He turned away from Sandy and the bodies in the river. He thought that if he just closed his eyes for a minute, he could imagine a normal wood without bodies and bullets and beer bottles for creek beds.

"That's pretty sick," Beau said, his voice thick. "Why would anyone do that?"

Rich turned back around to face him.

"Drug hit," he said, his face feeling unnaturally tight. "He's probably a dealer, and he made a mistake. He probably lost somebody money, or he probably lost some dope. It's like putting a thief's head on a spike in the town square. It keeps the other thieves from thinking they can make the same mistake and get away with it."

"It's still sick . . ." Beau started.

"Sandy," Rich broke in, "looks like you got everything under control. What do you need from me?"

"Well . . ." Sandy sighed and hitched up his pants. "I'm pretty sure Gerald is one of Raymond Smalls's boys. I heard you and Gregory had a run-in with him. Just wanted to know if you knew anything about this?"

"I don't," Rich said shortly. "What else?"

"Could you and Gregory have said something to Smalls that got him worked up enough to do this?"

"No," Rich said, not looking at Sandy.

He felt Sandy's eyes on him again, and it made his entire face flame. Sandy wasn't buying it, but Rich knew he wouldn't press. Not yet, anyway. Sandy didn't continue speaking until Rich looked at him.

"I could use some help on this too, Rich. We're short-handed. We need some people to help check out the hospitals and somebody to help with questioning. Anyway, I'd figured you could spare somebody since all you got is that Violet Hamilton thing. . . ."

"That it?" Rich asked, feeling sicker than Beau looked at that point. *Could you and Gregory have said something to Smalls . . .*

"Well, yeah," Sandy mercifully cut into his thoughts.

"You can have Beau," Rich said.

"But, but, but," Beau said to Rich's back.

And he had to say it to his back, because Rich advanced up the hill in long, clumsy steps. He almost fell twice and had to grab the ground with both hands to keep from falling flat on his stomach.

"Hey, hey, hey!" Beau yelled.

At first, Rich had decided to ignore him, but something in Beau's voice made him turn around. He stood halfway up the path. Beau stood at the bottom looking at him expectantly.

"What?" Rich snapped.

"Come here for a second," Beau said, not moving.

Rich was about to protest, but Beau's face stopped him. He slid down the hill until he stood face to face with the other man.

"You dropped this up there when you were doing your yoga exercises."

He held out a piece of pink paper, the note Kendra Hamilton had written him earlier that morning and the one he had shoved in his jacket pocket for what purpose God only knew. He snatched the note from Beau. He could tell by the look on the asshole's face that he had read it. He pointed a finger at Beau, started to say something, then changed his mind again.

When he reached the road, he leaned against a tree and vomited. A fourteen-year-old girl was dead because of him, because of something he did. If he wasn't convinced before that Raymond Smalls was a ruthless killer, he was convinced now.

Rich fishtailed the Monte Carlo back onto Johnson's Road. It took fifteen minutes for him to get back to Raymond Smalls's place in the woods. Normal speed would have gotten him there in forty-five, but he put the sirens on and weaved in and out of traffic until he reached the cabin. He didn't let himself think what Sandy would do to him if he fucked up his case. But now, it was personal.

The place was deserted, no cool Raymond, no snarling Thor. Rich leapt onto the porch, pounded the door until his hand stung. He shouted Smalls's name until he was hoarse. But there was nothing. Only silence. And when he kicked the door open, the perfectly placed furniture reminded him of a picture in a magazine. Cold as hell. And empty.

CHAPTER 28

Rich used to visit the train station with his father when he was a kid. His father—an old man even then—would tell Rich about the old days when the trains ran like an executioner's watch. Rich was the youngest of his three sons, and though his Pops was too tired to throw a baseball with him, his eyes would light up at the train tracks. He told Rich how they brought workers from San Francisco to work in Dunhill's fabrication plants or shipped canned goods to the East from Dunhill's two canneries.

The gravel Rich now stepped on used to be a paved parking lot. The weeds he crushed beneath his feet used to be under six inches of tar and rock. Even when he sat on the bench with his too-old father, the pavement had already begun to crack and the weeds had started to move in.

Now, over twenty years later, Rich walked to the edge of the platform and the place looked the same, only slightly more decrepit. Gregory, the sleeves of his white shirt rolled up, straddled a green bench. Two cups of coffee in Styrofoam cups and a brown bag stained with grease were balanced on the peeling paint.

"Donuts and coffee?" Rich said as he sat.

"I know," Gregory smiled. "A little bit of a cop cliché. I thought you might be hungry."

"You haven't been here long," Rich commented while taking the top from the coffee. He watched the white smoke disappear in the air around him.

"No," Gregory smiled and blew on his coffee.

"Why here?" Rich said.

"I don't know," Gregory looked around the railway station. "It's where Brock Gordon wanted to meet. He said that he always takes his lunch here and he was not changing it for us."

Yes, good old Brock Gordon, Rich thought. He had no idea who this guy was, but Gregory seemed to think that he could shed some light on the cross that Violet Hamilton and the other girls wore. Gordon was a buyer for a retail drugstore chain. Gregory had learned about him when doing his research on the cross and had set up a meeting here of all places.

"Besides," Gregory interrupted his thoughts. "You once told me that you liked coming here as a child."

"Liked, Gregory," Rich said. "Past tense. Besides, it was the company, not the place."

He shrugged his shoulders. "Oh well, it's good to get away from the office anyway."

He then slurped his coffee. Gregory was not a very graceful eater. He slurped his coffee, his soup, and his Jell-O when he had it, especially when he was nervous.

"What do you think about our April Hart," Gregory asked him now.

Rich tested the coffee with the tip of his tongue. It was hot, but not burning.

"Probably the same thing you do," Rich replied. He looked into the bag, and quickly closed it again. Usually, he had a pretty stable stomach, but he didn't know if he could handle a jelly-filled donut after the scene at the Elephant's Graveyard. Not today.

"You think he's killed her?"

Rich licked his lips and said nothing. Neither one of them had said what was paramount on both of their minds. Neither one of them had said who *he* was yet. The running argument had been either Smalls or Luke these last few days. Rich felt a pulse jump in his jaw. He didn't want it to be Luke. Gregory bent his head to one side and studied Rich.

"He has the only connection to them, Rich. The missing girls were seen at his clinic at one point or another for things like well-baby checkups or methadone treatments. And his alibi, Rich . . ."

"What about Smalls?" Rich interrupted quietly. He still wasn't convinced himself. Not yet. There was a part of him that would not let himself be convinced. "Those girls were heroin addicts. They also had connections to that bastard. He could have given Cassady the dope. "

"The bourbon," Gregory said softly. "And those glasses."

Rich's head whipped around to look into Gregory's face. "Forensics came back finally?" he said.

Gregory licked his lips. "Not exactly," he said.

"What do you mean, not exactly?"

"I went down there myself and took a whiff." Gregory almost laughed. "That was some very expensive stuff." His voice turned serious. "It's the same stuff, Rich, the stuff at Luke's party the night Violet Hamilton died."

Rich slowly nodded, willed his soul to be still. When he spoke, his voice was soft and quiet.

"I don't think your nose is admissible in court," Rich said. "Besides, Raymond Smalls was drinking bourbon at Tess and Tabby's. He was also at that same party."

Gregory smiled. "Tess and Terry's, Rich."

Rich stood up. "Whatever," he said. "Why are you so willing to pin this on Luke? It could have been Smalls or . . ." He stopped.

"Or Kendra," Gregory finished for him.

Gregory didn't say anything for a moment or two. Rich

sat down on the bench, ignoring the twinge of pain in his back.

"And there is the problem with Luke's alibi, Rich," Gregory persisted.

"What problem?"

Gregory sighed, stood up until he faced Rich. He told him that he had questioned Luke's party guests. Luke had disappeared between the hours of eight and ten that night. No one remembered seeing him.

"What about the girlfriend?" Rich asked

"The girlfriend?" Gregory raised an eyebrow.

"Yeah," Rich said. "The blue-haired lady the bartender told me about. You know, the one with the sagging tits? The ass-candy?"

Gregory nodded. He told Rich how he did talk to this one woman who swore Luke met with her for a little *private conversation* that night. She was sure it was at eight-thirty. Or nine-thirty. She couldn't remember; she had been a little tipsy that night. Luke had kept filling her glass with whiskey.

"So what are you telling me, Gregory?" Rich asked.

Gregory didn't speak for a while. Rich waited.

"Remember what Jiffy said about the man in the lobby of The Elite the night Violet Hamilton died?"

Rich nodded slowly, a ball of dread in his gut.

"Well, Luke was wearing dress shoes that night with his tux, Rich," he said. "It would have been very easy for him to not only change, but leave the party, get the bad drugs to Violet, and return to the room with his tipsy girlfriend. You know how smooth he is, Rich. He could have easily confused her about the time."

"But why go to all that trouble, Gregory?" Rich protested. "It doesn't make any sense. He could have given her the drug anytime. For God's sake, man, why did it have to be that night?"

"I've been thinking about that, too, Rich," Gregory said. "Maybe Violet knew something about the other girls. Maybe she was threatening to expose him. And the way she died, the way they all died. It's a statement, Rich. Whoever's doing this is trying to tell us something."

Rich closed his eyes. Just weeks ago, he remembered sitting in his office in the newly formed homicide division watching news coverage of the Amtrak crash. Despite the tragedy and the fact that Sheriff Freehold had tricked him into heading up the homicide division, the world seemed huge with promise and success. Evil and good, depravity and morality had existed side by side, but separated by a thick black line.

Men like him existed to make everything right for the rest of the world. He faced something about himself now. He had always wanted to be the hero. At first, there was baseball. He had visions of hitting the game-winning home run. And when that didn't work out, there was the sheriff's department, where he could work on the side of right and still be the hero.

There were still new discoveries to be made, things he would still have to figure out, but he had known one thing for sure. There were good people and bad people; good things and bad things. That had been his truth.

And now, the world had shrunk with each passing day to the size of a walnut. Clear lines between good and evil had been erased. He had slept with a woman he barely even knew, then betrayed her by searching her apartment. He had been the instrument in the death of a child, and now he sat here with Gregory implicating a man who was like a second father to him.

"It could easily have been Smalls at The Elite that night," Rich said softly.

"It could have been all three of them. Not at The Elite, of course. But all three of them—Kendra, Smalls, and Luke—could have done this," Gregory pressed, gently. "The question is, why force us to investigate? That's what I don't get."

Rich sat back down on the bench and leaned his neck over the back of it. He wished briefly that the edge of the bench were a blade that would cut his head off and just make everything go away.

"What happened to the babies? Were they killed, too?" Rich asked now.

"I don't know," Gregory said with a sigh.

Rich gave him a sidelong glance. "Oh, now you are all fresh out of theories, huh?"

Gregory turned his bony hands over until both his palms faced heavenward. He had given up. "Do you have any?"

Rich closed his eyes. For a moment, he saw complete darkness, then tiny pinpricks of light. He waited for a minute. He heard shuffling and a man asking if they had any spare change. Rich still did not open his eyes. He heard Gregory rustling, a wet voice saying thank you, then more shuffling.

"You know where he's going with that, don't you?" Rich asked Gregory.

"Rich," Gregory replied impatiently. "Your theory."

"Straight to the liquor store," he said.

"Rich . . ."

"Did you check to see whether Luke, or—"He stopped and swallowed. He wanted to say Kendra Hamilton but couldn't. He was sure Gregory noticed, but the other man didn't say anything. "Did you check to see whether they had any connections with adoption services?"

"No." Gregory said the word so thoughtfully, Rich imagined he could see it float along in the darkness behind his eyelids. "What are you getting at, Rich?"

Rich opened his eyes and looked at Gregory. He said what he needed to quickly, before he could change his mind.

"Luke Bertrand was going on and on during that party the other night about saving children. His face changed when he talked about it, as if he was getting his information straight from Him"—Rich pointed up to the sky—"and I thought to myself when he was talking that he sounded like a fanatic. But then I was thinking that it was in a good way."

"So you think it's Bertrand?"

Rich shook his head impatiently. "No, I'm not saying that. What if someone gets it into his or her head that they need to save these children somehow from growing up with a junkie?"

"Then that would be Kendra," Gregory said.

"Or Raymond Smalls," Rich countered.

"But why kill Violet Hamilton?" Gregory asked.

"Because of Kendra Hamilton," Rich said, emphasizing each word.

"I don't . . ."

"Jiffy said that Violet Hamilton was harassing Kendra, asking for drugs, showing up at the ER loaded."

"Kendra still could have . . ."

Rich waved his hands one over the other to erase Gregory's last words.

"No!" he said, his voice so loud it startled even him. "Would you listen to me for a minute, man?"

"Okay, okay," Gregory said.

"Kendra Hamilton killing her mother doesn't fit. It just doesn't. Because if she killed Violet, she would have to have killed those other girls. She doesn't fit the profile."

"Profile?" Gregory raised an eyebrow. "We have a profile now?"

Rich blew out a gust of air. "No, we have theory. And my theory is that someone killed those girls and took those babies because they thought they were doing a good thing—for the babies, I mean. Kendra wasn't even in the country when they died."

"But," Gregory said slowly, "still, why kill Violet?"

"To save Kendra Hamilton from more harassment," Rich said. He could see that Gregory was buying into the theory.

"So we are looking for someone obsessed with her. That could be Luke Bertrand," Gregory offered.

"Or Raymond Smalls," Rich countered. "Remember what Cassady said? That Smalls wanted her to keep an eye on Kendra's mother."

It seemed like a perfectly plausible explanation. Raymond Smalls killed Violet Hamilton because he didn't want her embarrassing Kendra anymore. He did it through Cassady, who gave Violet the tainted dope the night she died. Maybe it was good Sheriff Freehold had charged her. The man in the lobby of The Elite that night? Coincidence. Good people and bad people, remember? They could clear this case and go home. He could get back to his life.

"What next?" Gregory asked.

Rich looked over the cracked parking lot and saw that he would be granted a small reprieve. A 1980 maroon Cadillac rolled into one of the many empty spaces. The door opened, and a heavyset man twisted in the seat, braced a meaty hand on the door, and stepped heavily from the car. He carried a grease-stained bag in one hand and acknowledged them with a wave with the other. Rich watched Brock Gordon trudge across the parking lot toward them. He was a big man with a torso like a whale. His suit coat bunched under his arms and framed his protruding stomach.

Both Rich and Gregory stood as Gordon climbed onto the platform and shook both of their hands. His fingers were short and stubby, like sausages. Pink splotches stood out on his fat face. He sat down heavily on the bench next to them.

"I'm sorry to intrude upon your lunch, Mr. Gordon," Gregory said as he sat back down. "But I was hoping you could help us."

Brock didn't answer right away. He opened the paper bag and pulled out a can of Diet Coke. He reached down and placed it between his legs. He then pulled out a Saran wrapped double-decker sandwich.

"You know what," he huffed, still out of breath. "This place used to be somethin'. Used to come down here all the time." He twisted around to look at Rich and Gregory. "Actually, rode the train more times than I can count. Damn shame to see this place like this."

"Then why do you come?" Rich asked him.

Brock hunched his shoulders. "I don't know," he said. "Just trying to imagine it like it was, you know. When things were good in Dunhill."

"So you are from here?" Gregory asked.

"Lived here all my life." Brock grunted as he flipped the top off the Coke. It opened with a pop. "Did my fair amount of traveling, but this is still home. What did you boys want to see me about?"

Gregory reached in his pocket and pulled out the cross. He handed it to Brock, who put the sandwich on the bench beside him before taking it. He weaved the chain between his meaty fingers and stared at it for a second or two. Then he laughed, his big belly shaking up and down.

"Well," he chuckled, wiping his eyes. "I haven't seen this goddamn thing in twenty-five years. Where in the hell did you get it?"

"You mean you recognize that?" Rich asked, pointing to the cross.

Brock grunted. "Recognize it?" he said. "It's one of the biggest flops of my career."

"How do you mean?" Rich asked.

"I bought this from a vendor cheap, when our stores were first starting to get into the jewelry category. Because it's a cross, you see, and we thought that it was cheap enough that we would do a lot in volume, especially in the poorer neighborhoods. I ordered cases of this piece of shit."

"What happened?" Rich asked.

"Well," Brock said, "we did sell a lot of 'em at first. But you see this thing here?" He pointed to the miniscule diamond at the tip of the cross. "This damn thing kept falling off. Everybody kept returning them. We ended up pulling 'em out of the stores."

"Do you know anyone else who might sell them?"

Brock wagged his head no. "That vendor gave me what he called an *exclusive*. Besides, I don't know anyone else that would be as dumb as I was back then. Like I said, I haven't seen anything like it around in twenty-five years. It's a poor design, especially with that diamond off the end like that. Bound to fall off. I should have known."

"What did you do with the rest of them?" Rich asked.

"I tried to give 'em back to the vendor, you know, return 'em. But the guy went out of business. I kept them in a box in my office for a number of years, then I gave the entire lot to charity."

"Charity?" Rich asked.

"Yeah," Brock said, taking a swig of his Coke. "We have an arrangement with a few charity groups, you know. We give 'em vendor samples every now and then. You wouldn't believe how much junk I get from vendors in this business. Some I keep but them crosses, I packed the entire shit-load up and gave 'em to charity."

Rich's hands grew cold despite the heat. He asked the next question, already knowing the answer.

"What charity?" he asked. "Do you remember?"

"Yep," he answered. "Sure do. A colored fella I had dealt with personally from time to time. Pretty famous around here now, you probably heard of 'im. Fella by the name of Luke Bertrand. I packed the entire shit-load up and handed them over to Luke Bertrand."

CHAPTER 29

A cloud, thick and black, rolled over the baby blue summer sky and settled there on its heavy belly. Any minute it would bleed torrents of rain all over Dunhill County and surely parts of Oakland. But for now, it just lay there waiting for the exact moment to release. The blinds in Sheriff Freehold's office were open, but the steel skies did not reveal any light.

Rich and Gregory faced a grim Sheriff Freehold in his office in the newly remodeled side of the sheriff's department. Freehold sat behind his desk with his shirt sleeves rolled to his elbows. Springy black hairs covered his forearms. He clutched the report Rich and Gregory had spent all night preparing, along with the photos of the nine dead girls and the three still missing.

Rich had just finished explaining to the sheriff why they needed a search warrant for Luke Bertrand's San Francisco office and his Dunhill home. Rich even told him about the letters, because he was convinced that Luke had sent them. The son-of-a-bitch wanted to get caught. It was the sheriff's response that plunged the room into silence. It made Rich's thoughts retreat to that corpulent cloud covering the once blue sky. Sheriff Freehold spoke the word without hesitation and unwaveringly. *No.*

Rich pulled his eyes from the window and looked at the sheriff.

"No," Freehold said again. His face looked as if it had just been sprayed with dry ice. He pressed his lips together into a thin, hard line.

"I don't understand," Rich said, but he did understand. He understood all too well. Sheriff Freehold had his murderer. A junkie named Cassady Moon. No family, no connections, and no mess. Rich motioned to the pictures between Freehold's useless hands and was about to protest again. But then Gregory spoke in a voice uncharacteristically naive.

"Didn't you read the reports?"

Freehold didn't answer. Rich could tell by the tight skin around his mouth that Freehold had damn well read the reports. There was something else going on. It was something in the way he sat behind his desk, unmoving, like some damned ice sculpture.

"You knew about this, didn't you?" Rich said in a soft voice.

Freehold jerked like he had been slapped. He pushed the chair back from the desk, and it scraped loudly against the floor. He stood up and placed both palms flat against the sides of his head. Rich could see his bald pate sweating despite the coolness caused by that rain cloud over Dunhill. Freehold sighed deeply and sat back down heavily, his left hand falling against the face of April Hart. *The still alive April Hart,* Rich thought. She had to be still alive, Luke wouldn't kill her before the baby arrived.

"Know about what, Marvel?" he challenged. "A serial killer? You don't know about any damn serial killer, either, or else you would be asking me to send the FBI in here. Is that what you want?"

Rich thought about that. No, that was not what he wanted. He still believed they had a handle on the case. He didn't want the FBI coming here crawling all over the place, and, worst of all, he didn't want them taking all the credit for the bust. He kept silent. He looked over at Gregory, who also said nothing.

"I didn't think so," Freehold said. He stood up again, and Rich swore he heard the chair creak a sigh of relief. "You asked me if I knew about this. Let me tell you the *this* I knew about." He waved his hand at the reports on the desk. He shook one of the photos free.

"This girl here, April Martinez," he showed them a mug shot of a Latina girl with brown eyes and brown hair. "I investigated this case myself, had to be fifteen or so years ago. Drug overdose, nothing more. Same as the rest of 'em."

Rich couldn't believe what he was hearing. He leaned over to speak, but the sheriff held up his hand.

"We knew that some of these girls had some connection with Luke Bertrand. We knew a couple of them were pregnant. But that goes back ten years or so ago. I investigated. Thoroughly." He stopped speaking, and challenged both of them with his blue eyes. "Luke explained that some of them had come to him *before they died,* same as this little chickee." He flicked the mug shot at them again. "They asked him to place their babies up for adoption. He gave them a cross, so what? He tried to help them, but they all ended up back on dope. The only thing you've uncovered is a good man trying to find a home for these children while their junkie no-good mothers were sticking needles in their veins. That's it. Serial killer, my ass." He threw the picture on the desk.

"How did you remember her name?" Rich asked.

"Huh?" Freehold responded.

Rich leaned forward. "I said, how did you remember April Martinez's name? You said you investigated over fifteen years ago."

"What does it matter?" Freehold barked.

"You thought it was Luke from the start, didn't you?" Rich said. "You went back to your old case files to look for any similarities when Violet Hamilton died, didn't you? What made you do that, the fact that Violet had that damned cross?"

Freehold reddened, then shrugged.

"So what?" he asked. "So there were a few coincidences. They didn't mean a damn thing."

"Is that why you buried Beth Rinehart's autopsy report?" Rich taunted. "Things were starting to get a little too hot even before Violet Hamilton died, huh, Freehold? That's why you hid the fact that the Rinehart girl had given birth before she died."

It was only a hunch, but Rich played it for all it was worth.

"That's bullshit, Marvel," Freehold said softly.

"Why didn't you tell us about it?" Rich asked.

"I didn't tell you about it, Marvel, because it has nothing to do with this case. I told you that Luke was only trying to help these girls."

"Yes," Gregory said in a deceptively bored voice. "With adoption agencies all over the county, isn't it curious that they chose Luke? And isn't it further curious that the outcome of his counsel was death for, let's see"—he counted on his fingers—"nine of them? Maybe twelve?" he finished with a raised eyebrow.

"Look, smart-ass," the sheriff said, "I don't remember the number being as high as nine. I said a couple of them. But Luke explained it."

"And you believed him?" Rich asked. "Just took his word for it?"

Freehold sat down and interlaced his fingers on the desk. He leaned forward and pinned Rich with his eyes.

"Have you any idea the pull that man has in this city? You, of all people, Detective Marvel?" he asked. "You're damn straight I took his word for it. Even though I don't believe he had anything to do with it, in the end I had this one thought."

"And what thought was that?"

The sheriff grinned. "So what if he had anything to do with it? So what if a couple of hookers and drug addicts bought the farm. Just chalk it up to ole Lucas Cornelius Bertrand doing his part to clean up the streets of The Pit. I'm not the only one who thought so, boys. Believe me."

"You are saying that there are others in the department who knew?" Gregory asked.

Sheriff Freehold shrugged. He stacked the pictures one on top of the other. April Hart's photograph lay on top.

"Yes and no. There were people who had their suspicions, but they didn't have the heart to investigate it."

"Like Lindstrom Grady?" Rich asked.

The sheriff only shrugged his shoulders in answer.

"Why didn't we know?" Rich asked, angrily.

Sheriff Freehold looked at him. He stabbed April Hart's picture with his elbow as he leaned against his hands.

"Your partner, Gregory here, is an outsider. Some think he is a fairy. And you . . ." he stopped and looked at Rich.

"And me?" Rich prodded.

"You are too damn good, for one. They thought you would do just what you are doing now. Investigate, look for somebody to arrest. But in the end, a lot of people in the department don't feel comfortable with you because you are from there."

"The Pit," Rich said.

Freehold nodded. "Yes, The Pit, Rich."

"Tell me something, Freehold. Are you on the take? Is Luke paying you? Is that how you keep that young wife of yours in diamonds?"

He expected anger, denial, but Freehold's face remained calm and controlled. "If that's what you want to believe," he said with a shrug, "believe it. I don't give a shit. I told you all that I'm going to tell you."

"But why are you telling us all this now?" Rich asked, although again, he knew.

"The homicide department is being dissolved. All homicides from now on will be handled by investigations, Sandy's department."

Rich expected as much, but that didn't stop the breath from coming sharp in his throat. "Do we get to know why?"

"You mishandled the initial crime investigation for Violet Hamilton's death and kept back vital information regarding this case from this office."

"What vital information?" Rich asked.

"The potentially deadly drugs being distributed on the streets and the fact that Luke Bertrand was even a suspect. Rich, you drove around for God knows how long with evidence in your trunk." Freehold put his chin in his hands, which made him look like a gargoyle. He turned to Gregory. "Detective Atfield, you also harassed and embarrassed Luke Bertrand by questioning everyone at that party without permission and proper notification." He turned back to Rich. "You want to know the kicker, Marvel?"

Rich said nothing, just stared hard at Freehold, wanting to kill him with a single look.

"You fucked one of the suspects," Freehold stated dryly.

It was as if Rich's body had separated from his brain. Before he knew what was happening, he lunged across the desk toward Freehold. He was going for his fat throat. A gold clock and the pictures of the dead girls clattered to the floor. Rich felt the edge of the desk dig sharply into his stomach. All he could think of was squeezing Freehold's flabby throat between his fingers.

Freehold jumped backward before Rich could touch him. Rich felt Gregory's bony hands clasp his shoulders and pull him away. Jerking away and breathing hard, he somehow ended up standing on April Hart's picture. He could see a single blue eye staring up at him. Freehold didn't look angry, just wary, as if he had received the reaction he wanted. Rich knew that he probably had.

"Your guns and badges," Freehold said, unmoving.

"How do you know we won't go straight to the press," Rich asked. "Tell them about the bad drugs you are so concerned about? I could tell them you obstructed this case every step of the way. Were you responsible for the stall in forensics?"

"What do you think?" Freehold said. "Besides, if you go to the press, they will know as well as I do how badly you two fucked up this case. And you wouldn't want that green-eyed debutante to know that you strayed, now would you? Besides, they wouldn't believe your ass, anyway."

"So does that mean the entire homicide department is dissolved?" Gregory asked.

"Of course not," Freehold said. "Detective Blair was just operating under your guidance, wasn't he? I may keep him around to tie up a few loose ends."

"Was he your mole, Freehold?" Rich said, finding his voice.

"Let's just say he was protecting his interests. You once knew what that was like, didn't you, Rich? Protecting your interests?"

"Go to hell," Rich said.

"Your guns and badges," Freehold repeated.

Rich felt as if he had chopped a limb from his body when he took off his holster. He removed his Beretta and placed the empty holster together with his badge on Freehold's desk.

"The weapon's mine, Freehold," Rich said.

"Leave the bullets then," Freehold answered. "I'll be damned if I let you walk out of here fully loaded."

Rich emptied his weapon on Freehold's desk beside Gregory's surrendered weapon and badge. Rich felt as if his career had just slammed against a brick wall. He waited for the pain of impact but felt nothing. Just emptied out. He bent down and picked up April Hart's picture. Her eyes pleaded for help. It had been a long time since he'd had that feeling, the feeling that he wanted to help somebody, that he could be the hero one more time. He walked around the desk. A flash of fear flickered in Freehold's eyes, but Rich received no pleasure from it.

"You go on and do whatever you think is right for your political career," Rich said. "But when you close your eyes at night, you remember this girl. She may still be alive. Her life worth it, Freehold?" he asked. "Her life worth you spending a couple of more years behind this desk picking your ass doing nothing?"

Rich slammed the picture heavily into the man's chest. He walked out expecting to feel oddly naked without the shield he had worn for nearly thirteen years. But he didn't.

Instead, he felt fully aware of the job he needed to do. He knew now, more than ever, that Luke Bertrand was a big player in this. His last act as a detective for the sheriff's department would not be putting his shield on Freehold's desk. His last act would be to find out why Luke Bertrand murdered those girls. And he would find out on his own terms.

That green-eyed debutante waited for Rich in the parking lot. She stood beside his Firebird with her arms crossed and her face fixed in accusation. The wind whipped her black hair across her forehead. When he reached her, she snaked out a hand and slapped his face. Rich didn't speak or flinch against the sting.

"Haven't you anything to say for yourself?" she asked him.

"How did you know?" he asked.

"How do I know?" she squeaked. "You sleep with some Pit trash; do something that can totally humiliate me and ruin us, and all you want to know is how I know?"

Rich looked at Dinah. She wore a lavender pantsuit and a cream silk blouse open at the throat and cut so low he could see the swell of her breasts. He searched her face, looking for the hurt that he was so sure he had caused, but the only thing he saw in her eyes was pride. She was thinking only one thing—damage control.

"I'll tell you how I know," she was saying now. "Daddy received a call from Sheriff Freehold . . ." She stopped. Rich was laughing, softly.

"Daddy," he said. "Good ole Daddy."

"You may think that this is funny, Rich," she said. "But I don't."

"What do you want, Dinah?" he asked. He didn't mean for it to come out like it did, but he didn't feel like playing the contrite fiancé for Dinah's sake.

"What do you mean, what do I want?" She was starting to sound like a broken record, he thought. "For starters, how about an apology."

"An apology?" he said. "An apology? Don't you want to know why it happened?"

Her face changed, and he saw tears form in her eyes. She reached into her handbag and pulled out a tissue. "Don't you think I asked myself that all night?" she said. "But it really doesn't matter, especially since everyone knows we are engaged. We need to figure out how we are going to get through this . . ."

As she droned on, he realized why they had ended up together. She was concerned with appearances just as much as he was. He remembered Smalls's words the other morning— *all spit and shine.* Since she had decided that he was the one she wanted and announced it to the world, she had to make the best of it—no matter what. He remembered a question she had asked him the day Violet Hamilton died. *Why do you want to marry me, Rich? The money?* His gut reaction had been no, it wasn't the money. It was much more. He had wanted her as his girlfriend, wanted to marry her because that was the way it was supposed to be. He was the hero, and she was his reward for doing everything right in his life.

"I'm sorry, Dinah," he interrupted her.

"What?" She stopped, stared at him.

"I said I'm sorry. You picked the wrong guy."

She opened her mouth, closed it again. Her hand fluttered to her throat.

"Rich, you can't mean . . ." she started.

He knew he owed her more, but it was a debt he couldn't pay. Without looking at her, he opened the driver's-side door of his personal vehicle and got inside. He glanced in the rearview mirror. Shock and surprise rather than hurt marred her beautiful face.

CHAPTER 30

When Rich walked into homicide the day after meeting with Freehold, both Gregory Atfield and Beau Blair were there. Beau paced up and down the cramped office, alternately running his hand over his bald pate and cursing. Gregory sat behind his desk, calmly, one hand over the other. Rich ignored them. He strode over to his desk and pulled open the last drawer. It was empty.

"If you are looking for the letters, they aren't there," Gregory said quietly.

"What happened to them?"

"Freehold's already cleaned you out, old man," Gregory shrugged. "My bet is that he's got them. They may come in handy for him someday."

Rich felt a muscle jump in his jaw. He fought the urge to grab Beau by the waist and take him to the ground in an old-fashioned schoolyard fight.

"Anybody mind telling me what's up?" he said instead, trying his damnedest to make his voice mild over his beating heart.

Beau stopped pacing. He held up his hand to Rich in a gesture of concession. "Hey, man, let me just say first that I didn't know anything about this shit."

"I want them back."

"They're evidence, man," Beau said.

"They are my personal property."

"Bullshit."

Rich pointed a finger at him. "I swear to God, Blair—"

"I can get them back for you, for all the good they'll do. But only if you help me, Rich."

Rich ignored him and walked to his desk. *Correction,* he thought, *my former desk.* He didn't speak, just started dumping items into the cardboard box he had brought from his apartment. He picked up a picture of Dinah and looked at it for several seconds before carefully placing it in the box.

"Aren't you even going to say anything to me?" Beau asked.

Rich kept his silence. He picked up his baseball with the fake autograph of Reggie Jackson and placed it in the box. When he finally spoke, his own voice surprised him. He sounded tired, old, worn-out. And it scared him. He felt as if he were giving up.

"You're not even worth it, man," he said.

"Don't I get a shot at explaining what happened?" Beau asked, his voice wet with emotion. Rich stopped packing and looked at him. Gregory unfolded his thin body from his chair and stood up.

"Maybe you should listen to him, Rich," he said.

"Why?" Rich challenged. He turned around and pointed to his own back. "You see this spiky thing sticking up out of my back?"

Gregory said nothing. Rich whipped around. "Well, your boy put it there. And if you turn around and look at your own back in a mirror, you will find one just like mine."

"Rich, you should at least hear him out," Gregory said.

"I'm not keeping him from talking, am I, man?" Even as he continued packing, he listened, he wanted to hear Beau's explanation. Beau heaved a big sigh before speaking.

"He asked me and I tole him," he said with a shrug of his shoulders.

"What?" Rich said in disbelief. "That's your explanation? Freehold asked and you told him?"

Beau nodded his big head, reminding Rich once again of a big dumb sheepdog. The only thing missing was the hair covering his beady blue eyes.

"Yeah," he contended. "He'd come up to me, and say, 'Hey, Detective Blair, how are things going with the Violet Hamilton case?' And I'd say not good or okay, and then he would ask me for some of the details."

Gregory broke in. "From what Beau tells me, it looks like he kept him informed every step of the way."

Rich knew this error was probably due to Beau's newness to the team. During investigations, especially political ones, Rich liked to keep the details of the case close within the unit. Even from the brass. If they did ask for reports, he shaded them until they were meaningless. This allowed him to conduct investigations without unwanted suggestions or interruptions. Sheriff Freehold was not stupid, and this was probably why he went to Beau in the first place.

But there was still one thing that bugged the hell out of him. "You told him I slept with Kendra Hami—"

"No," Beau said before Rich could get the words out of his mouth. "I never said that, man. He must have guessed it, Rich."

Rich didn't respond. He didn't know what to say. The anger had almost left him. He turned away, and his eyes fell once again on Dinah's picture laying on the bottom of the cardboard box. She stared back at him, her eyes glowing like green glass. He had been so deep in thought that he hadn't heard what Gregory said until he repeated it a second time.

"Rich," he said. "Raymond Smalls is in the interrogation room."

"What?"

Beau came over and stood directly in front of him. "The sheriff turned this entire thing over to me," he said.

"What entire thing?" Rich looked from Gregory's soft pale face to Beau's big sheepdog head.

"Everything!" Beau said. "That drug murder, the two at the Elephant's Graveyard. Violet Hamilton. The whole nine goddamned yards." Then Beau walked back to his desk and sat down heavily.

At first Rich didn't know why Freehold would do something like this. But then he did. Freehold obviously wanted out of that campaign promise, and the only way he could do it was by proving the utter failure of the homicide department. He was able to suspend himself and Gregory because they had not kept him informed. Rich had sealed his own fate in more ways than one the minute he lay down with Kendra Hamilton.

But Beau. Beau had been the department's golden boy. He was the department's clean-cut cowboy who rode into town and declared himself a hero. Freehold couldn't fire him simply because he'd been assigned to a lead detective who didn't train him properly. After all, Beau was just following orders. But if he failed, utterly failed, the story would be different. Freehold would be able to disband the homicide department and go back on his campaign promise with his face intact.

"But that still doesn't explain why Smalls is down the rabbit hole," Rich said.

"I didn't know what to do," Beau confessed. "Sandy's team pulled some tire tracks from the scene, and they think they most likely belong to a Mercedes. I know Smalls owns a Mercedes and Gerald Smythe worked for him. Pulling him in seemed like a good thing to do."

"Did you impound his car?" Rich asked.

"We tried," Beau said. "But we can't find it. Gave us some bullshit story about selling it."

"What about a search warrant for his place? Did you toss his place?"

"Tried," Beau breathed. "But couldn't. Judge wasn't having any of it."

Rich placed his hands on his hips and whistled through his teeth.

"Sounds like you got a personal problem to me," Rich said.

"You are an asshole, Marvel," Beau said in disgust and stood up. "I'll take care of Smalls myself."

Rich chuckled. "Man," he said, "Raymond Smalls will eat you alive."

Beau looked at him. "So you gonna help me?" he asked.

"Nope," Rich said without looking at him.

"Richard," Gregory broke in, his voice gentle. "We can help here, even though it's not in an official capacity."

"Why?" Rich asked. He swiped the box off the desk. It clattered to the floor, and the baseball rolled toward the door. "I'm already fired. Hell, you're fired, Gregory. Why do you give a shit? Why should I give a shit?"

"But this isn't about your career, is it, Rich?" Gregory asked. "And it hasn't always been about that, has it?"

Rich's initial reaction was to ask his partner what in the hell did he think it was all about. But he swallowed back the words before they fell from his lips. Instead, he tried to remember a time when he had worked cases without his career in mind. He was good at what he did. And maybe for that reason, he would forget his dreams of fame and respect and throw himself into a case with all the purpose of a speeding train. He simply wanted to shine a spotlight on the evil, illuminate it so all the world could see it.

But lately, that feeling, that passion had left him. He could barely remember what it felt like. His mother brought him up to believe things happened for a reason. God set things in motion for a purpose. He had become disillusioned and had allowed himself to be raped by the promise of success. He closed his eyes and saw the speeding train, the cars slamming together like a line of dominos. He had to finish it with Smalls. It was his second chance to make him pay for what Rich knew that he had done. He had to see it through, because that was what he was supposed to do.

* * *

The three of them watched Raymond Smalls from the two-way mirror in the homicide squad room. Rich had studied the files and pretty much thought he could create a reasonable scenario as to what had happened.

The father had a twenty-two hidden somewhere on him. Smalls must have missed it when he searched him, which explained the bullet in a skinny redwood next to the road. The entire right side and back of Gerald Smythe's body was covered with dried mud from the creek bed, but the other side was not. That would have made sense if he was lying on his side when the body was discovered. But Gerald had been lying on his back, which led Rich to believe that he had somehow changed positions after he had been dumped. And that meant he had been alive when he rolled down that hill.

They looked down the rabbit hole at Raymond Smalls, who sat at the same square table where Cassady Moon had sat before. One hand was folded neatly on top of the other. To Rich, he looked monumentally bored, or was trying like hell to look that way.

"It may have been a mistake to pull him in this early, man," Rich commented to Beau. "All you got is the tire track? No car?"

Beau nodded, his face grim. "Says he sold it, remember? Probably dumped it."

Beau fell silent, his face pensive. Rich could tell that he was thinking about the young girl whose only sin was being her father's child. She was now lying on a slab at the morgue. Rita Sandbourne and Clint the nibbler were probably already hacking away at her.

"Did Sandy pull anything else from the scene?" Rich asked him again.

"Nothing we can go to the bank on. He did pull some fiber from the T-shirt the girl was wearing. Said it looked like a piece of white suede or some shit."

"He has an alibi?" Rich motioned to Smalls.

"He won't talk to me, Rich," Beau said. "He keeps saying he wants a lawyer."

"You didn't hear him say that, did you, man?" Rich asked in an idle voice.

Beau grinned, a big country-cowboy grin. "Not really," he said.

Rich turned away from him and walked into the hallway. He walked down a set of short metal steps spiraling into the basement. Using the key Beau had given him, he opened the door. Smalls looked at Rich and smiled darkly.

"What? No gun, no badge?" he asked with a raised eyebrow at Rich's gray ribbed T-shirt and blue jeans.

"It's my day off," Rich commented. He pulled a chair up to the table and straddled it. He rested his chin on the back of it. Smalls regarded him, his eyes black and his lips cold and unsmiling.

"How's Thor?" Rich asked.

"He misses you," Raymond said, the corner of his mouth lifting a bit.

"I came by your place later that morning, but you weren't there."

"Sorry Thor and I were not there to greet you."

Ignoring the comment, Rich threw the manila file on the desk carelessly, as if he didn't care if Smalls saw what was in it.

"I didn't know you were into that seventies shit, man," he said.

Raymond rewarded him with a confused look. "What?" he asked, his voice cool and level.

"You know," Rich said and sat up fully. "That seventies stuff. Afros, platform shoes. . . ." he let his voice trail off. Smalls didn't respond. "White suede jackets," Rich continued.

Smalls's eyelids flickered over his glinting black eyes. He had been caught off guard. He formed his mouth into a small yawn. Deliberately.

"I don't know what you mean," he said in that same level tone.

Rich stood up and turned the chair around. He sat down and scooted the chair closer to the table.

"You know why you here, man?" Rich asked.

"Your John Wayne told me something, but why don't you explain it to me in detail."

"One of your guys and his little girl got popped. The Smythes. You know 'em?"

Raymond didn't speak. Instead he looked at the mirrored glass before turning back to Rich. A shadow surrounded his smile. "Is that why you came back by my place the other day, to talk about these two unfortunates?"

"No," Rich responded, "I came by your place that day to beat the shit out of you."

Surprise flickered over Smalls's face, but he quickly composed himself.

"Did you know them, Smalls?" Rich asked.

"I think I may have known him," he said. "Vaguely."

"You own a white suede jacket?" Rich asked.

Raymond lifted his flat black hand from the table. "I don't know. You tell me."

Rich nodded. "I think you do," he said.

"Think?" Raymond lifted his eyebrow again.

Rich nodded. He looked at the table and pulled the files toward him. He knew Raymond would not be able to understand the scientific garble. He pretended to study the report.

"We found a tire track at the scene. It was from a Mercedes . . ." Rich stopped. He looked at Raymond. "Hey," he said as if just remembering. He shook his index finger at him. "You drive a Mercedes, don't you?"

"So?" Raymond commented. "I drive a lot of cars."

"Where did you say that car was?" Rich asked.

Raymond sighed. "I've already told Gunsmoke out there that I sold it."

"When?" Rich challenged.

"Recently."

"To whom?" Rich asked.

"I don't know."

"Do you have the paperwork?" Rich asked.

"It was a paperless deal."

"Is that so?" Rich said dryly. "What if I told you that we found your Mercedes with a trunk full of blood and one fucked-up seventies white leather jacket?"

Rich realized he had never heard Raymond Smalls laugh, not with real amusement anyway. Now he laughed so hard that tears shone in his black eyes. Rich sighed quietly to himself. At least he knew by Smalls's reaction that he had dumped the car. It was probably being melted down for scrap metal as they spoke. As Smalls's laughter trailed off, Rich cocked an eyebrow toward the window. He could almost feel Gregory's disappointment through the two-way.

"Bullshit," Raymond said unnecessarily.

"This is what happened," Rich said as if Smalls hadn't spoken. "You got real spooked when Gregory and I talked to you about the bad shit on the streets. Then you remembered that one of your boys came across a bad load a while back. You gave him orders to dump it somewhere, but he didn't. Or at least that's what you thought. So you had to take care of him, right?" Rich looked at Smalls, but the other man's face was as silent as death. "I mean, you couldn't have anybody out there Johnny Rotting you and doing whatever the hell they wanted, could you? So you and one of your boys went out to teach Gerald Smythe a lesson. You wanted to be there because you wanted to make sure he got what he deserved. Anyway, you wake them up in the middle of the night and you give them a chance to get dressed for some reason. I don't know. Maybe there's a heart beating in that chest of yours. The fourteen-year-old is so scared shitless that she puts on her panties and T-shirt inside out. Did you know that?" Rich stopped, in pretense of giving Smalls a chance to speak. But Smalls didn't say anything, and Rich hadn't expected an answer. He went on. "Anyway, your other boy caps the girl first with two in the back of the head, in front of the father to teach him a lesson. But you want him to suffer a little bit more, so you have your boy cut his fingers on his right hand off. You got anything to add to this?"

Raymond made that little motion with his hand again, a motion of feigned concession. "Why?" he asked. "You are doing so well."

"So you and your boy put them both in the trunk, and drive them to the Elephant's Graveyard, where you finish him off by cutting the arterial vein in his thigh. You dump her first, him second, and he rolls toward the creek bed and falls onto his side. You stand by the road, looking down, admiring your handiwork, but then something happens. He pulls out a little gun you guys didn't see him pick up and just shoots with his good hand, right?" Rich stopped. Smalls stayed silent.

Rich looked at Smalls a long time before asking the next question. "By the way, what blood type are you, Smalls?" Rich didn't get an answer, and again, he hadn't expected one. "You or your boy returns fire, and he falls backward into the creek." Rich held his arm above his head and leaned back into the position Smythe had been found in.

There was complete silence in the room when Rich stopped speaking. Raymond stared at him with a blank look on his face.

"You forgot one thing in your little narrative, Detective," he said.

"What's that?" Rich asked. "Please enlighten me."

Raymond leaned forward. "I wasn't there." He smiled. "I have an alibi."

"Oh, I'm not doubting that, Smalls," Rich responded. "Not for one second."

"Aren't you going to ask what it is?"

"Nope." Rich made a motion to stand up, as if he weren't interested. And in a way, he really wasn't. Rich was sure that Smalls had some alibi, but he was also sure it was as phony as hell.

"What time did your little fairytale take place?" Smalls asked.

Rich cocked his head at him. "You are trying to tell me you don't know?" Rich waited, but there was no answer.

"Okay. Between midnight and three the night before last." He shrugged.

Raymond leaned back in his seat and steepled his fingers near his lips. "I was with Kendra Hamilton." This time he leaned forward and looked at Rich with eyes so intense that Rich felt as if he had been stabbed. "All night."

"Bullshit." The word escaped Rich's mouth before he could pull it back. He felt like he had just been hit in the stomach by a wrecking ball.

"Ask her," Raymond said with a nasty smile on his face.

"You think she will testify to that?" Rich asked. The lowness of his voice negated the sarcasm he tried to infuse.

Raymond's fingers flew apart briefly, then came together again so the tips lightly touched.

"She will testify to anything I tell her." He paused before continuing. "Rich."

Up until that point, Rich had thought that the interview was going well. He had a good lead about the car and knew that they should start scouring junkyards for a start. Raymond didn't have time to do anything else with it. He also knew by Smalls's effort to keep his face completely still during his scenario that he had gotten some things right. If he gave Beau the right words, they might be able to get a search warrant to toss Smalls's place.

But when Smalls mentioned Kendra Hamilton, Rich felt as if someone had screwed off the top of his head and poured his insides out. Smalls's next words scattered Rich's thoughts into a thousand pieces.

"And another thing, have you thought about asking our little Kendra where her mother obtained her dope?" Rich said nothing, Smalls continued. "I can see by your face that you have. Repeatedly. Not that she will tell you the truth, am I right? So why don't you ask Cassady, that junkie that you think works for me?"

"Why don't you tell me, Smalls?" Rich spat.

Smalls shrugged. "That's not my place. Besides, I have no reason to tell you. I'm not desperate enough. Are you? Are you desperate enough to go to a junkie because your girl-friend won't tell you the truth?"

"So if I tell you what I know, what's in it for me?"

Cassady's eyes, flat black except for the glow of despera-tion, darted between the two of them. Rich and Gregory faced her across the table in the rabbit hole. Neither one of them spoke, just waited. Cassady continued.

"I didn't tell you something the last time I talked to you. You know, I kept a little something for myself. Just in case I needed it," she said into the silence. Her voice was husky. Rich and Gregory still didn't speak. She swallowed, then went on. "Peanut tole me I can get money, you know, for telling you guys stuff. Right?"

Gregory answered her. "It really depends on what you have to tell us."

"How much," she said, swallowing again. "I really need to get out of here, and I need some bread, man. I need a fix. What can you give me? A hundred bucks?" She looked hope-fully around at them. They didn't say a word. "Okay, fifty?" she entreated.

Rich let out a sigh of disgust. Dressed in bright jailbird orange and facing murder charges, all Cassady Moon could think about was a fix.

"Why don't you tell us first," Gregory prodded gently over Rich's snort of disgust. "Then we will decide."

Cassady looked down at her black canvas tennis shoes. They had to be at least a size thirteen. She then looked di-rectly at Rich. He could see in her eyes that she didn't trust them, but he could also see that she knew she had no choice.

"Violet had it going on," she said. "She never had to worry about bad shit or where her dope came from, never had a problem with her supply. You know what I'm sayin'? That's why everybody know somebody dropped her on pur-pose. But I didn't kill her. I swear that I didn't do it, man."

Rich sighed. "Get to the point."

"She got the shit straight from her daughter, from the doc. Every two weeks, like clockwork, the doc would find her and hand her enough dime bags to last her. But sometimes Violet shared it, to make friends, you know. The last time Violet got heroin from Kendra, we all had a party, and Violet ran out that first day. She tried calling the doc from pay phones and shit, beggin' for more. I heard 'em fightin' and, you know, Violet tole me that the doc was pissed. She said that the doc tole her that it was her fault that she used up all the junk in the first day and that she would just have to wait." Cassady stopped and swallowed.

Rich felt the ground beneath his feet slide open, the last of his control slipping away.

"Go on," Gregory prodded.

Cassady trained her eyes on Gregory. "Next thing I know, I show up at The Elite and Violet's got two dime bags. And you wanna know something, man? She wouldn't share it with me, so we get into a fight." Cassady touched her fat neck. "That's when I notice the cross. I did ask her where she got the new dope, you know. She looked kinda funny and said the usual place."

The room was quiet. Cassady's voice thudded on in the silence. "So the bitch killed her, right?" When no one spoke she said again. "Right? I don't have to go down for this."

Rich didn't know his feet had carried him to the door until he felt his hand twisting the knob. Rage carried him to his car. He was barely aware of Gregory's voice behind him yelling for him to stop, to wait. He felt an emotion so pure, it was almost divine. He simply wanted to kill.

April

That morning, with yellow sunlight streaming through the open door of the shed, the man who held her told her that sometimes God was tight-fisted. Sitting on the bunk and burrowing into her with his dark eyes, that was the word he used. He then closed his fist so tight, the veins of his wrist bulged. *Tight-fisted. He disguises most of his blessings, he had said, and it's up to us to pry open the fist and see what's in store for us.*

She didn't know why she thought of this now, sitting alone on her bunk with her knees drawn up as far as her pregnant belly would allow. For the last few days, he hadn't tied her up, and that was fine. It was part of her plan. When he left her alone, she scoured every inch of that place. She ran her hands along the wall looking for loose nails, small pieces of broken wood, anything that she might be able to use as a weapon. She walked every inch of the floor and even shook out her pillow case. She twisted at the metal bars in the headboard and when they wouldn't give, she lifted up the mattress. She had stared at the box springs until the twisted black metal looked almost unrecognizable.

She no longer begged for help or urged Sage to listen to her. She didn't cry or plead as he prayed over her. She just sat or stood meekly, head bowed. She practiced a faraway look in her eyes that she hoped would finally let them think that she had lost what little mind the heroin had left her. She needed an advantage. Maybe that was why Sage no longer bothered with the knife when she brought her breakfast.

And maybe that's why he let the door stay open while he sat on the cot beside her. Maybe that's why he started to tell her things.

She had thought of running, all right. She thought of springing up and bolting out of the door into . . . And that's when it hit her. Into what? She had no idea where they were. For all she knew, they could be deep in the woods. In the time she had spent here, she hadn't heard a car or a truck or any sign of the outside world. Besides, she was eight and a half months pregnant. They would easily catch her. She had to think of a different plan.

Tight-fisted, April thought again. *Disguised blessings.*

Was it a blessing that she was here, waiting to give birth before being killed by a madman? She knew that's what would happen, because he had begun to tell her about the others. And by a curse April didn't know could be so cruel, she remembered each of their names—Lorna, Rochelle, Kitten, and Beth. At least, those were the ones he told her about. She knew there had to be more. Just one look at his face told her that there had to be more.

They were all addicts, like her. They had all come to him voluntarily for help. *Pregnant and desperate, every single one of them,* he had told her. In the end, he had to keep them there. For if they left, he knew that they would feed their children the heroin they themselves so desperately needed, even begged for during captivity while on methadone. He and Sage delivered their babies when the time came. And then, when those girls were weak and relieved of their burdens, he would go to them with a dime bag clutched in his tight fist. He asked them to make a choice between the baby and the drug. She would be given that same choice, he had told her that morning.

"What happened to them?" April had said, not recognizing the sound of her voice. It sounded like a robin, thin and high and ready to break into pieces any second.

"They made the wrong choice," he said. "And they have been punished."

"How?" she had asked.

But he ignored the question, didn't answer her. He just went on and on about the children, how they were being raised by good families, good God-fearing families.

Tight-fisted. The man who held her here had been playing God with a dime bag clutched in his hand. The only blessing, April thought, was that the children would not have to be raised by drug addicts, by people like her.

"But what if they made the right choice?" she pressed. "What happens then?"

His eyes looked sad at the question. "My dear," he said. "No one ever makes the right choice."

April wondered what would happen if he came to her right now with a dime bag of heroin, a spoon, a syringe, and a Bic lighter. April always injected, that was her favorite way of getting heroin into her body. No matter what anybody said, the rush was faster and hotter. Would she have the strength to look the other way? She didn't think so. Didn't think so at all.

CHAPTER 31

at happened to diently." April had said not recently sound of her voice. It sounded like a robin, little and

Kendra Hamilton stood in the middle of her living room, a small suitcase beside her. She folded her arms and looked around the room. She hated to leave it, had almost grown accustomed to the place. But she needed the trip. Maria had agreed to come by and check on things for her. Dr. Willis would take over her duties at the clinic until she decided to come back. If she decided to come back.

She tried to remember the exact moment she had made the decision to leave. It had to have been when she was washing away the blood of a stranger with warm soapy water. But even before that night, her life had started to become out of control. First with Violet's death, then her split with Raymond, and now Rich.

She patted the pockets of her dark blue jeans to make sure she had the ticket. She needed some time, some space. She had decided to spend some time in Florida lying on the beach and looking out on the clear blue water. She hoped to find some answers there. Luke, of all people, had suggested it. He even paid for the ticket and the hotel.

The knock at her door was so loud that she would have sworn that she felt it before she heard it. Fear swelled behind her eyes. *Something had happened.* She walked to the door and placed her eye against the peephole, but couldn't see anything. It was blocked again.

"Who is it?" she asked through the closed door. But there was no answer even after she waited a few minutes. She knew she shouldn't open it, that she should just wait until the person on the other side went away. But something told her that what was waiting for her on the other side of that door was not going away. Not ever. She pulled it open. Richard T. Marvel stood staring at her, his face like an angry thundercloud. He looked down at her for a moment like he didn't know who she was. She tried to say something, but he pushed her aside before she could get the words out. He only glanced at the suitcase in the middle of the floor before turning to face her. He didn't seem to be surprised.

"Going somewhere?" he asked.

She shut the door behind her and regarded him. At first she thought he was angry because she hadn't returned any of his phone calls. But then, there was something else. He wasn't in uniform, or what she considered a uniform for him. He was dressed casually in a pair of jeans and a gray T-shirt. She could see no hint of a holster or badge.

"Yeah, vacation. Why?"

His eyes flicked over her skeptically. "Vacation, huh?" he said.

"Rich, I don't . . ." she started.

But he swirled around and went into the bedroom.

"What do you think you are doing?" she asked.

He ignored her and threw open the sliding closet door so hard that it bounced closed again. She reached up and grabbed his arm, but he shook her off. He opened the door again, more slowly this time. He bent down and grabbed the fireproof safe from the closet. He snatched it out and shoved it toward her.

"Open it," he said.

She looked at him and then at the safe in his hands. How in the hell did he know it was there? Then it hit her. The bastard had searched her apartment the morning after . . .

"You son-of-a-bitch," she breathed. "How dare you—"

"Open it!" He threw the box on the air mattress. It bounced off and clattered on the floor. He jerked her arm toward it. She snatched it away from him, returned his angry glare with one of her own.

"You can go to hell," she said, enunciating each word. A lump climbed into her throat, and she felt tears sting her eyes. She turned on her heel and walked out of the room. But he snatched up the safe and followed her. She went for her suitcase, but he grabbed her wrist and forced her to sit on the couch. He kept his fingers clamped around her wrist with one hand. With the other, he held out the safe to her.

"Open it," he said, this time his voice soft.

"No," she said. "Get a warrant." She tried to pull away from him, but he wouldn't let her go. For a minute she thought he was going to slap her. She was about to say something else when Gregory Atfield swung through the front door.

"Rich," he warned, "you can't do this. Anything you find here will get thrown out of court. You are wasting evidence and time."

Kendra turned her eyes to Gregory. He looked flushed and flustered.

"Bullshit," Rich said, never taking his eyes from Kendra. "Reasonable cause, Gregory. Reasonable cause. Open it."

Kendra realized that there was no way around it. If she didn't open it, they would simply come back later with a warrant. She wasn't stupid and knew that if they searched the place they would find evidence that Raymond had been there with a wounded man. Blood didn't clean up with soap and water. She looked Rich squarely in the eye.

"Take your hands off of me," she said. He didn't move. "I need to get the key," she explained.

She felt blood flow return to her fingers when he let her go. Rubbing her wrist, she walked into the kitchen counter to retrieve her key ring. She went back to the couch and opened the safe. Before she could get the lid up, Rich snatched it away from her. He rummaged through the few papers—

her birth certificate, her diplomas—until he found what he was looking for.

He held the bag of heroin to her face with his thumb and index finger. Then he snapped it back so fast that at first she thought he had hit her. She blinked against his stare. Rich turned and walked out of the apartment.

"I think we need to talk," Gregory said in a quiet voice.

Kendra felt as if she had dropped down a long narrow hole. The room she was in was circular and almost empty except for a square wooden table in the middle. One of the legs on the table was shorter than all the others. Every time she leaned on it, the table rocked to the floor.

She hadn't seen Rich yet. Gregory had slipped her around to the older part of the building and down the basement steps. He told her, not unkindly, to sit tight for a minute. Her throat felt dry and tight. She couldn't believe Rich searched her apartment. *Bastard,* she thought. She had thought for one night at least, they were not enemies. She didn't know why she had kept the dope. She should have thrown it away a long time ago. But every time that she thought about doing it, something stopped her.

Just when she thought that she would be left in the room forever, Rich walked into the room. He carried a manila file folder in his hand. Kendra noticed that he was still minus his holster and badge. She could tell by the hard set of his mouth and the pulse that beat in the base of his neck that he was still angry. He just had it under control.

"Let's talk about Raymond Smalls," he said, all business.

"Let's not," Kendra said in a hard voice. He looked up at her. She folded her arms and returned his gaze without blinking.

"Let's talk about why you were snooping around my apartment," she said. "You know, all you had to do was ask. You didn't have to fuck me."

He sat back in his chair as if she had slapped him. "Is that what you think?" he asked her.

"Yes, that's what I think," she responded without missing a beat.

"I put myself on the line for you, lady," he said.

She laughed bitterly. "Rich, I don't believe you put yourself on the line for anybody. Not in your entire lucky life."

He stared at her for a long time, then dismissed her statements with a wave of his hand. "Forget about all that," he said, "Let's talk about Raymond Smalls," he said again.

She cocked her head at him. "Let's not," she repeated.

"I don't have time to play games," he said.

"Then don't," she snapped. "Just get to the point and ask me what you want to ask me."

He sighed deeply. "Was Raymond Smalls with you three nights ago?"

"Is that what he says?" she asked him.

"Never mind what he says. I'm more interested in what you say."

"He was over at my place," she said, knowing it wasn't a complete lie. She just neglected to tell him that he was with somebody else.

"All night?" he asked.

"For the better part of the night," she answered.

"All night?" he pressed.

"I see you are back to playing games again, just ask me what you need to ask me and get it over with."

He leaned forward until he was inches away from her face. "Was Raymond Smalls with you between midnight and five A.M. three mornings ago?" he asked.

She looked down at the table and bit her lip. She looked back up at him and answered. "Yes."

He drew back and sighed in disgust. He shoved the manila folder at her. She had to reach out a hand to stop it from skittering to the floor. He motioned for her to open it. She pulled out two photographs. One was of a young girl curled up in a fetal position, and the other was of a man sprawled in an almost dry creek full of trash and surrounded by yellow weeds.

"You want to change your story?" Rich asked her.

She shook her head slowly at the brutality of it. Raymond. How could he? Rich thought she was answering his question. He snatched the photos away from her.

"What do you think we'll find in that heroin?" he asked her.

She was more surprised by his words than the sudden change of subject. "What are you talking about," she asked him. "What in the hell do you think you'll find, Rich? Heroin."

He stared at her for a long time, his face unreadable. But she saw something in his eyes that was not there several days ago. There were dark circles and heavy dark patches on his usually clear brown skin. She also noticed almost a day's growth of beard on his face. He still did not wear his badge or the holster. She found that strange, since they always seemed to be a part of him, of who he was. If the circumstances were different, she would have felt sorry for him.

But then he opened his big fat mouth and spoiled the entire effect. "Listen, Kendra, you can go to jail for this. You understanding me?"

She leaned forward and looked at him. "Tell me, Rich," she said. "What would you have done if she were your mother?"

Without taking his eyes from her, he retrieved the folder and stood up. He left without saying a word.

It had been only an hour since Rich left her alone in the room. When he came back his anger scared her.

"Did you kill her?"

She looked at him in disbelief.

"No." The word escaped her in a sob.

He put both knuckles on the table. He leaned into her, until his face was inches from hers. She could smell the mint on his breath, and it made him seem distant, cold.

"Did you kill her?" he breathed angrily, his voice quiet.

She pushed the chair away from the table. It made a scraping noise against the floor, but she had nowhere to go. Rich blocked her path. She folded her arms across her chest.

"How could you even ask me that—" she started, but Rich cut her off.

"Did you kill her!?" Rich yelled the words, accompanying every one of them with a fist thumping against the table.

For the first time, Kendra realized how much trouble she was in. The dope, the dope that Rich had found in her apartment, was poisoned with quinine, the same stuff that had killed her mother.

It didn't matter that she hadn't given Violet the dope that killed her on the day of her death. The fact remained that Kendra had planned to give Violet her regular supply of heroin days later. If Violet hadn't died that day, Kendra had the dope that would have killed her later. The very dope that Kendra secured for Violet so she would be safe, so she wouldn't have to prostitute herself or steal to pay for it, was poisoned. It was ironic. She wondered if the person who gave it to her knew. Had he given her the poisoned dope on purpose? But that wouldn't make sense, would it? He couldn't have known that it was harmful.

"Answer me!" Rich yelled.

Kendra looked at him, and tried to think of someone, anyone, she had ever seen as angry as he was now.

"Look, I didn't—"

"Tell me the truth!" he said, pounding on the table again, causing an empty chair to clatter to the floor.

"Tell you the truth?" Kendra said, matching the loudness of his voice, "or tell you what you want to hear?"

Rich swept over to her, pointed his index finger inches from her face. "Let me tell you what you are already looking at," he said. "You are looking at possession of an illegal substance. That carries a prison term, not to mention the loss of your medical license. Then there is the conspiracy to commit murder. Tell me, Kendra, were you and Cassady in on this together? She obviously hated your mother, and you said yourself that her death was a relief. Did you kill her, Kendra?"

A finger of fear touched her heart as his words sank in. He saw it and pressed on. "You are already facing prison. You need to be straight with me if I'm going to help you."

Still standing, she regarded him for a minute. He had dropped his voice almost to a soft whisper. She almost believed him until she saw the muscle jump in his jaw. He was trying some bullshit interrogation technique on her.

"You can go to hell," she said, incredulity in her voice.

Rich snaked a hand out to grab her, but suddenly, Gregory Atfield grabbed his arm and pulled him away. Kendra hadn't heard him come in, and Rich obviously hadn't, either. Rich jerked away from him. He turned his back on both of them and ran a palm over his head.

"Come on, Rich," Gregory said. "You can't be here, old man. All right? This isn't good."

Kendra swallowed, and looked at the cement floor. Rich said nothing.

"I'll take it from here, okay? You've been up all night. Why don't you go get some rest?"

"No," Rich said with his back to them. Then he looked up at the ceiling, and placed his hands on his hips. It was a stance of both hurt and disbelief. Kendra had seen it many times in other people when she delivered bad news. She couldn't believe that in this case she was the cause of all that pain.

"Rich . . ." Gregory began again.

"Fine," Rich said. He slammed out of the room, not looking at either of them. Kendra doubted he would be watching the session from the two-way mirror.

Wearing a white shirt rolled up at the sleeves, Gregory came over and gently picked up the chair that had fallen to the floor. He put the dingy Styrofoam cup on the table and gestured mildly to the chair. Kendra noticed that he looked tired. His blond hair stuck out from his head in several different directions. The tie he wore was so loose that it hung from the collar of his shirt and swung like a pendulum when he sat down.

He looked at Kendra, his gray eyes kind, but grim. "Sorry about that," he said, his voice hardly above a whisper. Kendra had to strain to hear him.

"What is this?" she asked. "Some kind of bad-cop, good-cop scenario?"

He sighed and looked at her. "You know better than that, Kendra."

She pushed a hand through her hair. It was tangled and hot on her head. She looked down at the table and massaged the back of her neck with her hand. It felt stiff. When she got home—if she was allowed to go home—she promised herself she'd have a long, hot shower.

Gregory waited a minute before speaking again in that same quiet voice. "Can I get you something to drink?"

"Please. Water."

Gregory left and returned a moment later with a paper cup. Kendra drank it in one long swallow.

"More?" he inquired.

She shook her head. Gregory sat back in his chair. "You have to know how this must look," he started.

Kendra looked at the mirror opposite her. In the corner of the mirror was a circular point of light. She knew it was a camera. As if reading her mind, Gregory pointed toward the mirror.

"Look," he said, "you say the word, and I turn that thing off so we can talk, honestly."

Kendra cocked her head at him. "What do you think I am? Stupid?"

Gregory shook his head. "No. I don't think you are stupid. But there is one thing I've come to learn about you, Kendra. You live by your own rules."

"If I killed her, why would I insist that you investigate the death? Why would I go to Luke?"

Gregory was quiet for a moment.

"We've considered that," he said. "And the conclusion

we've come to is this." He stopped speaking and leaned forward. "We never had focus on these drug deaths before. But right about the time your mother was killed, we opened homicide. James Freehold promised concentration on the violence in The Pit. You figured sooner or later we would put the heat on the investigation, and you came to us first because—"

"You thought I wanted to deflect suspicion from myself?" Kendra finished for him. She saw them sitting around the squad room, discussing her, talking about her motive for killing her own mother. She felt vaguely violated.

Gregory peeled pieces of Styrofoam from the cup. He nodded. He caught her eyes with his own. They seemed to bore into her soul.

"Does Rich think that, too?" she asked before she could stop herself.

Gregory picked up pieces of the Styrofoam and put them into the cup before answering.

"I don't know what Rich thinks," he said finally. "I doubt if he himself knows what he thinks. You need to give us something we can use, Kendra."

"Like what?" she said, surprised to hear a little cry in her voice. "What can I give you? I have nothing. I didn't kill her, Gregory."

"Where did you get the dope?" he asked.

She swallowed and crossed her arms over her chest. "You know I can't tell you that," she said.

"Okay," Gregory said, his voice quiet and careful. He let the silence close around them.

"What now?" she asked. "Am I being charged?"

He shook his head. "Not at the moment, no."

Kendra looked up at him in surprise. He smiled, a thin-lipped smile.

"Sheriff Freehold would like us to move carefully on this one," he said. "But that doesn't mean you won't be charged in the future."

He was lying. She saw it all over his face. There was

something more happening here, something that he was not telling her.

"Gregory," Kendra leaned forward. "Do you think I killed her? Do you?" She persisted.

He waited a moment before answering. Then, quietly, "No."

"Thank you," Kendra breathed.

"But that doesn't mean anything," he said, his voice urgent. "You need to give us something, Kendra."

This time, Kendra let the silence stand. A weight settled over her. It was the weight of Rich's eyes. Accusing. Unforgiving. Then Rich returned to the room, but now he didn't look accusing. Only defeated. And to Kendra, he looked like a man ready to lay everything on the line. He sat down in the chair opposite her, gripped the table, and took a deep breath. Mumbling something about coffee, Gregory left the room.

"Look," Rich began, "in the last couple of weeks, I've lost my fiancée, I've been suspended from my job, and I find out the man I admired more than my father may be no better than the perps in The Pit. I literally haven't slept for days, and I am tired as hell."

Kendra started to speak, but he held up one finger to stop her. "I need to finish this, Kendra," he said. "And I need you to help me do it."

"What are you talking about, Rich?" she asked. "What do you mean, suspended?"

Gregory walked into the room with three cups of coffee in a cardboard tray before Rich answered. Seeing the happy yellow arches on the side of the cup that Gregory set in front of her made her realize that what was happening was real. She wouldn't be able to change the channel, and there would be no rolling credits at the end.

"You take cream, sugar?" Gregory asked.

She wanted to tell him that she didn't drink coffee, only tea. But in her confusion, she nodded. Gregory reached in the pocket of his rumpled brown jacket. He pulled out several containers of creamer and three wet packets of sugar. Kendra looked down at her cup. She read the side of it to escape Rich's intense stare. CAUTION, CONTENTS MAY BE HOT. When she opened the lid, smoke twirled on the surface of the black coffee and rose upward. Rich waited until she had emptied two creamers and a sugar into the coffee.

"I'm asking for your help," he said.

It was the word he used, *asking,* that made Kendra pause when bringing the cup to her lips. She set it back down on the table.

"I still don't know what you are talking about," she said.

"Luke Bertrand," he said.

"Luke," she said, looking from Gregory to Rich. They knew. But how? "Is he hurt?"

"No," Rich answered wryly. "But you might wish he was after I finish telling you what I have to tell you."

"What are you talking about, Rich?" she said, trying to keep the scream from her voice.

He watched her for a long moment and then told her that he suspected Luke was the reason that there were so many drug deaths in The Pit. He told her about the party he had the night Violet died, how he disappeared for hours. Kendra put her hands over her ears, but Rich refused to stop. He started to tell her about the crosses.

"Shut up," she screamed, knocking the coffee over. The liquid fell in a brown stream over the side of the uneven table. It sounded like a pattering rain on the cement floor.

"You are a liar," she said. "You are trying to trick me, to make me say something to incriminate myself. I want a lawyer." She felt hot tears on her face and slapped them away furiously with the back of her hand.

"We think he may be holding someone up there, Kendra, at his place. Another one of these junkies."

"Shut up," she said again. "You two don't know what you are talking about. Luke didn't have to kill her that night, not when he had already given me the dope . . ." She stopped, suddenly realizing what she had said. But it was too late to take back the words now. Sighing, she continued. "I mean, if he wanted her dead, all that he would have had to do was wait, right? Wait until I gave her the dope. That proves that he had nothing to do with it."

"How long did Luke know your mother, Kendra?" Rich asked.

She didn't answer.

"Long enough to tell her secrets?" Rich asked gently.

"I don't know."

"I think that Luke could no longer control your mother," Rich said. "I think that she threatened to expose him. That's why he couldn't risk waiting until you gave her the dope."

No one spoke for a moment. Rich just sat there, his gaze skating on the surface of the table. He wouldn't look at her. Gregory leaned against the wall, studying her. They were both waiting for her to continue. Their faces gave nothing away.

"Did you hear what I said?" she asked. "I'm through talking to you. I want a lawyer."

"Did you hear what *I* said just a minute ago?" Rich asked her. "Both Gregory and I've been suspended. We have no authority to hold you here. You are free to go."

"Suspended?" she breathed. "But why?"

She could see something flicker over Rich's face. He was deciding how much to tell her. "Sheriff Freehold knew about Luke and the deaths in The Pit. He canned both Gregory and me when we got too close, Kendra. He insisted on charging Cassady Moon for your mother's murder."

"But he had to give you a reason. What was it?"

His face told her the reason. "My God," she said. "It was because of me, wasn't it?" Her laugh was bitter. "That's a little ironic, isn't it, Rich? After all, you thought that you were just doing your job." A muscle in his jaw twitched at the jab, but he kept his face as still as stone. "And you mean I can go?" she asked.

Rich nodded. She stood, walked as fast as she could to

the narrow door and put her hand out to touch the knob. Rich's voice stopped her.

"For now, anyway," he said.

She spun around and pressed both hands against the door. She stared at the back of Rich's strong neck. She could see a half moon of sweat underneath the collar of his T-shirt.

"Even if what you say is even remotely true," she said. "What in the hell can I do about it?"

This time Gregory spoke. "Kendra, despite all the evidence we have against Luke Bertrand, it's not irrefutable. Because of his standing in this community, we need a confession. We need him to say it."

"Don't you want to finish this, Kendra?" Rich asked. He turned around to face her, his eyes dark and smoky. "Don't you want to know?"

"I already know," she shouted at him. "You are both full of shit!"

Rich got up and walked up to her. When he was inches from her, he slapped the spot on the door right beside her head. She turned her face away instinctively.

"Rich . . ." Gregory warned.

But Rich ignored him and reached out and grabbed her chin, making her face him.

"Fine," Rich said. "Don't think about me or Luke or what he has done or the fact that he has someone up there. Think about yourself. You are facing possession of an illegal substance, not to mention possible murder charges and the loss of your medical license. If we find out that you helped Raymond the night he popped those people, patched up the shooter or something . . ." He stopped. It must have been the look on her face. How did he know?

He answered her unspoken question. "Do you think that I'm stupid, Kendra? You think I wouldn't be able to figure out why Raymond was with you that night?"

"And it helped that you had access to my apartment. What did you find, Rich?"

He ignored the comment. "Right now, you are dealing with two suspended cops who at the moment do not have a formal relationship with the Dunhill County Sheriff's Department. We can forget to tell them some things, Kendra. But first, you need to help us."

"You don't need me," she insisted. "All you need to do is find out if Luke Bertrand has any connections to adoption agencies. And those crosses, Rich—you have that. You could at least get a search warrant . . ." She stopped because he was shaking his head slowly.

"You haven't heard a word that we've been saying. We don't have any authority with the sheriff's department. If it weren't for Beau, we wouldn't be here right now. Plus there is a girl in danger up there. That girl you are looking for, April Hart? We think she's up there. We don't have time to fool around."

Kendra searched his face and then pulled her head up until she was able to free her chin. "Why should I trust you?" she asked.

"Right now, you have no choice," he said. When he spoke again, his voice was almost as gentle as Gregory's. Almost. "Kendra, we are asking for your help."

She wanted to run away, but knew that she couldn't. It was not only the sound of his voice that made her realize that there was no way out of this. It was the promise that she'd made to April Hart's grandmother. She had no choice.

"What do you want me to do?" she asked.

Rich asked her to sit back down and told her to start with where she had obtained the dope. She told him that she did get it from Luke, who purchased it from Raymond. Luke always got it for her, in small enough portions so if she did get caught, she wouldn't look like a supplier. She told him Luke insisted on doing it himself, because he wanted—she swallowed—to share the risk. After all, it was his fault that she had come back to Dunhill in the first place. She told him about Raymond knocking on her door the other night with the wounded man. She stole a look at Rich when she said this to try to gauge his reaction. But he managed to keep his face unreadable.

"What do you want me to do?" she asked again.

Rich leaned toward her and spoke. His voice was grim. "We want you to get him to say he did it. That he killed those girls. We want you to get him to say it, like he's dying to do."

April

What made her so special, he told her, was that she was just like the first April. He sat beside her on the metal bed in the garden shed. He pulled her hands into his lap as he talked, squeezed her wrists until her fingertips tingled and then became numb. He had left the garden shed door open again. The smell of honeysuckle and tea roses floated on the warm sunlight falling across her bare legs. He had become more talkative in the last few hours, even more than before. He babbled about this and that until his words became as meaningful as the chickens clucking in her Nana's yard.

There had been two Aprils, he told her. She was the second one with that name, the second one whose child had come to him to be saved. This April had come to him for help just as she had. She had been Latina, with huge brown eyes and a puckered knife scar that divided her bottom lip in half. And he had helped her, treated her with methadone for her addiction.

But as the baby grew larger and larger in her belly, he kept thinking about the life it would lead with such a creature. He had been around drug addicts for the better part of his life. He had seen what became of their children.

But April, this first April, went into labor a month earlier, had given birth in his house. He had delivered the baby as best he could. It was small and pink and mewling like a baby lamb. But the most significant thing, the thing she must understand, was that this baby was born with a veil over his face. It was a sure sign from God. He didn't know for what at first, but then, in the next weeks, it all became clear to him.

This first April had been stealing from him. He kept drugs in his house for another purpose, and she had found them. He discovered her sprawled out on the tile bathroom floor, in a heroin nod so deep that her eyes rolled back and her head lolled on her neck like that of a rag doll. He knew then what the veil meant: he had been commanded by God to save this child from this beast.

He had given her a choice—the dope or the child. He knew a lawyer that would help him adopt out the baby. He had the papers ready for her to sign. She looked from him to the dime bag that he had laid on the kitchen table and then to the baby in his arms. No sign that she heard its mewling cry. Instead, she scooped up the dope and left his house on foot. He had thought that was the end of it. But she came back two days later and demanded the child.

So he gave her a choice again. He laid everything out on the table again and gave that first April a second choice, a second chance. He told her she could either take the child and go, or take the dope and go. Again, she chose the dope, a dope he had made especially for her. She had taken it voluntarily and died in an abandoned factory in The Pit—a place where time still worked though everything else was broken. He hadn't killed her really, he hadn't killed anybody. Every one of those girls had made her own decision, their own choice.

And now God was sending a message through her, the second April. Her death would be special. Her death would serve a purpose.

"But won't I be given a choice?" she asked. "I can make the right choice."

But he looked at her, and his eyes told her that he would never let her leave like the first April. Not for a moment. *Your death,* he told her, *has already been predestined. The choice has already been made.*

CHAPTER 32

THE SAVIOR

tions. At first he told her he would come by her house to dis...
... but he changed his mind about it on the phone ... for a phone

Kendra Hamilton was in Rich's apartment with four men: Rich, Gregory, Beau, and a short balding man with forearms like meat hooks. Rich introduced him to Kendra as Detective Sanders, telling her to just call the man Sandy. As Sandy fitted the wire on Kendra, he complained about losing his job, about his twenty-five years on the force going to hell in a handbasket. Kendra sat on a glass coffee table, wearing nothing but a bra and the same pair of jeans she had on when Rich and Gregory "arrested" her. Correction, they couldn't quite arrest her, could they? But she hadn't known that then.

Rich himself had showered and changed into a red polo shirt that stretched over his broad shoulders. Instead of the familiar holster, he had a small gun stuck into the back waistband of his neatly pressed jeans. But he hadn't shaved, and the growth on his face gave him a tired, desperate look.

Earlier that night, before they left the station, she called Luke Bertrand from Rich's cell phone. They told her to act like she was upset, which was quite easy to do, since she was. They told her to stick to the truth as much as possible. A lie would have to be remembered.

So she told Luke about the entire fiasco with Raymond and about the cops coming around asking her a lot of ques-

tions. At first he told her he would come by the clinic tomorrow, but she insisted she speak to him tonight, at his place.

"I'll come to your apartment," he had said.

"No, no," she whispered. "I'm afraid of him, of Raymond."
She looked up at Rich, and he nodded his approval. She went
on. "I'm afraid he may be watching me. I'm afraid he may
try and do something to me. I need to see you, Luke."

He eventually agreed to let her come over. Sandy pressed
tape over the wire running between her breasts, the pressure
bringing her back to the present.

"I could lose my ass for this, Rich," Sandy said for about
the hundredth time.

"You already said that, man," Rich said tiredly, his eyes
on Kendra.

Beau ran his hand over his balding head. "He's right," he
said. "Maybe this isn't such a good idea."

Rich stood up, exasperated. "Both of you just plain shut
up. Beau, you are up to your ass in this, and now Rita is in it
too, since she tested that dope for you without using the
proper protocols. And, Sandy"—he pointed at Sandy, who
had reached around Kendra to make sure the wires were
connected to the box tucked in the back of her jeans—
"you'll have a hard time explaining what you are doing with
all this equipment checked out. The van, the wires, the works.
Let's just play this cool, and all three of you will come out
looking like heroes."

"What about you?" Kendra asked. The words surprised
her, because they came from her before she could call them
back.

He gazed at her steadily before responding. "This isn't
about me," he said. "Not anymore."

Sandy helped her pull a white tank top over her head,
careful not to disturb the wires. Rich picked up a bulletproof
vest from the couch and walked toward the two of them. She
could only stare at him horrified.

"I can't wear that thing," she stated emphatically.

"It's not the time to be squeamish, Kendra," he said.

"I'm not being squeamish. I can't wear that. It'll put ten pounds on me."

"Just like a woman," Beau said with a snort.

"No," she insisted, not bothering to keep the annoyance out of her voice. "I can't hide that under the shirt. He will know something is wrong."

"She's right," Gregory agreed. It was the first time he had spoken since they had all arrived at the apartment. Rich sighed and threw the heavy vest on the couch. Sandy helped Kendra button a shirt over the wire, then stepped back to admire his handiwork.

"It would help if you had a jacket or something to put over that," he said.

She shook her head quickly. A corkscrew curl came loose from the barrette in her hair and fell across her eyes. She was too nervous to brush it away. Instead, she breathed in and out deeply, trying to drive away the fear. She knew she looked ridiculous but couldn't help it. She didn't know what frightened her more, getting hurt or finding out what Rich said about Luke was true. She looked down at her cold hands, lying in her lap like two dead fish. Rich walked over to her and stooped down on one knee so they were at eye level. He stared into her eyes long enough to make the others in the room uncomfortable.

"I gotta go to the can," Beau said.

"I need a drink of water," Sandy said.

Gregory didn't say anything, just peeled himself from the wall he had been leaning against and left.

Finally, Rich took both of her hands in his and said, "Do you really think that the only reason I slept with you was to get access to your apartment?"

She averted her eyes. At this point, she didn't know what to believe.

"I can't change your mind about the reason you believe I stayed with you that night. Not in the time we have now before this thing needs to happen," he said. "But when you go in there tonight, you need to trust me." He paused because she tried to pull her hands from underneath his. He tried to grab her with his eyes, but she turned away from him. He used a hand to tuck the errant rope of curl behind her ear.

"Don't go in there risking your life," he said. "The minute— no, the second—you suspect something is wrong, you say so and get your ass out of there. We will be up that hill in exactly two and a half minutes. Do you understand me? Two and one-half minutes."

She nodded, her eyes still averted.

"Kendra," he said in a voice that told Kendra he was still not satisfied. "Do you hear me?"

"I said yes!" she said, and forced herself to look at him.

"Good," he said grimly, and stood up.

Kendra stood up as well and rubbed the sweat from her palms on her thighs. The others returned to the room.

"What's that you say, Blair?" Rich cocked an eyebrow at the big cowboy.

Beau grinned a big Texas ten-dollar grin and said, "Let's roll."

As Kendra parked her black Acura in Luke Bertrand's circular driveway, she kept seeing an image in her mind. It was an image of orange fire in a can. It stretched its red fingers to touch the sides and used a yellow tongue to lick the top.

She tried telling herself it was the fear manifesting itself into this image. But in the back of her mind, she knew it was what she had been trying to do with Violet all these years. She had tried to control fire by capturing it and placing it in a can. She had tried to infuse Violet's addiction with logic. She tried to control the addiction by supplying her with the drugs she needed to make her life bearable.

"Come on, kiddo," she mumbled to herself. "Get it together.

She fiddled with the wires running between her breasts and then jumped at the voice in her ear. She had forgotten the earpiece was there, covered by her wild hair.

"Take it easy, Kendra," Rich said. "Two and one-half minutes, remember?"

She didn't answer out loud, only nodded. The men were parked in a PG&E van about a mile and a half down the road.

"Kendra?" Rich asked with a little bit of urgency in his voice. "Answer."

"I'm okay," she said. "I'm okay. Don't do that again, all right. You scared the shit out of me."

He didn't answer her, but she hadn't really expected him to. She got out of the car and closed the door. It thudded heavily in the silent night. She looked at her surroundings before mounting the steps leading to the double teak door. Surrounded by five acres of rolling green hills and wild woods, Luke's house was in the most prosperous section of Dunhill. A narrow dirt road marked PRIVATE was the only way in or out of the property. Or so Rich told her earlier that night as he drove her back to her apartment to retrieve the Acura.

The house itself was a split-level ranch built probably in the early fifties. Circular brick steps flooded out from the double teak doors like ripples of water. Lights from the circular driveway illuminated the way to the front door. She placed a foot tentatively on the bottom step, then stepped up the rest quickly. By the time she reached the front door, she had regained some of her composure. Luke Bertrand had swung the teak door open before she could knock. A wide smile covered his face, and he spread his hands in a welcoming gesture.

"My dear Kendra," he said, "please come in."

He took both of her hands in his and guided her into the house. He went to hug her, but she stepped away, fearing he might be able to detect the wire. She could tell by the small flicker in his eyes that he noticed, but he didn't say anything.

"It's so hot, and I'm all sticky and sweaty. I wouldn't want to give you a nose-full by getting too close," she said with a laugh. She knew it was a lame excuse but didn't know what else to say.

He waved away her concerns and squeezed her shoulder. As Kendra walked inside, she couldn't remember the last time she had been in Luke's house. Luke's insistence on his privacy was legendary in Dunhill. The front door opened onto a wide expanse of room with white marbled floors veined with tan. Two tall columns stood at an angle some distance away. To Kendra's left, there was a sitting room with a couch made of soft white leather. Two black armchairs were on either side, and in the middle there was a marble coffee table the same color as the floor.

Fresh white lilies sprung out of a thick crystal vase in the middle of the table. The pictures on the wall were all abstract and probably worth a fortune. Kendra couldn't detect a portrait or a fruit bowl in any single one of them. In a cream shirt, black slacks, and white suede shoes, Luke himself seemed to be dressed in a manner befitting his home's decor.

"Luke, I'm so sorry to bother you with this . . ." she started, then stopped. She didn't know what to say. Rich hadn't helped with that part. He just told her to get him talking and feel her way from there. He told her to stick to the truth as much as possible. But he didn't tell her what to say.

Luke led her to the couch, where they both sat down. She cast her glance around the room and noticed a fireplace built into the wall. Stereo equipment stretched from the floor to the ceiling.

Kendra turned to Luke. "I think Raymond killed my mother," she blurted before she could stop herself.

Luke drew back and took a deep breath. "Go on," he said. He didn't seem surprised.

"I think he poisoned her," she looked up at him. "On purpose, Luke."

He regarded her steadily, his face as calm as still water. "Have you gone to the police?" he asked.

Kendra looked down at her hands. She quickly put her

left hand over her right to keep them from shaking. She hadn't counted on this. She hadn't counted on his being so calm. She thought a long time before she spoke her next words. She wanted to tread carefully. *Keep as much to the truth as possible.*

"That's just it, Luke," Kendra whispered, still looking down at her hands. "I don't know if I want to." She bit her lip and brought her gaze to his. He still said nothing.

"Luke," she tried again. "Remember when I was little, the first time I had ever gone into a foster home?" She waited for him to speak for at least a full minute. He said nothing. Kendra's heart began to beat faster and faster. He knows, she thought. He has to know. "Anyway, you took me to the circus, and there were these men there eating . . ." She stopped with a nervous laugh. "They were eating . . ."

"Fire," Luke finished for her. "They were eating fire."

"Yes, fire!" she said in a voice that sounded too dramatic to her own ears. "And I asked you that ridiculous question about what happened to the fire inside them, in their bodies. I asked them how did they . . ." She stopped, hoping he would finish it, that he would become more a part of the conversation. His laughter sounded like a relieving rain after a long drought.

"You asked me how they passed it," he said.

She laughed with him. "And you told me that they didn't, that they learned to control the fire inside of them."

Luke spread his fingers apart and regarded her. "Kendra, I don't understand what this has to do with why you don't want to go to the police."

"Because Luke, ever since that day, I thought I could control fire. I thought I could control Violet, but she got away from me, Luke. She got away, and she was making my life a living hell—calling me every five minutes for dope, showing up at the hospital with those damn purple tracks up and down her arms, risking everything that I had worked for. I wanted her dead, Luke." She said this last part so forcefully she stunned even herself. *Stick to the truth,* she heard Rich's voice again. She pressed her palms against her ears and shut her eyes.

"Explain yourself, Kendra," Luke replied.

She took her hands from her ears and looked squarely into Luke's face.

"I don't want to go to the police because Raymond Smalls did me a favor. The world is rid of one less junkie, and my life is saner without her. I didn't deserve a mother like her. Nobody deserves a mother like her, Luke. Nobody."

She waited for him to speak. Still, he said nothing. He looked over his shoulder. Kendra followed his gaze. She jumped because at first she thought she had seen a specter, a dark black ghost. A thin black girl with hair that had not been straightened stood looking at them with solemn brown eyes. Her bottom and upper lip looked as if they were glued together, as if she never had cause to part them and speak. The lime green dress she wore made her look like a bright beanpole. She had a nine-inch butcher knife in her black hand. She looked like some silent sentry ready to do her master's bidding.

Kendra turned back to Luke. He knew. She didn't know how, but he knew. She went to say something, but he pressed an index finger to his lips. Sage stepped closer.

"Now, you don't mean that, Kendra," Luke said smoothly. "You are just upset. Sage, please get Kendra a glass of chardonnay, won't you."

The girl behind her didn't move. He motioned for Kendra to stand up. She could hear the girl breathing behind her. Cold steel pressed the soft spot at her base of her skull.

Her heart beat wildly, and her chest heaved up and down. Surely they must hear that, she thought frantically. Surely they must hear how heavily she was breathing. But Rich's voice didn't sound in her ear.

"You know what I do when I'm upset," Luke continued. "I listen to some music. Are you fond of modern jazz?"

When Kendra didn't answer right away, Sage pressed the tip of the knife harder into the base of her skull. It was a kill spot. Kendra turned her face around so she could look at her. She wondered how this girl, so young, could know that. Sage grabbed a handful of hair and shook Kendra's head until the roots burned in pain.

"Yes," she answered.

"Good," he said. "I have this disc given to me by a friend of mine. It's new, and as a matter of fact, I was enjoying it before you arrived. Do you mind?"

"Of course not," Kendra said. Fear paralyzed her. She knew that she should say something; scream to warn Rich and the others. But her throat has closed, all possibility of making sound was gone. When she finally did feel the beginnings of a scream in the pit of her stomach, Luke pressed PLAY on the CD player. Music filled the room, drowning out Kendra's voice. He drew his finger down the middle of her chest, indicating that she unbutton her shirt. He shook his head and mouthed, *You disappoint me Kendra*. He then reached over and gently pulled away the tape holding the wire to her chest. Sage helped dislodge the black box. Luke carefully placed the entire contraption near one of the speakers.

He walked out of the room, and motioned for Kendra to follow. They walked past the two columns into a large kitchen with big chrome pots hanging from the ceiling.

"Don't speak, Kendra," Luke said as she was about to open her mouth. "This is not your doing. This is the Lord's doing. He has shown me what will happen. He has instructed me."

"Luke," she tried. "Please tell me what is happening."

She tried to reach for the old Luke Bertrand she had known, the man who had helped put her through medical school, the man who helped her with her drug-addicted mother. But when she found his eyes, she could see that the Luke she'd known was gone. Perhaps he never existed. This man's eyes glittered and his lips had the wet sheen of excitement.

"No more lies, Kendra. You see," he said, walking around her, "I asked the Lord what would happen after your phone call. I asked him for the truth of His Word. He told me to place the Bible on my lap and let the leaves of his wisdom fall open. Do you know where the pages fell, Kendra?"

Kendra shook her head.

"Psalm twenty-two, verses one through sixteen. It's the prayer of David to God asking why he was forsaken. When I put my fingers upon these words"—he held up a finger and touched the air as if he were actually touching the words of God hanging on the air—"I knew that I must suffer before I would be delivered to walk beside God."

"To walk beside God?" Kendra asked.

Luke just smiled and then looked at Sage. "Is the other one ready?" he asked.

Sage nodded. As if reading his mind, she shoved Kendra toward him. Luke grabbed Kendra's hair in a grip that told her that he'd had lots of practice. She felt his hard chest against the back of her head. She felt his forearm against her stomach as he drew the knife near her throat.

"Don't make the mistake of thinking for one moment that I won't kill you, Kendra. I would hate to do it, but if it is His will, so be it."

Kendra forced her body still. He opened a drawer on the island and pulled out a roll of gray duct tape. Kendra had a fleeting thought that she might be able to get away as he maneuvered to bind her. But he expertly gripped both of her wrists between his and taped them together, then, before she could react, he knocked her feet from under her and taped her ankles. Tape flew around her ankles in a gray whir. He grabbed her by the waist and dragged her outside. Her head fell against someone's lap as Luke threw her into his gold Lexus. She looked up and saw April Hart.

April's blue eyes stared at Kendra's bound hands and ankles, finally resting on her flat belly. Her hands resting serenely in her lap, April Hart turned her white, dirty face back toward the front without speaking. Kendra looked at April's bare feet, which were crossed simply and calmly at the ankles. The girl was not tied up. She was as confident and calm as an unexpected cool breeze on a hot summer's night.

April

It had been a long time since April had seen other people besides Sage and the crazy man who had been praying with her every day for months. April just wished that the first person she had seen was not as helpless and useless as the black woman whose eyes looked as frightened as a pig's before the slaughter. April turned her face away and let her mind drift to her last time in the shed earlier that night.

After the crazy man had left her, he didn't come back for a while. He hadn't even come back to pray. She remembered how dark it was in the shed. It was as dark as pitch. Whatever would happen would happen that night. She knew then what it felt like to be on death row. She understood what it felt like to wait one final time.

She was sure of one thing, though. He and Sage would have to hog-tie and gag her to get her to take that poisoned dope. She would never again voluntarily stick another needle in her arm. She thought about her first few days cooped up in this garden shed like an animal waiting to breed. Chanting. That was what had kept her from going completely insane. That was what had kept her from losing her mind.

She started with her name first—out loud. Her own un-used voice scratched at her throat. She coughed a few times to clear it, then tried again.

"My name is April Hart, I'm from Red River—" She stopped suddenly and thought about the other girls. She thought about them all the time now. Lorna, Rochelle, Kitten, Beth. And finally April, the first April. What had they looked like? April, the first one, he had said was Spanish or something and had a scar. But what about the others? Kitten and Lorna and Rochelle?

"Kitten, Lorna, Rochelle," she chanted, and leaned her head back against the wall. She noticed for the first time a hole in the roof. She saw a couple of stars, their tiny lights flickering on a field of velvet. She kept up her chanting, and with each name came a breath of hope.

She placed her hand on her belly, looked down at it. She watched it hunch up as if the baby was trying to sit up. Her heart felt like it was being pushed to her throat, and her stomach felt like someone had punched her in it. She told herself it was too early, that these were just the practice con-tractions that she had heard about. By her calculations, her baby wouldn't be due for two more weeks.

"Hold on, baby," she soothed. "Hold on."

Her stomach deflated slowly and she looked up at the stars. *Kitten, Lorna, Rochelle*. She stopped. *April*. Her stom-ach did that thing again, and this time she felt something scrape underneath her breast. It was the twisted nest of wires and rusted nails she had collected from the bedsprings and shed walls. The pain comforted her.

She knew one thing, destined or not, she was not going quietly.

"I ain't going quietly at all, you crazy son of a bitch," she said, her eyes on the glittering stars overhead.

The car jolted over a pothole, and she found herself sit-ting in the gold Lexus, riding along the dark road. April turned to see the black woman staring at her. She almost laughed out loud when she recognized who it was. It was that doctor from the clinic, the one who had told her that she was pregnant. The one who hadn't done her any good then, and probably would be just as useless now.

CHAPTER 33

"**W**hat's this shit?" Beau asked rudely from over Rich's shoulder. "Some kind of black man's country?"

The music had been playing for two minutes. Rich clasped both hands together and pressed them to his lips. His feet did a nervous tattoo on the floor of the van. Gregory slumped in the seat beside him, slurping coffee loudly in his ear.

"Something's wrong," Rich murmured into his hands. "Something's wrong, man. I can feel it."

"What's that?" Sandy said. "Everything seems to be all right." Sandy ran his fingers along the controls in the van.

"I'm not talking about the equipment, man," Rich said. "I'm talking about the setup. Something's happening. He should have cracked by now."

Rich replayed the conversation they had all just heard over again in his head. Though his heart skipped a beat when Kendra blurted that shit about Raymond killing Violet Hamilton, she had taken it somewhere that was very plausible. She not only sounded convincing, she sounded convinced. But Luke hadn't bitten.

"Hey, Blair," Sandy said loudly to Beau. "What shit-kicking part of the county you get those country-ass boots from? You look like you going to a rodeo."

"Fuck you, Sandy," Beau replied.

"Shut up, shut up," Rich jerked his hands at both of them.

They had been engaging in their good-natured banter ever since they'd stopped the van and watched Kendra drive up the hill to Luke's place. They had barely listened to the conversation between Kendra and Luke.

Three minutes had gone by. "Rich," Gregory said mildly. "What's going on?"

"I don't know." He rubbed his head. "Something's not right."

"Do you want to go up?" Gregory asked.

Rich didn't answer. He felt paralyzed in his seat. He wanted to get into the driver's seat and go barreling up the hill to Luke's front door and get Kendra the hell out of there. But he knew what the consequences would be if he did that and nothing was wrong. He needed more proof. Something was up.

Four minutes. The CD had started into the next song.

Luke. How could he have fooled everyone? How was it that no one saw? He remembered how Luke appeared at the party. He was so smooth that he floated around the room like he was rolling on a pair of greased wheels. And even when he didn't like something, he didn't show it. He made you feel like you were the only person that mattered. He thought about that young kid at the party, that jazz musician who maneuvered himself to stand next to Luke Bertrand. When the kid saw his moment, he thrust the disc at Luke and told him that he was his inspiration. Looking at that kid straight in the eye, Luke had taken it and proclaimed how much he liked jazz. How much it had thrilled him to be an inspiration to someone who had a part in such an art form. Rich smiled now to think of it. The kid walked away on cloud nine. But when he was out of earshot, Luke turned to Rich and said . . .

"I hate jazz." Rich didn't know he had spoken the words aloud until he found three pair of eyes staring at him in the PG&E van parked exactly two and one-half minutes from Luke Bertrand's house.

"I hate jazz," he repeated stupidly, looking at all of them in turn.

Beau shrugged. "Then turn the shit down. I can't stand it, either."

Rich jumped over Beau and stepped with both feet into the driver's seat.

"Hey, watch it, man," Beau complained. "You kicked me in the head."

Ignoring him, Rich started the van and put it into gear. He glanced in the rearview mirror and could see Gregory carefully make his way to the passenger's seat.

"What is it, Rich?" he asked.

"The music is a cover," Rich said. He slapped the steering wheel hard, but the resulting sting barely registered. "How could I have been so fucking stupid?"

Freehold. How long did it take the sheriff to call Luke and tell him what Rich and Gregory had suspected? He twisted his wrist so he could get a look at the face of his watch. The van swerved dangerously to the side of the road. Both Sandy and Beau swore loudly, but again Rich ignored their complaints.

By his calculations, the music had been playing four, maybe five minutes. Plenty of time for Luke to do what? He tried to imagine. If he'd decided to try an escape, he would have had to pass the PG & E van parked on the road.

He thought about the pack of letters Luke had sent him these last months. No, Lucas Cornelius Bertrand would not run. It was beneath him, and besides, he thought he was doing what was right. Why run from the truth? He knew that whatever Bertrand had planned, it involved Kendra Hamilton. She would not meet her fate in the sprawling house in the midst of those green hills. That place held no meaning for Luke, not for what he was trying to do. He was going to finish it where it started, somewhere in The Pit. But still, if Luke left his estate, he would have no option but to pass them as he descended from The Point.

"Beau," Rich said as he looked in the rearview mirror at Beau's big red head. "You got that map of the property."

Beau's head disappeared, and Rich felt pressure on the back of his seat as the big man steadied himself. Beau leaned over and crumpled the map on Rich's chest, causing the van to swerve crazily once more. Rich turned on the overhead dashlight and glanced briefly at the map.

"You sure that this road is the only way out?" he asked as he alternately looked at the van eating up the road and the swirls and lines on the map in front of him.

Beau sighed heavily. "I know that's the only proper road. But if someone wanted to get out, they could find a way."

Rich swore under his breath. He thrust the map to Gregory, who spoke after looking at it for what seemed like minutes, but was really only seconds. "It looks like he could have gotten out on this road here," he stopped. Rich felt his gaze on him. "Should we call for backup?" Gregory asked as they were pulling up in front of the house. Rich said nothing but grimaced. He wanted to answer yes, but knew they couldn't call for backup.

"Hell, no," Beau and Sandy said at the same time, but it was Sandy who finished the thought. "First of all, this situation is as illegal as hell. I don't want to get my ass held to the fire unless something is happening."

Their answers did not surprise Rich. This was not an official run for either one of them. They couldn't call backup until they got their story straight. He flicked the lights off the last thirty seconds or so of the ride so he wouldn't alert Luke. When they arrived at the lighted driveway, Rich jumped from the van with Gregory following closely on his heels. The lawn lights reflected from the surface of Kendra's black Acura. At least her car was still here. That was a good thing.

By silent agreement, Rich approached the door straight on. Gregory stayed out of view by leaning against the side of it, weapon drawn. Rich looked around for a doorbell, his heart beating fast. He resisted the urge to just kick it down. He lifted the brass ring in a lion's mouth door knocker and rapped it hard three times against the teak door. Out of the corner of his eye, he saw both Sandy and Beau go around opposite sides of the house. He waited for several seconds. Gregory breathed heavily beside him.

There was no answer.

He lifted the brass ring again, and let if fall. Again, no answer. He hesitated a split second, then jerked the handle down and stepped into the foyer of Luke Bertrand's sprawling ranch-style home. The big room must have been air-conditioned to well under seventy degrees. After the warm cocoon of the night, he felt like he had just been plunged naked into an ice-cold stream. Jazz music blared from the stereo equipment in the sitting room. The body wire lay on the marble floor next to the speaker. Goose bumps rose on Rich's forearms.

Rich took out his weapon, but he knew it was fruitless. The place was empty as a robbed grave. Gregory stepped behind him and pointed his weapon to all corners of the room. Then he went into the kitchen and went through the routine again. Rich just stood in the middle of the living room, the room swirling around him crazily as the truth dawned on him. They had missed them. Kendra and Luke were gone.

Gregory said nothing when he returned from the kitchen. He disappeared down a hallway off the sitting room and returned after a few seconds.

"Looks like the place is empty, Rich."

Rich didn't tell him that he had known the place was empty the second time he lifted the brass ring in the lion's mouth and did not receive a response. And besides, Luke's gold Lexus was not parked in the driveway.

"What now?" Gregory looked at him.

Before he could answer, they heard Blair's voice as he walked from the kitchen.

"Girls," he said. "You need to come catch a look at this."

Rich and Gregory followed the big man back through the kitchen and into a garden area. About twenty feet from the double French doors and slightly to the left there was a dilapidated garden shed. It exploded with light from the flashlight Sandy obviously had inside. Both Rich and Gregory walked inside.

The garden shed was close to empty. No rakes, no shovels, no merry little tools hanging from the pegboard caked with earth. Instead, someone had swept the dirt floor smooth and pushed a rusty bed with a thin mattress against one wall. A miniature green Bible, one with just the New Testament and Psalms, lay neatly by the bed.

Rich walked to it and picked it up. Someone had bent the pages so it lay open on the floor. An empty milk carton and a banana peel, still yellow, lay beside the Bible.

Rich picked up the Bible and pressed it to his chin so hard he half wondered if the words would be grooved into his chin. Luke Bertrand always talked about time, how there was always time for hope. He'd even talked about it during that first meeting with the sheriff. And he had this last baby, this one last baby he had to save.

"Rich," Gregory asked.

"Let's go," Rich stood up. "I know where they are."

CHAPTER 34

Luke Bertrand used a key to open the chain-link fence surrounding the abandoned factory that was the home of the only working public clock in all of The Pit. Besides the butcher knife that Sage clutched in her fingers like a cross, Luke had retrieved a small revolver with a stubby nose from the glove compartment. He kept it trained on Kendra Hamilton as Sage used the butcher knife to cut the tape from her ankles.

Luke ushered them all in, and they walked across the cement to the factory's entrance. The night had cooled with the coming morning. Used condoms and McDonald's hamburger wrappers stirred with the wind across the parking lot.

Kendra shortened her steps in an effort to slow Luke down, but she felt the knife tip press against her bare back. April Hart had not said a word during the entire car ride over. Kendra had tried to talk to her, but Sage had reached behind and punched her in the face, stabbing her left cheek with her knuckles. Kendra could taste blood in her mouth.

She stole a glance at April, who walked listlessly beside her. Kendra looked around the abandoned factory. The structure was about five stories high and very wide. Kendra had to turn her head if she wanted to take in the entire width of the building. Many of its tiny square windows were missing. The few windows that did have glass reflected the glow from the moonlight. As they approached, Kendra got the feeling they were about to be swallowed up by a grinning giant with great winking eyes and punched-out teeth.

"Why are we here, Luke?" she asked him.

He didn't answer, not right away. Then, as they walked through the front doors, he said. "We are here to pray, and to reflect."

Support beams stuck uselessly in the empty air like bent and broken fingers, reaching for a ceiling that was no longer there. What used to be the second floor had long since rotted, destroyed by the ravages of time and abandonment.

She thought most of the factory was like this, but then she and April were herded toward a darkened corner that looked like nothing but empty space. Yet there was a door with a heavy metal lock. Luke's keys clanged together as he found the appropriate key to open it. Kendra wondered why Luke went through so much trouble. Many people in The Pit thought the place to be haunted. Brave teenagers rarely went past the parking lot, and old winos knew enough not to venture past the front door.

He ushered them into the tiny room. For the first time, Kendra noticed that Luke carried a black medical bag. All three of them stood closely together in a weak pool of flashlight, reminding Kendra of campers ready to tell ghost stories. She could smell the musk covering April Hart, almost as strong as the rotted wood of the factory. Luke motioned for everyone to kneel and then prayed a wild, looping prayer that lasted five or so minutes and ended with Luke's apologies to the Lord for his inability to save more children.

When he was finished, he grabbed Kendra's hand and forced her to her feet. Though Luke's skin felt papery against hers, he gripped her hand hard enough to cause the bones to crush together. He stopped just before she screamed, just before he did any real damage. Still holding the gun, he brought her hands to his lips and kissed her fingers.

"These hands, Kendra," he said. "These hands have helped so many, these hands I helped create. They have done so much. Now they must do one last thing."

He let go. Kendra stared at him. Why hadn't she seen before how completely insane he was? How could she have been so blind? He handed the short stubby gun to Sage, who stood watching both April and Kendra as if she could cut out their hearts while preparing morning tea. Kendra knew she wouldn't be able to do anything with Luke if she didn't handle this Sage. She looked over at April. For the first time that night, April returned her gaze as if she was answering Kendra's latest thought in the affirmative.

Luke opened the medical bag and pulled out a scalpel. He grabbed Kendra's hand again and placed the knife in her palm. Sage stepped closer and placed the muzzle of the gun against her hand. Kendra looked at the knife, then closed her eyes. She swallowed, and both blood and fear traveled down her throat and settled in the pit of her stomach. When she opened her eyes again, Luke's eyes glinted at her.

"I don't understand," she said.

"You must finish this, Kendra. You must," he said. He held his palm up to April's belly. Dread hit her with the realization of what he wanted her to do. Dread and anger.

"Why did you kill my mother, Luke?" she asked now.

Confusion swept his face for a minute, and then he smiled. "Why for you, my dear."

"But you set me up with the poisoned dope," she stalled.

"I did," he nodded. "That was the original plan. Your hands should have been the ones to dispose of her. But she had become so insistent in her harassment of you, that it simply couldn't wait any longer. And she would have exposed me. I helped you, Kendra. Now you must help me." He pointed at April's stomach.

Kendra looked at the scalpel in her hand. "That's impossible," she said. "I won't."

Sage pressed the gun harder against her temple. She winced and closed her eyes again but continued, "I swear to God, Luke, you are going to have to shoot me. I won't perform a cesarean."

She opened one eye just in time to see Luke's imperceptible nod. At first she thought he was bluffing. Then she heard the hammer click back. She felt her nostrils flare as her breath came in and out. Fast.

"No, wait!" April Hart's voice surprised them all. "You can't. What about my baby?" Though her voice was soft and southern, it was the voice of someone who had not given up—who would not give up. April's voice shamed Kendra into wanting to fight again. If April hadn't given up in all these months, then Kendra certainly wouldn't now.

"I can't do it here, that's all," Kendra said quickly.

"This is where it will have to be," Luke said. "If you won't do it, I will. I am a trained medical doctor. I've done it before."

Kendra managed a short laugh. "Come on, Luke," she said. "You haven't practiced medicine in over twenty-five years. You were lucky with the other births. Your hands are weak," She stopped as Sage pressed the gun harder to her head at the insult. "I'm just telling the truth," Kendra said, unable to keep the sob out of her voice. "If you try to do a cesarean on a woman who is not sedated, you won't be able to control her. Even with Sage. You will only end up butchering this girl and killing that precious baby. You need me."

His silence told her that he knew what she said was true.

"We need to go to my clinic," she continued. "There's medicine down there, and I can do this in an almost sterile environment." She didn't say what was chief on her mind, that she could also buy herself and April more time. But more importantly, if Smalls still felt the need to look after her, maybe the gentleman in the black Nike jacket would be there watching over the clinic. And maybe this time he could do more than just open the door for her.

She could see Luke turning the idea over in his head. Finally, he dropped the key to the cement floor. Then he walked out of the room with the flashlight still in his hand, the light pooling around his legs and feet as if he were walking on water.

CHAPTER 35

Darkness filled the streets around the clinic with quiet. The white moon hung fat and low in the velvet sky like a watchful eye. Kendra Hamilton looked around for the man who had so startled her when she had come here to look through the files that night. But the surrounding streets were empty. Smalls had obviously felt no reason to protect her and her interests any longer.

The four of them entered the clinic, and Kendra turned on the light next to the door. Light flooded around them, but it was only for a second because Luke immediately turned it off. He then slapped her without a word. She brought the back of her hand to her busted lip and counted the stars behind her eyes. She prayed silently for the scalpel against her hand again. Once she had it, she would use it to slice Luke's face in half. When she opened her eyes, she saw that Luke had the flashlight on. He pointed it down toward the white linoleum.

"The exam room . . ." Kendra said and started walking toward the back.

"No," Luke said as Sage jerked her arm. "Here."

"But there is no place . . ." she started.

"I said here," he repeated.

Kendra nodded. "All right," she said. "At least let me get some blankets and start an IV."

"You will use this scalpel. No IV and no blankets."

Kendra licked her lips. She had counted on those blankets. If she positioned them in a certain way, Luke wouldn't be able to see what she was doing.

"I really need those blankets for the baby."

"No."

She looked at April. Her blue eyes skated across the room in abject fear. Kendra could see all the fight leave her like air being sent out of a balloon.

"This is no better than the factory, Luke," Kendra protested.

Luke hooded his eyes a little, and Kendra could tell that he was thinking about what she said. She knew that look, and it scared her that she knew him so well. In some ways at least.

"What harm can it be, doing it in the exam room?" she asked.

The long ensuing silence was fine with Kendra. This meant that Rich and the others would have more time to find them. That is, if Rich could guess where they were.

Finally Luke spoke. "Okay, the exam room. But no painkillers."

They walked to the same exam room where Kendra had first learned of the death of her mother. It was probably the same exam room where April Hart had found out she was pregnant. Now it was the same place that Kendra would either kill Luke Bertrand or be killed by him.

The cover on the exam bed crinkled noisily as April scooted up on it, crushing it with her weight. Kendra pulled a blanket up to the girl's chin. While she did so, she looked into April's eyes. *Don't give up,* she mouthed. *Be strong.* She turned and felt the stubby barrel of the gun against her sternum. Sage pressed the gun against her hard. Kendra knew she meant to hurt and that for some reason the girl hated her.

"Luke, I need to get iodine and a C-section kit. I may

have one here for emergencies." It wasn't a complete lie, but also she wanted April to have a chance to calm down as she pretended to look for it.

"No," Luke said, his voice firm, his eyes on April's bulging stomach underneath the blanket.

"Think of the baby, Luke," Kendra pleaded.

"The baby is in the Lord's hands. No iodine. No C-section kit. You will use my instrument."

He held up the scalpel. For the first time Kendra noticed little flecks of rust on it. She licked her lips as a fresh horror touched her. She recognized blood, even dried blood, when she saw it.

"It's not sterile, Luke," she said, trying to sound reasonable.

"It has the blood of the lamb, of the sacrificed," he countered.

Sage walked over to the door and blocked it while she pointed the gun at both Kendra and April. When Luke placed the scalpel in her hand, Kendra felt as if she had the advantage for the first time that night. Luke stepped over to the sink to make room for her, which made her feel better and worse at the same time. She looked at him to see if he had the butcher knife. He did. The hopeful feeling she had a moment ago dissipated, but only a little. *Where in the hell is Rich,* she thought. She almost laughed thinking that this was the first time in her life that she'd ever wished for a cop.

She grasped the blanket on April's chin and tried to pull it down. But the girl held on to it tightly. Her eyes were big as two blue dinner plates, and her pink lips trembled. Kendra tugged at the blanket, gently, and April let it go. She used the scalpel to cut away the filthy flowered shift April wore. When the girl's breasts were exposed, Kendra stopped suddenly.

"Luke," Kendra said pensively, using most of her body to block Sage's view. "You better come take a look at this."

"What?" he asked, concern in his voice. "What is it?"

"I don't know," she said, slowly. "I've never seen anything

like it." That was not a lie either. She hadn't ever seen anything like it.

"Give me the scalpel, Kendra," Luke said. Without turning around, she held out the scalpel to him. She felt it leave her hand and then heard it drop into the sink behind him. *Shit,* she thought. He walked over to her and stood behind her a minute.

"What is it?" he repeated.

"There, below her right breast. You see it?" she asked, knowing full well he couldn't.

"You are in the way," he said.

Kendra stepped back over to the sink and looked at Sage. The gun was still trained on her, and Sage's eyes glittered wildly.

"I don't know—" Then Luke screamed.

April, in a flash, had grabbed the weapon she had tucked under her breast and stuck Luke with it. Just as Kendra hoped, Luke's cries of pain unnerved Sage. But not for long, and not long enough for Kendra to snatch the scalpel from the sink.

While Luke and April struggled, Kendra tackled Sage. The girl still didn't speak, but instead eeked out a squeal that did nothing but egg Kendra on. The struggle knocked open the exam-room door, and they both spilled through the narrow doorway. Sage squirmed beneath Kendra like a fish, her sharp bones digging into Kendra's throat and stomach. Sage worked the gun around and pointed it into Kendra's face. Kendra squeezed Sage's wrist, screaming for her to drop the gun.

"It's over," Kendra yelled. "Let it go."

But Sage pulled the hammer back and then smiled while slowly squeezing the trigger. Kendra closed her eyes and waited for the impact.

But instead of a bullet, Kendra felt something hard step into the small of her back. Luke's foot hit Sage in the face, knocking her head against the wall. The blow knocked Sage unconscious. Luke reached down and pulled the gun from Sage's hand before Kendra had time to react.

Kendra struggled to a sitting position. She looked over at April who sat on the floor holding her torn dress over her exposed breast and belly. Blood soaked through the front of the dress as April cried softly.

"Get up," Luke said. "Now."

Kendra stood up. She heard paper crinkle and knew April was doing the same. Kendra looked at Luke. He had a bundle of twisted wire about a half inch thick sticking from his shoulder. Kendra thought briefly about the scalpel in the sink and wondered if April had managed to get it. But April's steady stream of tears told her differently.

Sweat ran down Luke's face and settled in the deep grooves on the side of his nose. His cream shirt was stained with blood and dirt. He motioned for them both to return to the waiting room. His eyes, his eyes were crazed and determined. As she backed into the exam room, Kendra saw pinpricks of light between the window and the blind. Relief flooded over her. It had to be Rich. She leaned over to April until her lips touched her ear.

"Run," she whispered.

April stopped her sobbing. She looked slowly over at Luke and then the gun and then back at Kendra.

"Luke," Kendra said in a hard voice. "It's over."

Before Luke could respond, April pushed past him and sprinted down the hall. Kendra prayed that she remembered the back way out of the clinic. Luke's scream pierced the air as he started after her. But Kendra ran after him and grabbed his arm. Whirling toward her, he raised the gun to hit her. But just before the blow landed, the front door burst open.

Rich stood there pointing his gun at Luke and yelling. Luke swiveled around and they faced each other. Suddenly all action stopped. All need for hurry and action simply ceased as Luke and Rich faced each other across the room.

"Tell him to drop his weapon," Luke ordered Kendra in a calm voice.

Kendra looked at him horrified. She wondered what made Luke think that she would do that. Then she heard Rich speaking to her.

"Kendra, move away."

She turned her eyes away from Luke's smug face. Her eyes collided with the gun Rich pointed at them. She turned back to Luke, and her eyes collided with the gun that he held on Rich. It was then that she realized with perfect horror her dilemma. Somehow, she had ended up dead center between the two men.

By pointing the guns at each other, they also pointed them directly at her. She looked at Rich, then at Luke, then at Rich again. She laughed—short, spurting laughs that threatened to turn into sobs. Incredibly, Luke started laughing with her. Kendra watched Rich's face grow confused but only for a moment.

"Kendra," Rich said again, this time more forcibly. "Please move away."

"Don't move," Luke countered. "Tell him to drop his weapon."

·Kendra felt as if she were the hub of a two-spoked wheel. When she moved a step, Luke moved a step to keep out of Rich's gun sight. And when Luke moved, Rich moved. She was the controlling center.

Kendra stopped the hysterical laughter. "Luke, please . . ." she started.

"Come over here," Luke commanded. "I have something to tell you."

She might have ignored him if she hadn't glanced over at Rich. The muscles in his arms tensed and flexed as if on a spring. His eyes told her that he wanted to shoot Luke. He wanted to shoot Luke with his entire heart. And again, she was just in the way.

She looked at Luke. Sweat bathed his face. His low afro glinted in the overhead lights that Rich had turned on. His full lips trembled as he tried to keep the cool, smug smile on his face. And his eyes sparkled with just one intent. He wanted to shoot Rich. He wanted to shoot Rich with all of his heart. For him as well, she was just in the way. She was the only thing that kept them both from pulling the trigger and entering into one more round of violence. She couldn't let that happen.

"Kendra," Luke said as if reading her mind. "I would have never hurt you. Never. You must know that." He used his most sincere voice. Kendra took a step toward it, toward the man she used to know.

"Kendra," Rich warned. "Don't listen to him. Move away."

But she could not *not* listen. All of her memories, all of the things that Luke had done for her were there in the midst of all this confusion. The bloodstained man disappeared. And in his place was the man she knew. The man who had always protected her.

"Kendra," Rich said in a careful voice. "Don't. You have been up for hours. You've gone through a lot of shit tonight. You're tired. Confused. Can't you see what's happening?"

She frowned, confused. She rubbed her eyes with her fingertips. Luke must have seen her confusion. He pressed on.

"You ever wondered why I've protected you, Kendra?" Luke said. "You've seen me kill for you. Don't you realize that you were the first child that I—"

"Shut up, Bertrand!"

Kendra didn't know where she was. She felt a wave of uncertainty crash over her. She smelled blood and sweat. Through the confusion, she thought she heard Rich, yes, maybe it was Rich, say "Too close." But then Luke was speaking again. She didn't hear his first words, but she could hear the middle.

"—saved. Kendra, it was—all f—"

But Rich did not let him finish. Suddenly, he dodged to the right and shot. The entire room went dark as he slapped out the lights. Kendra heard plaster rain onto the linoleum floor. The noise exploded as if it came from within her head. Luke snatched her arm and jerked her to his chest. He turned her until her back was pressed against him. His forearm crushed against her throat, and she could barely breathe. Luke used his gun hand to turn the lights back on. He then stabbed the gun at various points around the seemingly empty room.

"Rich," Luke said. "Please come out. I don't want to hurt you. I just want a head start."

Luke and Kendra had their backs to the front door. Rich had to be behind Maria's desk, which was now turned on its side. Papers and pencils littered the floor. Kendra realized part of the crash she had heard before was Rich diving behind the desk.

Her throat felt as fragile as an egg under Luke's forearm. She struggled for breath. "You're choking me," she spurted. He let her go. She gulped air as if she had just stepped from a vacuum-sealed room.

"You see, Rich," Luke said. "I don't want to hurt her. You must come out. I don't want to hurt you, either. You are both my children. Head start, that's all I ask."

He spread his arms out to his sides and held his hands out. The gun hung loosely from his fingers like he didn't know it was there. Kendra saw Rich rise from behind the overturned desk. He pointed his gun at Luke in a two-handed grip.

"It would be nice if you could drop your weapon, Rich, so we can discuss this."

Luke's voice flowed from his body as smooth as cream, and he had a perfectly sane smile on his face. Both lulled Kendra into a false sense of security. Maybe this was going to turn out all right after all. His demeanor must have convinced Rich as well. He relaxed his grip on the gun, but still he didn't drop it. He stepped out from behind the desk.

Kendra kept her eyes entirely on Luke's face. She was able to see the glitter in Luke's eyes before Rich did, and her only thought was to warn him. Without thinking, she stepped forward and yelled Rich's name. She heard her own name in answer, then twin blasts from both sides of the room. An electric current traveled up her arms. Then there was silence, and finally blackness.

CHAPTER 36

Kendra thought she was in heaven when she finally opened her eyes. Pricks of pain like white light growing larger and larger fell around her. The sting of the IV in the back of her hand brought her back to reality. She wasn't in heaven. Adam was not going to come and greet her with a big-toothed smile and tell her everything was going to be all right—forever, this time.

Instead, she was in a hospital room with white-painted walls, a TV hanging from the ceiling, and a bright blue blanket pulled to her chest. A strong odor of blood permeated the room. Her shoulder felt like someone had removed her arm and replaced it backward. Pain steamrolled her midsection. Her eyes felt heavy, and all she wanted to do was to close them again. But then she heard a voice. His voice.

"How are you feeling?" he asked quietly.

She blinked her eyes as best as the pain would allow. What happened to the self-inflicted amnesia that accompanied severe trauma? There was none for her. She remembered everything. Luke. The pain of the bullet. April Hart. She didn't want to cry. Not after all of this. She didn't want to lose it and start bawling. She turned her head to the side and saw Richard T. Marvel sitting by her bedside in a pair of clean blue jeans and white T-shirt. She knew at least a day had passed since the clinic. Although Rich's eyes were puffy with the need of sleep, his face was neatly shaved. He laced his fingers and pressed them to his chin.

"What day?" she croaked.

"May seventh," he answered.

She nodded. She had been out for at least a week. She waited for the next question to float across her brain.

"April?" she finally asked.

"She's okay. They got her in some rehab center. The baby's got some problems, but they think she may be all right. They will probably let her keep it."

"Ray Ray?"

Rich didn't say anything at first. Then he spoke in an unemotional voice.

"He's in jail for murder, Kendra. We found the car he used to move the bodies."

Kendra closed her eyes and nodded. She remembered Raymond's face floating across in a dream she'd had while she was out. It wasn't his face as she'd last seen him, but a little-boy face with the hope of the future. She laughed a little. Rich remained silent. She opened her eyes and stared at him.

"So Ray Ray really did it, huh?" she asked. "He really had it in him. Luke?"

"He's in jail," Rich said.

She swallowed. She needed to know something. Desperately. She concentrated on getting the words out, so she would make sense, so he would tell her.

"Have you seen him? Tell me everything. I need to know." She thought she was yelling but knew it was only a harsh whisper at best.

Again he waited a moment or two before speaking. He regarded her. Then, as if making a decision, took his hands from his chin and leaned forward in his chair. "He was very upset when you were hit . . ." He continued in an unemo-

tional voice, as if he were giving a report to a superior.
Kendra knew that it was his way of trying to keep control, of
making sense out of what had happened.

Luke had fallen to his knees and wept when she went
down. Law enforcement personnel entered and arrested him
on the spot. The round (and that's what Rich called it—the
round) from Rich's own Beretta had nearly severed Kendra's
arm from her shoulder. The round from Luke's weapon, which
was a .22, had pierced her side, missing all vital organs,
though it was still lodged inside her after several hours of
surgery.

For the time being, Lucas Cornelius Bertrand was charged
with one charge of aggravated kidnapping and another of
attempted murder. More charges, of course, were pending.
Kendra licked her lips and tasted salt. That's not what she
had wanted to hear.

"Did you speak with him?" she whispered.

Rich told her that he had. He went to see Luke in the
county lockup. In her mind's eye, Kendra could see Lucas
Cornelius Bertrand in jail, the only creature comforts a toilet
and a cot. But Rich said that Luke had treated that tiny cell
as if it were a royal palace and Rich a visiting subject.

"Rich, before I was shot, Luke said he had killed for me.
What did he mean by that?"

Rich brought both hands to his mouth and rubbed them
across his face. "I don't know," he said finally, his voice dull.
"Maybe he was talking about your mother."

She thought about that for a moment and then shook her
head.

"I don't think so," she said. She knew. Deep down, she
knew. The only person she had ever seen killed was the wino
at The Elite Hotel, the wino who waited for her to pass him
in the graffiti-stained hallway on her way to the bathroom
when she lived at The Elite with Violet. She saw a strange
man with glittering eyes choke the wino to death. Never touch
what's mine. That was what the man had said. Maybe all of
it, from that death forward, maybe all of it was her fault. "He

said that I had *seen* him kill for me," she continued, "and he started to say something else, just before- –"

Rich's sigh cut her off. "He's crazy, Kendra."

"What did he say, Rich?" She felt hot tears roll from her eyes. She knew that an answer was not forthcoming.

Rich didn't speak for a second or two. He ran his hands over his face. "I don't remember," he said. "I didn't hear him."

"Rich . . ."

"Besides," Rich continued. "It's obvious he's crazy."

"Well, there you are again, sleepyhead," a nurse said in a cheerful voice as she glided into the room. "Are you going to stay with us for a while this time?"

Kendra felt the first stirrings of a laugh. Now she knew how her patients felt.

"It's time for you to go, Rich. I can't break the rules for you again tonight. She needs her rest."

He stood up and walked over to Kendra's bed. He touched her hand for several seconds. She knew that he was waiting for something, but her fingers remained still. Then, without looking at him, she finally squeezed his hand.

"So I guess we will see you tomorrow?" the nurse asked him.

Without hesitation, Rich answered her. "Yes, you will," he said.

Kendra watched his broad back as he left. She could have sworn he was whistling.

Rich whistled as he walked out of Doctor's into the cleansing white sunlight. He had no badge, and the gun tucked into his waistband belonged to him. All his hopes and dreams had been blown to bits in the space of three weeks. But for the first time in his life, he felt an odd sense of freedom overtake him. His mind was open and the world still had possibilities.

EPILOGUE

April Hart told the Greyhound bus driver that the air in Red River, Texas, was so sweet that people had once talked of bottling and selling it. But by the time they reached the town, she understood that it was no longer sweet. The rains had come, and the ground was soaked through. A sour-smelling mist hovered just above the wet soil. The smell seeped through the Greyhound's closed windows, filling April with dread.

April fingered the AA medallion in her pocket. Counting the time she spent with Luke, she'd been clean over ten months now. Her baby, the baby bundled in her lap, was almost three months old.

"I got to let y'all out here, gal," the bus driver told her through the wad of tobacco in his mouth. "Unless you want to go all the way to town."

April didn't want to go all the way to town. That would put her at least two miles from Nana's place. And she was walking with a baby. When she stepped from the bus, mist pricked her skin. She could taste the bitterness in the back of her throat. She peered through it looking for something familiar, something that she knew. But there was nothing. It was pitch black. Starlight could not struggle through the quilt of dark clouds in the sky. A car's headlights glowed brighter and brighter as it passed her. She heard a hoot owl screech, and the sound of crickets filled the night.

Because she didn't have any choice, she started walking. And as she did, the darkness flanking both sides of the road took shape. At first she saw thin arms twisting in the mist, then broad branches attaching themselves securely to tree trunks. Trees, about eleven million of them, towered above her in the thick mist.

April touched the medallion one more time in her pocket. She was still scared to death. He heart thumped as if it would break, and she had no idea where this road would lead.

But thank the Lord, she was sober. Thank the Lord, she was finally home.

The following is a sample chapter
from Faye Snowden's eagerly
anticipated upcoming novel,
FATAL JUSTICE

It will be available in October 2005
wherever books are sold.

ENJOY!

PROLOGUE

The place is beautiful but the two standing under the
shimmering green leaves do not notice. They do not see
the thriving river or the gray blue water rushing over the
rocks. Sunlight sifting through emerald leaves and red flowers tucked at the bases of redwood trees are lost on them.
What they do see, however, is each other. How intent each of
their faces are, hers with determination and his with equal
determination but something else as well. Fear that he is
about to lose control yet again.

Maybe he never had control over this woman. Maybe he
was a fool to think so. The brown suitcase with the brass
buckles, the one she holds in front of her as she listens and
does not listen tells him that he has let things get out of
hand. The fact that she is packed and ready to go, contrary to
what they had agreed—no, what she had promised him—
tells him that indeed, he must have been a fool. And things

must be set right. But first he has a duty. He must at least try. So he tries to reason with her.

"Debra," he says. "This will not stand. It will never work."

"No," she answers. "It will. I know it will. It has to."

"You can run away all you want but you will never be able to run away from the world."

Her hands, the smooth brown fingers, the painted red nails reach for him. "When running away is all a person has, then running away is the only thing to do. I refuse to rot away doing the right thing."

He stops those reaching hands, places his own hand on her bare arm. He had once thought this woman beautiful. Her smooth dark skin and brown eyes reminded him of Cleopatra. But now he scoffs. The nails greedily clutching at him are chipped. But his job right now is to keep her calm. Her face grows cold as she begins to understand his intent. And as he watches, that face he has loved grows even colder, as cold as the water rushing over the rocks behind them.

He studies her and fully understands how it came to be that he is here in this beautiful wood pleading with this woman to do as he ordered her to do. Here she is, staring at him, her skin as smooth as a ribbon of flowing chocolate, her large brown eyes accentuated by the fake eyelashes, the full mouth now set firm with determination. He had allowed her to catch him like a bear in a trap. He caresses her arm but she jerks away. She stumbles backwards on those ridiculous white go-go boots paired with a miniskirt that only reaches mid-thigh. She had worn that skirt, which revealed her long legs, to enchant him. No, not enchant, to ensnare as she had done on the very first day that they met.

"You have no heart," she tells him. "You have no heart after all that we've been through that you can stand there and look at me like I'm trash."

"Heart?" he counters. "You tell me about heart? How many men have there been besides me, Debra? How many have you gone through before you found the sucker in me?"